Graced Land

Graced Land

Laura Kalpakian

Blue Heron Publishing, Inc.
Hillsboro, Oregon

Copyright © 1992 by Laura Kalpakian All rights reserved. Originally published in hard cover by Grove Weidenfeld 1992.

Published by Blue Heron Publishing, Inc.
24450 NW Hansen Road
Hillsboro, Oregon 97124

LIBRARY OF CONGRESS CATALOGING-IN-PUBLICATION DATA

Kalpakian, Laura.
    Graced Land/by Laura Kalpakian.
        p.   cm.
    ISBN 0-936085-39-8
    I. Title.
    PS3561.A4168G7   1992
    813'.54-dc2O   91-37852
                                                  CIP

Manufactured in the United States of America
Printed on acid-free paper

Book design by Dennis Stovall. Cover design by Linda Dalal Sawaya with counsel on digitizing and electronic composition by Michael and Erik Clyman. Cover art copyright © 1997 by Linda Dalal Sawaya.

First Paperback Edition 1997
10 9 8 7 6 5 4 3 2 1

This book is for my mother, Peggy Kalpakian Johnson, the famous "without whom…"

Acknowledgments

For sharing their time, their talents, their sacred yearbooks, I am indebted to Connie, Frank, Kate, Mary, Paul, Sandra, and Vicki. This book was written with the much-appreciated encouragement of Gail Fox, Juliet Burton, Charlotte Sheedy, Walter Bode, Margaret Ann Marchioli, and Meredith Cary. To Paola Rizzoli, *grazie mille.* My parents, William J. and Peggy K. Johnson, and my sons, Bear and Brendan, lived graciously with this book.

A grant from the National Endowment for the Arts made *Graced Land* possible.

Contents

Most wretched men
Are cradled into poetry by wrong;
They learn in suffering what they teach in song.

Percy Bysshe Shelley, Julian and Maddalo, *1819*

But by the grace of God I am what I am:
and his grace which was bestowed upon me was not in vain.

— *I Corinthians 15:10*

The Old Maid's Prayer

One

Testing. Testing. Emily Shaw here. Caseworker 1766. Today's date: April 9, 1982. Reporting on Home Visitation made Wednesday, April 7, 1982, County Case Number 68-46784. Address: 2924 Santiago Street. Living in the home is the client, Mrs. Joyce (aka Rejoice) Jackson, and her two daughters, Priscilla, age thirteen, and Lisa Marie, age nine, both in good health, as is Mrs. Jackson. The children's father, Warren James Jackson, Jr., pays some child support, but not reliably, though Mrs. Jackson seems to manage well. Mr. Jackson lives in the next county with another woman and children he has fathered by her. On her. With her?" Emily hit PAUSE, envisioning how this would look on paper after the typist got through with it. She reversed, erased, so the sentence had a neat ring to it and no doubts. "The children of this other woman…" Emily hesitated, playing with her engagement ring; she hated the cliché, *other woman*. So Gothic. "…are two sons. Mrs. Jackson has their pictures up amongst other family photos and seems genuinely fond of them, speaks of them in terms of such affection that, well, that seem unwarranted by the situation." Emily thought of Rick. She thought if Rick had fathered children on another woman, she would die. She would die first and then she would kill him.

"The Jackson home was clean without being neat. There was a lot of laundry stacked and ironing everywhere and there were boxes with neat piles of clean mended clothing marked MEN, WOMEN, CHILDREN, and BABIES and the ironing board was up and the sewing machine was open and it had sort of center stage. When I arrived, Mrs. Jackson had a mouth full of pins. She took the pins out of her mouth," Emily added lest the girls in the typing pool think Mrs. Jackson spoke through pins the whole time. "Mrs. Jackson is forty-two, older than most of my clients, though I do not think that age alone can answer for the, well, she's the sort of woman who gives the impression of, well—you know, 'age cannot wither her, nor custom stale'—" Emily reversed to *clients* and added quickly, "Mrs. Jackson was very gracious. I should perhaps here note Mrs. Jackson's undue, unusual attachment to the late Elvis Presley."

Emily hit PAUSE and stared at the dotted walls of the taping booth. Social Services had seventeen such booths so that caseworkers could record in privacy. There was no graffiti. Emily could not think why Elvis ought to be noted. He had already been noted in the file. Naturally. Elvis Presley had died five years before. But if she didn't say something, people might think she hadn't noticed. "We spoke of him briefly," Emily lied blithely, and continued. "Mrs. Jackson is a very able manager and her home is comfortable, not at all welfare-ish but really sort of middle-class" Emily said, before pushing REVERSE to take off the last few words, which suggested that welfare-ish was low-class and betrayed, moreover, her mother's sense of values. Emily detested her mother's invidious shorthand: there was LC and LMC, MC and HC. The best of these was high-class. The worst of these was LMC, suggesting that low-class types had tried to pull themselves into the middle class and failed, hung precariously by their thumbs from the lowest possible rungs. Emily had tried to stay free of these prejudices, even when they were cast theoretically and pompously at USC in Sociology 414: Class in American Society. Emily backed up to *able manager* and stopped there.

According to the guidelines given her in training class, she had touched on nearly everything required of her: names, dates, numbers, health, state of the home, family history, that's all, unless the family was *in extremis*.

In extremis was the phrase welfare workers used to designate a family in a state of emergency, of one sort or another. Every time Emily heard *in extremis* it made her think of Oscar Wilde, who spent his whole life in one extremis or another. She confused *in extremis* with *De Profundis* and pale anguish at the gate. But if the Jacksons were not *in extremis* or *de profundis,* then how to explain the hours she had spent there? Thirty or forty minutes would ordinarily do. Mere curiosity would not answer. Mere curiosity has no place in the social worker's quiver of aids.

The quiver of aids was a metaphor used continually by the man who had conducted their training class, Mr. Hansen. Mr. Hansen was a font of information and experience and metaphors like *the quiver of aids.* Emily wondered if she was the only one who thought of sex toys. Anyway, she wasn't simply curious. Emily wanted to help people, to bring the Less Fortunate into fuller participation in society and see people lead full and happy, useful lives. That's why she became a sociology major at the University of Southern California, though she had started out in English. By her junior year, though, she had to agree with her peers and parents and boyfriend that sitting around reading a bunch of novels and absorbing useless frippets of poetry "buttered no bread." Unbuttered bread (in her mother's parlance) was the metaphorical equivalent of sloth, decay, squalor, waste, and want. Welfare mothers went about with unbuttered bread.

Unbuttered bread was probably as good a description as any for the welfare mother's lot, but it was not what Howard Hansen had stressed in the month long training period. Howard Hansen had dutifully walked them through the Thou Shalt Nots of social work, the county and state regulations, forms for refiguring budgets and procedures should your clients, for any number of reasons, be caught with overpayments, but the thrust of his presentation what he had to teach, indeed, what he had clearly learned, was a sense of shared humanity. Mr. Hansen advocated listening skills, compassion, good-natured regard, sturdy, democratic tolerance, all of which sounded like something Jesus or Saint Francis might have practiced. But in her three months on the actual job, Emily had discovered that veteran social workers weren't the least like Jesus or Saint Francis. They did their paperwork, made Home Visitations, handled those cases in extremis, and washed their hands before they left the building. They did not take their jobs home with them. Nearly all these people were married.

Emily wished she could shake off the habit of looking first at people's left hands and imagining where they had got up that morning, from which beds and whether naked or clothed, if they had reached to touch or tousle a much-loved head or set bare feet on bare floors and gone directly to the bathroom. During the training session, these thoughts about her fellow trainees (some thirty of them) often usurped her attention from Mr. Hansen's instructions, particularly when he was waxing on about Procedure. In training class Emily had used the skills she had never perfected in Sociology 381: Statistical Analysis for the Social Sciences. She did a statistical tally of her fellow trainees: who was married and who was not. All the good-looking men were married. All the average-looking women. The really attractive women were not married, though Emily did not count herself, really, in that last category, at least not statistically, because she was engaged, and while that wasn't married, neither was it exactly single.

In fact, it wasn't exactly anything. Emily found herself clinging to her engagement ring as though it were a life ring thrown to her in rough, rude waters, there to keep her afloat in a sea of desire, need, expedience, and simple longing.

Emily longed to be married to Rick. She hated her smart new apartment in the Raintree complex with its three swimming pools, a pond with ducks, a sauna, and a tennis court, congenially close to the freeway, the soon-to-be mall, and the high-class chain restaurants. She hated driving by the no-man's-land of the dead and ripped-up orange groves, that desolation of weed and wildflower that soon would sprout a drywall, neon-new mall. She hated the Raintree's manicured landscaping and little camphor trees held up by wires. She hated her own bathroom with female things only and her mother's old Avanti towels. She hated the decor, motifs, and touches (finishing and otherwise) courtesy of the Blue Goose, a Laguna boutique her mother favored. Emily loathed geese. She loathed country blue. Politely, she never said so, and her mother never guessed.

An instinctively neat young woman, Emily kept her new apartment tidy, except for the bedroom, which fell into sloth, the squalor reflecting the disarray of her most intimate life. Clothes and towels, like wounded in battle, lay where they fell. Unanswered mail hunkered in the corners and a trail of *Cosmo, Redbook, Glamour,* and *Mademoiselle* led to the bathroom. The novels she devoured at night were stacked by the bed until they too fell over into a rubble of print and glossy covers. Always an avid reader, at particularly unhappy times in her life Emily read bulimically, binging on novels, searching for fictional solace. Every night she read till she could not keep her eyes open, but before she went to sleep, Emily always reached across the double bed to the undented pillow where Rick should be. In the half-light her rocklike diamond ring mocked her. Engaged indeed. Emily Shaw wanted the man in her bed and the plain gold by-God band that tells the world you are a married woman. That was all she wanted. Sometimes she was afraid it was all she would ever want, feared that when she got it, she would cramp up from lack of longing and collapse. This was not quite the same thing as being fulfilled.

Of course, she wanted to be independent too. Naturally. That's why you go to college and train yourself to have a career and your own life and sense of self-worth. Self-worth cannot be dependent on your husband. First, though, you needed a husband. Emily needed Rick. To be married to Rick. Some mornings she wrote this feeling off to her being old-fashioned. "You're old-fashioned," she said to her pretty image in the mirror, applying Estée Lauder makeup. She had Renoirish coloring and bright blue eyes. "Just an old-fashioned girl." Expertly she fluffed her light brown hair. "Woman. Just an old-fashioned woman."

In an old-fashioned way, Emily had been excited about law school for Rick when they both graduated, University of Southern California, class of '81. But in August—after a summer of tennis and swimming and sailing on her parents' twenty-eight-foot sailboat, *Breaking Wind*—Rick had left for Georgetown University. Rick left and Emily was left with the discovery that, while being a wife might be a full-time job, being a fiancée was not. For the first time ever, her life was not mapped out with required lessons, school, sorority functions. She had no place to go and nothing to be. Rick, by contrast, filled his days with new friends, experiences, challenges. He told her so on the phone. The present was far more exciting to him than his shared past with Emily, or their mutually assured future: after law school, Emily's father had promised him a place in the prestigious Newport Beach firm Shaw, Shine, Brill, Syme, and Turlock.

In September, Emily's parents had suggested she join a couple of Tri Delts touring the European capitals. Emily declined (without saying that her parents themselves had forever soured her on cold churches, mute pictures, and oversized monuments during their European trip after she graduated from high school). She had had quite enough, thank you, of the Old Country.

Perhaps instead she would explore a new country: while Rick was in law school, Emily would get a job. She had a degree in sociology. She would be a social worker, which, she figured, would be a lot like being a Candy Striper. She'd always enjoyed being a Candy Striper at St. Luke's Hospital By-The-Sea, helping patients, going to meetings, planning events to cheer the less fortunate. Emily took the social worker tests, the interviews, and the job in St. Elmo County when it was offered to her. But it was not at all like being a Candy Striper. Deserty St. Elmo was not like Laguna Beach. The people she came in contact with were not like the grateful patients at St. Luke's By-The-Sea. The meetings did not plan events to cheer the less fortunate, but clumped over needless acres of barren bureaucratic ground, during which Emily doodled sailboats. That was not the worst of it. Worse, by far, to go home to the empty apartment, to have no friends, no fiancé, no sorority sisters. No one. Emily felt cut off, left out, abandoned, and lonely, pictured herself getting on a plane, flying to D.C., finding Rick, and the two of them eloping on the spot. She jokingly suggested as much to him on the phone. He said he'd love to, but studying consumed his life and he would have no time for a wife, and Emily would be cut off, left out, abandoned, and lonely.

Bravely, Emily set out to find friends. She went to one ghastly meeting of the St. Elmo Chapter of the USC Alumni Association, which met the first Thursday of every month in a banquet room at the Cask and Cleaver for dinner and drinks. The whole experience was so dreadful that Emily was forcibly reminded of that gruesome scene in Michener's *Hawaii* where the new arrivals to the leper colony, people yet whole, got pounced upon and mauled by the really ghastly lepers. She did not return, despite repeated entreaties from some of the alumni, mostly married men.

At work she struck up a lunchtime acquaintance with another social worker, Penny Pitzer, who was about thirty, single, and seemed to have a perfectly full and happy life. Penny urged Emily to come out for softball on the county team, but Emily begged off (without quite saying she was unequal to any sport that required physical finesse beyond the ability to zip up your own pants). Anyway, Emily didn't need the exercise. Lunch with Penny Pitzer was enough to kill your appetite and a good way to shed those extra five pounds, because it was very hard to eat while Penny talked about her caseload. Penny had five years' experience with the welfare department, and all her clients, it seemed, either were being or had been beaten, molested, robbed, mugged, drugged, raped, arrested, abducted, defrauded, or were defrauding somebody; their teenage children were always running away with someone who had VD and their little children were caught shoplifting. Every one of Penny's clients was either violent or retarded.

"Don't you have anyone normal?" Emily had asked plaintively.

"If they're normal, they're not on welfare," Penny replied, biting into her Whopper. "You've got to remember—there but for the grace of God…" Penny grinned. "Take it in stride."

Perhaps, Emily thought. But it did not seem quite the spirit of shared humanity that Mr. Hansen had stressed in training class.

She thought she might be able to share a little humanity and make friends around the Raintree apartment pool, taking her novel and a diet Coke and suntan lotion and a towel. Friendship was out of the question, and even acquaintance unlikely, because the young women at the pool regarded her as just more competition for the few men. Emily tried to make it clear she wasn't looking for a man. She was engaged, after all. She kept mementos and gifts and pictures of Rick up all over her apartment, so that anyone who came over would know she was engaged. But no one came over.

At work she drank her coffee from Rick's valentine mug and kept their engagement party picture on her desk in a charming country blue ceramic frame. In the picture Rick wore his Winning Team Smile and Emily beamed in her Laura Ashley party dress. In the messy sprawl of welfare paperwork, Emily sometimes eyed that picture, wishing she could crawl back inside that framed moment, just about a year ago now at the Laguna Hills Country Club. No one had had a more splendid engagement party than Rick and Emily. Right out of *Gatsby*. All their friends said so, but in the year following graduation those friends had had weddings, and Emily once reckoned up she'd spent over a thousand dollars on their weddings, on presents, clothes, and travel. That was the way she saw it on bad days. On good days she did not doubt that true love was beyond all calculable worth, that Juliet would as soon be inconstant to Romeo, Desdemona to Othello, Antony to Cleopatra, that the moon would be unfaithful to the tide and the stars pay no worship to the garish sun before she, Emily, would slacken her devotion to Rick. Stout of heart. Clear of purpose. She returned to her dreary caseload and the omnivorous paperwork spread out on her desk and put from her mind that glorious engagement party, with its three hundred guests, its nine-piece orchestra, buffet supper, champagne enough for everyone to toast the happy couple, for everyone to think, even if they did not say, *Imagine the wedding. If this is the engagement party, imagine the wedding!*

But when Emily fathomed the vast desert of time between *imagine* and *the wedding*, she canceled her subscription to *Bride*. By the time she got married, all the fashions would have changed. Of course she understood how important it was that Rick have an eastern degree to join her father's firm. This scrap of time was but a small price to pay for their high-class future. But there were moments when Emily Shaw didn't give a shit for the high-class future, would trade it all for a tender present. Sometimes she had to ask Rick to explain it all over again when he called twice a week, regularly, reliably, at 8:03 Pacific time. Occasionally he surprised her with a call, which pleased her more than the twice-weekly expectables. Occasionally she called him on impulse. But the time difference argued against it. She knew how Rick hated to be waked up once he had got to sleep.

When he called, Rick would tell her of the challenges of law school and funny stories, anecdotes about people he had met. Emily would laugh without thinking they were funny. She wondered if his laughter was equally unfelt when she told him funny stories about her work, especially her supervisor, Large Marge.

Marge Mason had been a WAC and she still wore clothes with a martial air, uniforms of checked dresses, gray gabardine skirts wrapped round her impossible bulk, and white polyester blouses rippling over her enormous breasts. Marge wore support hose and sensible shoes and her steel gray hair was cut in a no-nonsense bob. She had a way of sucking on her bottom lip that made Emily shiver. When Marge's heavy-hooded eyes met Emily's during staff meetings, Emily always remembered what she'd left undone, or done wrong, felt tarred with inadequacy and feathered with silliness and she doodled whole pages worth of sailboats that might take her away from all this.

When Mr. Hansen had introduced the supervisors to the trainees, Large Marge had prefaced her own remarks with words that Penny Pitzer later recited right back to Emily over their Whoppers at the Burger King on Brigham Boulevard. "I'll bet Large said, *I have raised three children on my own and no one knows better than I the daily demands on a single mother.*" Penny dipped one of her french fries in the ketchup and nibbled it. "Something like that?" Emily nodded. "Did she tell you about the son who graduated from Chico State and the daughter who graduated from Long Beach State? And did she save it up for last about her son at the Air Force Academy?"

"Well, yes, she did."

"A sorrier bunch of emotional cripples you've never laid eyes on."

"You've met them?"

"The county Christmas party is an obligatory event. She always brings them. We call them the Geek, the Gook, and the Grubber. The Grubber's the one at the Air Force Academy."

(When Emily repeated this bit of folk wisdom to Rick on the

phone, he chuckled, though admittedly he did not shriek with laughter as Emily had when Penny told it.)

"You watch out for old Marge," Penny cautioned when their mirth subsided. "She's a ball-buster."

"But I'm not a man.

"Have you ever slept with a man?"

"Well, yes, of course. I'm engaged."

"Did you enjoy it?"

"Naturally, but I don't see—"

"That's enough for Large. Think about it. Who do your clients sleep with?"

"Men."

"Right. That's how they get knocked up and have a lot of children they can't support, but they never learn, do they? They go to bed with men who go to prison, with men who dump them for other women, with men who spend one night and are gone in the morning. They end up pregnant and poor and it doesn't stop them. They fall in love. They hit the sack. And since Marge hates all men, it follows automatically, she hates all women who love men."

The clarity of this argument was not lost on Emily, not exactly, though she asked in the interest of understanding, "But that's everyone. Everyone in the world."

"Almost."

"There's only men and women."

Penny shrugged.

"Well, how did Marge get—"

"The Geek, the Gook, and the Grubber? Adoption. The military can do whatever they like. Sweep children right off the streets and give them to ball-busters like Marge. It's a shame, really." Penny bit into her Whopper and chewed thoughtfully. "I probably shouldn't tell you this, but why do you think Sid quit fieldwork? Sid Johnson, that black guy who had your caseload? That man is a born social worker, but he asked over and over for a new supervisor, and they said no. Finally Sid just told Howard Hansen the truth about Marge. Old Sid, he really laid it on the line. He had to leave after that. Lucky for him he got transferred to a different division, or he'd have been out of a job. Nothing can budge Large. She likes to cut and slash clients' grants, benefits too, if she can get to them. She spends whole days at it and you can see the satisfaction on her face while she's working up how much they owe, or how long they're going to be without grants. Oh, and it's all legal. That's what she likes best. Sid said there was one of your cases, old Marge wouldn't even let the file go down to Library for his first two years. Every time he wanted that file, he had to ask Large. She kept it in her desk."

"I don't suppose…did Sid mention the name?"

"Can't remember. It's those people, though, there at the corner of Santiago and Sultana—Westminster Abbey for Elvis. Heartbreak Hotel. You can't miss it. It's only about half a mile from the county complex. You know the one: Flags! Flowers! Music! You don't? Over on Santiago? Everyone drives right by it on their way to work."

"I don't. I live out the other direction."

"Well, you should drive by just to see it," said Penny emphatically. "In five years it's become a local landmark, like the old Mormon Adobe downtown. Florists donate flowers. People drive by just to look. Like some kind of holy shrine—and you ought to see it on Christmas and Easter! And if you think that's a circus"—Penny wadded up her Whopper wrapper—"you ought to see it January 8!"

"What's that?"

"Elvis's birthday. Oh, you wouldn't believe it, Emily. She puts big signs out on the porch, HAPPY BIRTHDAY TO THE KING. All day long she plays the same Elvis songs loud, so you can hear it all up and down the street. It's unbelievable. She gives cookies with 'E.P.' in sugar frosting to passersby. You pull up at the stop sign in front of her house and she's there, giving out goodies in honor of his birthday. On August 16 she does the same thing, only then she just plays the gospel songs. She stands in the street there at the stop sign and gives away candy. *In memory of the King,* she says when she comes up to your car."

"What's August 16?"

"The day Elvis died. Oh, this woman is a fruitcake. A fearless fruitcake. Sid told me that she goes to garage sales and buys all the leftover clothes at the end of the day, takes them home and washes and mends them, and then she'll just go right down anywhere in this town—and there are some pretty rough areas in this town, if you haven't noticed—"

"I've noticed," Emily confessed.

"—and go up to people's doors and say, *Here, Elvis Presley wants you to have this coat, or this warm sweater. Here, Elvis wants your little girl to have this dress.* Sometimes she goes to that halfway house, the one for drug addicts and ex-cons. She walks right in like there's not a perv in a hundred-mile radius and gives them boxes of clothes, everything neat and washed and starched and mended. Looks like it came right off the shelves from Sears. Sid says the guy who ran the halfway house found out Sid was her social worker and called Sid and wanted to know if this woman was nuts."

"What did Sid say?"

"He said it depended on your taste in music. This woman is really a fruitcake. They had this article in the paper a couple of years ago, her friends went to the bank and set up this fund for anyone who wanted to contribute so that she could fly to Memphis, fly there and see Elvis's house, and Elvis's grave."

"I bet Large Marge loved that."

Penny snorted. "Large called up that bank like she wants to contribute to the fund, finds out what she needs to know, and gets ready to pounce on that woman the minute she lays hands on the money. And it was a lot! The paper said this woman's friends collected enough for a round-trip ticket to Memphis—hotel and everything. And she never touched it." Penny finished her Whopper.

"What do you mean? Did she just leave it there?"

"No. She gave it away. Honest. There was a picture in the paper of her with the bank manager, signing the check over to the principal of Adobe Elementary for the children of that school."

"Adobe's that school—" Emily pointed vaguely to the east. "The one out by the flood channel where there's all those shacks."

"Migrant workers. Send kids to school who can't speak a word of English." Penny clucked sorrowfully. "Anyway, she told the principal and the bank and the paper that she would never forget her friends' kindness and their love, waxed on with all that rubbish, but if Elvis was alive, this is what he would do with the money. She said something like—she could better serve Elvis Presley's spirit here in St. Elmo and she didn't need to go to Memphis. Well, we all thought it was a hoot! Sid Johnson, he even has the balls to go up to Large and ask if she saw that in the paper and didn't she think that was nice."

"Why did I have to get Sid's caseload?" Emily moaned. "Why did I have to get Large Marge?"

Penny grinned. "Well, all I can say is I hope you like Elvis."

Emily didn't. Neither did Penny. The two young women agreed that long before he died, Elvis Presley was nothing but a relic of the Age of Greasy Kid Stuff. Unsophisticated music, compared to punk rock, and nothing in comparison to Air Supply or Foreigner or Journey. Elvis and his bedroom voice and doo-wop music and all those goofy gyrations. Funny. Fat. Pathetic. Neither Penny nor Emily could understand how people could get so worked up, so broken up, when Elvis died.

"I got sick of it," said Penny. "They played nothing but Elvis for a week on the radio."

"They played his music in Italy too. I was in Europe that August with my parents, in Rome then."

"When in Rome!" Penny sucked up the last of her diet Coke.

"When in St. Elmo," Emily replied without enthusiasm.

Two

Emily pulled the county car under the jacarandas lining Santiago Street. She thought, Oh shit, without quite saying it. Her client's house was at the corner of Santiago and Sultana: 2924. Heartbreak Hotel. No mistaking it, but thirty years ago this tract was new and raw and these houses all looked alike: three bedrooms, one bath, separate garage, a scrap of lawn front and back, a parkway with jacaranda plunked, one in front of each house. The jacarandas had grown and prospered and now the lacy leaves formed a near-canopy across this forlorn street where the houses, by contrast, had shrunk into motley, sun-faded, hunched-over, ill-kept ranch-style stuccos with cement porches and fake shutters. She dreaded the coming encounter, although by now she'd been a social worker three months and knew how to conduct a Home Visitation. But was she ready for this? These people must be as weird as owl pellets.

She checked her briefcase for notes, a ridiculous gesture that only proves that hope springs eternal because (contrary to all Mr. Hansen's instructions in training class) Emily had not read the case histories prior to her fieldwork. The time she ought to have been dutifully acquainting herself with the paperwork on welfare clients, Emily had been busy writing something funny and clever and cute and caring to Rick. She put something in the mail to him every day, so she would always be present, there, in a manner of speaking, waiting for him when he came home from a hard day at law school.

She locked the county car and wondered if her supervisor had singled out this family for special contempt because Marge hated Elvis. Impossible thought. Aside from Sousa marches and possibly *From the Halls of Montezuma*, music alone would not have moved Marge Mason in the least.

A rusted BEWARE OF DOG sign hung on the chain link fence, and Emily felt about in her purse for her Mace canister. ("Not necessary, but not unwise," that's how Howard Hansen had phrased it.) But no dog approached and no barking disrupted the drowsy afternoon. She opened the gate and started up the walk, which was flanked on either side by slender gray crepe myrtle trees with long black satin streamers fluttering from their lower branches. The grass was dry and brown, but neatly clipped and clearly swept. No dead leaves gathered in the crevices of the steps, which were covered in carpet remnants of sky blue. The whole porch was an immaculately maintained open-air chapel sacred to the memory of the late Elvis Presley.

Nailed up across the two front porch windows there was an American flag and a Confederate flag and below them, a picnic table covered in a sheet, bleached, starched, and ironed The table reverently displayed a Gideon Bible at either end. A wreath of plastic daisies lay before a poster-sized picture of the mature Elvis wearing a white spangled bodysuit with a flaring cape, his knee bent in a posture at once dramatic and humble, emphatic and supplicating, tense and intense; he held the mike in a white-knuckled grip. Emily gulped and turned her engagement ring several times. The picture was framed in quilted black satin with four satin rosettes at each corner, and long mourning ribbons twitched and gyrated at the behest of the April wind. Also on the white-clad table, smaller pictures of the young Elvis sat, some cut from newspapers, all in cheap metal frames, and at either end a vase of tall gladiolas in clear, unyellowed water. More red glads were tucked in the flag holder on the porch posts above yet another picture, Elvis in a Hawaiian lei. Nailed to a trellis, a huge hand-lettered sign read:

Sacred to the Memory of This Prince Among Men
Elvis Aron Presley
1935–1977
Long Live the King
His Truth Goes Marching On

Twining up the posts around the signs, encircling the big, black-framed portrait, strung between the two flags, and draped across the white sheet on the picnic table were hundreds of Christmas lights of the tiny, twinkling variety. The wind, more insistent now, bristled uncomfortably at Emily's temples, ruffled her denim prairie skirt, and lifted the sheet covering the picnic table. Underneath, between two speakers, she saw the biggest, hairiest, strangest-looking mutt she had ever seen, who seemed to be shredding a blanket with his fierce, sharp teeth.

Emily's hasty knock was answered by a woman with a mouth full of pins. She removed the pins with one swift gesture and hollered, "Get out of here!" Emily was appalled, speechless really. This particular contingency had never been addressed in training class, the recalcitrant client, perhaps, but never this. The woman yelled again and the dog tore out from underneath the picnic table and ripped around the side of the house.

"That Colonel," said the woman. "He knows this porch is Sacred to the Memory of Elvis. He has shade around the back. He just always wants what he knows he can't have." She gave Emily a look of complicity. "Like any male, right?"

Emily nodded affirmatively.

"You must be the new social worker. Mr. Johnson's replacement."

The woman was green-eyed and fair; she wore no makeup and her hair, darker at the roots, was neatly caught in a barrette. She was about the same height as Emily (except Emily was not barefoot) and she wore a loose Mexican dress, bold colors in a fine weave, which surprised Emily as most of her welfare clients wore clothing frayed and drab as their lives. Emily introduced herself, adding gallantly that she had indeed taken over Sid Johnson's caseload, but everyone said he could have no replacement.

The woman smiled. "I'm Joyce Jackson, but I guess you know that. Come in, Miss Shaw, and get out of this heat."

In the dim living room, starched, ironed clothing hung from the doorways, dismembered dresses pinned to patterns lay on the floor, and clean clothes still stiff from the line were folded and stacked in boxes marked MEN, WOMEN, CHILDREN, and BABIES. The ironing board and the sewing machine competed for preeminence, and Elvis was everywhere. Emily asked her professional questions and noted Mrs. Jackson's responses on her clipboard. Then she mentioned she had a headache.

Joyce Jackson moved her to the La-Z-Boy, told her to take her shoes off, brought in two aspirin, a glass of iced tea, and a selection of generic cookies. For the first time since she had moved to St. Elmo, Emily felt the pleasures of shared humanity. Never mind that Joyce was almost twenty years her senior, clearly LMC, and dined on unbuttered bread. Emily relaxed into the La-Z-Boy, up against a comfy quilt, while the swamp cooler sluggishly keeled air currents about the dim room, cool with the smell of spray starch and something else—sweet, reminiscent, but elusive. Pigeons cooed up close to the house and their fluttering contentment seemed contagious. Across from Emily, Joyce sat, knees tucked up, stitching a hem while they chatted about music and men and money. The county, of course, paid Emily to talk with Joyce about men and money, but music ought not to have been on the agenda. How could you help it with Elvis pictures, Elvis posters, Elvis all around you, clustered on the table, filling up the top of the upright piano, tacked even on the lampshades? "You certainly have his whole life here," Emily remarked politely, "young and old."

"Well, he never got to be old, did he, Miss Shaw?"

"Emily, please."

"He died at forty-two. That's exactly how old I am now. Forty-two," Joyce sighed. "Leaves you with a lot to live up to. Look at all the good he did in just those few mortal years, the gifts he gave the world. Are you a fan?"

"Oh yes," Emily lied blithely in the service of good manners. "I'm so glad to hear that. People who don't like Elvis, well, you can't trust them."

"Oh, you can trust me." Emily's gaze rested on the young Elvis in his leather jacket, slender, dark, intense, and beautiful, on a framed poster from *King Creole*.

"That's an original," said Joyce, as though Monet were under discussion. She launched into a funny tale of how she and her best friend, Sandee, had seen that movie a dozen times and lusted. "And that's the right word, Miss Shaw—"

"Emily."

"—we lusted after that poster. That was Elvis's favorite of all his movies. It was a real early one, '57, in those glorious early days before he went in the army."

Joyce took the ironing board down and cleared stacks of folded laundry from her path, put them beside the open sewing machine while she continued telling how she and Sandee had snatched not one, but two posters right off the wall at the old, long-vanished Dream Theater right downtown, one of those great old theaters with a ticket booth shaped like a wave. How she and Sandee had run into the ladies' room, strapped the posters to their thighs with masking tape they'd brought for that very purpose, and how, under their full skirts, no one ever guessed. "We went back in and watched the movie for the seventh time. Of course, peeling off the tape was no fun," she added. "Sandee got hers too close to the short hairs. Now Emily," she said, stepping over the patterned dress and going to an old stereo, "I'm so glad you love Elvis! It means I don't have to convert you. You just choose your favorite song. Name it. I have all his music."

"I'm not very good at titles," Emily confessed. Neither had she been very good at Interdisciplinary 451: American Pop Culture—The Postwar Years. She should at least have learned a few Elvis titles from Dr. Parks, a huge man who reminded her of the Jolly Green Giant, though he was not at all jolly. Quite the reverse. He was sallow unto greenish, with a grizzled, balding head, and he seemed gigantic because he walked so that his hands swayed in front of him and brushed against his knees. Dr. Parks gave Emily a C. Her GPA was high enough to keep her in the Tri Delts, but C's seemed to dot her grade reports, a spray of crescent moons. To a more perceptive mind than Emily's, her image of crescent moons alone might have suggested why her grades were so mediocre. Emily was afflicted with imagination—not, alas, the focused sort that betokens great things in the big world, but the other sort. Random and inappropriate thoughts ricocheted constantly across her mind like the lights and bells of a pinball machine, and the stimulation from all this flash and noise distracted her continually. In class she found herself wondering what the professor looked like naked (even someone like Dr. Parks, where the thought was really too too terrible) or wondering what he'd be in his next life, maybe a frog, wondering if he might suddenly sizzle down and hop away. Bits of verse suggested themselves to Emily at inappropriate moments, snippets of plays and poems and lyric; Shakespeare and Yeats and Louisa May Alcott elbowed their way to the front of her mind and stayed there, pushing out dutiful thoughts that had been waiting in line for a long time. She couldn't always quote these poems or bits of fiction correctly, but they stayed there, taking up space that ought to have gone to Interdisciplinary 451. Sometimes Emily spent class time wondering, if you were a fly, would you rather drown in cognac or honey?

Emily had confessed this failing to Rick and he said it was part of her charm. Anyway, he said, he would be the brains of the family. This was doubly comforting: clearly he meant to have a family with her, and Rick was very smart. Got very good grades. Top grades in his frat. Would do splendidly in law school (everyone said so), would come back to California, pass the bar exam first time through and join the lucrative butter-slathered practice of her father's Newport firm, Shaw, Swine, Swill, Slime, and Turdlock, which is the way Emily usually thought of her father's partners. Rick did not think this funny at all. Quite the contrary. He reminded her that Shaw, Shine, Brill, Syme, and Turlock would enable the two of them to have a lovely, opulent Laguna Beach life where they would entertain lavishly and tell their guests funny stories about the time they'd had to spend apart, he at

Georgetown in D.C. and she in St. Elmo. Their dinner guests would laugh, St. *Elmo! How* did *you ever stand it, Emily? I hear that's the Armpit of the Nation!* Emily would roll her eyes and raise a glass of sauvignon blanc and say with a smile, *Oh, it's not that bad, it's worse!* Everyone would laugh, because of course those deserty counties were sinks of smog and poverty and desolation, except for Palm Springs, but someone would say even that wasn't the same, and then the conversation would shift. The comfort Emily gained from these mythical dinner parties always waned when she realized Rick would be years in law school and she would be years and years alone in St. Elmo. Years and years and years and

"Who? Excuse me, I—"

"Elvis. There never was a man like him, born a poor boy that God gave a great talent and a great destiny."

Emily sipped her iced tea, nodded, remembered Dr. Parks nattering in Interdisciplinary 451 about poor white trash Elvis Presley whitewashing black music. Elvis was a musical phenomenon only because he made black music respectable—which is to say white. Presley's success had more to do with his being a good-looking white boy than any so-called talent. The history of Elvis, Dr. Parks said, dismissing him in about ten minutes, properly belongs to the history of marketing and has nothing really to do with music. Dr. Parks said Elvis could only play three chords on the guitar and, as for his famous shake-them-up-and-make-them-scream electric pelvis, well, black performers had been doing that for years in black clubs. But when Elvis brought this sort of thing before white Americans, they thought he had invented it. In truth, he'd only plundered and pillaged black art. Dr. Parks said, at the end of his life Elvis Presley was a great fat bloated toad of a drug addict who could hardly speak, much less sing. Dr. Parks said you need only look at those sequined capes and gaudy bodysuits to know that money could not buy good taste. He concluded with the observation that Elvis was one of those American pop icons morally, mentally, physically, spiritually, and emotionally unequal to his own success.

As Emily sat in Joyce's dim living room with *Love Me Tender* billowing across the room, pushed in slow, alluvial currents by the swamp cooler trailing an elusive fragrance, she recollected standing in a coffee line beside Dr. Parks and noticing he had big blackheads in his ears. She marveled now that she could have even listened to, much less taken seriously, a man who had blackheads in his ears. The line from *A Midsummer Night's Dream* rang in her head: *With the help of a surgeon, he might yet recover and prove an ass,* she thought, forcibly returning her attention to Joyce. She wondered how they had got from Elvis's destiny to marriage. She was interested in marriage.

"The man you marry—I tell my daughters—can be rich, or poor, or plain, or beautiful. Girls—I tell them—you can marry the broom monkey at the Union 76 and you won't hear a word of complaint from me, but never, *never* marry a man who does not like his mother. A man who doesn't like his mother will never like you. Wedlock will feel like headlock, deadlock. Terrible."

Emily could not remember if Rick liked his mother. Could not remember his mother.

"The man who does not like his mother is the man to have an affair with, but not to marry. My husband, Jack, he was a devoted son to his mother. Devoted."

What was that woman's name? Emily had been a guest in their Pasadena home and Rick's mother was—Frances. Right. Frances. Did Rick like her? "Did Rick—I mean, did Elvis like his mother?"

"I tell you, Emily, Gladys Presley was the most important person in his life. Ever. You don't know how close I came to naming Cilla, my first girl, Gladys, after his mother. And I would have too, if I'd known she was going to divorce him."

"Gladys?"

"No. Priscilla, his wife. She divorced the King in '73. Gladys was his mother. She loved Elvis absolutely unselfishly. Why, you know the first record he ever cut, he did it for her, right there at Sun Records in Memphis. He paid to record it. My *Happiness* and *That's When Your Heartaches Begin.* He gave her the record for a birthday present. She died in '58 when he was only twenty-three. Imagine."

"I'm twenty-three," said Emily, without anything more substantive to add.

"You can see pictures of him, when he got out of the service in 1960 and came back to a house with his mama gone, dead—it breaks your heart to see his sweet face. The look on that sweet face. He was never again that close or loving with another human being. His whole life would have been different if Gladys had lived. Who knows what suffering God allots us and why—and what that suffering means." Joyce dropped her sewing, her lips twisted with pain. "At the end of Elvis's life, the suffering on his face—" She gulped, swallowing emotion. "They say he took massive amounts of drugs at the end, that he was so drugged and fat, he was a zombie. They make cruel fun of him for that—the boy who didn't drink or smoke, the King of Rock and Roll who snorted drugs like a pig. Oh, it's terrible what they say. Don't they understand? Drugs were part of his punishment. They were part of his suffering. No one could save him from the suffering. No one. He sang himself to death because he loved us, all of us—the fans, the audience. He needed us as much as we needed him. You can tell that just by watching his movies. He didn't need the camera, he needed the people." Joyce's eyes filled with tears. "He loved us as much as we loved him. He died for us."

Emily sat spellbound in the La-Z-Boy, wishing like mad she'd paid closer attention in training class, where no doubt they had covered this sort of thing—Dealing with the Crashing and Inexplicable Sorrow of a Perfect Stranger—while she, Emily, had been tallying up who was married. Emily extracted herself from the La-Z-Boy and sat beside Joyce on the loveseat, patted her back, expecting that Joyce would say, *Oh, you'll have to forgive me…* People always did say that, wanting to be forgiven for having emotions and showing them, but Joyce did not. Her shoulders shook and she wept for the suffering of the man whose death had broken the heart of the world. Emily went to the box of Kleenex on the TV and pulled a few, placed them gently in Joyce's hands.

"The drugs only prove he was human, born to suffer like the rest of us. We're all born to die and sin and suffer. The drugs were a disgrace, of course they were! Didn't Jesus suffer disgrace? Wasn't the cross a humiliation? The crown of thorns? What was that? There's no disgrace in his suffering. There's only his humanity."

Emily patted her again and thought, oddly, of Howard Hansen and his earnest face and voice.

Joyce blew her nose. "You remember your First Corinthians."

"'Suffer the little children'?"

"'By the grace of God I am what I am.' God gave Elvis the sweetest, most powerful voice He ever gave to a mere human being. God never bestows grace in vain, does He?"

"You wouldn't think so," replied Emily with what she hoped was an affirmative tone.

"You know, when I'm out, at a restaurant, or shopping, or even just in the car, and his music comes over the radio, I just have to smile because I know he's present. His voice was a gift of God and he's still giving to us. His spirit's in his music and his music is everywhere." Joyce toyed with her Kleenex, smiling. "When I wake up in the morning, every day, one of his songs is right there, at the edge of my mind, playing when I wake up, and I know, whatever song it is, that's the way the day's going, that there's a reason for it. I know if it's going to be a *Peace in the Valley* day, or a *There's Good Rockin' Tonight* sort of day, or a *Wear My Ring Around Your Neck* day. When I hear his music, Emily, on the bus, or the Muzak at the mall, I just turn to whoever's nearby and I say, well, the King's still with us, isn't he?"

Emily glanced at the pictures of Elvis all around: the sideburned, heavy-jowled man, the near-boy with his openly vulnerable, invitational, appealing expression; the too-groomed, too-smooth, slick Hollywood face; the artist photographed in the intensity, the act of spontaneous creation: music. "He was certainly very good-looking."

Joyce blew her nose. "Elvis wasn't just good-looking, honey. Why, I could walk out of this house and point to half a dozen men who are good-looking." She chuckled. "Well, maybe not out of *this* house, but looks—looks are nothing, only fleshly clothing. When you die, you drop them like a pair of pants before you get into bed. Your spirit goes naked. What Elvis had was spirit, Emily. It wasn't painted on him. It came from here." Joyce hit herself squarely in the solar plexus.

"I guess I just don't remember very much about Elvis. I wasn't even born till 1959."

"You poor girl. You missed everything, didn't you?"

Joyce went into the kitchen for some more iced tea and Emily walked slowly back to the La-Z-Boy, wondering what she'd missed. She'd been to USC, after all. She was a Tri Delt. She was engaged. She looked at the laundry stacked in plastic LMC baskets and the starched ironing hanging in the doorways, the patterns lying dismembered on the floor. The eyes of Elvis everywhere seemed to bore into her and she reluctantly returned his burning gaze.

Joyce came back with her face freshly washed, hair brushed, and a bright sash tied around her loose dress. Emily was struck with the paradoxical evidence: Could a woman be beautiful without being glamorous? Impossible. All Tri Delts know you must be beautiful *and* glamorous. And rich. You have to be all three. And yet, here was Joyce Jackson, on welfare, middle-aged, manless, maintaining an LMC shrine to a drugged-up rocker, but she had the air of wanting for nothing. She carried a tray with a plastic pitcher of iced tea and more generic cookies. The tray was as LMC as they come, yellow metal with the names Joyce and Jack twined around wedding rings, and the date, June 24, 1959. She offered the iced tea with a palpable generosity of spirit that had clearly kept her buoyant. Her mouth was poised between candor and concentration and her green eyes were at once shrewd and innocent. She went to the stereo, pulled out a two-record set, and the needle clunked down on a rasping, oft-played *Jailhouse Rock*. An irresistible flush of energy filled the room, enlivened even the sluggish swamp cooler, and Joyce picked up her hemming, humming, and between the music and the work in her hands she seemed whole, complete.

Emily Shaw fought a sense of envy. Wrongheaded, ridiculous envy, she told herself, rounding up all the usual suspect phrases—*I am young, pretty, educated. I have wealthy parents and a career and prospects and I'm engaged to a wonderful man who will be rich and prominent.* She arched her left hand for comfort and played with her ring.

"That's the most beautiful engagement ring I've ever seen."

"Thank you. My fiancé chose it. Rick. Rick has very good taste."

"Well, anyone can see that. He's engaged to you, isn't he? When are you getting married?"

"Well, I—we, that is, he's in law school back east, but he'll come to California this summer, during their break. This summer he'll be doing paralegal work for my father's firm. I call them Shaw, Swine, Swill, Slime, and Turdlock, even though that's not their real names— except for Shaw, of course. Rick hates me to do it, even though I promised him that when he gets to be a partner, I wouldn't do that to his name. Our name," she corrected herself. "Rick thinks I should be more respectful."

"Why?"

Emily pondered. "Well, I guess because, well, because it's the law and whatever the law thinks is supposed to be right. Personally"—she lowered her voice—"I agree with whoever it was in *Oliver Twist* who said, 'If that is what the law thinks, then the law, sir, is an ass!' But I wouldn't say that to Rick. He doesn't like novels. He thinks books are full of unbuttered bread, except for lawbooks, like those." She pointed to a stack of 1934 lawbooks, footstool high before the loveseat. "Are you interested in the law, Joyce?"

"No. Those are family heirlooms."

"Rick is very interested in the law. Very smart. Works very hard." And then, never mind Howard Hansen's instructions re Listening Skills, and never mind that spilling your guts is not exactly in the quiver of aids, Emily found herself going on about Rick. Sort of non-stop about Rick and how Georgetown was second choice and he'd been turned down by Harvard Law School and how the rejection was such a blow. The worst thing that had ever happened, and "You can't believe how devastated he was, Joyce."

"Oh yes I can."

"He thought his life was over and he'd just go—go be a broom monkey or something. He wanted to die. What was the use living without Harvard Law School? It was just awful, you know, 'That White Sustenance—Despair.' He was in a perfect coma of despair and it took all my strength and passion, really, passion, to get him to come out."

Joyce dropped her sewing. "Of the coma? Oh, Emily—"

"No. Out of the Motel Six. He took a room at the Motel Six in Inglewood and refused to come out. I had to bang on the door and beg him to listen to me, to let me in." Emily paused and then gave Joyce a rather more prim version of the incident there in front of room 132 at the Motel Six in Inglewood, where she had knocked, then fist-and-flat-palm pounded, shouted that she wasn't going to let him think his life was over because Harvard had turned him down. *That's shit, Rick! Shit!* she had screamed, and because they were in Inglewood, passersby paid her not the least bit of attention. "I finally convinced him it wasn't the end of the world and Georgetown was very nice. It was like 'The King's Breakfast,' you remember? The King wants butter for his bread and there isn't any, and the Queen says, well, 'Marmalade is nice if it's very thickly spread,'" she concluded, wondering where that had come from.

"You saved Rick's life, Emily."

No one else had ever thought Emily had saved Rick's life, but perhaps she had. "I guess it was a sort of far far better thing that I did than I have ever done before."

"That's the way it is," Joyce sighed. "Men will always need us more than we need them. You just have to feel sorry for men. They're just not independent like women are. Oh, you probably don't notice it so much, young as you are, but you just wait till you get a little older. Honestly. A middle-aged man without a woman is just pathetic."

Emily considered this thoughtfully with her generic cookie. "But you almost never see a man without a woman, young or old. You see a lot of women without men." The Old Maid's Prayer. The cookie went down dryly.

"That's because men are afraid. Why do you think they're always scrabbling after women?" Joyce bit her thread. "It's the fear that moves them. The old gut-thumping fear."

"Of what?" Emily cast back through her subscriptions, *Cosmo, Redbook, Glamour* (to say nothing of *Bride*). "Why aren't there a lot of men's magazines telling them how to shed ten pounds, or cook well and look good and make up so they'll always be pretty and have orgasms and keep a nice house and manage their time?"

"Oh, that's just gnats dancing, Emily. None of that matters. The truth of it is, a woman can look after herself and a man can't. It's that simple. Women always have a lot of friends and family and people at work and church, neighbors. They're not afraid to get personal and listen, tell stories, call someone up just to laugh and scratch, have a few beers or a cup of coffee."

"Or an iced tea."

Joyce grinned. "But a man? A man is only allowed to have a woman. And the truth is, a man can't relax with a woman until he gets her into bed. Poor bastards."

Emily decided right then to cancel her subscriptions. She did, though, mention a story in the April *Cosmo* about a man "'who was all torn up, worried that his wife was having an affair. Mostly you always read about women who are bent out of shape wondering if their men are, well, screwing around. But in this story, you got to feel sorry for the man.

"You should always feel sorry for men. Men can't look after themselves. Cradle to grave, they're always asking women, *Where is my...?* Start to finish. If they couldn't say that, they'd be mute. They begin with their mothers, *Where is my...?* And end up asking the visiting nurse, *Where is my bedpan?* Pathetic. Women don't do that. Women know how to take care of things and people, starting with themselves." She held up the skirt she was hemming, nodded, put it aside, and started ripping the seams in a pair of pants. "I have to take out all Sandee's pants. She just refuses to buy a size eighteen."

"Still," Emily returned to the question of constant fascination, "you need men. Well, you need *a* man. A husband. You have to be married. If you don't get married, you end up an old maid. Oh, I know people don't use that expression anymore, not like the Old Maid's Prayer, but you can still *be* an old maid. People still think of you like that. Like the card game." She shuddered: the hideous, lost, alone old maid, to be stuck with her was to be the loser.

"Oh, Emily, that's got nothing to do with marriage! Why, my sister Bethany's an old maid and she's been married for twenty years!

She's a grandmother! It's love that saves you from that kind of aloneness, not marriage! Look at me. My husband's not here right now. Sandee's always telling me, Joyce, why don't you just dump Jack, divorce him and get a new man? And I just say, why should I? I'd have to fling the new man out the back door when Jack comes in the front. And he's coming back. He is coming home." Joyce lifted her chin, awaiting the placating, professional social worker's response with its implicit *harrumph* and form-thwacking, but Emily (who had not read the case file) only said the weekends were the worst if you didn't have a husband, if you were on your own. Joyce picked up the refrain from *Are You Lonesome Tonight* and said the King knew all about it.

"I don't mind being alone, really, it's just—" Emily slumped. "I feel like while Rick's in law school, I'm in jail. I'm serving out a sentence. I'm a prisoner and I have to wait for him to bail me out."

"When you love someone, time is nothing, time is just as false as the flavor in a frozen burrito."

"Oh, I *know* that! I love Rick like Juliet loved Romeo and Desdemona loved Othello and Cleopatra loved Antony and Elizabeth Barrett loved Robert—you know what I mean? But it's awful, because the nights I wait for—the nights I love and look forward to—those are the nights I dread! I sit there every Wednesday and Sunday night and I do my nails, and the closer it gets to eight, I'm chewing my nails. I'm afraid the phone won't ring."

"Does it?"

"Yes, but I can't stand the tension! It's terrible. It's like—" And then she was telling Joyce this story, *The Operator,* she'd read once in a magazine, about how a woman's fiancé had to move to a new city far away, and she tried to call, tried and tried and asked the operator to help her, and when she finally got through, a woman answered the phone. "I keep thinking of that story, of the last line. I can't remember what it was, but I can't get it out of my head." Emily went to the TV to get some Kleenex. She admonished herself to be professional and not get worked up. Listening Skills. The quiver of aids. Sociology 414. She vowed to sit and listen to Joyce's story. She would have a story. They all did. Probably something about the Jack on the yellow tray who Lost The Best Thing He Ever Had. In her three months on the job, already these stories had begun to furrow and rut with repetition. Emily had read hundreds of case files, and there, on paper anyway, these tales all had the flavor of coming attractions recollected in tranquility. Wasn't there always a husband, a dim and distant memory, the pledge of promise unfulfilled, the wedding picture with color going to yellow in all the faces, as though the wedding party all suffered hepatitis of the heart? Or, if not a husband, then some Other Man Who Didn't Work Out and left her with the infant token of a night's pleasure, his smile and the light in his blue eyes, and the sweet baby then brought squalling to his mother's arms and breast, where love bloomed anew. The baby who, according to the files, inevitably grew up to be a smart-mouthed, bad-assed, snot-nosed kid who had his old man's blue eyes and found himself some girl he could...

"Where did you learn to do that?"

"What?"

"Sew like that. I've never seen—" Joyce's hands flew over the dismembered dress that had been pinned to a newspaper pattern, remembering the dress swiftly, certainly, and without a single pause. Joyce seemed to carry the tensions of her body in her shoulders and hands and wrists. "How can you do that so quickly?"

"Oh, I was born being able to sew well. It's nothing, but you should have seen me in home ec at SEHS," Joyce chuckled. "They had to pass you if you were warmblooded, but me and Sandee, we got the only D's in the whole class. We just loved to watch Miss Gruski get her dander up. We'd take a pillowcase up to her five times in a row, sewn inside out. Miss Gruski! Imagine her, teaching a bunch of teenaged girls home economics—and her never having a man or making a home, or any idea what any of it was like except what she'd read in a book."

Emily winced as though manacles cuffed her to Miss Gruski's manless and pathetic fate: the Old Maid's Prayer.

"She taught us to sew cute little aprons," Joyce went on without looking up. "Heart shaped over the bosom and gathered at the skirt, but we were never supposed to wipe our hands on them when we cooked—if you could call it cooking." Joyce laughed out loud. "Eggs goldenrod. That was Miss Gruski's idea of cooking. That and Jell-O salad. Can you believe it? Oh, kids like Jell-O well enough, but did you ever meet a *man* who wanted to do anything with Jell-O except maybe lick it out of your belly button?"

Emily endured a pleasurable shiver concocting a scene with Rick in her own double bed. Peach Jell-O. The very next time...

"Me and Sandee worked for those D's. Even the retarded girl got a C."

"But look how talented you are!"

"Yes, but it was 1957."

Emily had no idea what this meant and her face showed it.

Joyce clarified. "I didn't give a shit."

"You mean home ec was a required course?"

She quit sewing and smiled. "No, honey, I mean it was 1957. It was *too much*. The world had only just discovered Elvis, and rock and roll was only just born and bringing us all to life, liberating us, really, and that's all we could think about—rock and roll, and Elvis and having a ball, and boys and cars, and parties and sneaking out of the house. Well, Sandee didn't have to sneak out. But there were parties in the orange groves—where there aren't even any orange groves anymore. It's just no-man's-land now, all torn up and—" Her hands rested briefly in her lap while she looked soulfully to the young Elvis on top of the upright piano. "Anyway, how could anyone be expected to care about eggs goldenrod when you could be—*All Shook Up?*" She laughed to hear that very song come on the record player.

"When I was in high school," Emily offered (after all, she had not missed *everything*), "home ec was an elective and you didn't have to take it if you didn't want to. I didn't." It would have been too LMC for words, but Emily didn't say this. "I was college prep."

"My girls are going to college. UCLA. Cilla especially—so smart! And Lisa Marie, she's smart too. What an imagination! But she's lazy and Cilla's a go-getter."

Emily glanced from her clipboard to the yellow metal tray, noting the nine years between 1959 and Cilla's birth in 1968. "You must have postponed having children for a career." This is what all Emily's married friends intended to do. "Were you sewing professionally then, Joyce?"

"No, Emily, I was crying my eyes out. I guess it was a career. It certainly was a full-time job." Joyce paused thoughtfully. "Though, you know, when I watched Elvis's '68 comeback special on TV with Sandee and I had my baby, Cilla, in my arms, rocking Cilla and watching Elvis, hearing him sing like the King that he is—I thought for sure we were both safe and free."

"You and Cilla?"

"No. Me and Elvis. I guess he was for a couple of years there. Till Priscilla left him and then—well, you know what happened then."

Emily had no idea what happened then, but since she had billed herself as a fan, she nodded knowingly.

"Me, I was all right. I had my baby and I knew my husband would be back. I knew we'd be all right." A fleeting look of pain crossed her face. "Of course we weren't, or you wouldn't be here now, would you, Emily? I guess all that muck and misery is plastered on paper somewhere in the files of the welfare department. "Joyce straightened her narrow shoulders. "It's not the whole truth, Emily. It's not even the whole story."

Emily, who had not read the files, squirmed visibly, opened her briefcase, wishing she could find there some human response that would not make her sound like a bureaucrat or an idiot.

"I know what everyone at the welfare department calls my house. What everyone calls it. Heartbreak Hotel. That's just not true. But I don't care. Call it whatever they want. Elvis was an eagle who soared over all our lives and freed us."

"'Does the eagle know what is in the pit?'" asked Emily for lack of anything more pertinent. "'Or wilt thou ask the mole?'"

"You really are a fan, aren't you? You really understand about Elvis."

Emily shrugged. "'Can wisdom be put in a silver rod? Or love in a golden bowl?'"

"The King has lots of fans, but not many people understand him. They make fun of my porch. They think I put that shrine up for publicity, or some other low reason. But that porch is there to honor Elvis, to honor the eagle that he is. I'm honoring his goodness, which he didn't want anyone to guess at, his genius and his energy, his humbleness and his music. And his spirit," she added simply. "And of course, they're one and the same. You hear Elvis's music and it's just like you're standing, palms up, in the spring rain. That shrine is on that porch to educate people, Emily. To teach them about Elvis Presley."

"Yes. Well." Emily cleared her throat. "Education is very important. Education is the key to independence." She clipped efficiently through the files in her briefcase, that quiver of county aids offering acres of acronyms. "The county has this program, the GGP, the Good Grades Program for AFDC mothers on Family Assistance, and if you keep your grades up, the county pays your fees at SECC, St. Elmo City College. Or your books. Maybe they pay the fees but not the books. I think they help out with the gas and parking too. Something like that. Anyway, it's sort of like a sorority. You can stay in the GGP as long as you keep your grades up. You should go to St. Elmo City College, Joyce. You could do anything you set your mind to." Emily glanced at the 1934 lawbooks stacked footstool high. "You could go to Georgetown Law School if you wanted!"

Joyce scoffed, "My law school was the county courthouse."

"Well, what do you want to do with your life?"

"I'd like to carry on Elvis's work."

Emily coughed, shuffled her papers. "You want to be a rock-and-roll star?"

"That wasn't his work." Joyce walked to the stereo, flipped the records over, and one clacked down like an old man's dentures. *Burning Love* came scorching out. "That was his job."

Not until they heard the back door slam and Cilla called out she was home from school did Emily look at her watch. Inwardly she groaned and the generic cookies roiled in her stomach. And of course by now she had to pee because she and Joyce had shared the whole pitcher of iced tea, to say nothing of having shared stories and swapped histories, Emily offering up the long sweet saga of her and Rick, from their memorable first meeting during Rush Week to their glorious engagement party. In return, Joyce shared her stories of Elvis, his being born in poverty, just like the lyrics to Dixie, one frosty morning in the Deep South, the gospel roots of his music, the genius that was just a gift of God, the destiny that connected him to Sun records, his traveling the South in the mid-fifties, playing any gig he could get, electrifying everyone who saw him. He wasn't even twenty-one when he signed with RCA and started going on national TV, where, even on those tiny gray screens, people thought he was dangerous. Small-minded, tight-livered, pump-sucking righteous types, like Joyce's own father, hated Elvis, accused him of obscenity. It got so bad, Joyce confided to Emily, that on the Ed Sullivan show once, they only photographed him from the waist up. That's how afraid they were. No matter. Elvis drove the fans wild with his voice, his posture, and just one hand free. But after he sang *Peace in the Valley,* Ed Sullivan himself came out and assured the American people that Elvis Presley was a fine person. Emily and Joyce had got through all this (plus how to survive in St. Elmo without air-conditioning) while they worked their way through the pitcher of iced tea and the drowsy spring afternoon.

When Emily came back from the bathroom she shook hands with Priscilla, an immaculately starched and polished girl. She was dark, strong-jawed, probably the image of her absent father, tall for thirteen and perfectly poised. In five minutes Priscilla Jackson had reckoned up Emily Shaw altogether, from the rock on her left hand to her Pappagallo shoes, figured on the Christian Dior lingerie and Estée Lauder cosmetics. She figured up the cost, the maintenance, and the implications. She was shrewd, swift, and nothing got past her. "Where's Mr. Johnson?"

"He got transferred," Emily explained.

"He is a saint," Joyce declared. "It was Mr. Johnson noticed Cilla needs braces last year. He said, *Joyce, I bet that girl needs braces. Take her to the orthodontist.* Show Emily your braces, Cilla. Two thousand dollars, right there in that girl's mouth, Emily. Can you believe it? I bless MediCal every night."

"I hate them. They still hurt."

"I used to have to wear braces." Emily grimaced.

"Is that why you smile with your mouth closed?"

"Do I?"

"Oh, Cilla, would you run down the street to the Phans' and bring Lisa Marie home? I told her she could go there after school."

"Can't I call?"

"They don't have a phone, Cilla." Joyce turned to Emily. "They're Vietnamese and you never met such workers in your life, but there's so many of them and they're just getting by. They don't have a phone because only the little girl can speak English. The adults, they're still just wrestling with English."

"They should take ESL!" said Emily, making some notes on her clipboard, without considering that if the Phans could not speak English, they could hardly read the brochures, but she vowed to send some extra night school material for Joyce and information on the GGP and SECC especially for mothers on AFDC. She packed up and prepared to go, first reflexively fluffing and refolding the quilt on the La-Z-Boy. "I see a lot of country quilts at the boutique my mother shops at, but they are nothing like this." She fondled the hand-sewn hem. "Those are just run up on a machine to be sold. You certainly can tell the difference."

"It's an antique," said Cilla.

"It's been in the family for years." Joyce picked it up and put it in Emily's arms. "It's yours now."

"Oh no. I couldn't. I don't think it's allowed." Emily knew it was not allowed. In training class, Mr. Hansen had specifically addressed this issue, which was a Strongly Suggested unto Thou Shalt Not: Never get chummy with clients. Even given our shared humanity, Mr. Hansen had said, you can best serve your clients by keeping the relationship professional. If you once let it get personal, you open up the possibilities of heartbreak. For everyone. Mr. Hansen cautioned them to use good judgment. A cup of coffee on a Home Visitation, fine.

Gifts, personal phone calls, a few brews outside work, no. "I can't, Joyce. Thank you. Really."

"We have lots, Emily. My grandmother made lots of these the last years of her life."

"Could she sew like you?"

"Better. Even with arthritis and old as she was. We've kept all her quilts, but I know she would want you to have this one."

"It's so sweet of you, but I just can't—"

"Please. Take it. If you have this quilt, you won't be so lonely in St. Elmo."

Emily's resolve wobbled at the mention of loneliness. She bit her lower lip. "I shouldn't have gone on so about myself."

"We're all pilgrims and strangers on this earth, aren't we? We just have to comfort one another when we can."

Emily hugged the quilt, hugged Joyce, Cilla too, and moved toward the door, which Cilla held open for her. But there on a drop-leaf table in a forest of family photographs, a huge magnolia bloomed out of a Coke bottle. So that was the sweet, elusive scent. Emily bent down, breathed deeply into its creamy golden heart, its ancient fragrance. She noticed a glossy color picture of two little boys.

Joyce dusted the photo off tenderly. "Aren't they just the cutest little peaches? Justin's almost five and that little sweet pea there, that's Little Jack. He's just two."

"Are they your nephews?"

"They're little bastards."

"Cilla Jackson! You say you're—"

Cilla sulked and apologized while Joyce explained that these were her husband's children by Dorrie Vardy, the woman he lived with over in San Juan County.

"Hmm," said Emily, who would have known that if she'd read the case file.

Cilla hustled Emily out the door and off the porch and had her nearly to the gate when the Colonel ran from the back and jumped Emily, covering her with dog kisses, dropping his dirty blanket at her feet. Cilla collared him and dragged him off. "Don't take it personal," she cautioned. "He'd do the same for the Hillside Strangler." She shooed the Colonel away and opened the gate. "I guess Mr. Johnson didn't tell you then, huh?"

"You mean about your dad"—Emily coughed— "living with…away from home?"

"What? Farty Vardy? What a whiner. We don't know how Dad stands her. My mother treats those boys better than Farty does any day. If Farty was my mother, I'd beg to be adopted. No, I didn't mean that at all."

"About what then?" Emily rummaged for her keys.

"About coming—you know, coming in the mornings. See, I called Mr. Johnson a long time ago. I told him, don't come in the afternoon. Sometimes me and Lisa bring friends home from school. But if you bring someone home and the county car's out front and the social worker's in there, well then everyone knows, don't they?"

"Knows what?"

Cilla gave her a look of exasperated beatitude. "Look, I tell everyone my parents are divorced—there's no shame in that. Lots of people are divorced. I tell them my dad's a drug buster always out on dangerous assignments, or maybe a fire fighter in the mountains. Something like that. But no one knows we're on welfare and that's the way I want it. At school I'm one of the Bobbaloos. You think I could be a Bobbaloo if I was poor? Poor people stink—but I guess you know that, being a social worker."

Emily could not bring herself to comment on this, but she felt oddly humbled by this candid girl, her protective pride and submerged pain. "You can count on me, Cilla. I'll always do Home Visitations in the morning." Emily shook Cilla's hand, gravely, not knowing a brush of yellow magnolia pollen yet remained on her nose.

Three

Emily's three other Home Visitations that afternoon were, as the saying goes, short and sweet as the Old Maid's Prayer. Emily loathed this expression, but had to endure it constantly. It was one of her father's favorites and he used it all the time: to wrap up consultations, conclude phone calls, on memos to his secretaries, even as a way of dealing efficiently with his family. Never mind that the Old Maid's Prayer had come to be—like racial epithets and slurs against non-Protestant religions—socially unacceptable, he found it a convenient phrase and always funny. Though if, perchance, a listener had not heard the expression *short and sweet as the Old Maid's Prayer,* John Shaw would roll his eyes to heaven and cry out, *Oh Lord, send me a man!* And if this failed to elicit an immediate laugh, he was fond of clarifying, *Don't you get it? The old maid doesn't care what kind of man! Any man will do!* Practicing corporate law, John Shaw seldom dealt with anyone this phrase might offend. It offended Emily. She felt its pathos and encroaching horror: the conviction that marriage alone could butter a woman's bread.

Her last three Home Visitations got about ten minutes each. Thank God none of them was *in extremis.* Even shortchanging these families, Emily did not pull the county car into the county lot till 4:55—well past the 4:30 deadline. She stuffed the antique quilt in her briefcase, closed and snapped it with difficulty and hotfooted it into the Department of Social Welfare. Family Assistance was one vast wing of this building. All the social workers and supervisors worked in a huge, fluorescent-lit, high-ceilinged room with windows along the back wall only. Their desks were set in neat groups of five with the supervisor's desk set singly nearby, like the nest of a broody mother duck. That's what Emily always thought.

She pushed past co-workers who were leaving the office. Large Marge had just turned and shouldered her purse like a carbine. "Have trouble budgeting your time?" she asked Emily.

"Oh—maybe. Just a little. Some tidying up to do here. That's all. A few minutes."

"Did you get through all your Home Visitations? What's that on your nose?"

Emily rubbed at the magnolia pollen, blushed to think of the last three homes she'd visited with bright yellow on her nose.

"Who did you see today?"

"Let me think. Isn't that incredible! I can't remember their names!" Emily smiled, expecting that Large would return that smile, even if in a halfhearted fashion. Nothing of the sort happened. "Let's see. Who? Hmmm. Yes, well I saw the Dudley family today."

Marge shook her head. "Three generations on welfare."

"And the Santoyas."

Marge quacked under her breath.

"And the Washingtons."

"Which one?"

"Ruby."

Marge groaned. "Ruby is lucky she can get herself and those kids dressed by dinnertime."

"Well, they were dressed when I was there. Most of them," Emily added, without saying the Washingtons were her last visit.

"Who else?"

"Ackerman, Ramirez, Nguyen—or however you say that—and the Jacksons."

"Which one?"

"Let me think. Hmmm. The ones on Santiago Street."

"Every time I drive by that Elvis shrine, it puts my teeth on edge."

"Don't you like Elvis?"

Large gave Emily a withering look. "It sets my teeth on edge because I've been through all the books and there's nothing I can use to stop it."

"To stop it from what?"

"There's no law," Marge explained, "that says a welfare mother may not use her Family Assistance grant to pay for a shrine to a rock-and-roll star, a hip-swinging degenerate and a poor white trash drug addict, if I make myself clear at last, Emily."

Emily tried a smile, but it would not come. She swallowed hard and muttered words to the effect that the Santiago Street shrine was not exactly Mount Rushmore.

"It's not a question of relativity," Marge went on while Emily did a mental jig around the notion of $E=mc^2$, though she kept her mouth resolutely shut. "That shrine costs money, to pay for the lights and the music and the fresh flowers. All that costs. The posters and pictures cost money. Keeping that up costs time that woman should be giving to her children, or looking for a job. That woman has been on and off welfare since 1968. If she worked, she wouldn't have *time* to have a shrine in her front yard. But no. The county supports her. She has had MediCal, food stamps, and a check from St. Elmo County every month since 1977. Figure that."

"I'm not too good at math."

"You wonder how long that Elvis shrine would stand if her neighbors knew they were paying for it."

"They are?"

"They're taxpayers, aren't they? You have just taken a sworn statement from her today in Home Visitation that county aid is all the money she gets. Isn't that right? Family Assistance, welfare—" Large lingered over the words as though sucking marrow from them.

"Yes. I think so. She might have had some money from her husband."

"That worthless, jailbird, philandering husband of hers doesn't pay support!"

"Jailbird?"

"Didn't you read the file?"

"Yes. Of course. Jailbird. I just got them confused with some people I used to know in Laguna."

"That woman is defrauding the county. I'm certain of it. She lives too well." Large's heavy-hooded eyes narrowed up and involuntarily Emily shuddered, picturing Large as a barn owl with a field mouse hanging limp and dead from her indifferent lips. Large commented that Emily looked pale. "Anyone *in extremis?*"

"Oh no. Everyone's fine, just fine. It's just that—" Emily wanted to say that nothing in Sociology 387: Aspects of Poverty in Postmodern Societies had prepared her for the squalor and ruin and hopelessness of a family like Ruby Washington's, where half a dozen children under six played in the Cheerios on the floor and then ate them; how Sociology 387, with all its charts and graphs, had made no mention whatsoever that poverty in postmodern societies could be like a fat shiny tick sucking hope and blood and juice from actual lives. Sociology 387 did not seem to know that down by the unvarnished ugliness of the St. Elmo flood channel, there were black men hunkered in what shade they could find, who drank wine from paper bags and stood up drunk, peed in the gutter or against the side of the building, where it evaporated instantly. Sociology 387 addressed poverty theoretically, which was not at all the case in certain areas of downtown St. Elmo, where runaway teenaged girls strutted their stuff and, if they couldn't sell it for cash or drugs, they slept in doorways or under tarps strung between palms in the park. Sociology 387 neglected the aspect of poverty you'd find if you drove out to the Tumbleweeds district and found a house far back from the road and drove up a track set about with trash and mattresses and interviewed a pregnant teenager who swore she didn't know who done it and her mother's boyfriend sat right outside the door, so close you could hear him sucking on his teeth and listen to him light his cigarette, blow out his match. Aspects of Sociology 387 completely ignored someone like Eddie Regis, five years old, who (Cilla was right) smelled bad. His brothers smelled bad and his mother smelled bad and his house stank; he had climbed into Emily's lap and cried there the whole Home Visitation. When she left, Emily smelled bad. It was contagious. Sociology 387 never told you that. "I guess I have a lot to learn."

Marge agreed, said good night, and left. They all left. Emily found herself alone, save for a single social worker who was on the phone, *in extremis* across the acres of desks. His voice rang out declamatorily in the emptiness and finally he hung up and fled. Emily was alone with the janitor, who began at the other end of the room, swinging metal trash cans into the big basket on his trash cart, where a transistor radio wailed out tinny country-western tunes into the void. Alone with the janitor and the Jackson case file.

Emily took a deep breath, plunged into the case history of County Case Number 68-46784. Preferring always mythology to methodology and inspiration to perspiration, she flipped forward and backward, shuffling, ruffling through pages impaled at the top on sharp fasteners that nonetheless nailed down nothing. This two-inch-thick folder might have cast more light on Joyce's story if someone had put a match to it, but this much history was clear: On June 20, 1968, Mrs. Joyce (Rejoice) Jackson had first asked the county's aid. She was pregnant, impoverished, unemployed, and her husband had recently gone to prison for two years for aggravated assault. Interspersed through the file were allusions to, notes about, and copies of Warren James Jackson, Jr.'s police records, his arrests and convictions, an erratic, repetitive account of malicious mischief, aggravated assault, assault and battery, drag racing, disturbing the peace, unlawful betting, speeding, and sundry other breaches of several sections of the penal code that suggested the unstable chemistry of alcohol, male ego, motorcycles, and unemployment.

The most serious charge was unarmed robbery in 1965. The evidence, taken as a whole, suggested this was less than a carefully hatched, premeditated robbery. It better resembled a dispute over money that came to physical blows, coupled with loud threats and noisy, blustering demands for payment. Judge Vernon Eliot found Warren James Jackson, Jr., guilty of unarmed robbery in 1965, but the conviction was subsequently, shortly overturned and the prisoner released. The prosecutor had botched presentation of the evidence. Warren James Jackson, Jr. continued unreformed until 1968. He was arrested again, albeit on a relatively minor charge, aggravated assault. He pleaded not guilty. The judge was Vernon Eliot. Judge Vernon Eliot remembered that his earlier verdict had been reversed, and when given this opportunity, he threw the proverbial book at Mr. Jackson, sentencing him to two years for aggravated assault.

Emily rubbed her eyes and tried to imagine what she would do if Rick went to jail for two years. Couldn't. Couldn't imagine him anywhere near a jail. Not even as a lawyer. Clean corporate law. That was Rick's style, not dealing with motorcycled malicious-mischief-making machos like Warren James Jackson, Jr. No wonder Joyce had cried her eyes out for a career.

When Warren James Jackson, Jr., got out of prison, he returned to his wife and daughter and, if he was not an altogether model citizen, his breaches of the peace and penal code were minor and he had managed to support his family. County Case 68-46784 went into Inactive until 1977, when Mrs. Jackson (now with two daughters) was once again impoverished, abandoned by her husband, who had bolted the Santiago Street home and moved to San Juan County. He now lived there, unmarried, with Miss Dorrie Vardy, who had gone on the San Juan County welfare rolls when she became pregnant with the child who was born in July 1977. When Warren James moved in with Miss Vardy, she went off welfare. Someone had noted that County Case 68-46784 ought to be cross-indexed with San Juan County's Vardy case and to check police records under Denby.

"Who's Denby?" Emily asked the thick folder, and finally it emerged that Denby was Joyce's maiden name. Her brother Stan had been born Noah Denby, changed his name in honor of the great Stan Kenton, and was known to the authorities as an out-of-work musician, a small-time marijuana peddler, and for the occasional petty theft. In 1971 he had been convicted for smoking marijuana in the park and in 1972 another conviction, this time for drunk walking. "Drunk walking?" Yes, said the file, and willful destruction of property while he was at it, playing the drums on mailboxes and crosswalks and shop windows while under the influence.

The throb in Emily's head worsened as the janitor moved closer, the warbling of country music punctuated only by his tossing trash cans and the occasional *whoosh* of his broom, sweeping all the lyrics up, words about unfaithful women and hard-living men, hard liquor, hard times, hard beds, coffee you could chew and tobacco you could spit. Emily massaged her temples, concentrated hard, changed her mind, and resolved to go about this in a systematic fashion. "Begin at the beginning," she declared. "Go to the end. Then stop." It seemed like very good advice.

On June 20, 1968, when Rejoice Jackson first approached the county for aid, she had brought with her those documents the system demanded before they could offer succor even to the most desperate cases:

1. Social Security card and/or driver's license.
2. Marriage certificate if claiming to be married.
3. Birth certificates of any children.
4. Note from the doctor if claiming to be pregnant.

Joyce Jackson was claiming to be four and a half months pregnant, but she had the doctor's note and this first social worker had checked each item and then signed below:

Marjorie Mason

"Oh Lordy," Emily whispered, coming up for air. "Oh Lordy."

The janitor, still overturning trash cans in a fairly rhythmic manner, was close enough to her to grin when she looked up. She gave him a tiny wave, wincing when he smiled back: his mouth was a checkered array of yellow teeth and black spaces, reminding Emily of a whorehouse piano, not that she had ever played a whorehouse piano, or even seen one. But the thought came to her that the music was not from a radio at all, that he was playing it on his own teeth. The thought made her rather faint, especially when it looked as if—

hairless, toothless, and slack-jawed as he was—he might be coming over to have a little chat. She instantly bent her head down over the file. If he comes, she told herself, I'll say my husband will be here any minute. Wednesday night! She had to be home by 8:03 for Rick's call. She still had time. It was only 6:15, after all. Concentrating on the file seemed to have the desired effect of warding off the slavering janitor, and Emily read on.

In 1968, Marge Mason had only noted the equivalent of name, rank, and serial number in this first interview, concluding,

> I approve this twenty-eight-year-old client for county aid, satisfied that her statements are true and her documents are in order. During this eligibility interview she was noncommunicative, not helpful, and refused to answer any but routine questions. I was explaining to this woman the state and county rules governing the Family Assistance benefit program, when she began to laugh. Her laughter was so intense and inexplicable and certainly not in keeping with her situation that I suspect the use of mind-altering substances. I inquired point-blank. She refused to answer and continued to laugh. In a gesture of outright insubordination, this woman reached over and touched my cheek. I reprimanded her instantly. I add this information to the file as it suggests a very bad attitude. This woman bears watching. There is something peculiar about her.

"That's true," Emily conceded, "there is something peculiar about her." Large had been Joyce's social worker for about a year, and then the case passed through many hands and many voices reported to the file. Emily Rebecca Shaw followed this progress (at the Cheshire Cat's advice) chronologically, doggedly, though she got very discouraged. This shaggy pile of papers told her virtually nothing about Joyce Jackson. All these ramshackle attempts to catch and preserve, to nail Joyce Jackson's life and story in little coffins of prefab phrases and labels mandated by the state, to fit round her these regulation words, all that failed. It would fail (Emily began to see) for any of us. Cast thus, understanding evaporated, dried here and blew across her eyes as punctuation-dust, then flew up off the page in flocks of words, swirling overhead, winging their prepositional way into the high vault of the office and beyond, into the dusk tumbling purple at the window: word-birds, noun-nuns hurrying toward vespers whispered in some distant roofless nave beneath bare ruined choirs where darkness enveloped, absorbed, obliterated them all. And that's what finally fluttered up from these dense, typewritten pages: darkness, not illumination. Not lies, but limitations. Emily hyperventilated, fathomed without quite understanding that we are—any of us—but prisms of light and water. We hold one another up to the light, but what we see is constricted everywhere by what we are able to see.

The people who had murmured these valuations of Joyce Jackson in the confessional quiet of the taping booth seemed content with, unto oblivious of, the darkness. They held Joyce up to no light whatever, but described her variously as a victim, a dupe, an object of mirth or pity, a fruitcake, an Elvis fanatic, a dangerous obsessive, who handed out cookies like communion wafers on January 8 and August 16, who created and maintained Heartbreak Hotel, a woman with bad taste in men and music, a good mother, except that she clung to the fiction that her husband would return, and this (as well as her adoration of Elvis) kept her from getting on with life, facing reality, from implementing goals and plans. But at least (and the sigh was all but audible in the pages of the file) Joyce Jackson was never *in extremis.* Joyce accepted the county's financial grant, food stamps, and MediCal, but she consistently spurned any social worker's pious reflections on poverty, on the suitability of trimmed-down hopes and advisability of her seeking out some minimum-wage undertaking commensurate with her lack of marketable skills (she could not type, after all) and her high school education.

Only Sid Johnson disagreed. He wrote on the occasion of his first Home Visitation: "If Mrs. Jackson had had other opportunities in life, there's no end to what she might have achieved. She is able, intelligent, imaginative, and resourceful. Moreover," he added in a rather testy and emphatic tone, "I disagree with social workers who believe that Mrs. Jackson erected her shrine to Elvis to get publicity, perhaps notoriety. I feel strongly that these condescending newspaper articles about the shrine should not have been admitted to this file. The evidence suggests that Mrs. Jackson's husband left her (apparently for good) on or about the same day that Elvis Presley died. How can we underestimate the shock of these two losses? How can we know what Elvis meant to Joyce Jackson and how can we judge the measure of her grief?"

Mr. Johnson's was the only entry in the entire file to end in questions. Everything else was cast in thick statements and meaty assertions, their very solidity, substance, and rotundity suggesting austere judges on a grim bench, meting out sentences in which the words, once written, all flew away like butterflies, with the grace of indifferent butterflies, and the verdicts thus robbed of all their pain and terror.

Which crashed upon Emily when the trash can clattered behind her and spun crazily on the floor, the janitor so close his radio crooned *Your Cheatin' Heart* right in her ear. She had not heard the janitor's approach. She had heard nothing at all. And now she looked up to see the janitor victoriously emergent from Large's trash can, his whorehouse-piano teeth parted over a half-eaten Hershey bar. He grinned, slack-jawed, and stepped so close to her she could smell the chocolate on his breath. She sat there, speechless, helpless—the man and moment frozen before her—until he laughed hollowly and then moved on, pulled his cart and *Cheatin' Heart* toward the next set of desks, and Emily turned back to the files spread before her to find that what she had read and constructed into so shapely a story with some grace and grandeur was really nothing but paper lumps of sorrow and loss, infidelity and despair, defeat reeking of the jail, the latrine, the unmade bed where sweat and wet and seed and anguish all stained and stank. All this gleamed before Emily like oyster turds in the fluorescent light that hurt her eyes since full dark had fallen outside. The light itself became like water. Emily knew she was in over her head.

"Emily?"

"Mr. Hansen?" she screamed. "Mr. Hansen!"

"What are you doing here this late? Are you all right?"

"Oh, Mr. Hansen." Emily began to cry. "Mr. Hansen, I can't stand it—think of them, all of them, everyone, everyone who's alive and even those who aren't, they—we—all commit such follies and do such crazy things in the name of love." Emily gulped. "I mean—it hasn't changed since *Greensleeves.*"

"What?"

"'Alas my love you do me wrong to cast me off discourteously—'" Emily splayed her hand over the Jackson folder and flung open her file drawers with April's cases all lined up in neat alphabetical order. "All these knocked-up girls, Mr. Hansen! They've existed since the beginning of time! And think of it! They—we—all—we get here in the same way, with two people we don't even know screwing their brains out! Everyone does it. Why should it be so endlessly fascinating? Why do people have to call it love and write songs and poems and stories about it? It's not fascinating. This isn't." She pointed to the case files in the drawer and the Jackson folder before her. "These aren't great love stories! These are squalid little histories. Every one of these women—and every other woman, living or dead or yet to be born— every one of them who has a bunch of kids hanging on her hem, she watches for her man, and one day he just doesn't come home, or he dies or he gets hanged, or marched off to war, or prison, he turns to drink or he takes up with another woman, and every last one of these people, do you know what they said, Mr. Hansen? Do you?"

"What did they say?"

"*Oh shit.* That's what they said. *Oh shit, what's going to happen now?* And the only thing that happened was they went on screwing and working and sweating and sleeping and swearing—and then, they died. Is that what you meant about shared humanity? In training class? You can say what you want, Mr. Hansen, but the human race is lucky to be out of the tar pits!"

"I don't think humans were ever in—"

"And love! 'Alas my love,' oh, when you love someone you just feel like—" Arm outstretched to the empty office, Emily declared, "'When he shall die, take him and cut him out in little stars, and he will make the face of heaven so fine that all the world will be in love with night and pay no worship to the garish sun.'" She wiped her eyes with the flat of her hand. "Oh, Mr. Hansen! That's shit, isn't it?"

"No, Emily. I think that's Shakespeare. *Romeo and—*"

"When poetry, I mean poverty, comes in the door, love flies out the window, but sex doesn't."

"What window?"

"Heartbreak Hotel," she wailed. "We're all just lodgers here at Heartbreak Hotel and it's like, it has a revolving door." Tears splashed into her hands and she bit her lip. "It's sex that makes people crazy and married, and it doesn't have anything to do with love or law school. Oh!" She clapped both hands over her mouth. "Law school!"

"You shouldn't be here this late, Emily. You're working too hard. Let me buy you dinner and a couple of beers."

"I can't," she wept.

"Why not?"

"I'm expecting a call and it's already late and you can't."

"Of course I can. I'm over twenty-one. Aren't you? That means you can drink in this state."

"But you're married." She had certainly counted him married in her statistical tally in training class. She'd heard roundabout there was a Mrs. Hansen. "Aren't you?"

"I used to be. Once. I'm divorced."

"I'm sorry to hear that."

"It was just another boring family tragedy," he said, folding up the Jackson folder and putting it in her desk. "Like all the rest of them." He closed the file drawer and handed her the bulging briefcase and her purse. "Let me take you to Zacateca's. You have to be a local to know Zacateca's. Best Mexican food in town. In the world."

"I can't! I can't miss my call. It'll be—"

"Mascara," said Mr. Hansen, after he took out his handkerchief and wiped her cheeks.

Emily stared at him. She'd always regarded him as the guiding guru of the training class in particular and of the Department of Social Welfare in general, so naturally she'd assumed he was middle-aged. She realized now he was in his early thirties. He had thinning dark hair and a moustache and wore glasses over level, compassionate brown eyes. His features were rounded but his shoulders were not. They were broad and straight.

Mr. Hansen smiled. "Come on, let's go to Zacateca's."

Emily hesitated; spontaneity of any sort is always depressing to someone whose life has been premeasured, neatly slotted into prescribed activities with prescribed people, the social calendar filled out well in advance. Nonetheless she took up her purse and, in a dispirited fashion, followed him. Threading through the desks in the enormous office, she realized randomly that this was probably the first impulsive thing she'd done in nearly five years, since that day in Italy.

Howard Hansen interrupted her thoughts, inquiring if she was parked out back. Emily said yes. "Good," he replied. "That will make everything easy. You follow me to Zacateca's in your own car and then, after we eat, you can go right home and get your phone call."

Emily nodded wanly. She'd already missed her phone call, the first Wednesday night call she'd missed since Rick had gone to Washington, D.C. The lapse seemed unduly dire, a sticky premonition, as though the stitching of her life had frayed and might completely unravel, because in fact, Emily had no wish tonight to listen to the challenges of law school larded up with words of love and the cultural excitement of living in Washington, D.C. She didn't want to hear it. Any of it. She wanted, needed, something far more modest: shared humanity, a few laughs, a few beers, a friendly face across the table in a well-lit Mexican restaurant. Imagine wanting so very little. It was embarrassing and out of place in the rest of her life. In impulsively accepting Howard Hansen's invitation, Emily felt oddly as she had in Italy when, lost and wandering with her parents, she had simply forsaken them, walked away—and foolishly almost missed the train back to Rome. That entire day she had felt unmoored, and yet expectant. But once back at the Excelsior Hotel in Rome, it all seemed a mere spontaneous aberration, more like a dream than a memory.

Following Mr. Hansen now, Emily passed the janitor, his cart, his noisy transistor radio. His whorehouse piano teeth curved into a crescent of a smile. Emily shuddered, picked up her pace, lifted her chin like the heroines she had read about, girls facing grimly altered circumstances. Okay, so Howard Hansen did not have a Winning Team Smile, nor Rick's athletic grace and electric personality. So be it. She wasn't going to marry Howard Hansen, or sleep with him, or any of that. She was going to accept what he had this evening to offer. He stood there at the door, holding it open for her. That was all she wanted right now: to escape the echoes of empty trash cans, escape the ring of collected refuse, of what had been cast off discourteously, to escape tinny country-western tunes resounding in the fluorescent vastness of the Department of Social Welfare, where ignorant metaphors clashed by night.

Four

Early in the morning, the dining room of Rome's Excelsior Hotel was deserted and, in its marble splendor, all sound heightened into clarity; even the pages of the *International Herald Tribune* crackled when they should have whispered. A portly waiter clicked his heels and inquired if Signor Shaw and his family wished another caffè latte. As he poured (silver pots in his gloved hands), the waiter glanced at the two-column front-page picture of Elvis Presley in full regalia. *"Triste,"* said the waiter in a clucking tone, *"la morte di Elvis,* the death of the very great singer, the King of Rock and Roll, *è triste,* sad, yes?"

"Right," said John Shaw, crisply as though the word were a head of lettuce.

The waiter offered another caffè latte to Emily, who declined with a practiced *grazia.* That word, along with *per favore, buongiorno,* and now *morte* and *triste,* formed the whole of her Italian vocabulary. Emily wondered why all the Europeans she had met on this trip had endured the trouble of learning English, only to use it as waiters, clerks, or travel agents. If she could ever master a foreign language, she would want to be a diplomat. At the very least.

The doorman came to their table, respectfully informed Signor Shaw that their car and driver awaited their pleasure. His manicured English, *sotto voce* tone were commensurate with the gold and cream decor, the huge floral displays, and rosy pink marble of the dining room. John said they'd be there directly. Barbara, Emily's mother, said she was ready for anything that would get them out of Rome's beastly heat. She said again it was a pity they must come to Europe in August. The heat. The crowds. Terrible service. A September excursion would have been so cool and satisfying.

John and Barbara both (and probably without meaning to) looked exasperatedly at Emily. It was Emily's fault they must travel in August because in September she would be a freshman at USC. This wonderful European trip was her parents' gift for her high school graduation. Emily was piously grateful, but she knew the trip had been occasioned by John Shaw's tawdry involvement with one of the lowlier secretaries at his law firm. The affair itself was absolutely undiscussable, and so Emily's parents had filled the six weeks with pleasanter topics, like John's making Barbara late to her sister's wedding in 1966, Barbara's snubbing John's mother at Thanksgiving dinner in 1972, his speculating with their insurance in 1968, her spending habits, running up the credit cards and thinking he was made of money. Despite all this, the Shaws' marriage was durable, functional, and ugly as an old garbage scow. John Shaw was indeed made of money. In effect, he and Barbara were quarreling over the price of his lapse. The secretary episode was but one more weapon in Barbara's arsenal of moral superiority.

At eighteen, Emily recognized that only shared expediency united her parents. She thought it rather degrading, but as an only child lacking allies against the adult world, she ignored the obvious. John and Barbara would have been shocked at Emily's insight and judgment, not simply because the judgment was so harsh, but because she had always been so pliable, polite, the prim, incurious product of an Episcopal upbringing and an ocean-view home. Moreover, Emily was one of three (count them) virgins to graduate, class of 1977, El Capitan High School. John and Barbara never guessed at Emily's sophistication and they would not have believed she could come by that sophistication with so little experience. But Emily read. Emily devoured books—novels, poetry, biography, mysteries, Gothics. She kept books stashed all over the house, as a glutton hides bonbons. Her literary acquaintance ranged from Romantic poets to romantic sagas, Daphne Du Maurier to Daniel Defoe, James Michener to Henry James; her taste was catholic, wide-ranging, intense, and as a result, her knowledge was far broader and deeper than eighteen years in Orange County, California, would ordinarily have granted a girl.

When Emily had taught herself to read at the age of three, her parents believed they had a prodigy, but Emily never again did anything the least bit prodigyish and flunked all tests for Gifted. She was merely odd. She got odder by the year and would occasionally come out with a line of Frost or Brontë that shocked her parents far more than a good, hearty *shit*. For her fourteenth birthday, they took her to a much-touted performance of *King Lear* and she mystified them by noisily crying her eyes out because she was so moved.

Though Emily had failed as a prodigy, her parents took comfort in the fact that she did not give them any anguish. Conventionally pretty, her smile testified to the orthodontist's skill, and she dutifully took piano and tennis lessons. Practiced. Played Juliet in the high school production but showed, mercifully, no deeper inclination to Act. She did not get pregnant, or arrested, or have accidents with her car. Did not even get tickets. Did not get drunk or high. She had dates, but no special boyfriend. She seemed, in short, soft-center compared to the gleaming, keen-edged daughters of their friends. Barbara and John assured themselves that the challenge of a major university and a good sorority (Barbara had been a Tri Delt) would put some polish on Emily, season and sharpen her, as would this wonderful European trip.

The six wretched weeks—England, France, Belgium, Switzerland, and Italy—were now mercifully drawing to a close in Rome. Hot, impossible Rome with its savage armies of juvenile pickpockets, overrated ruins, and nasty foreigners. That's how John Shaw saw it; travel confirmed his every xenophobic preconception. Travel confirmed for Barbara that anything worth having she could buy at South Coast Plaza. John and Barbara mentally counted the hours until they could be in Pan Am's first-class lounge, sipping drinks. You could be certain of things in the first-class lounge, as you could be certain of little else in Europe.

The trains, for instance. Hot, disgusting, and filthy. Even in first class. On their journey down from Florence to Rome they had shared their first-class compartment with a garlic-soaked priest who carried on a noisy conversation with two other Italians, fanning his garlicky breath about the compartment with expansive hand gestures. "I thought priests were committed to poverty," John had whispered to Barbara. "What's he doing in first class?"

After that dismal experience, John went to the concierge at the Rome Excelsior, slipped him a fat tip, and asked him to make arrangements for a car and driver to take them to Assisi. They wished a leisurely trip through the Umbrian countryside. This day-trip to Assisi was not originally on the Shaws' agenda, but resulted from a chance encounter on the Zurich-to-Milan flight (first class, of course) with a La Scala violinist, native to Umbria. "To come to Italia!" he cried, "and to miss the region of Umbria is to have a love affair and not go to bed!"

It was an unfortunate allusion, given the Shaws' marital situation, but the violinist could not have known that. For the entire flight— and in his charming, excellent English—the violinist waxed on about his native region: the wine, the landscape, the tremendous cultural, religious, and political events that had marked its history. Umbria! The land of saints and generals! Unsullied Italia could still be found here, only a few hours from that cesspool, Rome. Umbria! Where towns and villages subscribed to the old customs, where the old family values had not been defeated, bought off by the ugly invasion of (he looked quickly around him) British, German, and Japanese tourists. Americans, he added, were welcome.

"If you go to but one city in all of Italy, it must be Assisi!" he cried, glowing with his third or fourth cognac. "In Assisi one feels the stamp, the very shadow of a man who has been dead for nine hundred years! Imagine! What *forza!* The strength of that personality! To be felt so many years after death! Saint Francis was born to a rich family but gave away all his wealth, forsook possessions, position, forsook his parents, dressed in poor rough robes, begged for his bread. He followed only God's command, *Restore my church!*" boomed the violinist, evidently taking the part of the Almighty in this dialogue. "And Francis did. His spirit was grander than any pope's, and yet he remained so humble, he would sing to the lowest sparrow. I tell you, he lives still! His spirit lives on! You will feel him present in Assisi!" The violinist fell back, exhausted, and ordered one more drink before they landed.

On the strength of the violinist's exuberance, the Shaws that morning left the Excelsior dining room, went out to find their car and driver awaiting them in the blue morning shadows of the hotel arches. It was early yet and the day's freshness as yet undimmed.

They were disappointed in the car, which, particularly in contrast to the grand Excelsior, had a shopworn air. Their driver was smoking, lounging with the radio on, tapping one hand nervously to Elvis Presley singing *Don't Be Cruel.* He wore no uniform, and he was sweating profusely; rings circled the armpits of his dark shirt. He was a slight, narrow-shouldered man of indeterminate age and he wore a cap and black sunglasses and had an unappealing stubble of beard across his narrow jaw. At the Shaws' approach, he removed the cap but not the dark glasses. He tossed his cigarette and came to a theatrical *Attenzione!,* opening the door with a flourish. Then he stepped smartly to the driver's side, snapped off the radio, placed his cap back on, and saluted. "Assisi, okay!" He closed the plastic partition separating him from his passengers, turned on their air-conditioning (his side had none), and grinned at them in the rearview mirror. He had very bad teeth.

John muttered that he had paid for better than this. Paid a good deal, in fact. (To say nothing of the concierge's tip.) The car had a sad, tattered, fifties air to it, the seats frayed and shiny where a great many anonymous bottoms had nestled deep. The passengers sat well back and were thus protected from the prying, rude populace, but protected as well from seeing anything. Unless they leaned uncomfortably forward. As a nod to modernity, a small frigobar had been awkwardly installed. It held little bottles of wine, water, and fruit juice.

Emily opened a peach juice and retreated, as best she could, into any one of the half-dozen stories she continually told herself to make this European excruciation bearable. Sometimes she was a princess traveling incognito with unlikely Americans. Sometimes she was an incognito spy. Sometimes she was a diplomatic courier with documents of the utmost importance. Sometimes she was Joan of Arc—or someone like her—on her way to meet a Great Destiny. But the game (and in this instance, any game) proved impossible to sustain. Getting out of Rome was tedious, harrowing. Their driver drove like a madman, darting in and out of traffic, nearly crashing, his haste and anger evident from the way he leaned on the horn and shouted at the other drivers. John and Barbara's frustrations took up the old refrain, Christmas 1965, when John and his oafish brother had showed up late and drunk. Emily burrowed into one of her many guidebooks, reading about Umbria, Assisi, and Saint Francis (ca. 1181–1226), readying herself for yet another day of cold churches, cavernous museums, mute walls.

Once out of Rome, though, the Shaws' mood lightened. The countryside lived up to the violinist's enthusiasm as they moved into Umbria. High, ancient hill towns looked like Leonardo backgrounds rising out of the plains. Ancient cypresses gnarled along the roadsides like thick arthritic fists. John was about to comment happily on the natural beauty when their driver took an abrupt, unsuspected turn. No one had seen a sign that said Assisi. No one had seen a sign at all. Emily suggested perhaps this was the scenic route. They had asked for a countryside ride. Perhaps he was taking them off the beaten path.

"No kidding!" cried John as they bounced up twisting roads. Before you could say *Saint Francis of Assisi,* the road narrowed yet again: two cars could hardly pass, and when a truck came from the opposite direction, the Shaws' driver put the car in reverse and inched down the narrow track to a minuscule turnoff, cursing all the while. As the truck passed, he exchanged obscene gestures with the driver before he bounced back on the road. Through their plastic partition, they watched the driver bring a bottle to his lips.

John's imagination, scrawny though it was, began to entertain dark thoughts. The Italians were great kidnappers. John realized he had not notified the American embassy in Rome of his monied presence. Obviously he was a rich American, senior partner in a California firm of corporate lawyers. His thoughts of the Red Brigade were interrupted by Emily's retching. John banged on the partition and the driver turned to him, cigarette dangling from his sneering lips. The driver had no English beyond the *okay* he had already used, and John could not explain how Emily was susceptible to being carsick. Finally, John just stuck his index finger in his open mouth and made gagging noises.

The driver pulled over. Emily got out and vomited onto the land of saints and generals. John stepped from the car, pulled himself up, spoke sharply to the driver. "Return to Roma!"

The driver exhaled a long, blue ribbon of smoke, pointed to the radio, where Elvis wailed. "No, signor, *Heartabreakahotel.*"

"Return to Roma!"

"No. *Arrivederci, Roma,* eh?" With a coarse laugh and brusque gestures, he pointed John back in the car. He made Emily get in the front seat with him. He pressed on the gas pedal. He meant business.

John Shaw considered himself a risk-taker. He had cheated on the LSAT to get into law school. He had embezzled money from his own firm to cover a bungled real estate deal. He had forged his wife's signature on a deed of trust. He had trod the risky, mined fields of adultery with many willing women, including his partner's wife, the now ex-Mrs. Brill. But now, here, in this car and for the first time in his life, John Shaw kicked himself for being a fool. He could have bought Barbara a new Mercedes to make up for screwing the secretary. He didn't have to come to Europe at all. The garlic-smelling priest was but a small price to pay for the safety of crowds and public conveyance. He hated himself for staying at the expensive Excelsior, for renting a suite instead of a room, for listening to some stupid goddamned wop fiddler tell him he should go to some stupid goddamned town and feel the presence of a man who was such a goddamned fool that he would give away his riches and talk to a bunch of goddamned birds.

Barbara's hand inched over his thigh. Her face was pale. He took her hand, as much for his comfort as hers.

Emily, for her part, had no thought of the Red Brigade. However, she was alarmed at the driver's drinking, which he now took no care to conceal. His driving became increasingly cavalier as the roads got narrower and they circled higher into the hills. They narrowly passed a motor scooter and she wondered how, since she spoke no Italian, she might offer some comment on safer driving. She pointed to herself brightly and said, "Emily. Signorina Emily Shaw."

"*Mi chiamo* Carlo," he replied glumly.

"*Buongiorno,* Carlo."

"Ah, signorina!" Carlo whipped off his glasses. The stubble on his chin notwithstanding, he was clearly a good deal younger than she'd first supposed, perhaps in his mid-twenties, not much older than Emily herself. His face was full of pain and he struggled with a storm of feeling. His lower lip trembled, ash from his cigarette fell to his pants, but he brushed it away without blinking. His dark eyes raked over Emily's face. "Ah, signorina!" he cried again and again, babbling on, wiping his eyes, explaining frantically as he lit cigarettes one after another. He spoke swiftly, swilling from the bottle, offered it to her. "Grappa?" Emily declined with thanks (in Italian) and he glugged down more, drove on, heedless of the ruts and potholes, crying, choking, wiping his nose on his sleeve, explaining everything. Everything.

Emily thought he seemed especially comforted when she nodded, so she did, over and over, but she caught almost none of what he said, save for the words she had just learned this morning. "*Morte?*" she inquired as another Elvis song, *Are You Lonesome Tonight?*, came on the radio. Carlo broke into a fresh paroxysm of weeping. Emily touched his shoulder consolingly and made tut-tut noises, though she thought it odd that an Italian should get so worked up over the death of an aged American rock and roller. Even Elvis's music was so clichéd, all you could do was sigh or giggle. Still, Emily offered Carlo the words of her Excelsior waiter. "Elvis Presley, *morte. Triste, si.*"

"*Mamma e' morta!*" cried Carlo, "*Mio Dio! Mamma mia!*" His hands flew off the wheel and he wrung them before God as the car careened toward a cliff. They were moving high now, up into the Umbrian hills, and the road (like the much-vaunted path to Virtue and Wisdom) was steep and rocky. Steam began to plume from the hood of the car. Carlo kept drinking, smoking, and with every new Elvis tune on the radio, he shook his head, muttered, until *All Shook Up* burst into the car and then he seemed to jump out of his seat, throttle the wheel, shout, pointing into the distance. At the top of the hill, Emily could see the pink and apricot walls, the medieval towers of a small city, a village perched up high with wide skirts, fields flouncing down the hillside, fields of corn and bronzed sunflowers.

Emily leaned forward. For six weeks now she had dutifully responded to pictures, monuments, museums, churches, icons of cultural significance. She'd obeyed tour guides and timetables; she'd endured the maid's mocking reply to her question about the bidet. She had borne the unbearable proximity of her parents. But now, as Carlo drew in on this high town embraced still in its medieval wall, encircled with fields, its towers bathed in the noonday light, for the first time since she had come to Europe, Emily Shaw was actually interested in the vista and experience before her. They were not going to Assisi. They were not going anyplace where a guidebook might be of use. They were going to some undiscovered country where, she felt certain, the language would come to her easily, expressively, where, indeed, she might very well be native.

Pulling through the narrow city gates that gave onto an even narrower street, Carlo began tooting his horn wildly, waving at pedestrians and bicyclists alike, shouting them from his path. Men, women, children flattened themselves against the walls and jumped into doorways as Carlo barreled through the threadlike lanes. A car, going in the other direction, seemingly pulled into a greengrocer's shop to allow Carlo to pass, and as he passed, people reached out to touch the car with their hands, some bringing fingers to their lips and crying out his name. The car climbed past shops and churches, under banners of laundry strung between the buildings, up streets so narrow only the noonday sun could penetrate to cobbles otherwise steeped in ancient shadows. Church bells tolled as they pulled through an arch and into a courtyard surrounded on three sides by crumbling buildings of vanilla-colored stucco, cracked and mottled with age. Thick webs of laundry festooned the windows. There was a low wall where a neat garden of peppers and tomatoes gleamed on carefully tied stakes, and in the distance, the Umbrian hills surrounded them in a dry, rugged embrace.

Carlo jumped out taking the key with him. He dashed up a broad stone staircase and vanished into the green darkness at the top. News of his arrival seemed to bounce around the courtyard, echoing back into the street, rolling amongst the stone buildings like the tolling of a church bell.

Ignoring her parents, Emily got out and walked to the wall, looking over the hills toasted everywhere to a Franciscan brown, where corn and drooping sunflowers sloped far below her. She heard a high, fragile train whistle and saw a distant plume of smoke fall back, exhausted, against the fields. The train itself was invisible. Overhead the sun burnt brassy, and heat reeled round her like a saint's unsubtle halo in a medieval painting. Emily felt suddenly light-headed and would not have been at all surprised to rise and fly, swoop over the burnished fields, as you would in a dream, where the old dull laws, like gravity, vanish and new laws prevail. This conviction grew girth and weight and radiated substance: something wonderful was about to befall her. Love, maybe. Her senses were, each one, sweetly sharpened and she felt enhanced, even ennobled. She carried this freshly minted conviction almost visibly as she walked to an old cistern where water plopped from the mouth of a stone lion.

John got out of the car, rumpled and sweating. "Don't be an ass, Barbara! Does it look like Assisi?"

Barbara wobbled uneasily after him. "How do I know? How do you know? God, it's hot!"

"Where did the goddamned driver go? Where is he? The little bastard!"

Barbara suddenly clung to her husband. "John, please get him to take us back to Rome. Please. Pay him anything. Maybe he'll take a card. Anything. Just get him to drive us back to Rome."

"He won't take you anywhere," said Emily, at last understanding what had escaped her entirely in the car. She drank from the cistern, rinsed her face, arms, neck, dried with the hem of her colorful cotton skirt, and turned to her parents. "His mother has died. In there." She nodded toward the arched, shadowed stairway "Carlo never had any intention of taking us to Assisi."

"*Carlo?*" demanded Barbara. "Since when are you so chummy? Did that little wop make a pass at you?"

"I'll have his Italian ass in a sling!" vowed John, adding he'd have Carlo's job as well; he'd tell the Excelsior, the American embassy. Worse, he hinted darkly, he'd tell American Express.

Barbara reminded him that none of this could come to pass until they got back to where they had been. "Which is going to be hard," she added sourly, "since we don't even know where we are."

"We are in a catholic country." Emily spoke translating for these foreigners. She explained without elaborating, "The country of the imagination is always a catholic country."

John and Barbara regarded their odd daughter with undisguised bewilderment that quickly dwindled into indifference as they volleyed blame for last year's Mazatlán vacation. "Remember the mule trip?" Barbara remarked savagely. "*That* was your idea! Just like this! I have to pee. You'd better find us a ladies' room, John. Fast."

A ladies' room proved impossible, but eventually they found a unisexual hole in the floor behind a closed door, with a moth-studded light bulb screwed into the wall and a hallelujah chorus of flies. This was in a bar. Before they had found the bar, they had inquired of people met on the street, *Bathroom? Bathroom?*, reduced to finally the expedient, *Toilet?* Wherever they asked, their American voices made people stare boldly and rudely. Walking down the town's narrow central street, they created their own, uncivil procession. From open windows overhead came a medley of opera, Abba, and Elvis; scratchy TV voices, wavering radio combined with chattering songbirds, their cages hung in the windows. As the Shaws' English floated upward, Italian matrons came to the windows and called out dourly to one another. Emily often heard Carlo's name in the exchange. Clearly, the sunny slogans of the Italian tourist board did not ring true here in the unsullied Italia.

They found the bar. They found the toilet. Barbara first and then Emily preceded John into the room with the hole in the floor. While they waited for her father, Emily watched flies play over sandwiches stacked on the counter. She absorbed hostile stares from the people in the bar, perhaps a dozen of them. The violinist had assured them only British, German, and Japanese tourists were despised in Umbria. Americans were all right. Emily tried the universal passport: a smile. Not valid here.

Blue Suede Shoes came rolling out of a vintage radio, followed by *Jailhouse Rock,* and the woman washing glassware turned up the music and wiped her eyes on the edge of a stained apron, her sad gesture totally at odds with Elvis's young voice, his unvarnished sexual energy. Emily cleared her throat. "Elvis, *morte. Triste, si?"* People in the bar became voluble, if not altogether friendly, and when John came out of the toilet, he was surprised to see the locals talking at Emily, if not to her, and Emily making the same tut-tut noises she had used with Carlo.

"Ask them how we get to Rome," John demanded. "Ask them if someone speaks English. Someone in this goddamned town has got to speak English."

Perhaps. But the Shaws never found this mythical English speaker as they wandered from shop to shop, buying bread and fruit and mineral water, trying to ease and pave their way with lire as they inquired how they might get back to Rome, absorbing the locals' unconcealed curiosity and ill will. Finally, with a great many hand gestures, much mental effort, and cobbling together a number of responses, Emily figured out there was a train. They could catch the train. There. In the distance. Down. Low. In the fields. Where? There, at the bottom of the hill. The train will take us back to Rome? Where goes the train? The train will take them, well, somewhere. The train would take them somewhere.

They started down the hill while all around them screens came down and shutters slammed shut. The orchestration of exclusion was deafening. The town shut up and shut down for the long midday meal and nap. Not like in the big cities, according to the Umbrian violinist. In the big cities shops stayed open all the time and Italians there had "lost everything of value while they suck up"—really, Emily had been surprised to hear so cultured a man use so vulgar a phrase— "to the almighty dollar—or rather deutsche mark." Well, thought Emily, as the streets emptied, clearly this was the old Italia.

A stout woman carrying a chicken slung over her shoulder hurried past them. The chicken's head at the end of its long, wrung, hapless neck was swinging with metronomic regularity across her black-clad back as she retreated down the narrow street. Hypnotically, Emily watched the swinging chicken head, feeling, oddly, that she might have been following a woman in 1177, rather than 1977, down this very street and out these gates, the time of Saint Francis himself, when people worked the sloping fields by day and returned here, atop this hill, at night. Behind these high stone walls, families had hunkered over bread and wine, alert always for the glimmering watch fires of invading armies. What were tourists but yet another invader? Behind her, her parents exhumed Mazatlán in 1976 as they all passed through the city gates and followed thin, dusty trails that Carlo's ancestors had trod through the corn and ruffling sunflowers. A hot wind dried her sweat and parched her lips. On the lathe of history, Emily turned story after story, imagining herself carrying a rake, a scythe (instead of this plastic grocery bag and her own purse), leaving the town daily at dawn, walking down this path and climbing back up it at night, working till-death-did-you-part from Adam's curse, from earning your bread with the sweat of your brow. From the time of Saint Francis, these people—none of them with Francis's *forza,* all of them anonymous as the dirt beneath Emily's feet—these people had stooped and sweated and shivered till they dropped and died and were buried. But where? Emily had seen no cemetery. Where did Carlo's ancestors do their dust-unto-dusting? Where would they bury Carlo's mother, who, like Elvis Presley, had died in August 1977: a chunk of time broken off as bread could be broken off, as knowable and subject to decay as bread.

"It wasn't the mule trip that ruined Mazatlán," snarled John. "It was your goddamned sister, bitching and moaning and—"

"My sister was sick! You never let up on her! You never…"

Emily hastened her step to escape them. Their very presence seemed a sort of wart on the imagination, a blister on the conviction that something extraordinary was about to befall her. However, she had begun to doubt it was love. Love—well, true love (and why bother with anything less?)—would need to speak English, after all. So perhaps it wasn't love, she reasoned, walking swiftly, but something less predictable. She reached the train tracks long before her parents and dawdled there, absorbing every scent and sound, the most mundane of which must surely have its significance. It would all—she was certain—be made manifest.

Approaching the tracks, Barbara brandished the simpering specter of John's college girlfriend. "Your own mother told me so! God, it's hot! Your own mother told me you wanted to marry Cherie!" Barbara drooled over the name as if it were a Goo Goo Cluster. "Would your mother lie? Of course, she only said it in the first place to be mean to me."

"Here's the goddamned track," said John, turning to Emily. "Now, where's the goddamned station? Where do we catch this goddamned train? My mother never said any such thing."

Emily abandoned them to their unsavory past and walked up the tracks with a dreamy dignity befitting one of the last three virgins in the class of 1977. She walked till she heard the sputtering of a car and could see the solid lineaments of an ancient farmhouse, thick walled, faded tiles sloping down the roof. The farmhouse outbuildings backed up to the track, and nearby there was a railway maintenance shack on one side and, across from it and down a bit, a shelter of sorts, obscured by a canopy of vines. It was old, unkempt, and it had a withered timetable under glass. Every weekday there were two trains. A northbound at 12:18 and a southbound at 3:10.

In the shade of the vines, Emily sat on the bench and tore off a chunk of bread, ate it slowly, alternately with the dripping peach. Looking up, she could see the high town glowing in the unreal Umbrian sunshine. The peach dripped off her wrist and she licked it casually. She twisted open the bottle of mineral water and took a long swig, wiped her mouth with the back of her hand, much as Carlo's ancestors must have done, taking their midday meal in these fields, long before there was a railway, a shelter, or any timetable beyond the sun and moon. She winced to hear her parents approach; they had moved from the base to the debased, from the unmentionable to the unspeakable.

"As God is my witness, Barbara! I swear, that secretary—clerk, really—she never meant anything to me and I never went to bed with her."

"Liar!"

"Look, Barbara, let me make this short and sweet, like the Old Maid's Prayer: I never screwed the secretary. Okay?"

"Liar!"

"I was tempted, I admit, but—"

"You dirty fucker! Fuck you! Do you think I'm a fool? You've fucked everything that walked into your office! You fucked Ilsa Brill—your partner's wife! Ex-wife now. You were fucking her brains out for a year! I should have divorced you right then! So help me, I'll do it this time. You'll have to split everything right down the middle and—"

"Try it! There's not a lawyer in Orange County who will represent you against me! If you think…"

Emily rose, dropped her peach pit, left the bread, the bag, her purse, forsook possessions, position, deserted her parents and walked away, as though she could simply granulate into the August light. She went toward the farmhouse, turned the first corner she came to, and caught the scent of food and a sweet-sad waltz. *I Can't Help Falling in Love with You.* Elvis again. She came upon the farmhouse courtyard and stood behind a leafy lattice where she was hidden from their view.

Through the lattice she could see a table set for perhaps a dozen people in the shade of an arbor. Little children rolled and tumbled in the sparse grass, and women carrying plates from the kitchen to the table sidestepped chickens pecking about the yard. In a semicircle, interspersed with potted geraniums, old men in shirtsleeves and suspenders quarreled volubly. A middle-aged woman barked commands at her teenage son, who ignored her, ducked the cuff she intended to deliver, and vanished into the house. A young mother kept trying to give a crying baby over to husband, who would have none of it. The baby's cries competed with the radio commentator rattling in non-stop Italian, and then Elvis warbled out *Ready Ready Ready to Rock and Roll.* The young mother thrust the baby at her husband and left them both there. She went into the kitchen. He joined the garrulous old men, entering into the argument while he ineffectually bounced the baby on his knee.

With an arch look to her husband, the young mother brought out a bowl mounded high with something plain and grainy-looking. It was the sort of dish—indeed, the sort of meal, wine, tableware, and company—Emily did not recognize, since her experience had been limited to churches, museums, and the dining rooms of places like the Excelsior Hotel. Here before her were not the sort of people who would eat at the Excelsior, nor drink in Pan Am's first-class lounge, nor shop at South Coast Plaza. Why then should Emily envy them? But she did. A clean, clear, somehow invigorating slice of envy. For the first time in her eighteen years, Emily Shaw experienced envy outside a darkened theater or the pages of a book.

As the family began to convene at the table, the fast song finished and the DJ next played Elvis singing *Santa Lucia,* simply, eloquently, and (Emily was surprised) in Italian. Someone in the kitchen turned up the volume and music floated out to the table like an invisible guest. But at that moment the teenage boy burst into the yard, laughing, clutching a guitar, and raucously rendering *Houndadogga* till his mother snatched the guitar, pointed him to the table, and clearly asked God what she was to do with such a son. For his part, the boy lounged in his chair, still snickering.

Emily wished she could have been that boy. From the protection of the lattice she looked up and down the table, wishing she could have been that boy, or his old mother, or the young mother (who held her baby), or the husband, or the cantankerous old men, wished that, like any one of them, she could act on impulse, emotion, instinct.

From the radio Elvis rang out *It's Now or Never;* the boy stood and, to a round of indulgent applause, sang an exaggerated operatic *O Sole Mio,* but to Emily, *It's Now or Never* seemed a cue, a command—oh, not anything so grand or shattering as *Restore my church!* but a call to act. Act on impulse, emotion, instinct! Act! And be empowered by the imagination! Act! And create a story that will free you and defy your circumstances, those random vagaries of time and place. Time must be denied. That's essential. Because time—like sequential chunks skewered on days and decades—takes always its pound of flesh, history grind-and-granulating, powdering people into dust and ash and pausing for no one, no matter how *forza,* certainly not for Carlo's mother, not for Elvis, not even for Saint Francis. History is so unbearable it must be dignified with story. That's why and how people dignified battle with bravery, dignified lust with love, dignified digestion with cuisine, dignified sleep with dreams and death with Last Words. In a story, no one ever dies without Last Words. Oh, they might die gruesomely, but it is always to some dramatic purpose; without dramatic purpose, they would not die at all and you know that from the beginning. But in history, people just croaked. Look at Elvis. What did the morning paper say? Emily fought to remember what she had thought merely trivial. Elvis had been found on the bathroom floor, fallen ingloriously off the toilet. The King fallen from the throne. The man who could move and touch so many disparate lives, could he truly be found mute, facedown on the bathroom floor? Not in a story, he couldn't. But that's how real people died. That's why Carlo raced to get here, knowing that justice and Last Words are only guaranteed outside of history, in that storied catholic country where imagination reigns and rewards gallant gestures.

It's Now or Never finished and the boy finished *O Sole Mio* and Emily took her cue, that fearful step, moved from the embrace of the lattice, liberated herself from puritan restraint, from history, and opened the low gate, empowered now to walk through and into their lives. The family laughed and chatted, forks pinged, plates passed, glasses lifted before they finally noticed her there, like her own ghost, moving joyfully toward them, her empty hands outstretched, the moment sliced precisely in half with the nearby whistle of the train. Adhering to its timetable, the train's metallic shriek caught Emily tangled in the August sunshine, as you get caught, tangled in a dream, twisted, only to find the sheets wrapped round your wrists and ankles, shackling you to history, when you wake.

Starlight Coupe

Five

I watch them rev up and tense, athletes I mean, on TV. They get this
look on their faces and I know just what they're feeling here, right
here where the old ribs join up. That's the way we do the garage sales.
Me and Mama and Lisa. Like athletes. We got a team. We got a track
record. We got a coach. We go for the gold. *Money, Honey.*

Friday nights we do the dishes up quick. Winters we spread the
classifieds on the kitchen table, but most of the time we take our classifieds and city map out to the front steps, where it's cool. No one sits
on the porch. No one. Our porch is Sacred to the Memory. We flip
on the stereo so Elvis's music comes out on the porch speakers. He's
our coach. We got him before us always for his excellence, for his
goodness and his struggle against suffering and poverty. Born to poverty, he rose to be the King. He suffered and he died, now five years
ago. Same night Mama tried to kill my dad. The ruckus woke me,
glass breaking, screaming, shouting. I went out back to the cement
stoop and even in the darkness I could see them fighting on the grass.
Mama told me to go back to bed and then she came in and sat on
the edge of the bed and sang to me. Dad's motorcycle started up and
left. Next day she's cleaning up the mess in the kitchen, and it comes
on the radio that the King is dead. The grief near killed us.

Heather Wilkes thinks I'm nuts to love Elvis. The whole eighth
grade at Palm Junior High just melts over Journey and Foreigner, Olivia

Newton-John and Air Supply. Those singers couldn't lick the lint off the King's blue suede shoes, that's what I said when I gave my report on Elvis in music appreciation class. The teacher says Elvis wasn't what she had in mind when she said classical. I stood up at my desk. I said: *Miss McGahey, if you can hear* Young and Beautiful, *or* Love Me Tender, *or hear Elvis sing* The Battle Hymn of the Republic, *and not cry your eyes out, well then, you just got a heart of pure gristle.* And I sat down.

Of course we don't play those heartbreakers when we're revving up for the Saturday garage sales. While we're getting ready for the competition, we play the stuff that sends your blood rocking on through your veins. Even the Colonel, he drags out his dirty blanket and lies on the front step and flaps his tail to *Hound Dog* (which is true of the Colonel, the whole song of it). Mama sews antique quilts from the scrap box while Lisa Marie reads from the classifieds and I trace out our route on the city map. It's like anything else—you want to win, you got to have a strategy. I am captain of the Palm Junior High girls' softball team, and garage sales are just like softball games, only the field is different. Just like you'd send your best hitters up first, we hit the best neighborhoods at 7:00 A.M. Sharp. I lay out the route on the map and sometimes I just say: *Well, sorry, we can't do that garage sale, it's too close to Heather Wilkes's house.* Mama says fine. She knows Bobbaloos don't do their shopping in other people's driveways. Bobbaloos can't be poor. They got to have everything. Looks. Clothes. And *Money, Honey.* And if you don't have *Money, Honey,* you got to have brains and practice, just like softball.

Practice and you get so you know the classifieds' lingo. Even Lisa Marie, fourth grade, she knows ANTIQUE SALE means everything's overpriced. GARAGE SALE, that could mean anything, depends on the neighborhood. YARD SALE means there's no shade. MOVING SALE is the best because people don't want to haul their stuff to a new address, and lots of times they don't even want to make money, they just want to be shut of the junk. ESTATE SALE is a moving sale for someone who's moved to the Other Side. REDECORATING SALE means they're getting divorced, selling the house and splitting everything and they don't want to say it in the city newspaper.

Saturdays, we're up at the el cracko of dawn. We have to eat. Just like athletes. If you don't eat, you lose your stamina by midmorning. Day-old cinnamon rolls, bacon, ketchup on hard-fried eggs. Cash in hand. (We only truck with cash.) Keys to the Plymouth Valiant. Newspaper. Map.

One for the money.

Two for the show.

Three to get ready.

Four to

Go! Mama does the serious looking. Me and Lisa Marie do the jawboning if it's needed because sometimes people don't like to sell to you unless they can jaw you up and pat you on the head. Sometimes they like to give you something just for being little and cute (Lisa's got this one down), some toy or half-naked doll, or a puzzle without all its pieces, a half-used box of paints (no brush), or a banged-up Tonka toy if all they had was boys.

I remember once, a while back, these old folks were having a moving sale and Mama's checking it out. The man says how cute we are. He goes over to the toy box. He hands me a snorkel, like it was a pearl of wisdom. Lisa Marie, he hands her this brown bunny with hangy-down ears and stuffing hanging out and both its eyes hanging off the ends of short threads. Lisa Marie says thank you, but she gives me a look that says *rat bait rat bait*. But Mama makes a big fuss. *Isn't that bunny cute! Can't you just tell it will be magic? Can't you just tell by the way it's been loved, all the love it has to give? It just looks like magic.* Well, that bunny looked like it had been beat, but no one said so.

That night Mama sews the eyes right back up and mends the rip in the ear and fluffs it a bit and hands it to Lisa Marie before she goes to bed. And Mama was right. Brown Bunny did have some kind of magic. It had love and it had it to give. Lisa still sleeps with that bunny. Nights she loves Brown Bunny, but by day it's Barbie Barbie Barbie—and if she could find him, Ken. We got Barbies up the wazoo and, okay, some of them have only one arm and one's bald as a bell. People are always kicking out their Barbies, but no one ever throws a Ken away. Garage sales galore and you never see a Ken. Why is that? Why go waxy over Ken? He's nothing like Elvis. Not in your wildest dreams.

I love giving Lisa a hard time over Ken, especially when she's setting up a Barbie wedding. She chooses the best-looking Barbie for the bride and the others all have to be bridesmaids. Right before the ceremony, I like to come by and say mean things like, *How would you like it if you never got to be married just because you were bald or only had one arm? They got laws against that now, Lisa. They call it discrimination.* Lisa launches herself at me like a rocket, knocks me down even if I am bigger. Sometimes she sits in the dirt and screams.

Then, one day, Lisa's doing a really big church wedding, a long checked tablecloth leading out of the Colonel's doghouse, which has a rounded door. She's lined the path with jasmine and bottlebrush. She's singing *Chapel of Love.* The Barbies are all dressed nice, clothes made from the scrap box, veil and flowers for the bride. I bring my book and Popsicle out on the back step and I wait. Just when they're coming out of the doghouse church, I say to Lisa Marie, *So where's the groom? Where's Ken? Pretty hard to have a wedding without a man. You gonna marry her off to Brown Bunny? Put in the pages of the* St. Elmo Herald: *Society Beauty Marries Brown Bunny?*

I wait for Lisa to scream, but nothing happens. Then she looks at me, cool and confident, like a grown-up woman looks. She says: *If you can have a marriage without a man, I don't see why you can't have a wedding without one. Why don't you just go in and ask Mama the same question, Cilla? Why don't you say, Where's Dad? Where's Jack? Where's the man in this marriage? How can you be married without a man?*

I call her a pig and give the whole Barbie wedding a big kick and the bride and all the dolls fly into the dirt. Then Lisa starts her caterwauling. Even the Colonel wakes up and evil-looks me, and Mama comes flying out of the house, thinking Lisa's being stuffed into the incinerator, while I hotfoot it into the garage, through the canvas flap that used to be the Colonel's before he got the doghouse.

I squat there and pull the flap just a little so I can see Mama sit right down in the dust and take Lisa into her arms, Lisa boohooing about how mean I am, while Mama smooths her little golden curls.

Oh, it's enough to make you gag, Lisa and her golden curls and her baby browns. But Mama rocks back and forth and says, *Honey, I promise you, honey, the first Ken doll we see, it's yours and I don't care how much it costs.*

This don't mean Mama would buy it new. Don't get me wrong. There's a limit to what we'll buy new. Underwear. Lipstick. Socks. Groceries. (Though once we got five gallons of corn oil at a garage sale and just kept pouring it into a bottle that says "Extra Virgin.") When you're on welfare, you figure all this out pretty fast. There's bread and cinnamon rolls at the Wonder Thrift. There's coupon books and food stamps. There's bulk buying at the Big Top supermarket, where it's so stripped down they don't have any Muzak and everything's generic black-and-yellow, black-and-yellow, black-and-yellow. You walk out of there depressed and seeing black and yellow. We used to go from market to market looking for the cheap fruits and vegetables till one day we happened to be in that nice new Thriftway over on Far West Boulevard and Mama starts up this conversation with the assistant produce manager. Turns out he graduated St. Elmo High in '57, the year before Mama and Sandee.

That night, Sandee comes over and they sit around with the old yearbooks and a few beers and they have a great time yukking it up over Chuck Sullivan and his duck's-ass hairdo and his checked sport coat and his goofy girlfriend, Florence Paxton. But the next time we go to the Thriftway, Mama's wearing makeup and her hair's freshly washed and hotrolled and, of course, she always looks nice, but that day she has on this Saint Germain jumpsuit she'd just made over the night before and it's hot off the ironing board. We go into the produce section and she's talking with Chuck Sullivan again, about how he was captain of the wrestling team. (No, he says, he wasn't captain. He was just on the team.) But, Mama says, *you were the top woodshop student that year,* and *Yes,* he says, *that's true,* and she asks how many children he and Florence have and listens all about them, and all about Chuck's little brother, Denny Sullivan. They have a long jaw about Denny, and him going from security guard to city policeman. Me and Lisa Marie are bored out of our socks. But after that, we go to the Thriftway every Thursday evening, late, after the regular produce manager goes off, so Mama can get the pick of what they're going to throw out anyway. You'd be surprised how much of that is still good and what you can do, even with what's not.

My mother says once you got quality, fashion is easy. Shop the best garage sales, and your clothes are from the best shops. She can tear a whole dress apart in an hour, stuff her mouth full of pins, and when the pins are out of her mouth and that dress is all put back together, you look like Cheryl Tiegs. Sometimes a couple of pins get left in. So what? Heather Wilkes says, *Oh, Cilla, where did you get that darling outfit?* I say, *Oh, that smart shop at the new mall. Now what is its name?* And, naturally, Heather or one of the Bobbaloos comes up with a name of a shop where they have admired the clothes. They fill in their own story, you might say. No one would ever guess the dress I'm wearing on Monday was lying in a rubble of garage sale clothes on Saturday night.

Sometimes we go back to the best garage sales Saturday night, when they're closing things up, and we offer, say, five dollars for the leftover clothes. We get these piles of clothes home and first we see if there's anything for any of us (me and Lisa go to school lots of Mondays in new clothes, new-looking clothes anyway). Then Mama picks through the stuff, and what can be saved or salvaged she mends, washes, irons (she likes to iron), and puts it in one of the boxes we keep on our living room floor. One each for men, women, children, babies. When the boxes get filled up, Mama delivers them here and there, homes or shelters, schools, a small neighborhood grocery store maybe. We don't do churches because Mama says they're too picky, giving only to their own believers. Sometimes we go over to the county complex, leave off the children's box at Juvie and the babies' box at County Hospital, places like that. It's good to know we can carry on the King's work, just like he did it, not making a big fuss, just helping, quiet like. He did it so quiet that people don't even know he helped, but it's true. From the start, real early on, he never forgot that he'd been poor. Once, before he was even real famous, he sang at a county fair in Mississippi, where he was born, and they paid him five thousand dollars. He gave it all back, to the poor children of that county. But people still don't believe it when you tell them. They think Elvis was just a singer. We had this social worker once, before Mr. Johnson, she was snotty as a nose hair. This woman says, *Oh really? Elvis used to give away clothes to people like you're doing, Mrs. Jackson?* And Mama says, *Elvis gave food and clothes and shelter to people and he never told anyone. He helped the sick and the people whose hope had died and he asked nothing.* And this woman says, real snotty, *Well, Elvis could afford to. Elvis wasn't on welfare.* And Mama looks right at the social worker and she says: *If you don't have it to give, you don't have it at all.* And the woman says, *Have what?* And Mama says: *Have anything. Love, money, anything. You got to have it to give, or you don't have it at all.*

This woman, her nose wrinkles up, like yeah, sure, really. I mean this woman really had a case of the moral zits. I wanted to go right up to her and yell, *We can afford it!* But I just zipped my lip shut and sat on it. You know if they get hold of anything even close to Unreported Income, your butt's on the burner.

But we can afford to because after we been through the garage sale clothes and taken out what we want and what we salvage and give away, then we take the really ugly stuff, so ugly that no one would wear it, so ugly, if someone was to say, *Wear this or go forever naked,* you'd say, *Okay, naked it is.* We take them and it's my job to cut them up into neat little squares for the scrap box. Mama sews these scraps into antique quilts and we sell them. We always say our grandma, ninety, near blind, sewed her arthritic little fingers right down to the bones making these antique quilts. (Never mind my one grandma's dead and the other don't speak to us.) Mama sews the quilts up quick, but she hand-stitches the hems. That's all people look at anyway. People think a hand-stitched hem must of been done by angels, sitting by cozy fires with the kettle steaming, buttered toast, snow outside, and a little dog at their feet.

There was this one old woman, a grandma herself, who stood in front of one of our antique quilts, rubbing a red velvet square between her fingers, tears streaming down her face. Sandee goes up to her and says she better have a sit-down and a glass of water and a Kleenex. The woman brings the quilt with her, puts it across her lap, dabs her eyes, and tells us all this Heartbreak Hotel of a story about a quilt her mother had made with a family tale for every piece in it. And then, "My mother died and I tell you, my sister snatched that quilt off her deathbed and the rest of the family never saw it again. I'd know this quilt anywhere."

Me and Lisa and Mama and Sandee, we listened without looking at each other, without saying that red velvet had been cut up from a pair of bell-bottom pants, just the ugliest things since the Gila monster. We all shook our heads to the woman's story and said, *Really? Is that so?*

Later, Mama's counting out the money and she says, "Let that be a lesson to you, Priscilla. It never matters what something really is, it's the story you tell about it. It's not the thing itself, but the story that you bring."

Sandee comes along and says: "What your mama means, Cilla honey, is that you call it trash, it costs a quarter. You call it antique and it's four and a quarter. It don't matter which is true."

"They're both true," says Mama, tying up the fivers in packages of twenty. "But which one are you going to remember? Which one is going to matter to people?" She starts to work on the one-dollar bills, licking her fingers and snapping them down, while Sandee and me just look weird at each other. She's counted out five packets of ten dollars each before she turns to us. "The story, of course. As soon as that trash *means* something, it's antique."

So, our family, we buy at trash, sell at antique. And it's just like Elvis says: *Money, Honey.* A business like any other. Mama can spot antique under a foot of trash. Bent spoons, warped knives, cupless saucers, most old magazines, all old *National Geographics,* Mason jars, kettles, china dogs, tin plates, old luggage, fringed shawls, windup alarm clocks, speckled coffeepots, anything with "Mickey Mouse Club" on it, tea towels of Charles and Di's wedding last year. Anything that's not 1982 can just about pass for the Blue Danube. I seen it all. People weeping over old 78s from the forties and a Shirley Temple cream pitcher, getting misty over *Anne of Green Gables,* opening up the book, you'd think to read, but no, it's to smell it. People tell themselves stories about trash, and Zap! Antique. *Money, Honey.* My mother's got a kind of genius for it. She can see the value where no one else can. She's been wrong, of course. That's why we have that whole set of California lawbooks from 1934. She got all fifty-seven volumes for fifteen dollars and she said it was a steal. Sandee said, *Yeah, a steal of your fifteen dollars.* We still got those books. Lisa Marie used to sit on a couple to bring her up to the table. We got some in the living room for a footstool and we use them for doorstops and a stepladder in the bathroom. When the leg broke off the chair, we just put a couple of lawbooks under it. When Dad brings those Vardy boys over, they make them into forts. But every six months or so (because Mama's never gonna give up on selling them) I have to carry them out to the Valiant, all fifty-seven volumes, for our antique sales.

Takes us ten days just to get ready. Sandee helps when she's off shift from Inland Trucking, and my uncle Stan comes over with his Bronco, Charleen takes a couple loads, and Uncle Phil has a pickup truck. (He's not really my uncle, but he's Sandee's brother so he might as well be.) Sandee's worthless man, Ray, he don't move butt from the beer can and the TV, while we're doing all the work. I don't know how Sandee stands him, but we got to put up with Ray because the antique sales have to be at Sandee's house. We can't risk it. We only live half a mile from the county complex and what if someone sees the ad in the *St. Elmo Herald,* or drives by on a Saturday and knows we're on welfare, figures out we're making *Money, Honey* we don't report? If you're on welfare, you got to report income, even if all you do is turn in your pop bottles for a nickel each. You don't, and they make you pay it all back. They can send your mother to jail and put you in a foster home. Anyway, everyone knows you got to handle Family Assistance with kid's gloves. They catch you with an illegal quarter and they take away your food stamps and MediCal too. That's the trouble with welfare. You can't live on it, but you can't live off it, either.

There was only that once that Mama got told a story. She got told this antique story by a trash Studebaker Starlight Coupe that had to be towed into our garage. And then, last week, TRAUMA had to tow it out. It never did run, but it's like it could hum or whisper, words or a tune only grown-ups could hear. To me and Lisa it just said *rat bait rat bait.* But you could tell it was singing to TRAUMA. You should of seen his face when we found him in our garage, kneeling by the hubcaps, listening. Maybe it was whispering *pay cash pay cash.* That's what I think. TRAUMA had the same look in his eyes that Mama had when she paid cash. Oh, that car, it was *Money, Honey,* all right, but it was not business.

We were down near St. Elmo City College, not far from the tracks, a crummy, dumpy neighborhood is what I'm telling you, and it's hot, August hot, and the end of the day. Me and Lisa Marie weren't champs back then but kids kicking and sniveling, hungry and hot and tired. We go to the gas station and Mama pumps two dollars' worth and stands us in the shade, squirts us down with their hose. She does her own feet and arms, and she's getting a drink from the hose when she looks up and sees nailed to a telephone pole: FIRE SALE.

Fire sale's on a street with no sidewalks and squat houses, some with boards nailed over windows, sunflowers and foxtails, trash blowing through the yards. Finally we see a sign hanging on a blackened-up chain link fence: FIRE SALE. Almost the whole yard was burnt to a stubble and there was a burnt-out shell of a house and, beside it, a lopsided trailer. Lisa says she's scared the ground is still on fire. We hold hands and follow Mama to the trailer, where there is a man on the stoop and some kids. Stuff was laid out on a couple of plywood sheets and it smelled of smoke and fire. The man didn't say nothing, and the kids looked at us like they were mad we had money to come to their fire sale at all.

There's nothing here for us, and we turn and walk back over the ashes toward our Valiant, when Mama stops. She looks over at the only patch of tall weeds left standing. The wind comes up just then and the weeds start tossing and moving, rustling, and she leaves us and wanders over. She stands in front of an old car, near buried there with all these foxtails tall as grown-ups grown up around it. Dry dead weeds stick out all over like Apache arrows. Burnt-up beer cans and bean cans lying everywhere and the paint blackened and blistered, peeling from the fire. Dust so thick you could of cut it with a chain saw, and inside, great thick webs hanging from the sun visors with dead flies and spiders. In the window there's a sign:

4 SALE
$600 or best offor

The man comes up and stands beside Mama. He's got a great big gut and no belt and you could see his crack. "Fire never touched it," he says. He has hairy arms and hands and yellow stains on his shirt. "Fire that night burnt everything right over our heads. Nearly burnt us too. We was lucky to get out with our skins." He lights a cig, like the mention of fire makes him homesick. He blows out the match and stomps on it. "But I tell you, the fire came right up to this here Studebaker and stopped. I mean, it was like the hand of God come down and said: *No further.*"

"Is that so?" says Mama, soft, like she doesn't want to wake the car.

"Fire department got there right then too. That very minute." The man puffs his cigarette. "Nice little car. You never see a 1946 Studebaker Starlight Coupe."

"Used to run good," says the wife. She shows up so fast, I think she got there on a broom. She stands beside her husband, a flat, pale woman with bad teeth and eyes like Brown Bunny before Mama fixed him, like her eyes have slid down on short threads. "It ran real good for a long time. We bought it off a Mexican who kept it up good. Mexican had it since 1951. We're the third owners. Hardly anything wrong with it," the woman goes on. My mother says nothing. "Roy woulda fixed it, but we already got a car. That's why we're selling it." She nudges her husband and he gives her a cigarette. She lights hers off the butt end of his. "Junkman's offered me four hundred fifty for parts alone."

Wind dies down and everything stays real quiet while Mama walks round and round the car. Finally, she clears her throat, licks her lips, and asks when was the fire.

"Lemme think," says the man. "This is Saturday, so ten days ago, maybe."

"August 16," says Mama.

The sun is burning into the backs of our necks, and long flat rays of light and dust twist in and out of the tall weeds that shake and bend up close against the car buried deep in all this dryness, like the very dryness protected it from the black-scorch all around. I go up to Mama, about to pull on her arm and go back to the Valiant, when she starts to talk about Elvis, low and quiet, about the sweetness and power of his voice and the joy in his music, the reverence too, how he'd struggled up from poverty, about his goodness. "Elvis bought food for the hungry and gave shelter and money to the sick, but you never heard of that, did you?" she asks. "No one ever did. He kept all that secret, but a car, oh, that was different. Elvis would buy a car for someone, anyone who was poor or hurt or struggling, who showed him the tiniest bit of pity or caring, not because he was a great singer—and of course he was just the greatest singer who ever lived—but because he was a man, like them, just a simple man, mortal and born to die like the rest of us. Then it would get in the papers. KING BUYS CAR FOR POOR FAMILY. Like the King was just tossing his money to the wind." Mama stretches out her arm, like to include this wind blowing these weeds. "Like he was foolish, but it wasn't that at all. Elvis knew what it was to suffer. Elvis's money was a burden unless he could ease the suffering of others." Mama takes a deep breath. "And if he was here, right now, if he was right here beside me, I tell you, Elvis Presley would buy this car for me."

"Personal friends with the King, were you?" The man hee-haws. When Mama says nothing, he looks at me and Lisa, like we ought to do something. We just sort of grin. What can we do?

The woman with the hangy-down eyes says Elvis ain't here. He died a long time ago.

He didn't exactly die," Mama corrects her, "he passed through."

"Through St. Elmo?" asks the woman.

"He passed through time like it was a sieve." Mama moves her hands out like slow, five-fingered wings. "He left off his suffering flesh. His spirit just passed through that sieve like steam, no different than water heated up turns to steam and gets free of the kettle, passes through the air, invisible so you can't see it, but you can feel it. Oh, I been crying my eyes out, all this past year, of course, and last week, August 16—it just broke my heart all over again, to know that every year I'd feel his loss and Elvis—"

"Oh, who cares about Elvis!" the woman butts in. "I cried my eyes out too on August 16, but it wasn't for Elvis Presley! This August, 1978, August, I cried! I watched everything I had burn up!"

"That's not true." Mama gives this woman a tender smile. "Not at all. There was a hand that came between you and all that death, that spared you the truly everlasting grief. Don't you see? Look. Here are your children. They are well and with you. Here is your husband. Your family has been spared destruction." The woman with the hangy-down eyes starts to cry. The man puts his hand on her shoulder. My mother goes on, not even talking to them anymore. Not talking to anyone. Her face has got this brightness, this pink glow. "This very car, this Starlight Coupe, is meant to knit my life back together. That's why it was not destroyed on August 16. It is a sign from Elvis. A gift. That's why I have been brought hither. Elvis wants me to have this car. Truly," she says sweetly, "verily. It's a gift from Elvis. A gift when no giver's in sight."

The woman quits crying, wipes her nose quick on the end of her shirt, and says, "Cash—cash money."

Mama laughs, and still laughing, she walks away, but I know it's false, like a tin of canned laughter opened on TV.

"Five hundred today," the woman calls out. "Six hundred tomorrow."

Mama turns around, her old self all over again. "It's near six on Saturday night. How can I get five hundred dollars cash on a Saturday night?"

"That's the offer."

We get all the way to the Valiant and Mama hollers back to the fire sale people, "I'll be back before nine. I'll have three hundred dollars."

"Three hundred fifty!" the woman screams. "And you get it off our property and you—"

"I'll have three hundred dollars and a tow truck!" Mama shouts as we're pulling away. Then she says to us, "That's a lot of antique quilts, girls, but it's going to be worth every bit of it. Every penny."

"For a beat-up, dirty, crappy car that don't even run?" I say. "For a car bought at a *fire sale?*"

"I know what I'm doing."

"Yeah? Like the 1934 lawbooks?"

"I'm taking you girls to your Aunt Bethany's."

Lisa Marie starts to wail and blubber.

"Oh, please, Mama. No. Look, I'm sorry, Mama. You buy the car, but please—"

"I'm only taking you there for a bit, honey, so I can hustle around and do what I need to do. Stop crying, Lisa. It's not a punishment."

"Fat lot you know," Lisa whimpers.

Aunt Bethany and her husband, Uncle Don, they live in one of those houses so neat they don't even have a laundry basket. You know their clothes are so well trained that they come off their bodies and march into the washer. They're afraid not to. Bethany and Don got gewgaws everywhere, so a kid can't turn around or sneeze without some little gimcrack falling off the toilet tank and the kid getting in trouble. They got pictures of Jesus in every room. Their kids are grown and married and gone. Their grandkids hate them. One of them told me so.

Bethany wants us like she wants antlers. She puts her hands on her hips and says to Mama, "I suppose that worthless Jack's come back again. I suppose he's got back on his motorcycle and left his other woman and come back to you. I suppose you're going off with him again. When are you going to learn, Rejoice? When are you—"

Oh, Bethany goes on and on, dumping on Dad and calling Mama a fool, but my mother's face still has that pink glow. She just cuts Bethany off with a laugh. She says, "Say what you want, Bethany, but living with Jack was living in overdrive. Jack Jackson has taken me places in this world."

"To bed. And to the cleaner's."

"To go to bed with Jack is like going to another country, Bethany.

When I'm in bed with Jack, I know I'm alive, and I'll bet you can't say the same for old Don in there, can you?" She doesn't wait for an answer, bebops off in the Valiant, waves to us before she gets in and leaves. Bethany looks at us. "I suppose you're hungry."

It's way past dark when we get picked up, after ten. Mama says, "Wake up, girls! I need your help. I bought it. It's ours! Sandee's already at our house and we're going back and the four of us are going to clean out the garage and make room for the Studebaker Starlight Coupe! The Studebaker Starlight Coupe! The Studebaker Starlight Coupe!" She's so happy. She says it over and over like it's the words to a song. She sings it all the way back to our house.

We get home and the garage door is open, the overhead light's on, and Sandee's there with a wheelbarrow moving stuff from the garage, where we kept everything we bought at trash and haven't yet sold at antique. The garage is full of it. "Wait a minute," I say, "—where is all this stuff going?"

"In the spare room," says Sandee.

"What spare room?"

After that night, me and Lisa shared a room always. They had moved Lisa's bed into my room so they could fill her room with stuff from the garage. We are, both of us, whining and griping and tired, but nothing matters to Mama except that Starlight Coupe. Never mind little Lisa's crying and fussing and I'm like a zombie. No one cares about us. Oh no, we got to slave and sweat and haul stuff from the garage, move everything, make room for—what? Some filthy old car. We get dirty as pigs, sweaty, dusty, yucky beyond belief, and when we're done, Lisa just grabs Brown Bunny and falls asleep in her clothes, sprawled on her bed. Me, I got my nightgown on, but not my teeth brushed, or face and hands washed, but I didn't care. It was way past midnight when I fell into the sleep of the dead.

I wake up hearing the Colonel bark his heart out. I get up and I know something's happening, like the way you feel an earthquake in your sleep and know, quick, to go stand in a doorway or get under a table. I go out and stand on the back step. Out at the garage I see a lot of flashing yellow lights and first I thought it was the cops, but it was a tow truck and people with flashlights. My uncle Stan's Bronco is backed up across Sultana Street, brights on, beaming into the garage. With a flashlight in her hand, Sandee's standing in front of his car, just in case someone driving down Sultana Street might not see a Bronco with its brights on, parked in the middle, in case they might not see the tow truck with the 1946 Studebaker hanging off the back, might miss a Starlight Coupe backing into the garage.

Driving the tow truck is Dogleg Wilson. (Don't ask me where he got the name. His legs look all right to me.) Dogleg weighs in at about three hundred pounds and has a beard and a ponytail. He plays keyboard in my uncle Stan's rock-and-roll band, the Eastbound Express. Once a month on Saturdays, the Eastbound's got a standing engagement in the bar at the Cask and Cleavage. They just pick up other gigs where they can and they all got day jobs. Days, Dogleg works at McDonough's Union 76 and Triple A Towing. It says so on the side of the truck. Even young as I am, even I know what McDonough don't know: where his truck is and that it's being used (for free) to tow a 1946 Studebaker Starlight Coupe for a woman who's lost her mind and three hundred dollars besides.

I stand there on the back step and I feel the August wind flapping my nightdress around my ankles and the night sky has gulped down the moon, swallowed it whole. I remember how I'd stood here on this very step that night a year ago. I saw Mama trying to kill my dad and I remember thinking: He's leaving for good. She wouldn't be trying to kill him if he wasn't leaving for good anyway. And I had cried out and lifted up my arms, high like sadness was a huge ball that some heavenly hand could scoop from me, lift off and away. But Mama calls out, tells me to go back to bed, and I do and pretty soon she's there by me, singing Elvis songs. The motorcycle started up and left. I fell asleep. How could I of fallen asleep when Elvis was dying? We loved Elvis so much, we should of known. There should of been some weird light in the sky, or a chill in your blood that hot August night, something. But we each went on, sleeping, or singing, or driving in the night, and knowing nothing. Not then, anyway.

McDonough's Triple A tow truck gets caught at an odd angle in the street and so it takes them a long time, a lot of cursing and creaks, a few crunches and groans, but finally the Studebaker gets backed into the garage. They yell, *Hallelujah!* I know enough to hotfoot it back to bed. I lie there and I listen to all four of them come into the living room, flop down, and say with one voice they're all going to die. They're so beat, they're going to die.

Then one of these near dead, I don't know which one, gets up and goes to the stereo and on comes *Jailhouse Rock,* and with that—I am here to tell you—comes the Resurrection and the Life of the party because pretty soon the phone's ringing off the hook and there's car doors slamming and you hear the slice off the top of bags of tortilla chips and chairs scraping back and the snap of pop-tops and the sewing machine gets pushed against the wall and the squeal of protest the ironing board makes when it comes down. You could hear all that for a time. But then you couldn't hear anything but the music—oh, not any of those heartbreaker songs, but his early stuff, fast, hard, alive, those songs that your feet can't stand, music that downright carbonates your toes and even if *you* didn't want to get up and dance, your feet would just desert you and go man go by themselves. The music pumps up and everyone in the living room is all shook up and dancing the hop-boppa-do-woppa-shake-down-shimmy and you can feel it in our bedroom. Never mind what you can hear. If you was deaf, you'd know there was dancing and happiness. You'd know grief had flown out the window. Lisa wakes up and rubs her eyes. We look at each other, and Lisa's eyes get big and she smiles.

I say, "There hasn't been music or laughing like that in this house since Elvis—"

"Since Dad left," says Lisa.

We get up and crouch down in the hall and watch everything through the heater grate. There's Dogleg and Stan and Mama and Sandee, of course, then there's Uncle Phil and his girlfriend Diana and Charleen and her new husband and Bruce and some of the other bartenders and a couple of waitresses from the Cask and Cleavage (which, it's past two so they're off work). And there's a bunch of others we don't even know. One by one, the Eastbound guys from my uncle's band show up. Meatball and Eldon and Candy, who always wears his John Deere hat sideways. They didn't any of them bring their instruments, but they brought their feet and they are all dancing, even Eldon. They're dancing with anything that will move and some that won't. Dogleg's got hold of the ironing board, pulled it up close to him, making it promise not to step on his *Blue Suede Shoes,* and Charleen is dancing with the busboy from the Cask and Cleavage, who's young enough to be her son, but who cares? Her husband is dancing with a barefoot woman in a pink disco dress and he don't care, because next it's *Money, Honey,* flailing out of that stereo, and after that they're rocking and rolling and even the Colonel's in there too, dancing with his dirty old blanket. The hall door opens fast and it's Uncle Phil, and he laughs out loud and picks up me and Lisa, one under each arm, puts us on the couch, and says, "What is it you love, girls? Let me hear you!"

"Rock and roll!"

He snaps his fingers, keeps the beat in between songs, the record rasps, and he shouts, "And what's your mama taught you is the two best words in English, girls? Quick!"

"*Tutti Frutti!*" We sing, right along, dance on the couch. Sandee grabs Lisa and swings her around, Mama swings me around, and they trade when we come to *Shake, Rattle and Roll.* My uncle Stan picks up a couple of clothes hangers and beats on the upright piano, and Dogleg flips that piano open. Its keys are all yellow and black, but who cares? Stan and Dogleg, they play backgrounds for Elvis like he is right here with us, singing in this very room. Mama starts to do the shimmy, starts standing, works her way down, and she looks pretty good too, everyone clapping time, and when my uncle Stan beats out that drumroll, every verse, everyone in the room, everyone in the house, everyone in the whole world, shouts out:

STUDEBAKER! STUDEBAKER! STUDEBAKER! STUDEBAKER!

Dancing, hands held over their heads and beers held high, a whole lot of shaking going on. I was there. I saw it. I heard it. The thump of feet, the cry and shout, Dogleg on the upright, Stan playing clothes hangers, and laughter like it was just ripped out of the walls, like lathe and plaster turned to laugh and plaster, joint jumping, pictures bouncing, all our Elvis pictures, even that big framed *King Creole* poster on the wall, bouncing like the King was happy at last to hear us happy. There was thunder in the floor and I felt his presence here with us. Thunder in the floor, like the stone had been rolled away from his tomb, and then I knew, right then, there was no tomb that could hold Elvis or his music. It's just like Mama says, he passed through. That's why we didn't know he was dying that night. He wasn't dying. He was just passing through time and now here he was, passing through this living room. His music fell on us like rain and we were, all of us, ready to grow again.

Well, there was thunder at the door too, but it was the cops. Two of them. They got helmets on and nightsticks and guns in holsters. Someone has to turn the music down so they can come in and ask who lives here and who are these minors (me and Lisa) and did we know it was near to dawn? Did we know that the music from this house could be heard all the way down at the county complex one-half mile away?

"Oh shit," says Sandee. She makes her way through the crowd to the stereo. "Someone hit the switch, Joycie. The music's been coming out from the porch speakers too."

Mama says she's sorry.

Cop says it's not funny.

Mama says she didn't mean it to be funny.

Cop says: "Why're you laughing then?"

"I can't help being happy."

Right then, the Colonel drops his blanket, snakes through the living room, jumps the cop with a bunch of wet dog kisses.

"Oof! Eeuw! Ach!"

Mama grabs the Colonel by his collar and tells him, "Down boy!" She holds him, kneels there on the floor with him, and then she looks up into the cop's face and she says, "Hey, aren't you Denny Sullivan, Chuck Sullivan's little brother? Aren't you Denny? St. Elmo High, class of 1959, and isn't your brother produce manager at the Thriftway?"

One day, maybe a week later, I knew my dad had been here. He wasn't home when me and Lisa Marie got back from swimming lesson, but we knew. We could tell from the motorcycle drippings in the driveway. We could tell because the house smelled like him, like leather and motor oil and his kind of cigarettes and his kind of sweat. We could tell because the toilet seat was up. We could tell because Mama was in her bedroom and she was crying and she had pushed a dresser or something in front of the door and she wouldn't answer us when we knocked and called her name. I got on the phone and got hold of Sandee at Inland Trucking Company, where she works, revolving shifts. Sandee said she'll call in another dispatcher and be there soon as she can.

I fix Spaghetti-Os and toast and jam and ice cream for supper. Sandee comes over and she knocks on Mama's bedroom door. Mama lets her in the room. Finally.

By the time Sandee comes out, me and Lisa are sick of watching reruns. She makes a pot of coffee. While it's perking, she puts Lisa to bed, tucks her in, and sings her a couple of songs. Sandee comes back in the living room, lights up a Newport, and tells me she's going back with Mama and I should just go to bed and that everything will be okay in the morning. It won't be great, she says, but it will be okay. "I think she just never…"

"Never what?" I ask. "Come on. I want to know."

"Well, there's only so much room for sorrow, so much and no more. Joycie's grief for Elvis filled all that space up…well, kind of like how we got Lisa's room all filled up now. There's nothing else can fit in there. We had to make room in the garage for the Starlight Coupe to move in. So for Joycie, when one sorrow moved out, the other sorrow moved in."

"You mean for Dad? You mean Dad's sorrow moved in?"

"Your dad moved out." Sandee stubbed out her Newport like it had peed on her foot. "I told her he's not coming back. She didn't believe me then and she doesn't believe me now. I said, Joycie, you'll see Elvis in this house before Jack Jackson comes back here to live. Coffee's done."

I followed her back into the kitchen. "She bought that car for Dad? I don't believe it. She bought it for Elvis. Elvis wanted it, wanted her to have it."

"What does it matter? One story's as good as another. You've sat behind the cashbox at the antique sale enough times to know that, Cilla."

"What's that dirty old rat bait of a car got to do with my dad?"

"Your dad drove a Starlight Coupe, back when him and Joycie first met. She was still in high school and he was—well, he was Jack Jackson. Just like he is now. No different. No damn different."

"You mean that Studebaker was *his car!*"

"Who knows? He used to have one. He drove a Starlight Coupe."

"What happened to it?" Sandee turns off the stove and said it didn't matter. I said it did. I wanted to know what happened to my dad's Starlight Coupe.

"He drove it into a ditch." Sandee got down a pot holder and picked up the percolator. "'Jack did to that Studebaker what he did to everything. He wrecked it. He drove it into a ditch and broke its axle. He had to put a sign on it that said FOR SALE, YOU TOW. And someone did."

"Are you saying he broke Mama's axle?"

"No. He broke your mama's heart, Cilla," she said like she was spitting ice cubes. "More than once."

"That's not true! She still loves him! He still loves her!"

"Well, I'm sure you're right, Cilla." Sandee took two mugs off hooks.

"That car was for Elvis—or from Elvis, or—anyway, it was Elvis."

"Maybe Elvis did want her to have it." Sandee shrugs. "What does it matter? She bought that car at trash and she can sell it at antique. She can make *Money, Honey.*"

Next day, Mama goes out to close the garage door, like you'd slam the covers shut on a book. But when they were towing the Starlight Coupe in, they'd hit the spring and the garage door wouldn't close now. So the Starlight Coupe just sat there, four years, facing the street, and no one ever touched it. New dust and spiders moved in and the old dust and dead spiders stayed put. Weeds stayed stuck in the bumpers. The FOR SALE sign came out of the window. That was all.

Even with the sign gone, though, sure enough, five, six times a year, someone comes to the back door, says: *Say, how much you want for the 1946 Studebaker Starlight Coupe?* Everyone who asks calls that car by name, Starlight Coupe. Mama always says three thousand dollars and they laugh and say, *For a car that don't run?* Even our social worker, Mr. Johnson, he asked after it. To him she said it wasn't for sale. She was storing it for her brother Stan.

Then, just last week, I see a BMW park across the street. It has vanity tags that say TRAUMA. A man gets out who has grayish hair but a springy walk. He's wearing light clothes, cords, a cotton shirt, and tennis shoes. He goes into the garage and I call Mama and Lisa Marie.

"I see those license plates go by all the time," says Mama. "He must be a doctor over at County Hospital."

We all three go out to the garage, and sure enough, there's TRAUMA kneeling down at the hubcaps of the Starlight Coupe, touching it like it's about to have puppies. He stands up, says he can't help but notice the car. Noticed it every day for four years. "I drove a Starlight Coupe in high school." He looks in through the windshield. "I crashed it and it died. I should have died, really. I always felt like that Starlight Coupe saved my life." He looks up at the garage rafters like they will rain down pity. "That's why I work ER, crisis care. I almost died in that crash, but the car saved my life and I vowed if I lived, I'd…" He looks at his shiny watch. "Well, I can't be late for my shift. How much?"

"Three thousand."

He shakes his head, thanks her, and starts back up toward his BMW.

"Two thousand," she calls after him.

"You mean it?"

She smiles. "Cash."

Six

Coming home from school Friday, I meet the mailman at the back gate (even the U.S. Postal Service isn't allowed on our front porch). He hands me a big envelope. It's from the county. "I see you sold the Studebaker," he says, digging for ads and flyers.

"No. It was my uncle's car and he just came and got it." Keep your stories straight and they're easier to remember, cut from one piece, you might say. Of course, we don't have to worry about the new social worker asking Starlight Coupe questions. Emily never even saw it in the first place.

I find Lisa playing Barbies and the Colonel fighting with his blanket in the backyard. Lisa tells me I better hold my nose when I go in. "You know what they're doing in the kitchen."

I can smell it before I set foot inside. Mama's head is all buttered over with coloring stuff and Sandee has the frosting cap on and Mama is pulling her hair through it with a crochet hook. They are wearing garbage bags with holes cut for the heads and arms so they can protect their clothes and skin. Mama asks me to open the county envelope. Out falls two brochures and a letter.

SEHS NIGHT SCHOOL
TOOLS FOR ALL THE TRADES
Advance! Enrich! Enroll!

I turn down the radio and read the letter out loud.

April 8, 1982
Dear Joyce—

I have lived in St. Elmo now for four months but no one has made me feel so truly welcome as you. I keep thinking of E. M. Forster's famous line about connecting and how that's all we need to do.

"What?" says Sandee.

I cannot tell you how much the gift of your grandmother's quilt means to me. It's beautiful beyond description and time has left it full of memory and warmth. I wrap up in it and I can feel your grandmother's soothing hands.

Sandee chuckles. "Your grandmother never so much as soothed a chicken on its way to slaughter."

"Emily doesn't know that. I gave her the quilt, let her bring what she wants to it. Go on, Cilla."

A person who is gracious and courteous to strangers is truly a citizen of the world and not a lonely island, but a continent, or something like that. Thank you again. I will never forget your kindness to me, a stranger.

Affectionately,
Emily Shaw

PS—I hope this brochure helps your Vietnamese friends down the street. (ESL classes are on page 6.) If you see anything here that might appeal to you, let me know, although I don't suppose there's any reason I should know. You certainly don't have to let me know. I hope you will, and that I can be a help to you and your girls. I have asked the staff here to find the brochure on the Good Grades Program and they will be sending that to you, and I called St. Elmo City College and asked them to send you their materials as well. A woman with your pluck will soon be on her way to independence.

"What's pluck?" asks Lisa, coming in for a drink of water.

"Luck that's been peed on," says Sandee, lighting up a Newie and picking up a brochure. "Hmmm. *You and Your Journal, Ecogardening.* Well, it ain't what they called *night* school in the old days."

Her and Mama crack up. They been friends since Mama's family moved from Hammath Hot Springs and they met in junior high. Just like me and Heather Wilkes. They're the same age, but Sandee's kids have all grown up. If you ask about her husbands (two of them) or any of her other men, Sandee says *woof woof.* If you ask me, the guy she lives with now, Ray, is as *woof woof* as they come. I'd rather sleep with the Colonel. Days, Ray lays cable for the cable TV people. Nights, he lays in front of the TV. Sandee is a shift dispatcher for Inland Trucking.

She rereads Emily's letter. "Is your new social worker goofy as this letter makes her sound?"

"She's pretty goofy," I say, "but she's pretty, too.

"Cilla, honey, get us all some iced tea, will you? I'm like to die in this garbage bag. There's nothing wrong with Emily that getting older won't cure. She has a good heart. She's just real young. You have to feel for her."

"You got it all wrong, Joycie. She's supposed to feel for you. You're the one on welfare. She's got the good job and the education. I bet she's traveled to Hawaii, Europe, has nice clothes, a nice car—"

"Maybe. But I got all of you and Emily's alone."

"She's engaged," I say, wrestling with the ice trays. "You ought to see the rock on her finger." Lisa waits for me to do the work, then puts the ice in her glass and goes back out. "Her fiancé's back east somewhere."

"You have to wonder what kind of guy gets engaged to a girl like Emily and then goes off, leaves her for law school," Mama says.

"A guy who wears his balls above his belt," Sandee cautions.

"Well, I never met anybody as lonely as Miss Emily Shaw. You ever hear of a social worker who stayed three hours?"

"Hell no. Forty minutes. Tops."

"Mr. Johnson used to do it in twenty," I say.

Mama laughs. "Oh, Mr. Johnson, he didn't *want* to know anything. Wham, bam, thank you, ma'am, and Mr. Johnson was gone. Emily's different."

"Really different," I say, crunching on my ice.

Mr. Johnson was a great big black man, taller than my dad. His hair was gray on the sides. Mr. Johnson never snuggled down into the La-Z-Boy like Emily. He asked his questions, did his business before the ice in his tea could melt. Clipboard. Pen. *Now let's see, Joyce, it's you and Cilla and Lisa Marie living here. Have I forgotten anyone?* (He has to ask that, so if Family Assistance finds you are living with a man, they can cut you off without a cent.) *And I'll bet these girls are both doing well in school. They're both so smart.*

Then, pen flying over his clipboard, he goes through *Food* (which, Mama tells him where to get the best price on whole-bodied chickens). *Clothes* (he can see all around him). *Transportation* (How is the '62 Valiant?). And in the middle of all this, without so much as making a dent in the conversation, he asks after Dad and what he's up to these days, like maybe Dad's an airline pilot and doing the Hong Kong–London route. Then: *Anything else I can help you with, Joyce?*

Not unless you can bring Elvis back among us, Mr. Johnson.

Clipboard back in the briefcase, he stands up: *I never met anyone who could manage like you do, Joyce. Your girls are always nice and polite and they look just like little fashion plates. Your home is a pleasure to come to.*

I always tell my husband, Fine, Jack, have a few beers and I don't care if you smoke, but no cans in the living room and empty the ashtray. If Dorrie lets you leave butts and cans around, that's her problem. Not in my house. Not in—our house. Not in this house, she finishes, getting it right at last.

Then Mr. Johnson says he's off. Others need him. Anyone can see we don't. Twenty minutes. Twenty-five at the outside.

While Mama's tugging her hair with the crochet hook, Sandee reads us all the ways you can spend your weeknights at SEHS: parenting, computers, wine tasting, conversational Spanish, designing your own clothes.

"You should be teaching that class, Joycie. Designing clothes. If you grew up in Paris instead of St. Elmo, you'd be a designer right now. You'd have clothes and perfume named after you. Just like Channel."

"Sha-nell," I say, getting out more iced tea. "In Beginning French, that's how they say it: Sha-nell."

"Will wonders never cease?" Sandee says to Mama. "French in the eighth grade. Say me something in French, Cilla."

So I ask if this is the pen of my aunt. And then I say, *"Voilà! Le iced tea.* Now, Sandee, you say, *Mer-ci beaucoup.* It's easy. Just say it."

Sandee did, then she stubbed out her butt. I empty the ashtray. We got a two-butt limit in this house.

"Will you look at this, Joycie? In the old home ec room, they're teaching Using Your Wok. Oh, imagine Miss Gruski's ghost flapping overhead and screeching out, *Wok! Wok! Wok!* You think those Vietnamese down the street from you would like to take Using Your Wok? Maybe they got a recipe for dog."

"Oh, Sandee—" Mama rolls her eyes.

"Really! Bobbi Jo Barton—you remember her—there's Vietnamese down the street from her and she told me in the grocery store they eat dogs."

"I don't believe it."

"Honest, Joycie, Bobbi Jo says they raise them just like chickens. To eat them. You watch out for the Colonel. You find him missing one day—he's chop suey."

We all laugh like to collapse on that one. The notion of anyone eating that half-setter, half-collie hairball Colonel is enough to make you choke.

"Who did Bobbi Jo marry?"

"Oh, first that guy, that big dumb jock, oh, you remember, Mr. Which-Is-Bigger-His-Brains-Or-His-Balls."

Well, then they're off and running and I end up knowing all about Bobbi Jo's sex life (her second husband was just as *woof woof* as they come), her and everybody else, because Mama and Sandee have got the goods on everyone in this town who ever went to SEHS. Which was everyone for a long time because SEHS was the only high school for a thousand years. I love to hear about the old days at SEHS, the great days of rock and roll, the giants, Elvis, Buddy, Jerry Lee, Phil and Don, Little Richard, Little Anthony, cruising Brigham Boulevard, the car clubs, and the jukebox at Ruby's Drive-In after school. Slip your dime into the slot, let the good times roll till Ruby came out flapping her apron, saying she'd lose her license if they didn't stop dancing.

"She did lose it too, but not for that. Her husband was making book in the back." Sandee starts singing *Chantilly Lace* along with the Big Bopper on the Oldie-but-Goldie station.

"Well, it's just a crime about SEHS nowadays. It looks like prison or a reform school. Graffiti everywhere and bars on the windows." Mama pulls extra hard on Sandee's hair. "I'm so glad we live in the Hacienda High district. I'd move before I'd let my girls go to SEHS nowadays. It's not safe for girls. I'd send them to Holy Rosary."

"Oh, Joycie, you slay me. You couldn't afford Catholic school if—"

"Jack's a Catholic."

"If the pope was Jack's brother. You couldn't move if Mount St. Helens popped up in the middle of Santiago Street, what with Jack's folks renting to you and not raising the rent since—when?—'76?"

"Jack's stepmother makes that old man keep to his promise. Jack's dad is just—" She looks over at me and says I should go out front and wait for the paperboy.

"Why should I wait for Donny Roncker? He's only Mr. Zit USA."

"Donny's not the paperboy anymore. It's someone new. He's been throwing the paper on the porch. Two days now. Knocked over the glads yesterday."

"Oh, you just leave him to me." I polish off my iced tea.

"Turn up the radio on your way out, will you, honey? They're due for another—"

Right then the DJ comes on, blathering fast about the KLMO Memory Jackpot. "Up to eight hundred and ten dollars this afternoon. We're 1220 on your AM dial and the pot goes up, twelve twenty added to the Memory Jackpot for every question that YOU can't answer! Hey—hey! Whaddo you say! Get that ball and go, St. Elmo! St. Elmo loves KL-MO! Somebody's gotta hit it big! We'll take the tenth caller. Are you ready, boys and girls?"

"We're ready!"

"Okay: What was the name of Dion's first Top Ten hit? The name *and the year!* Tenth caller—"

"A Teenager in Love!" shrieks Sandee. "Quick! Cilla! Bring me the phone."

"No—" Mama clutches the crochet hook, closes her eyes. "That was Dion and the *Belmonts.* He just said Dion…Dion…Dion…"

I quick hand Sandee the earpiece and hotfoot it back to the wall to dial. (We keep KLMO's number right there with the fire and police.)

"Runaround Sue!" Mama jumps up and down. "That's Dion's first, 1961! I'm right! I know I'm right."

And she was, but we weren't the tenth caller. I turned the radio off. "We don't need their old Memory Jackpot anyway. We already hit it big with the Starlight Coupe."

"Two thousand dollars," Sandee sighs. "Maybe we ought to go to Hawaii, or buy one of them new video things. You know you can watch a movie right in your own home? On your own TV. No commercials."

"No," says Mama. "That money is going with all the rest of it. Cilla and Lisa Marie are going to college—and I don't mean St. Elmo City College, either." She cracks down on the words like sunflower seeds.

I leave them there in their garbage bags, trying to decide where me and Lisa would do best. Sandee's sister's girl went to Long Beach State, but Mama holds out for the university. Mama's got her heart set on UCLA.

I get Lisa Marie and the Colonel and we all three go round the front to wait for the paperboy. The Colonel's part in this is easy, he just needs to look nasty. No one knows what a wimp he is. We three sit on the steps, not even needing to talk. We know what to do. We been through it all before. Since Elvis passed through, we get all kinds past our porch, Sacred to the Memory. Scoffers, unbelievers, people who drive by and laugh or cry, shout nasty words or yell out things like, *I bet your neighbors really love this shit, lady!* Some mornings we found smashed whiskey and beer bottles thrown on our porch. Kids once hopped the chain link fence and spray-painted the whole Sacred to the Memory, even the flags. Mama heard them and called the cops. It was Denny Sullivan came again, caught three of them. Denny Sullivan said he'd give us an extra patrol at night. Denny remembered what Elvis did for him too. "Did for all of us," Denny says.

Mama puts her hands up over her face and starts to cry. "He saved my life. When I thought I was going to die of the pain, Elvis saved my life."

Officer Sullivan pats her shoulder, tells his partner to take down the spray-painted flags, gives us ten dollars toward the new ones.

So after Denny Sullivan gives us the extra patrols, we got toilet-papered once or twice, a beer can or two, but only one grandma vandalized us. Tough and small as a spitwad and in broad daylight, she flies up our walk and starts slashing, smashing with her umbrella. "Devil's music! Filth! The sounds of Satan! Godless! Jungle!" On and on while the glads and Gideon Bibles go flying.

Mama wasn't home. It was just me and Lisa. I said we should loose the Colonel on her, but Lisa says, "What for? So he can lick her to death?" So I take a big breath and go out.

The grandma screams, "Elvis Presley took sex out of the bedroom in 1956 and put it on TV and it's been there ever since! He is filthy and his music—"

"You're too late," I tell her, "Elvis is gone. He isn't here anymore."

She looks at me sort of breathless, sad and surprised, her arm upraised, her umbrella ready to beat me or Elvis or anyone, really. She says again how he was scum and filth.

I just keep picking up the glads and stuff. I tell her, "I'm sorry. You missed him." I hold the wreath of daisies and sort of shrug. "Elvis isn't here."

She lowers her umbrella. She leaves, still miffed, slams the gate so hard, BEWARE OF DOG falls off.

So, sure we been attacked by fruitcakes and music haters and Elvis-baiters, but there's mornings we look out and someone's tossed flowers in our yard, sometimes whole bunches of them. Once a guy in a VW van, hair down to his belly button, parks his car, walks over, opens the gate, and without a word leaves on our step: a piece of evergreen, a stick of incense wrapped up in a *World Tribune,* newspaper of the Nicheren Shoshus. He sits in the lotus position, chants, gets up and leaves. Couple of times we had some really spacey types who stood, palms out, under the jacarandas, *Om'*d our house. Then we had some people said they were from the SRF and who knows what that was? I thought they'd come to check on the Colonel's tags and I said he'd had his shots, but they just wanted to leave a flower at the shrine of the King.

Just last month there's a car circles our intersection on a Saturday morning. I thought she's checking out the Starlight Coupe, but she parks and walks up to the front gate, a woman Mama's age, waving a thick book and screaming, "This book is the truth! This book is the story of his stinking life! And it's the truth! He was shit! Shit! He couldn't sing and he couldn't act and he—"

Mama opens our front door, goes right down to the gate and opens it, like to say, *Well, come in and say it to the King.*

She pushes that book in my mother's face. "Read this! Read it!"

"I wouldn't wipe my butt with that book," says my mother. "I wouldn't wipe my dog's butt with that book. I have more respect for my dog than that. I have more respect for his butt."

"Oh yeah? Did you ever see Elvis in concert? Well, I did. I paid good money to go see him in Houston in 1975. Good money! And there he was—he stank! Stank! He couldn't sing! He couldn't even make noise! He was so, oh God! He was just sickening! And now I know why!" She thumped the book again. *"The Impossible Dream,* hah!" She spits at my mother's feet.

"He needed your pity in 1975."

"What?"

"You heard me."

"He wanted my money!"

"He was singing himself to death for you. Elvis Presley was singing himself to death, right there in front of your eyes, and you couldn't see it. You must have been blind and heartless."

The woman bursts into tears and leaves.

So whoever this paperboy is, we are ready for him. I been through this a hundred times. I seen it all before. Lucky for us he's on foot and not on a bicycle. Fifteen, maybe. Taller than Donny Roncker and not as zitty. He's got that fat boy's walk to him and he carries the bags of the *St. Elmo Herald* like they was the wages of sin. He's smoking a cigarette. We meet him out at the gate. "You blind?"

"Whuh?"

"I asked if you're blind. Don't you got eyes? Can't you see our porch is Sacred to the Memory of a great man."

"Elvis?" Snort, snort.

"Elvis Presley is the greatest man who ever lived, except for Jesus." Lisa holds tight to the Colonel, like if she lets him go, this paperboy is sausage. "He didn't smoke and he didn't drink. He cared for the poor and the sick and the suffering. He reached out his music to all humanity and if Elvis was still alive, there wouldn't be any juvenile delinquents like you in this world."

"I'm no juvenile delinquent."

"Well then, you must be some kind of retard," I say. "Elvis was a great man and the world is a dimmer, darker place now that he's gone, and no one's ever gonna say the same about you when you pass through."

"When I whuh?"

"Gimme that newspaper. What's your name?"

"Alex." He flips his cigarette butt into the gutter.

"Well, Alex, at *this* house, the paper goes on the back porch. If you ever throw it up here on this Sacred to the Memory front porch, we call the cops and tell them you're disrespecting private property."

"Whuh?"

"You heard me. They'll have your butt in Juvenile Hall faster than you can spit."

"Oh, piss off," says Alex, handing me the newspaper. "And take Elvis with you."

The Book of Acts

Seven

Sandee always said you could tell who had lost her virginity on Saturday night by the way she walked on Monday morning. At lunchtime Sandee, Joyce, Charleen, and their girlfriends (who collectively referred to themselves as the Bombs—hydrogen, of course) sat in the dusty SEHS quad, six girls on a graffiti-scarred concrete picnic table. They munched green apples, elbows resting on heavy texts with names like *Traditions in Literature* and *Modern Math*. They watched the procession of crew-cut white boys in lettermen's sweaters. SEHS classrooms were integrated, but the grounds were informally partitioned by race; a black kid in the quad would have lasted as long as an orchid in the snow. (A Mexican got in once, though; he was campaign manager for Brad Pelich when he won senior class president.)

"She did it," Sandee said authoritatively, pointing to a ponytailed girl walking with Mike Lance.

"With Mike?" asked Debbie.

"You can't tell who *with*," Sandee explained patiently. "Only that she did it. Look how different her walk is."

"Looser," observed Delrene. "Definitely a looser walk."

Joyce nodded. She knew what was under discussion, though she could not hear what was said. She had taken an Elvis Pill on the school bus, as she did every morning, and the volume inside her head had escalated to near deafening. She chewed her apple to the internal thump and beat of *Hound Dog*. Personally, she couldn't tell any difference in the ponytailed girl's walk, but she trusted Sandee in these matters. Sandee had been dating since she was fourteen and a half. She had a boyfriend now, Ralph Strech, and though Sandee had certainly not Done It, she was sophisticated and experienced and correct. Joyce was none of these things. Joyce Denby was not allowed to date, to wear lipstick, jewelry, tight sweaters, nylon hose; she was forbidden dancing, boys, cruising, and rock and roll. She wasn't even allowed Sandee, for that matter.

Joyce Denby and Sandee Sloat had been friends since they were both eleven, the year the Denbys moved down from Hammath Hot Springs. Harmon Denby claimed he had left Hammath Hot Springs because there were only Indians and a mad, half-Jap writer living up there, but in truth, the owner had sold the property, hot springs and all, to a developer. Evicted by the developer, Harmon torched the shack they'd lived in and moved to a rural, impoverished area loosely known as Tumbleweeds. His eldest daughter rode the school bus to Rancho Junior High in St. Elmo proper, where she met Sandee Sloat.

Godless as the Sloats were, Harmon tolerated the friendship until that summer when Sandee was fourteen and overnight bloomed into womanhood. Always a big, horsey, athletic girl, Sandee sprouted breasts, hair, hips, a discernible waist, and three inches in every direction in a single summer. When Harmon Denby noticed this (and you could not help but notice; a blind man could have smelled it on her) he forbade his daughter Rejoice (who was still wearing undershirts over breasts that looked like poached eggs) Sandee's company. He did this without a single scruple or compunction; he was the father, after all, and stood in relation to the family as God stands in relation to the world. It never crossed his mind that he would be axiomatically disobeyed.

From Rejoice's point of view, her father's prohibition against Sandee was so unjust that it did not even warrant tears, much less compliance. It must be ignored. And it could be, Rejoice decided, as she sat one day in science class, watching the teacher slice an earthworm in half, in full sickening view of the class. Each side lived on.

Disgusting, but instructive. After that, she split, visibly, into Joyce and Rejoice.

Rejoice was a modestly clad, God-fearing girl who sang in the choir of the Church of the New Disciples, prayed continually, and believed rock and roll came from the devil. Rejoice, the dutiful daughter, dropped Sandee Sloat at her father's command. Joyce, on the other hand, lied with the ease of someone who had hell tattooed all over her afterlife. Joyce was only slightly alarmed at the grace and conviction she brought to these lies and at her parents' unblinking acceptance of them.

Thus, she found she could effect a daily and increasingly effortless transition, from Joyce at school to Rejoice at home and at the Church of the New Disciples. The faith of the New Disciples, like their church, was stripped to a hard, splintery, unsoftened core. They did not permit themselves the amelioration of air-conditioning, nor did the summer sun burn through stained glass, nor fall on softened pews. Communion was the prisoners' fare of bread and water. New Disciples distrusted what was not dry, unleavened, impoverished like most of the New Disciples themselves. Their slit-eyed suspicion of emotion touched everything in their lives, including their relations with one another. The New Disciples in general, and her father in particular, prized only suffering, humility, and obedience. Rejoice Denby was constitutionally unable to live like that, and from the time she was a little girl, she took the only avenue of escape available: music. Feeling the organ throb beneath her feet as she stood on the bleachers clad in her stifling choir robes, Rejoice released emotion, learned to transfuse lyric with rapture, with requited (if unseen) love of God. Rejoice had a full, clear alto voice and she could sometimes tilt her head back, lips parted, and believe the music itself to have become, not simply audible, but visible and palpable, notes like golden motes, like smoke or dust or steam, notes that rose from her throat, winging against gravity, till they fell back upon her open lips, touched her tongue, sweetened her breath like powdered honey.

So it was but a small leap from the church choir to the Elvis Pill, except the Elvis Pill required no church. You could take an Elvis Pill anywhere. Invoke an Elvis song, any song, and perform upon it a sort of musical communion: eyes closed, a sharp intake of breath, the song pressed into a wafery round—sweet, hard, fragile as the coating on a Jordan almond—Joyce laid this gently up against the roof of her mouth, neither sucking nor insisting, just her tongue pressing gently, firmly, till she could feel the music dissolve, the volume diminishing into her blood, rising up through her bones. The Elvis Pill allowed Joyce not simply to hear his music, but to have it. When Joyce Denby crossed the SEHS quad, her still-virgin's walk moved in evident rhythm to an unheard melody; her fingers snapped, gum cracked, feet tapped in tune and time and time again, music, Elvis's music, soaked her more fully than the Reverend Throckmorton ever had that day when she was twelve and she and a dozen other New Disciples had waded into an irrigation ditch in a St. Elmo lemon grove. The Reverend Throckmorton's hot palm hit her forehead and she went under, into the yellow-brown waters, a baptism of total immersion in the irrigation ditch. She came up silted, sputtering, and in a state of grace.

With the Elvis Pill percolating music up through her marrow, every school day Joyce Denby got off the school bus and went directly to the H building girls' bathroom, where Sandee and Charleen were having a smoke. Joyce used one of their lipsticks, took off her starched cotton prim blouse, put on a borrowed, tit-hugging Orlon sweater. If it was a cardigan, one of the other Bombs buttoned it up the back. She put on her Elvis charm bracelet (guitar, treble clef, hound dog, and a picture of Elvis in a heart). Linda took Joyce's thick hair and ponytailed it before the bell rang. "Roll over, Beethoven," said Sandee, running her smoking butt under the faucet. "Go cat go."

They got through the day. Somehow. And at the last bell (while Rejoice was doing something respectable with Youth for Christ), Joyce and the Bombs sashayed over to Ruby's, where there was always a whole lot of shaking going on, where for the cost of a dime tossed into the slot, Joyce could hear Elvis outside her head as well as inside. Elvis and every other rocking bebopper. For thirty-five cents, two girls could double up on a soda, flirt with boys in lettermen's sweaters, boys in leather jackets, boys in car club jackets. The girls might even get asked to ride in one of the sleek, shining cars, scoot their bottoms over white tuck-and-roll, check their lipstick in a rearview mirror that had angora dice hanging from it, and cruise: two Bombs in the front with the driver, three or four in the back, where vibrations from the transmission shook right up through the chassis, rattled your thighs, and rolled everything else till you went cotton-mouthed listening to the radio, KLMO *(Tomorrow's Hits Today)* rocking out as you cruised up and down Brigham Boulevard, that broad thoroughfare named for the great Mormon leader, who (like Beethoven) would have rolled over—grave and all—to see these goings-on. No doubt whatever of the Great Brigham's answer, had he been asked the musical question: *Devil or Angel?*

Harmon Denby was bedeviled beyond endurance with Rejoice. Girls were a curse. They grew up to be women, who after all had brought with them into this world sin, like a wrong set of keys to the human ignition: sex. They had invented and foisted on men the splendor and grief, the murk of sex. Women were correctly denied revelation, church office, and authority. Pretty girls were the worst, like that musky friend of Rejoice's. Put pretty girls together with all that jungle music, that Elvis-devil, and all the rest of that Negro thumping and you had real trouble. *Trouble pass me by,* that's what Harmon Denby said in effect, as he forbade such music, radios, and television (which he could not afford anyway). He boarded up the devil's entrance into his home. And in doing so (and because angels have a way of slipping, like drafts, through the cracks of our resolve, of making trouble, shrugging their wings, and calling it fate), Harmon became the instrument of his own undoing.

Syllogistically, you could make the case that it all came from God. There was a windstorm that night, just like in the Book of Acts; the sounds came from heaven of a mighty rushing and it filled the house where they were sitting. At supper. The family was at supper the night that windstorm hove and flung itself through St. Elmo, shake, rattle, and rolling the clapboarded house in Tumbleweeds. The house was sheltered from the sun by a grove of encircling eucalyptus, huge shaggy trees whose rough branches rubbed and creaked together, banging percussively in the wind, moaning like Rachel, like Hannah, like all the Bible's childless wives. Wind shook the wooden screen doors and the ill-fitting windowpanes.

Opal Denby was at the stove dishing up barley stew. Opal wore a grease-splashed skirt and a man's shirt. Rejoice served her father first, then her father's father, who was deaf as a post. Next Grandma, who heard everything. Then the younger children, Bethany and Rhoda. Baby Noah (cooing to himself and flailing with his fork) had to wait till Opal sat down. Rejoice served herself and her mother last. When Opal took her place opposite Harmon, their heads all bent in unison and prayer, which was emphatic, without emotion, spoken in a low, dull drone of gratuitous thanksgiving.

She heard it then. In the midst of prayer and even over the croak and groan of the old house in the wind. Rejoice heard the radio she had left on in the bedroom she shared with Bethany and Rhoda. Under the bed where she kept it hidden, but on. On and tuned to KLMO. *Oh Jesus,* Rejoice prayed over the barley stew. *Help me, Jesus. If ever you loved me, please turn my radio off. How could I have left it on? Oh, I beg of you, Jesus, help me and turn my radio off.*

The radio did not precisely belong to Joyce. She had found it, when they moved into the house, in a box that also had some *Reader's Digest* condensed books. Also left were a three-legged card table, a rain-damaged couch and chair, a box of copper tubing (which Harmon sold), chipped plates, an enamel coffeepot with a hole in it, and a lawn mower that didn't work. The furniture and lawn mower testified to some more comfortable day when this had been a rural chicken ranch. In those days there must have been a lawn. Now there were only overgrown, empty coops at the back of the property and foxtail patches, raw, ugly, random as the mange on a hound dog's back, speckled here and there with the yellow grunge of sunflower, mustard flower, and dandelion, everything soaked in that heavy, camphory smell of eucalyptus trees, whose rusty bark peeled off and fell to the ground, lay there with the leaves in deep, dusty profusion.

Unlike the lawn mower, however, the radio had always worked. It worked now. Over the thrash of the wind through the eucalyptus and rain gutters rattling, Rejoice heard the music—worse, the rolling banner of Elvis's voice promising *Any* Way *You Want Me.* And she knew, without words, what Harmon Denby would do and why: because you could hear in Elvis's voice what you could see on Sandee Sloat: someone plucking that taut string connecting imagination to desire, ringing out that complex chord of pitch and gristle. Clearly, in the beginning was the word, and the word was *Bee bop a reebop a grim goddamn* or letters to that effect. It could only have been instinct for Harmon because nothing in his shuttered-up, nailed-down emotional life could have taught him this. Never, or by any stretch of the imagination, could Opal Denby have oozed or dripped nectar, that thick femininity that Harmon recognized in fourteen-year-old Sandee Sloat. Never would Opal have implored Harmon to love her tender or any other way, never would Opal have knelt between his naked knees, vowing *Any Way You Want Me.* So Harmon's understanding of these things was inarticulate, instinctive, reflexive as the daily roiling of his bowels.

But there, around the Denby supper table, it was one for the money, two for the show, three to get ready for the wind when the song changed and Elvis caterwauled out the catalog of what he would endure in defense of his *Blue Suede Shoes.* When Harmon looked up from his plate, Rejoice pinched Baby Noah under the table and he howled. Opal calmed him in an abstracted fashion. The girls got in a quarrel stilled by Grandma thumping Bethany on the head and smacking Rhoda on the hand. And then Rejoice piped up loudly how Sister Meadows had given her the solo in choir on Sunday. *Blue Suede Shoes* finished. Rejoice bolted her barley stew.

"What's that?" Harmon chewed phlegmatically.

"'Scuse me." Rejoice scraped her chair back.

"Siddown. Stay where you are. That's *I Got a Savior Way Over Jordan,* ain't it, Ma?"

"No." Grandma refitted her upper plate with both thumbs. "That's something else. Listen to the words." Grandma quit eating.

"Same tune as *I Got a Savior*," she said at last, "but them words are different. Words sound to me like *I Got a Woman Way Across Town.*" A man of studied moves was Harmon Denby, as though he distrusted alacrity in anything, and so he slowly rose and Rejoice heard his tread down the hall toward the girls' room, Hog the Dog following, snuffling, sniffling, as though Hog too sensed the intruder, the threat. Joyce heard her narrow bed creak when her father sat down on it, feet planted apart. She heard him pull the radio out from underneath the bed. It sat there between his feet while he listened, his big hands looped over one another, to *I Got a Woman Way Across Town,* very like, indeed (except for the lyrics) indistinguishable from, the gospel song. Sitting at the table, Joyce hunched, head down, fists clenched as though she herself were to take the blow she knew was coming, did come, smooth and in one fluid motion. The music died in its final chord and the radio died with it. But then, as if their collective death had somehow angered the angels, the wind gripped the eucalyptus trees, throttled and yanked, tore them limb from limb, flung those limbs down, one right after another, one right on the roof of the girls' bedroom, where it crashed through the ceiling, literally scaring the shit out of Hog the Dog and missing Harmon Denby by inches.

"An Act of God," said the landlord as he stood in the yard and surveyed the damage. He said Harmon Denby could fix it himself. Harmon said he couldn't; he had a fear of heights. "Then find someone who don't have a fear of heights and get him to fix it," said the landlord.

Harmon said: "Okay, you'll pay?"

"Hell no," said the landlord. "Check the lease. Tenant pays for all Acts of God. You're only paying twenty-eight dollars a month rent, and for that you can fix the goddamn roof yourself."

Harmon Denby worked at the 7-Up bottling plant in St. Elmo with a man whose son worked construction. He said the son would not be averse to picking up a few nonunion bucks. The son said he would fix the roof, sight unseen, for sixty dollars. Cash and up-front. Harmon said he'd think on it, but in the meantime, he said, his three daughters were all sleeping in the living room and there was no peace for anyone. You're lucky you got sons, he added sourly.

The following Saturday Harmon Denby found some old newspapers under the front porch and a book of matches and went out to the back of the property, where stood the remains of the chicken coops. They smelled wistfully of feed and dust and feathers and droppings. Harmon spread the newspapers inside the coops. He lit the corner of the matchbook and tossed it in.

He backed off, squatting on one knee in the weeds, holding Hog the Dog by the collar, scratching him between his long floppy ears while the coops burnt. They went quickly and without protest, like penitent heretics, and then the fire snapped and flame—slurped the nearby weeds, dry brush, and foxtails overgrowing the coops. Harmon called for Rejoice to turn on the hose and bring it. Fast.

Opal stood on the back porch beside the wringer washing machine, Baby Noah on her hip, hand shaded over her eyes. Grandma sat on the back step, leaning against a splintery post, rolling her lips over her gums, and Grandpa waved his arms, shouting the way deaf people do. Harmon put the fire out before it spread too far with the collapse of the coops. The stench of wet droppings, long-dead feathers, old wood and wire wafted on whatever breeze could bear to carry it.

Harmon got out his keys. "Come on," he said to Hog the Dog.

"Aren't you going to change?" Opal asked. "You smell like fire. Like smoke and ash."

"Don't you have a brain to play with, woman?" Harmon motioned for Hog the Dog to get in the back of the family Dodge. He drove to the landlord's and said there'd been another act of God. He said it was lucky the fire didn't spread. He said he needed seventy-five dollars to fix the roof.

Two days later Warren James Jackson, Jr., showed up driving a 1946 Studebaker Starlight Coupe. He came to get his money. Harmon stood on the porch and counted out the sixty dollars. Warren said he thought he could finish it up in three weekends maybe. Harmon reminded him that in this house he could only work on Saturdays. Sunday belonged to the Lord. No one here worked on Sunday.

Rejoice came out of the house hoisting a basket of laundry. She watched Warren James Jackson, Jr., all the way to the clothesline, where she bent over, picking pieces up and pinning them to the line. Warren took the pack of cigarettes out of the shirtsleeve he had rolled into a pocket. His lips bent over the pack. He drew one up. He looked at Rejoice. Quickly she turned back to the clothes. He lit the match, pulling it up the thigh of his tight blue jeans. He said: "Cool, daddy-o, Saturday it is."

Saturday was one of those late-September days that should have been cool and wasn't. The long band of morning clouds burned off by nine-thirty. By that time Warren James Jackson, Jr., had already been on the roof for an hour, having driven his father's truck over with the ladder and tools in it. By ten the sun began to scorch and climb. Despite the shade offered by the eucalyptus, light glinted intermittently from his jagged saw and his leather tool belt baked around his hips; sweat stained his T-shirt in a V down his spine and armpits. By noon, the heat came down as if shaken from a roll of foil, and Warren James Jackson, Jr., took his shirt off. His tanned shoulders pinked and heat dried the pomade in his long hair where he had slicked it back. Over his forehead, one curl fell loose as he worked.

"Would you like a 7-Up?" Rejoice called from the foot of the ladder.

"Coca-Cola's a man's drink," came the reply.

"All we got's 7-Up."

"No beer?"

"No beer in this house."

"Cool."

She returned with the 7-Up and called up to him, watched him come down the ladder, the muscles in his back working against one another. His jeans were rolled up at the cuff and unbelted, though he filled them out and they did not hang slack as they did on the bodies of boys the Bombs dubbed Buttless Wonders. He took the bottle from her, tipped his head back, and drank. Eyes level with his chest, Rejoice watched the sunlight gleam in perspiration dotting the mat of black hair, hair so thick you could not see his nipples. Not unless you looked closely. The odor of his sweat and fresh skin brewed with the unseasonal heat, the baking eucalyptus, foxtails, the smell of wild mustard. It was the heat, probably, that made her feel light-headed. Sunstroke. Or something very like it.

"What's your name?" he asked.

"Joyce. Well, Rejoice here at home. Joyce at school."

"St. Elmo High?"

"There isn't any other school."

"I used to go there."

"I know you did."

He lounged against the ladder and his full lips curled into a grin. "How do you know that?"

"There isn't any other school," she repeated.

"What else do you know?"

Oh, the devil hath a hundred tricks and bricks to put in mortals' paths, to trip, tease, and tempt, to test our spindly mortal sinew. Sometimes Rejoice just wondered why the devil was so democratic, while God only bothered with saints or apostles or people in olden times. The devil went after everyone, no matter who you were or when you lived. Maybe it was the devil at work right here. What thoughtless angel would have put this mortal brick of sweating, twenty-one-year-old male flesh, half-naked, right in front of her? Perhaps she ought to pray to gentle Jesus, meek and mild, lead me as a little child. But she didn't. She knew she wouldn't. She kept her eyes on the dark hair curling over his chest; it gathered in a thin seam down his hard belly and disappeared into his pants. Her gaze fastened on a drop of perspiration hanging from his chest; she watched it gain weight and color, knew it was about to drop, felt she must, or could, or might lean forward (slightly; she was that close), leading with her tongue, to catch that drop of sweat, taste what she could already smell. Resolutely she licked her lips, raised her face, and met his dark eyes with the kind of candor unbecoming on a virgin. A woman older than Rejoice would have seen in his face the mature man he would become, or the boy he had been, but Joyce Denby saw him only as he was. And for her, as he always would be. "I know you graduated the same year as Phil Sloat. He's my best friend's brother."

"Phil Sloat, sure." His laughter seemed to bubble up from some deep, unpicketed place in his body, untainted by shame, or regret, or self-consciousness. Rejoice had never heard anything so musical. "Phil Sloat was in a different car club. Phil's a Baron. I'm in the Chieftains."

"I know," she said stupidly.

"I think you know a lot you're not telling me.

"No," she lied swiftly. She did know a lot about him; Sandee had been very obliging with the gossip. According to Sandee and others, Warren James Jackson, Jr., was just like his old man, a brown-eyed handsome hell-raiser. The Jacksons had given St. Elmo at least a week's worth of delicious Domestic Wrath headlines when Warren James, Sr., left his wife and four children and had the gas and electricity and the phone all cut off as soon as he was out of the house. When Mrs. Jackson found herself in the dark with no heat and no phone, she threw her four children in the back seat of the De Soto and hunted her husband down, him and his whore-girl-friend, sniffing them out like a bloodhound. He had a number of women, but when she finally found him, she drove the De Soto virtually right up on the steps and into the living room of the girlfriend's house. Warren, Sr., came running out, naked. Mrs. Jackson put the car in reverse, backed off the porch, then plunged after him, chasing him through the streets, to a schoolyard where he leaped over the fence and she fruitlessly rammed it. She spent overnight in the county jail for this, but she was not sent to prison.

After her front-page passion, Mrs. Jackson settled down to bring up a family of hardworking Catholic kids, was a model mother, save for the burning anger, hate, rage, and bitterness she carried with her. Perhaps it was this taint, desire gone rotten, that made the eldest son opt for the cloister and become a priest. They sometimes heard from him, living in Bolivia. One girl was a Miss St. Elmo runner-up in 1953 and left town to go to nursing school. The other married an insurance salesman and moved away. Jack (as he was now known, Warren James being out of favor as a family name) was the youngest, his mother's favorite, but his father's son for all that. Even as a kid he reeked of danger and rebellion. Never mind, his mother doted on him. When he graduated from high school, he started working construction (and playing serious poker) and he continued to live with his mother, easing the loneliness, paying the rent, insisting finally that she quit her nurse's aide job when her health faltered, when, perhaps, all that chronic bitterness curdled somewhere deep inside her.

He had a lot of girlfriends. More than that, he'd had a lot of girls. Charleen said nice girls wouldn't go near him. Not by day. He was rumored to have knocked up the 1955 head cheerleader Bonnie Baith, though he denied it and Bonnie finally admitted that the father was really a dumb cluck she was ashamed to have slept with named Dougie Barker, whom she subsequently married. While little girls like Sandee and Rejoice and Charleen were giggling in the junior high lunchroom, Warren James Jackson, Jr., was collecting around himself rumors, story shards, circumstantial, half-limned, unlovely episodes of road games, drag races, fights, underage drinking, and wild parties down by the flood channel, out in the orange groves, and up in the canyons and the foothills. Phil Sloat said Jack Jackson was a bad cat all around: too smart, too smart-mouthed, too good-looking for his own good. He said that Jack had a scar from a knife fight and a cracked rib from a chain fight and he had once beat the living crap out of a guy who alluded loosely to his mother's having attempted to murder his dad with the De Soto. He had played first base for the SEHS Varsity Knights their championship year. He lavished his time and affection on a 1946 Studebaker Starlight Coupe.

"Phil Sloat said you played baseball," Joyce said. The bead of perspiration dropped from his chest into the dust and eucalyptus at his feet.

"Old Phil tell you I'm going into the army in November?"

"No."

"Well I am. Drafted. I don't care. Army's only way I know of for sure to get out of this rat's ass of a town." He looked over her shoulder as though something beyond had caught his attention. "Once I get out, I'm real gone. I'm never coming back."

"Lucky for you there's no war on."

"You think that's lucky, do you, Joyce-Rejoice? You think you'd cry if I got killed?"

"No." Despite the heat, she crossed her arms resolutely over her chest so he would not see that her nipples were lit up like Christmas lights. She knew they were. She could feel them flashing and blinking inside her bra.

"You want to go out with me?"

"No. I don't go out."

"You want to go for a ride in my Starlight Coupe?"

"No."

"Boyfriend won't let you?"

"I don't have a boyfriend, and if I did, I wouldn't let him tell me what to do."

"That's good. I like a girl with spunk."

She looked up into his brown eyes to see if he was kidding. He wasn't.

"I got a girlfriend," he went on. "And I don't let her tell me what to do. I'd like to take you out, Joyce-Rejoice."

"I told you, I don't go out. I'm too young. That's what my daddy says." She looked back down, studying her bare toes sticking out of her sandals. "I'm only sixteen. I'm not old enough."

"When you get old enough, you give me a call."

"Girls don't call boys."

He brought his heavy boot right up to the edge of her sandal, met it, toe to toe. "I ain't no boy, Joyce. And anyway, you're wrong about that. Girls call all the time. They just don't use the telephone."

"Rejoice!"

She glanced over and saw her father, wondered how long he'd been standing there. Jack handed her the empty 7-Up bottle and she took it without comment or looking back.

All that afternoon (and in a manner of speaking) Jack pounded on top of her. He hammered and sawed and sang to himself. When the noise ceased, she went to the living room and stood in one of the long dirty windows. She smudged the dust with her arm, the better to see him amble out to his father's truck, unbuckle the tool belt, throw it in, light up a cigarette, put the truck in reverse, and gun it. She wondered where he would go from here. Home probably. For a shower and a shave and then out on a date. It was Saturday night, after all. Then she wondered how many girls had walked differently on Monday morning because they had gone out with Jack Jackson on Saturday night.

"I curse that boy."

"Curse the eucalyptus tree," said Opal as she folded Noah's diapers and laid them, one by one, on the threadbare arm of the chair.

"I curse the money I already paid him."

"Curse the wind that brought the tree down."

"He's been coming here every Saturday for a month—for near on two months! And he ain't finished yet. He shoulda been finished. He woulda been. He'd of been outa here if Rejoice would quit hanging around him, bringing him drinks, listening to that devil's music he plays on the car radio. I put a stop to that. I told her there'll be no more of that."

"Then what's she doing out there now?" Opal nodded through the living room window.

Some distance from the house, Jack had parked the Starlight Coupe. The driver's door was open and a blanket lay on the ground. He always turned on the radio, KLMO, and lay on the blanket while he ate his sandwich and waited for Joyce. He was never disappointed. She always came, with the excuse of bringing him a 7-Up. He patted the blanket and she always sat down. A good distance from him, but she always sat down nonetheless. There wasn't a damn thing Harmon could do about it, unless he wanted to pay someone else to finish the roof.

"Damn that girl!"

"She don't need you to damn her, Harmon. She's doing her own work."

"That girl is leading me the devil's own dance."

"I thought you told Rejoice she couldn't go out there and sit on that blanket with him."

"I did," said Harmon glumly.

"You told her more than that once, didn't you?"

"Oh, shut up," Harmon snapped. No need to tell Opal he had got a mouthful of biblical sass from Rejoice, quotes suggesting that Harmon had a low mind, an un-Christian heart, that he was uncharitably disobeying Paul's commands in First Corinthians. It was then that Harmon Denby began to fear his daughter, feared that breaking her will might test, or undermine, or break his own.

On the last Saturday he was working on the roof, Jack brought his father's truck so he could take the ladder back. Come lunchtime he put the blanket out, opened the door of the truck, and turned on the radio. KLMO. Loud. Really loud. Louder than ever before. He lay down on the blanket and put his feet up on the running board.

Joyce was washing dishes at the kitchen sink. She saw Harmon stalk out to the truck. His face was red and puffed and angry. His fist was clenched. She could not hear what Harmon Denby said, not from that distance. He stood above Jack, who did not move. He let loose a volley of abuse. He reached into the truck, turned the radio off. He gave Jack a nudge with his foot, not quite a kick. More words passed between them. He reached back in and turned the radio on. Lower. He whistled for Hog the Dog, got in the Dodge, and left, roaring, raising a cloud of dust behind him.

Joyce dried her hands, went to the fridge, and took out a bottle of 7-Up. She walked out to the truck. Jack was lying on his back, feet twitching, fingers snapping to *Shake, Rattle and Roll*. As she drew closer, she approached more gingerly and her breath went into escrow.

"Come on, Joyce. Just a couple of steps further. Come closer, Joyce. Stand right above my head."

"You'll look up my skirt."

"I'd die for a look up your skirt. You know I would. I'd die to have your skirt over my face. Closer. Come closer."

"I can't."

"Another step. Two. Kneel down right here. Put your skirt over my face and let me kiss your knees, let me kiss your thighs."

"Please don't say that. Don't say anything."

"You want to, don't you?"

The song finished and the DJ nattered a lot of nonsense for all the cats and chicks out there tuned in to KLMO. Rejoice stood poised, so it seemed, between heaven and hell, worse, feeling the heaven might be worth the hell.

Jack rolled over, stood, took her by the wrist, and pulled her tight against him. She dropped the bottle of 7-Up and splayed her hand across his chest. "I'm leaving Tuesday, Joyce. Basic training. Fort Ord. You going to write to me?"

"No."

"All right then, kiss me. Now, before I leave."

"I can't. I won't. Let me go. My mother's at the kitchen window."

"What does that matter? What does any of it matter?"

"You're too old for me. You have a girlfriend and a bad reputation."

His grip on her tightened and his arms encircled her, brought her up against the warmth of his body, crushed her flesh with his, and the Christmas lights sparkled and flashed everywhere, from every pore. "Let me go, Jack, you're hurting me."

"I'm not hurting you. I probably will, though. One day. I swear before God, Joyce, I don't want to. You remember that. Promise me you'll remember that. Because one day you'll need it." He kissed her hard and long, pushed her lips open and thrust his tongue into her mouth, and then, before he let her go, his lips lingered tenderly on hers. Abruptly he released her, bent, picked up his tool belt and strapped it on. "If you forget that in the next two years, you're not the girl I think you are."

Whistling, he returned to the ladder, climbed up to put the finishing touches on the roof. Joyce was left standing there, the bottle of 7-Up at her feet, with KLMO asking *Why Do Fools Fall in Love?*

She left the bottle where it lay and walked back to the house, and when she came in the kitchen, her mother gave her a look of matronly contempt.

"Don't tell Dad," Joyce pleaded. "Please don't tell Daddy what you saw. I don't know what you saw, exactly, but it wasn't what you think.

I didn't want him to. I didn't ask for it. Don't tell Dad or he'll go after Jack."

"I won't have to tell him." Opal was taller than Rejoice, narrow shouldered like her, but stooped and so seemed weaker, smaller, pale and tired, as though all emotion and volition had been bleached from her. "The graveyards are full of girls like you, Rejoice. Girls who thought they knew better than their parents. Girls who defied and denied and rebelled and went their own way. Girls God's had to punish. The graveyards are full of them."

"What's all this talk of graveyards? Do I look to be dying?" She picked up the towel and began drying the dishes. Ferociously.

"You are dying, girl. You're dying for something that is going to take you right down to hell, Rejoice, and I ain't talking about the afterlife, either. There's no hell on earth like a bad man."

"He's leaving! He's going on Tuesday to the army."

"Too bad there's no war on."

"Oh, Ma! What a wicked thing to say!"

"Too bad for you, Rejoice. It's the girl who pays. Always. It's never been any different and it never will be. It's the same old story." Opal took a small sharp knife and potato skins began to fly. "And at the end, it's the girl who pays. Not the boy."

"He's not a boy."

"I can see that, Rejoice. It's all over you."

"What! What is all over me? What?"

Opal concentrated on her potatoes. "Go change your clothes before your daddy gets home, girl."

Joyce looked down. The front of her white blouse bore flecks of sawdust imprinted from his body; the odor floated up to her: sawdust and the scent of a man's sweat and something else, something she had no name for, even though she recognized it without its name, fathomed, as she saw the sawdust stain between her own young breasts, that there was indeed a land of milk and honey, only its hills and valleys were sculpted from flesh, fired with imagination, with that old pith and suction, damp with desire: the baptism that could only be total immersion.

Eight

It is not particularly difficult to forge the signature of a barely-literate man. Whenever Joyce Denby cut school, Rejoice wrote a note for her in an erratic scrawl signed with a ramshackle *H. Denby.* Joyce elicited her teachers' sympathy (all except Miss Gruski) by dusting flour on her face and using Vicks VapoRub like My Sin so she would smell convincingly medicinal. Unfortunately there was no opportunity to work these theatrics on the attendance secretary, a deceptively fragile, leaflike woman given to headaches, who, except for the headaches, had little to fill her life or time, and so, often she would take her work home with her, combing through students' attendance records. She noticed an alarming pattern in Joyce Denby's attendance, much of it coincident with that of her locker partner, Sandee Sloat, and another student, Charleen Van Acton. The attendance secretary checked the records for the year before, when these girls were sophomores, and brought the entire matter to the attention of the girls' vice-principal, who studied it and called their respective parents.

The Sloats had raised three children before Sandee, and if practice does not make perfect, it certainly makes predictable, which is how the Sloats dealt with this problem. Charleen lived with her mother and stepfather, who had two children from his other marriage and three of their own; they both worked full-time and they were too busy to make much of a fuss beyond reprimands, and tears on

Charleen's mother's part, tears that had more to do with the utility bill than Charleen's attendance record.

But Harmon Denby was different. Harmon Denby's response was like that of the Old Testament God, swift, assured, and terrible. The girls' vice-principal called him at the 7-Up bottling plant. He was waiting for Rejoice on the front porch when she came home from school. Harmon recognized the heart of this matter and it had little to do with cutting school: Harmon had been persistently and unequivocally disobeyed; a man who can't control a mere girl can't really call himself a man. Harmon's rage was all the more potent because his pride had been impugned and the Church of the New Disciples forbade him even to feel pride. But they did not forbid him wrath. And when Rejoice came through the eucalyptus trees toward the porch, he rose, he dealt her the first blow before she reached the door. She whirled against the wall, her books tumbled, and her purse flew open and the Elvis charm bracelet flew out. Its brightness caught Harmon's eye. He left Rejoice there, sprawled, dazed, by the screen door. He picked up the charm bracelet with its heart-shaped picture of Elvis and he knew for certain that the devil had got into his daughter and he would have to beat the devil out and the devil's music too. He pulled Rejoice to her feet, clamped his hand on the back of her neck, bent her double, and pulled her into her room, where he tore apart the bed and dresser, found nothing more terrible than a glow-in-the-dark Elvis, newspaper clippings about him, and a cracked 45 of *Love Me Tender*. He broke the record across Rejoice's face and shook her, slapped her till Opal sent in the grandmother to tell him to stop. *If your right eye offends thee,* said the old lady, eyeing Rejoice critically, *then pluck it out.*

Harmon dragged Rejoice out to the Dodge, threw her in the back, drove to Juvenile Hall, spewing oaths and Scripture, prepared to pluck out, cut off, cast out the offending daughter. He drove to Juvenile Hall with every intention of leaving her there with the other godless scum who didn't deserve decent homes.

In a tiny airless cubicle, a social worker listened to Harmon Denby with rapt solemnity. When his intentions became clear, she gradually brought him to understand that the state of California could not allow him to cast out his daughter because she'd listened to the devil's music, done the devil's work, lied and defied him at every turn and for years. Rejoice was his legal charge until she was eighteen, but at that time the state…

Joyce took an Elvis Pill. Collected herself enough, pulled enough of her bruised flesh over her bruised spirit to take an Elvis Pill, not to press it gently against the roof of her mouth, but to swallow it whole, *Jailhouse Rock,* turn up the volume instantly so she could not hear the maundering social worker, nor see the brutal graffiti, nor breathe in the air of institutions built up, for, and around Things Gone Wrong. The social worker's face came up to her, a bricklike mouth pursed in an expectant look. Joyce knew she'd been asked a question. She sneered. She said, *Tutti Frutti.*

The next time he might very well kill her. And Joyce knew there would be a next time. Harmon, for his part, succumbed to forbidden pride, believed that he had taught his daughter an emphatic lesson in obedience and, in teaching Rejoice, that he had also visibly instructed Bethany and Rhoda. Noah was too young; the lesson was lost on Noah. But Harmon might have been right about Bethany and Rhoda; certainly they never followed Joyce's path. They lived obedient, hunched-up, humorless lives governed by suspicious minds and empty hearts. For Joyce such a life would itself have been death. She resolved—without drama or declaration—that if she were to risk death, at least she would be certain she had lived.

Three and four times a week (certainly every Friday and Saturday night) Joyce Denby lay awake in her bed, clad in a plain white flannel nightgown, with her clothes folded up beside her under the covers. She stared in the darkness at the picture of Jesus on her wall; however bedraggled she might be on Sunday morning, Rejoice would still stand up and donate her voice to the bright banner of music in church; she felt no sting or taint of wickedness. Had she not gone down in the silted waters of the irrigation ditch, come up with the conviction of grace? If Jesus would not have approved of her behavior, she felt certain, neither would He have taken it personally. Shortly after ten, almost invariably, the house rang with snores. (Harmon subscribed to early to bed, early to rise; thus, so did everyone else.) With consummate stealth, Joyce took her clothes and shoes, plumped up her pillows, pulled the blankets over them (and Bethany and Rhoda, even if they were not asleep, had been terrified into silence). She eased the window up on its already well-greased ropes and slipped out, closing the window gently to about half an inch above the sill. She made her way barefoot through the eucalyptus leaves, an elusive, white-clad figure moving through the shaggy trees toward the road, where a car silently waited, headlights doused, until she got in. There was a flicker of light and laughter, feminine voices, hushed, hurried conversation, and then the car started up and they were off and running. Fast.

Fast was the reputation that came to gather around Sandee and Charleen and Joyce. It began as a kind of whispered innuendo, collected momentum in the lingering looks boys gave them and the sporty superiority other girls assumed, girls who were not Fast. The old, easy alliance of the Bombs smashed up. Linda, Debbie, and Delrene knew you could not be thought Fast and be an officer in Girls' League or Dominettes, Pep Squad or Sub Debs. Debbie and Linda and Delrene were often pictured in the SEHS *Weekly Knight:* pom-pom girls, candidates for class secretary, Junior Darling, and leaders in leadership class. Sandee, Joyce, and Charleen, on the other hand, collected around themselves that aura of recklessness that goes with parties in the orange groves, where there was cold beer and hot dancing performed in the garish glow of headlights, music provided by KLMO. Even more indiscreet, on leaving the groves, they went with boys who drove them up to the Point, with its view of greater (and duller) St. Elmo. So dangerous were these girls' reputations, boys often dared to drive them up the unlit byways of Spanish Canyon, to park in the foothills near Hammath Hot Springs.

Sandee Sloat's parents did not bother to restrain her. Charleen Van Acton's parents could not afford to restrain her. And nothing could restrain Joyce Denby. That much was absolutely clear after the sock hop where Joyce Denby danced with that colored basketball star, Erwin Walker, and (Linda and Debbie and Delrene discreetly, swiftly retired to the girls' bathroom as soon as) Joyce Denby kicked so high her underpants showed. Joyce Denby was the only white girl at SEHS who could do the shimmy squatting and not fall over.

After Delrene started wearing Pete Polland's class ring around her neck, she quit speaking to Sandee, Charleen, and Joyce altogether. Word went round that at one of these orange grove parties, Joyce had left with Pete, gone to his panel truck, and rejoined the group with her capri pants on inside out. (Her pants were on inside out, but not thanks to Pete Polland. Joyce had gone off into the orange groves to pee and, feeling tipsy and uncertain because of the beer, she'd simply taken the capris off, unknowingly put them on inside out.) Pete Polland himself started the rumor about the panel truck, and it passed for truth because SEHS was ready to believe almost anything about Joyce Denby, Sandee Sloat, or Charleen Van Acton. They had good looks and bad reputations.

"What the hell do we care?" said Sandee, filing her nails and lighting up a Newie. "The other day Linda goes right past me, doesn't even speak. Gives me a look like I'm supposed to roll over and die." Sandee settled herself against the pink stuffed poodle on her bed.

"That's because Danny Lance took you to that last party at John Nasen's. She's had the hots for Danny Lance since seventh grade." Charleen blew on her Fire and Ice nail polish.

"Danny Lance is cute, but he's a Mormon. All those Mormon boys are—well, what do you think, Joyce? How does he kiss?"

"Danny's a Tin Woodman." The girls had developed a sort of shorthand for evaluating kisses: boys were either Scarecrows, Tin Woodmen, Cowardly Lions, Munchkins, or the Wizard of Oz. Joyce had never kissed anyone in the Wizard category except for Warren James Jackson, Jr., and she never told anyone about that, not even Sandee and Charleen.

"Well, personally, I don't care what any of them think. They can just take their Junior Darling and senior secretary and pom-pom girl and Girls' League and—"

"Hang them out to dry." Joyce gave an emphatic crack on her Juicy Fruit and pulled Sandee's stuffed Hound Dog into her lap. "Delrene thinks she has Pete Polland around her finger because she has his ring around her neck. I could kiss him in front of the whole admin building if I wanted to."

"Hey, I could kiss every last one of those boys, in a month's time if I put my mind to it." Sandee swung her white bucks to the floor and eyed her friends knowingly. "Let's do a bet. Everyone puts in five dollars, and whoever can kiss every boy in the Chieftains Car Club first gets the whole fifteen dollars."

"I don't have five dollars," said Joyce.

"Maybe you'll win."

"Cripes!" Charleen cried, "there must be twenty Chieftains!"

Sandee put her Newie out in a Coke bottle, fanned the smoke out her window, and grinned at the other two. "Winner take all."

"I hate him!" Joyce wailed. "I hate Brad Pelich!" She bent forward, weeping into her skirt, lipstick smeared, hair awry, sweater clips dangling from her cardigan by a single set of teeth.

"Shhh—" Sandee counseled, pulling her bathrobe more tightly around her. They sat on the cement back step of Sandee's house, Joyce having roused her with a handful of gravel flung at the bedroom window, totally unnecessary, really, because Brad Pelich had already wakened the neighborhood when he angrily peeled out.

"It all happened so fast, I mean, it was over before Little Richard finished *Lucille,*" Joyce sobbed, raking through her fair hair. "I was only making out with him b-b-because of the Chieftains bet, and he kisses like a Scarecrow, Sandee, really. He does. It's awful, but I didn't mind it as much after a couple of beers, and I said to him, *Okay, now Brad, it's time to stop, no Brad,* but he shouldn't have p-pushed me back down like that, Sandee, and my head was under the steering wheel, and he shouldn't have done that, Sandee, pulled my s-sk-skirt up over my face and—" Joyce leaned over, retched into the geraniums, stood and reached for the garden hose. She put her face into the water as if it ran from blue Galilee. She wrung the water from her hair

134

and mopped her face. She dropped the hose and swallowed a great hairball of humiliation. "Now I can't even get home. When my dad finds I've stuffed pillows in the bed, he'll kill me. I hope he does. I want to die."

"Don't worry about that. When Phil gets in, we'll take you back."

"What if Phil stays out all night?"

"He won't. He's out with Mary Martinelli. Her dad waits up for her. So don't worry. Everything will be fine."

"Everything will never be fine, never, not if he beats me again."

"Beat? You told me he dragged you into Juvie, but you never said—Did he use a belt?"

"He didn't need a belt."

"Oh, Judas H. Johnson! Why didn't you ever tell me?"

Joyce sat back down beside her friend and ran her hands over her face. "I couldn't. I couldn't tell anyone. If I once said it, if someone else knew besides me—and him—" She hugged her knees. "I can't explain it. It seemed like silence was the only power I had."

Sandee hugged her and began to cry too. "Don't you ever let him do that again, Joycie. Don't you ever let anyone do that to you again as long as I'm alive." Joyce broke into fresh weeping and they leaned together, holding each other. "You come here, Joycie. You understand? You come right to this house, even if you have to walk, you come here if he ever tries to hit you again. Oh, Joycie—"

"I thought he was going to kill me, Sandee—"

"Oh, it makes me sick. I just thought he kept you home from school for a week for punishment, I thought that was all he—"

"He would have sent me to school, all purple and green and busted up like that, but I wouldn't go. I said, *You can beat me all over again if you want, but I won't go to school looking like this.* He might have made me go anyway, but that meddling social worker called up and wanted to come over and see me and have a little family talk." Joyce wiped her nose with the back of her hand. "I just stayed in my room all that week and I sat on the bed and I kept my eyes on that picture of Jesus and I took one Elvis Pill after another, just one after another, so I couldn't hear or think of anything but Elvis, and now—" Her voice broke again. "Now what would Elvis think of me? He'd think I went down with Brad Pelich for a few beers and a ride in his father's Hornet. He'd think I was a tramp, a cheap slut, and he'd lose all respect for me."

"You think Elvis Presley is a virgin? He's Done It a thousand times. A million maybe! Elvis is no virgin," Sandee went on authoritatively. "Anyway, who's going to tell Elvis? You're never going to Do It with Elvis. You'll never even meet him, or see him! You think Elvis Presley is going to come to a dump like St. Elmo?"

Joyce looked up, her face streaked with disbelief. "You don't understand, Sandee. I don't have to Do It with Elvis to love him. Or see him, or meet him to love him, any more than I have to Do It with Jesus to love Him."

Sandee Sloat was not mentally equipped to split doctrinal hairs, or bricks, or beams for that matter, and could not say quite *why* she was sure that Not Doing It with Elvis was not the same as Not Doing It with Jesus. She said, "Everyone does it."

"Oh—and on Monday everyone will watch me across the quad and they'll know I'm not a virgin. Just to see me walk."

"No they won't."

"Think of all the girls we've watched on Monday, just knowing for sure what they did on Saturday night."

"Hey, Joycie, you never guessed from the way I walked, did you?" Joyce brought her face up from her hands. "You didn't."

"Yes I did."

"And you never told me! How could you! I don't believe you! Who?"

"Ralph Strech."

"Ralph Strech! But that was—that was more than a year ago!" Joyce gasped. "And you never told me?"

"How could I? All the Bombs were virgins. You'd have thought I was a tramp, a cheap slut, and lose all respect for me."

"I'd never think that of you! You're my best friend. Why did you do it with Ralph Strech?"

"Why did you do it with Brad?"

"That didn't count. That's what's so terrible." Joyce sniffed. Tears were past, leaving only the rusty residue of disgust and regret. "I don't even like Brad Pelich. And the first time! The first time it should have been with"—she thought of Jack Jackson working on the roof, shirtless and the patina of sweat glowing over his back, of sitting on the blanket with him in the hot crush of eucalyptus leaves and the kiss he'd given her before he went in the army—"someone thrilling, someone dangerous and daring and exciting, someone romantic who made me feel alive and in love."

"There's no one like that around here."

Joyce sighed and said Sandee was right. "Anyway, it shouldn't have been a guy I was kissing for a kissing contest jackpot. I never even took my clothes off. I didn't even see it," she added sourly. "I've Done It and I don't even know what it looks like."

"I saw it. Ralph's, anyway. It's this sort of pink long thing that you wonder where—"

"Oh don't!"

"Well, I didn't love Ralph either, if that's any comfort to you."

"But you went around telling everyone you did! We all thought you were nuts for loving Ralph Strech."

"Well, I had to love him! What if I got preggers? I'd need him! Every time I'd get my period I kept vowing I'd *never* Do It again, but, well—I—it was—you'll never know what I suffered, Joycie."

"Oh yes I will. The fate of the damned. My mother was right. It's the girl who always pays. If Brad Pelich has got me pregnant, I'll kill myself. The graveyards are full of girls like me."

"Relax. You never get preggers the first time. Not in real life. My mother told me that."

"Your mother!"

"Don't forget, my oldest sister, Betsy, had to get married, and Ceci, my other sister, who's married now, well, there was a time she was really worried. And it wasn't the guy she married, either," Sandee added with a knowing nod.

"But did you tell your mother you were worried?"

"Of course not!"

"How did she know?"

"It was strange. One night I'm sitting on my bed and my mother comes in and closes the door and leans against it, folds her arms, and says, real quiet and icylike, *You been talking a lot about Ralph Strech, Sandee. I been hearing about how you're in love with Ralph Strech.* And of course, I had to say how I was in love and all that. I'm going on and she says, *You better learn your lesson, Sandee Sloat, and you better learn it fast. Mr. Wrong comes from a family of all boys, and don't you forget it.* And then she just turned and walked out."

"What did she mean by that?"

"Well, I'll tell you. I figured it out. Right after that was the day of the big Key Club car wash, you remember that Saturday, and me and Ralph are supposed to go out that night—go out to the movies and end up in the orange groves—but anyway, he says I should come help out at the car wash, that lots of girls are going to be there. So I said okay. The Key Club's all there, all the SEHS Big Boys, Pete Polland and John Nasen and Brad Pelich and—"

"Don't say that name!"

"Sorry. Anyway, I'm not just helping out, I'm doing all the work. These guys are all standing around and it's then I see, wow, my mom was right. They *are* all from the same family. They're taking in all the money! The girls were doing all the work! Finally, at lunchtime Ralph takes me over to that little twenty-four-hour Mexican place on Sunkist, what's it called?"

"Zacateca's."

"Yeah, and Ralph's going on about how much money the Key Club is making and how good he's doing on debate team and the new tuck-and-roll his old man is buying for his car. I thought, If boring was a capital crime, this guy will be in the gas chamber before he graduates."

"They all should be."

"Well, Joycie, I ate my whole taco and enchilada and chili relleno before Ralph even got the guacamole on his. Finally, I just butted in and I said, *Ralph, eat your enchilada and listen to me. I don't love you, Ralph. I never did love you and I never will and I'm never Doing It with you again.*"

"What did Ralph say?"

"He choked."

"You mean—like gagging, sort of?"

"Cripes, Joycie! What do you want? Marlon Brando to act it out for you? He choked. He took me home. And I never went out with him again."

"Well, at least Ralph didn't go around telling everyone you were a slut or—"

"Of course he did! Mr. Tennis Team, Mr. DeMolay, Mr. Key Club, Mr. Debate Team—he has the biggest mouth in St. Elmo."

"Not as big as Brad Pelich's. Mr. Class President, and All-Star Wrestler, and Young Republican."

"Maybe not," Sandee conceded. "But why do you think I'm five Chieftains ahead of you and Charleen in the kissing contest? They're all dying to go out with me because everyone—everyone except for you—knew I went down with Ralph Strech."

Headlights strafed the garage and Phil Sloat pulled in. He got out of the car and said hello to the girls. He had a goofy look on his face. Mary Martinelli always did that to him.

Phil and Sandee drove her back to Tumbleweeds, half a block away from her house, doused the lights, killed the engine, and coasted. Phil hit the switch so the inside light would not go on when Joyce opened the car door. When she disappeared into the darkness, he started up again and slowly pulled away.

Joyce tiptoed through the eucalyptus leaves, stirring up their camphory scent, found the bedroom window just as she'd left it, hoisted it quietly on its greased ropes. She put one foot in and gave herself a boost, her head inside the window and one foot on the bedroom floor when Harmon Denby's hand wrapped around her arm, yanked her to the floor in a thin pool of moonlight, just enough to illuminate the trajectory of his hand so she could duck that blow, but not the next one, nor the one after that.

"Lying! Godless! Disobedient! Slut! Whore! Devil!"

Bethany and Rhoda woke up screaming, their cries echoing Joyce's screams as she tripped on Rhoda's bed, fell against the dresser.

Harmon's hand came down, missed Joyce, and slid across the top of the dresser and everything flew off. Harmon grabbed her shoulders, pulled her up, and rattled her till her teeth shook. An unseen hand turned on the overhead light and Joyce saw in Harmon's eyes the unvarnished anger of a man defied, denied, thrust into fuming impotence because he could not control a girl he outweighed by almost a hundred pounds, a girl who, by biblical right, ought to have obeyed his every word. Opal shrieked and tried to stay his hand, but he flung her off. Opal rushed from the room, calling for the grandmother, who alone might have been able to stop Harmon Denby. He had Joyce trapped against the dresser. His feet planted apart, his hand came down again and again.

Joyce slid down the dresser; needle-bright light converged overhead and she took the only route possible: a deep, painful breath—then, under, went under, into, beneath, not the mud-silted yellow-brown waters of the irrigation ditch, but into that blue Galilee, that cool vision of salvation, sank where the waters closed over her head and protected her, as Jesus would have if He could. With a single, upraised hand Jesus would have protected her. As Elvis would have protected her, stepped between her and this cruel rain of blows, taken the blows himself. Returned them. Elvis would have saved her if he could have. Elvis would have saved her if he could.

Nine

She woke in an unfamiliar room, dark, with flowered drapes, sun eking through them to light up the old-fashioned silhouette of a sewing machine against the wall and disembodied clothes hanging around like ghosts. She tried to move, hurt. Oh yes.

Harmon had taken the family to church that Sunday morning. All except Rejoice, who had heard the Dodge leave and then, mustering every bit of strength and denial, got out of bed. She had put a sweater over her dress from the night before, which was ripped and torn, and shoved her feet into shoes. She had walked out, leaving Hog the Dog yapping, leaving the door open, leaving Tumbleweeds and Rejoice behind her forever.

Joyce tried to move and couldn't. Her face hurt. Her whole body hurt. She touched her eye and winced. The door opened and a current of air fluttered through the hanging clothes. Carole Sloat softly called her name. Carole Sloat was a big, bony woman, built like Sandee. She wrung out a washcloth in a bowl; the water dripped quietly in the dim room. "I've called your mother, Joyce. I told her you were here so she wouldn't worry. I've told her you were going to stay here for a while. Sandee's dad and I have talked it over, and there's plenty of room here and it's just a few months till graduation. We want you to stay. We think you should."

"What did my mother say?"

Carole Sloat murmured something noncommittal, did not say that Opal Denby's message was that Rejoice would be punished for her willfulness, her wickedness, her disobedience, her rebellion. Opal Denby had said the graveyards were full of girls like Rejoice.

"I'm here on God's errand. We're all disappointed you have not returned home," said the Reverend Throckmorton about two weeks later. He sat across from Joyce at the picnic table on the Sloats' patio. He was a youngish man whose hair and eyes and skin were all of a gingery color that clashed with his severe dark suit and rusty tie. He spoke, always exhorting, as though some unseen pulpit hovered before him. "We fear for your soul, Rejoice! This is a godless home." He scowled at the narcissus ringing the patio, in thick belated bloom, their heavy odor lying seductively on the air. "Your path and duty are with your father. Honor thy father and mother. Your father has asked God's forgiveness for his—his—his—" Reverend Throckmorton faltered, looking for a word he might have dropped beneath the picnic table.

Joyce brought her green eyes up from her hands. "His what? What did he tell God he'd done?"

"He's repented. All he asks is that you do the same, Rejoice."

She returned her gaze to the grain in the wood of the picnic table, listening to his brimstone-and-brown-sugar speech. He was clearly enjoying it. She drew a deep breath, congealed an Elvis Pill out of *Peace in the Valley*, the simple, declarative tune granulating into a wafer, which pressed against the roof of her mouth, dissolving slowly, too slowly to altogether extinguish the Reverend Throckmorton.

"Pray with me, Rejoice!" The reverend suddenly reached across the table and grabbed her hands, clutched them in an iron grip while his eyes rolled back in his head and his chin tilted toward heaven. "Pray that your sins may be taken from you! Let God forgive you! He wants to. He wants to banish that devil from your side! I see that devil! He's grinning, Rejoice, grinning! That devil has got his heavy breath there at your neck, Rejoice! Can't you feel it, sister? Fight off damnation, girl!"

Joyce snatched her hands back and stood up, swallowing her Elvis

Pill in one gulp, brushing her skirt and shoulders as though truly some pesky devil might be loitering there. "I'm not going back, so you're just wasting your breath, Reverend."

"Eternity, Rejoice! You'll burn and have hot pokers pressed into your flesh for disobedience. God hates rebellion. God loves obedience. God will punish you."

"I don't care." She started back toward the house.

"God will not let such wickedness pass! God *will* punish you! God will smite you!"

"Well, let Him!" she called as she opened the door to the house. "Let Him."

"You'll regret that, Rejoice."

"Let Him," she repeated, slamming the door behind her.

In the spring of 1958, her senior year at SEHS—thanks to the fact that Brad Pelich did have a big mouth—the names of the boys Joyce Denby dated read like a roll call of St. Elmo's finest, best-known, well-heeled, most desirable young men, many of whom went on to achieve distinction—of one sort or another. Danny Lance became St. Elmo's mayor in the late seventies. Brad Pelich went on to Stanford, came home, and teamed up with that smart Mexican kid who had run his senior-class president campaign (Richard Garcia, the first Mexican to make it into the white quad before the SEHS race riots in 1968 changed everything). Richard was smart, poor, and power hungry. He slaked his power thirst through Brad, told Brad he could make him Senator Pelich. He actually did get Brad into the California state Senate, but it all went smash in 1977 when Brad was arrested in the Sacramento Greyhound bus station for soliciting sex in the men's bathroom. John Nasen became a dentist and committed suicide. Pete Polland (Student Council, leadership class, and straight A student) almost didn't graduate from SEHS. (Never mind he'd been accepted at Northwestern). A black janitor caught him pilfering the answers to a physics final from the teacher's desk drawer after hours. It was Pete's word against his. In 1970 Pete was busted for drugs, arrested by Erwin Walker, the black basketball star and All-Jive dancer who became a narc.

With the exception of Erwin Walker (naturally), all these boys had fathers who belonged to Rotary and Kiwanis. Their mothers did volunteer work with the Junior League and the Hospital Guild. They had homes where someone Japanese cut their grass and someone Mexican mopped their floors. They had nice cars, and when they went to the senior dances or DeMolay gatherings, leadership class parties, they took girls like Debbie and Linda and Delrene. But when there was an informal gathering in the orange groves, or at the apartment of someone who'd already graduated, or the night the Chieftains brought beer and firewood all the way up to Hammath Hot Springs (where they never did build that damn resort), built a fire, drank the beer, danced to the music on KLMO—and skinny-dipped in the hot springs—to these events they took girls like Joyce, Charleen, and Sandee.

When Delrene heard about the Hammath Hot Springs party, she dropped Pete Polland as if he had sprouted mucus on his teeth and hair in his ears. Or vice versa. She gave him back his class ring and said moreover their date for the prom was off. She was going with a *man* from Pomona College. Naturally Pete got drunk. Just to piss Delrene off, he asked Joyce Denby to the prom.

He double-dated with Neal Puckett, who had asked Sandee, but when Pete's panel truck pulled up in front of the Sloats' modest tract home to pick up the girls, Neal alone got out and rang the doorbell. It was nothing, he said. Pete wasn't quite ready. A mix-up with the rented tux.

Sandee's corsage was a spray of yellow orchids. Joyce's (which she adjusted carefully in the mirror) was a spray of pink orchids and contrasting pale carnations: perfect for the fuchsia gown she had cut down from a bridesmaid's dress Ceci Sloat had once worn. The girls pulled on their elbow-length gloves and Al Sloat took their pictures. They walked out, and Neal lowered his voice and said they shouldn't worry or anything but Pete was, well—Pete was spread-eagled in the back of the panel truck in his rented tux, holding a half-empty bottle of Jack Daniel's. When word had reached Delrene that he was going to the prom with Joyce Denby (that cheap slut and Delrene's erstwhile friend—and everyone knew Joyce's own father had flung her out of the house because she Did It with everyone), Delrene had announced she was *engaged to* the Pomona College man. What else could Pete do but drink Jack Daniel's? He couldn't afford Wild Turkey.

He sobered up a bit at dinner, but the four of them split a six-pack on the way back to the gym, and there, in the back of the panel truck, Pete ran his hand up Joyce's leg, lifted her skirt. "Oh Jesus," he panted, "your panties are hot pink too." She slapped his hand and told him to keep out. "Oh baby." He gave a low, guttural groan. He nuzzled against the back of her neck, naked because she'd pulled her hair up high, in a French twist.

Joyce pulled away. "I mean it, Pete. Keep your paws off me. I'm going to dance tonight and not hang out in this panel truck in a drunken orgy with you."

By the time they arrived at the prom, music throbbed all the way out to the parking lot right behind the gym and the quad. Sandee and Joyce did the stroll all the way to the door, where the vice-principal and leadership teacher, Mr. Roncker, looking slightly less pervy than usual, took their tickets. He noted the cigarette packs in the boys' jackets and the alcohol on their breath, started to say something, but Joyce and Sandee did the stroll right past him.

"Sophisticated Silhouettes" was the theme, fittingly vague, suggesting a lot of black-and-white, art deco, and some Gershwin thrown in. But instead, they'd set up a platform for the KLMO DJ, who was broadcasting all over town that night from the SEHS prom, no commercials, save to mention all the sponsors who'd given their air time free tonight, "So we can bring you these Sophisticated Silhouettes, this memorable night, the 1958 St. Elmo High prom," the DJ crooned in his deep, artificial voice. "This magical, memorable night when all the cats are hep and all the chicks are beautiful. Okay, cats, lets groove to it. *Let's Go to the Hop…*" He followed this with *Hail Hail Rock and Roll* and *That'll Be the Day, Party Doll, Get a Job,* and *Tequila!* Then he came back to the mike and said he'd have to play a few slow ones. "Time for everyone to cool down, cats. The vice-principal's getting *All Shook Up.* Am I right, Mr. Roncker? Ha ha ha."

Joyce, her hair tumbled down, moved in a swirl of fuchsia and pink to *Earth Angel.* John Nasen cut in for *Love Me Tender,* Danny Lance cut in on him for *Catch a Falling Star,* which was guaranteed not to shake anyone up, and through the other slow numbers, other boys cut in on Pete while their dates were in the girls' bathroom. The slow stuff hit a comatose low with *Twilight Time,* and just as everyone was about to wilt, the DJ hit *Blue Suede Shoes.* Erwin Walker cut in on Pete Polland.

"You can't do that," said Pete. "This is a white girl."

"This is a dancing girl, Pete," Erwin replied. "And I am a dancing man, if you dig me."

"What?"

"Ask the lady."

"Go have a cigarette, Pete."

To ease his discomfort, Pete chuckled and remarked to Brad Pelich that it was Saturday night and he was going to get laid. Brad said he wanted a cigarette too, and that coloreds were getting really uppity lately. The two walked outside together.

Basketball star that he was, Erwin Walker lifted Joyce Denby high in the air, she whirled and kicked so high that her underpants (dyed fuchsia for the occasion) showed, her shoes flew off, and whether it was the sight of the black basketball star dancing with the white girl, or whether it was just their dancing, people drew back and gave them room. Having taken an Elvis Pill early in the evening, the volume inside Joyce's head balanced with the volume outside her head: music pressing inside and out and song after song, she wasn't sure if she was dancing or flying, and she didn't care. Finally, the KLMO DJ gave them all *Jailhouse Rock,* which swept the school gym, and the joint was jumping, the girls were letting go, the guys were rocking, the place was rolling, the DJ was coming all undone, prancing up and down the platform, gyrating, pulling off his tuxedo tie, and it seemed the perfect moment for life to imitate art: strobing police lights from the front door pierced into the gym and squawking police radios counter-pointed Elvis, but the DJ kept on dancing while the rest of the St. Elmo cellblock, including Joyce (who quickly scooped up her shoes), Erwin, Charleen and her date, Sandee, Neal, Debbie, Delrene and her Pomona College man, all flocked outside to the quad.

Two police cars, four cops wading into a rocking Saturday night roil of tuxedoed bodies, flying feet, flying fists, oaths, a hot time in the old quad tonight. The cops pulled them, one by one, from the heap, pushing, shoving the boys back, nightsticks flying as the boys fought and stumbled, their white tuxedos pink with sprays of blood, wiping their lips with bruised knuckles, flinging down crushed boutonnieres, and spewing four-letter words. At the center of the carnage, Pete Polland lay, flailing on the ground, till a cop pulled Warren James Jackson, Jr., off of him.

Joyce had not seen him since the day he had kissed her, just before he left town. He was older. Of course. A year and a half in the army changes a man. He wore a dress uniform with corporal's stripes and his hair was cut short, but there was no mistaking Warren James Jackson, Jr.

He brushed his thumb across his lips. Looked at the blood, gave a quick, practiced feel across his teeth. He bent, picked up his hat, spat at Pete's dress leather shoes. "You sonofabitch."

"That's enough," shouted the cop. "Shut up. Prom night or not— it's the St. Elmo jail for all of you. Now, does someone want to tell me how this started?"

The crowd drew back and a lot of cigarettes got lit. Someone handed Pete Polland a handkerchief for his bloody nose and the rest of them adjusted their cummerbunds. The vice-principal stepped up, said that he had called the police, that he had seen the whole thing and Jack had started it. He added that Jack was not an SEHS student and had no business here.

The cop sucked his lip. "I can see he don't belong here, Your Honor. I can see he's in uniform, ain't he? But I want to thank Your Honor just the same." He turned to Jack. "What's the problem here, Corporal?"

"Sonofabitch has a mouthful of shit. If he wants to talk shit, he might as well eat it."

Pete lunged for him, but John Nasen and others caught at him. Brad Pelich stepped forward. He used the same gravity and demeanor that he would perfect in later years in the courtroom, doing a lucrative business in other people's misery, that he would use when he ran for office, and that he no doubt used in the men's room of the Sacramento Greyhound station. He said, "Officer, I'll tell you what happened. A bunch of us were out here having a smoke in between dances, when this—this hood"—he nodded toward Jack—"he comes out of nowhere, walks past us, turns around, calls my friend Pete here a name I won't bother to repeat, and punches him right in the face. Look at him bleed, Officer. Isn't that the way it happened?" Brad turned to his friends.

"We couldn't let him beat the crap out of Pete," John Nasen whined. "We had to help our friend."

"I'll beat the crap out of all of you before I'm through," said Jack with no particular malice.

"Just cool down, Corporal. Why did you hit this guy? He wasn't bothering you."

"Fucker had a mouthful of lying shit."

"It's not shit!" Pete cried out. "Half the seniors in this school have been in Joyce Denby's pants! She'd go down for—"

Jack ducked, darted behind the cop, ran full tilt into Pete, knocking him off his feet.

"Cuff him," said the cop, and Jack found himself wrestled by two men, hands yanked up behind his back, cuffs snapped on with metallic finality.

The cop nodded. "I remember you now. You're Jack Jackson."

"No, I'm the frigging Wizard of Oz."

"He is, too," Joyce said to Sandee.

"You were a real hell-raiser here, a few years back, Jack. I'd of thought the army would of shaped you up, Corporal." The cop waxed on at great sarcastic length about how the army was supposed to make a man of you, while he beat his nightstick into the palm of his hand.

Jack sighed, as though sitting through the coming attractions for the hundredth time, and then he raised his eyes to meet the cop's face, but instead he saw Joyce Denby in the surrounding crowd. His gaze never left her green eyes and he seemed not to hear whatever question the cop had asked him. The cop poked him with the nightstick and Jack mumbled something. Then he winked at Joyce.

"Whadidchu say, Corporal?"

"I said, yes sir, Officer."

"That's better. Now, where are you stationed these days? I don't reckon it's the high school quad."

"Fort Riley, Kansas. Sir."

"Well, that's real interesting, Jack. What the hell are you doing here, besides kicking the shit out of high school boys?"

"I was kicking his—" Pete cried.

"You want the cuffs too, son? They'll go nice with your tuxedo. Now just shut up or your daddy gets a late-night call." He turned back to Jack. "Answer me, Corporal."

"I'm home on compassionate leave. Sir. I just got here this morning. My mother had a stroke two days ago. She's in the hospital."

"Then why ain't you compassionately at the hospital?"

"I've been there since seven this morning. It's almost midnight. The doctor told me to go home. He said she wasn't going to get any better tonight. He said she wasn't going to die tonight either."

"So why didn't you go home like the doc said?"

Jack twisted his broken, bleeding lip. He met Joyce's eyes again. "I heard it on the radio, on KLMO. I heard the DJ say he was broadcasting from the prom and I just came, thinking maybe I could dance, but I got here, Officer, sir, and I heard that sonofabitch over there"— he nodded roughly toward Pete—"sharing a mouthful of shit with his chickenhearted buddies. I only hit the one guy, Officer, sir—the others"—Jack shrugged—"they jumped into it, so I had to hit them too."

The cop drew his hand over his face, so hard he might have pulled his features off and flung them to the ground. "You boys"—he nodded to the tuxedo-clad lineup—"you go back in the gym or it's the drunk tank for you and a single call to your old man. You, Corporal, being as your mother's in the hospital, I'm not going to take you in either, though I should. I'm going to take the cuffs off you and you're going to get the hell out of here." He nodded to the other cop, who unlocked the cuffs.

Jack rubbed his wrists. Jack was as tall as the cop. The cop outweighed him. He met the cop eye to eye. "I didn't come here looking for trouble, sir. I didn't start it. I came to dance. That's all. I mean to have a dance."

"Oh, don't let me be hearing this right! Because if I am, it's the drunk tank for you! Breach of compassionate leave, Corporal! I don't think the army—"

Joyce Denby elbowed through the crowd, pushed through the tulle and hair spray and ribbons falling from corsages, past Chantilly laces and pretty faces, the creaking underwire bras and wilted boutonnieres. She moved quickly and without hesitation. With her gloved fingers, she unpinned the pink orchids from her dress. She threw them at Pete Polland and hit him squarely in the face. "You're a dog." She added in her best biblical fashion, "And you may return like a dog to his vomit." She found herself face to face with Warren James Jackson for the first time in nineteen months. That's how long it had been. She had kept count. She put on her high heels. "I'm ready," she said. "Now I'm ready. I wasn't then, but I am now."

His eyes combed over her face. "You are so beautiful, Joyce. I never quit thinking about you. Not in all this time. I never forgot you."

"I never forgot you either."

Jack took her arm lightly, steered her toward the Studebaker Starlight Coupe illegally parked in the gym lot, where the cop cars still squawked and flashed. He opened the door on the driver's side, and gathering up her fuchsia skirts, Joyce slid across the seat. Jack glanced back over his shoulder, as though he expected trouble to follow. And it did, of course, uninvited, all but assured. But neither of them knew that. And if they had, they would not have cared. In this Book of Acts, this was the only one that mattered.

Ten

For the next year or so, Joyce Denby defied everything and everyone, even the odds, and did it all with a kind of careless grace fired by a singular passion. All passions are singular; if they're not singular, they're not passions. You know this by instinct or you don't. It can't be learned.

In taking up with Warren James Jackson, Jr., Joyce followed her instincts. The local wags and gossiping girls all said she was just another girl, one of many he would diddle and drop, bed and be done with. But it did not happen that way. Recovering slowly from her stroke, Jack's mother moved directly from the hospital into a convalescent home, and Joyce moved in with Jack, living in open sin, contemptuous of God, gossip, or anything else. What Joyce felt for Jack was love, by any standard—even time, that cruelest standard of all. They played loud music, made loud love, pressed sweet wine from the sweat of their bodies, licked it, got drunk, and made love again. They were in love as they might have been in debt, or in trouble, some inextricable, inexorable condition; they were in love as they might have been in France, some country with a population of two, its own customs, currency, and language; they might make treaties with the rest of the world, but no one else could truly cross their frontiers.

When Jack's mother died, Joyce stood beside him at the funeral. His brother, the priest, did not come from Bolivia, but the married sisters were there, outraged that an eighteen-year-old girl should be sleeping in their mother's bed and living in her house. Jack was so comatose with grief, he scarcely noticed their ire. Joyce drove him home in the Starlight Coupe, took him into the bathroom, took off his clothes, pulled him into the shower with her, made love, and then held him while he wept for his loss. *I'll never leave you, honey,* she promised. *You'll never lose me, not while we're here on this earth. You'll have to die first, Jack, because I will never leave you.*

And she never did.

Sandee stood beside Joyce in the courtroom where, on the judge's lunch break, they got married in June 1959. Also attending the wedding were Charleen and her (first) husband, Phil Sloat and his (first) wife, Mary Martinelli, and Jack's father and his third wife.

After the ceremony, once out in the marble halls and contrary to all courthouse rules, Sandee flung rice at the newly married couple. She had a whole bag of it stashed in her purse and everyone reached in and tossed rice, which clattered on the hard floor and chattered against the banisters and fell down the stairwell like hardy white rain. Joyce, in the vanilla-colored dress she had made herself, copied from a picture she saw in *Vogue,* leaned over the banister and looked down two floors to a bevy of secretaries laughing and looking up, covering their heads from the shower of rice. Joyce tossed her bouquet over the banister, down two floors to anonymous, unmarried secretaries on their lunch breaks.

After the wedding, they had four days. They drove down the coast to Mexico, to Rosarito Beach, and stayed in the big hotel, walked on the beach and drank margaritas and danced. Coming back north, they drove through Tijuana, where Jack bought her a straw hat and a white fringed shawl. They had their picture taken with big sombreros on a donkey cart. The last day they stayed in Del Mar, where the fairgrounds were close by the beach and crowded at dusk, as the beach was not. They walked along the beach, and a thin hangnail of a moon swung overhead with a single star tacked against the sunset. This close to the lagoon, the air was thick with crickets; frogs thumped and lusted audibly. The train, when it rattled over its trestles, percussively dimmed the crashing waves. The beach lay golden and unpocked before them, tide up, the smear of foam colored peach by the twilight. The future seemed to lie unpocked and golden as the beach, colored peach by the conviction, correct and untainted, of their love. It's terminal, love like that. Jack kicked a pile of seaweed from her path, and at that moment the wind came up, caught her hat, blew it into the water. She waited, clutching the white fringed shawl to her shoulders, as he chased into the surf, captured the hat, returned to her, soaked to the waist, the long curl of his hair lying loose on his forehead. He gave the hat back to her, straw smell heightened by salt water, and the sun completed its arc, fell into the horizon, and pulled the coverlet of night up over it. In the brackish lagoon, reeds languidly kept time to music of their own making and carnival lights from the fair appeared in the black water, reflecting like late-blooming stars; lights from the Ferris wheel swam and winked in the lagoon. Joyce stood mute with happiness, rooted, because just as surely as the high tide receded, visibly, she felt the indelible promise of the future, even though the present ebbed from her, retreating, swallowed up in fog and a whisper, the past, the dreamless plain.

In the years between 1960, when Elvis Presley got out of the army, and December 1968, his comeback special on TV, Sandee had three children (and one illegal abortion). Charleen had two children. Delrene and Debbie and Linda had, among them, ten children. Anyone could do it. Bonnie and ugly Dougie Barker had three more. Bethany had children. Rhoda had children. Phil and Mary Martinelli Sloat had three. Anyone could have children. Everyone had children. Joyce had miscarriages. Four of them.

The brutal cramp, splash of blood, the rush to County Hospital, the carnival ride on the gurney, her body rebelling, repelling, expelling. The pain without product as they rolled Joyce over and stuck a needle in her backside, gave her something for the pain and she gave herself, as best she could, an Elvis Pill, forming the wafer, hearing his voice, low and slow and sweet, because the Elvis Pill was the only medication effective against that other pain: the loss of hope in the first trimester, the pain of failure and unfulfilled longing, being denied the opportunity to love.

Each time, Joyce lay in the women's ward at County Hospital, where the eastern sun crossed the floor like a copper stain and what they gave her for the pain sucked her down a dream-drain where everything twisted and converged, then spit her back up, beached her, splay-legged, before a procession of finally faceless ob M.D.'s employed by the county of St. Elmo, who were baffled by her repeated miscarriages, who referred to the lost, the mourned, the would-have-been baby as a fetus, who invariably said ha ha ha think of all the fun she and her husband would have as they tried and tried again because if at first you don't succeed...Joyce closed her eyes. *Just* give *me something for the pain,* said Joyce, I have taxed God's patience, just *Return to Sender* and let the Elvis Pill dissolve.

But increasingly, Elvis himself dissolved, granulated into the big screen at the Dream Theater; he vanished—ironically, where he was most visible—into the movies. Twenty-seven movies in eight years. In 1960 Joyce and Sandee paid their money at the great silver wave of a ticket booth and entered the Dream Theater, its lobby smelling of fresh popcorn and stale cigarette smoke, the carpet worn through to wooden floors as they walked down to take their favorite seats there before the red velvet curtain rusty with age. They watched *G.I. Blues* with a good deal of surprise, since they had been expecting more of the old sizzle inherent in *King Creole, Jailhouse Rock,* or *Loving You,* where Elvis smoldered, then blazed to life in the musical numbers. The movies that followed, *Wild in the Country, Blue Hawaii, Kid Galahad, Follow That Dream,* were pale, but not as anemic as *Girls! Girls! Girls!, It Happened at the World's Fair, Fun in Acapulco, Roustabout, Girl Happy.* Elvis seemed always to play a version of the same inoffensive boy in need of money and a girl he seldom kissed, but always married. These girls (with the exception of Ann-Margret in *Viva Las Vegas,* which Joyce and Sandee saw four times) were all interchangeably vague, actresses who could convincingly convey a range of emotions from petulant to pouty. Soon it was clear, even to Sandee and Joyce, that Elvis movies were being made very much like sausages:

no one cared very much what went into them as long as audiences would bite.

By the mid-1960s Joyce and Sandee took to entering the Dream Theater with their fingers crossed, hoping that *Frankie and Johnny* might redeem *Harum Scarum,* that *Speedway* might make *Spinout* seem the exception rather than the rule, that the stale antics in *Double Trouble* might mark an all-time low, that surely *Stay Away Joe* could not be nearly as bad as *Clambake,* where moviemakers defied nature, placed mountains in Miami and had the sun set into the Atlantic on the coast of Florida. In the stuffy embrace of the Dream Theater, Sandee and Joyce endured Elvis's films, much as Elvis seemed to endure them, long past the point where his acting ambitions had got submerged, even drowned, in mechanical repetition. Their expectations certainly diminished, and Joyce might have given up altogether except for a moment in *Tickle Me* when her vision unclouded and her understanding suddenly deepened. After that, she could watch any and all of the King's movies with a kind of loyal immunity.

Sitting through the brutally stupid *Tickle Me,* Joyce was suddenly startled by the flash of Elvis's unguarded eyes. In that moment he betrayed his anguish, and Joyce could all but hear the clank of fetters that chained him even as he clowned and cavorted across the screen. He seemed, in that instant, to beg Joyce's understanding, to ask for— and simultaneously offer—pity. And when the instant passed, Joyce rubbed her eyes to see once again the mechanical windup male doll who lurched from song to song while the camera trained its indifferent eye on the breasts and buttocks of surrounding starlets. Joyce understood: Elvis was up there, on-screen as routinely as any shopgirl or clerk-typist going to her dreary job, working there to collect his paycheck and take his punishment. Elvis was being punished for the sheer raw energy, the excitement he'd so effortlessly generated in his early days, and clearly he *was* dangerous. He was so dangerous they put him in irons made of schlock, musical manacles, movies where he remained an everlasting boy (indeed, getting younger as the years progressed) and never was allowed a man's pain or a man's pleasure, a man's needs or a man's response to women, not even a man's music, just prescription tunes with which the audience was to be dosed at regular intervals. Joyce could not watch the end of *Tickle Me*. She waited for Sandee in the lobby of the Dream Theater, which, in 1968, closed down in disgust after a final showing of *Live a Little, Love a Little*. The gilded doors were nailed shut and the great silver wave of a ticket booth drooped sadly, silver paint flaking like fish scales.

Easy Come, Easy Go is what Joyce might have said about her third pregnancy: she seemed to ride the gurney through County Hospital's revolving doors as Jack went round and round through the county jail's revolving doors. In a sort of random, often repetitive way, Jack was arraigned for disturbing the peace, unlawful betting, malicious mischief, assault, resisting arrest, speeding, cited and his license revoked for the high-speed chase that ended in the wreck of the Starlight Coupe; Jack went to jail briefly and the woman who was his passenger was treated for minor injuries. FOR SALE, YOU TOW, he put in the cracked window of the Starlight Coupe, and after that there was a string of cars. A string of bars. A string of women. A string of jobs. Three were long drives to Vegas to win money (more speeding tickets) and long, impoverished drives back. There was the small matter of a forged check, tidied up outside the courtroom—thank God. There was the charge of unarmed robbery that wasn't robbery at all: the guy owed Jack money from a poker game and he wouldn't pay up. It was a misunderstanding that came to blows, Joyce explained as she drove around St. Elmo (past the graveyards that are full of girls like her) trying to borrow bail money from her friends and relatives to get her husband out of jail.

Joyce was right in telling Emily Shaw she had cried her eyes out in those years as a full-time job, but she also worked at the sewing machine, making prom dresses, wedding dresses, altering everything from business suits to bathing suits, busy seasons and slack seasons, year after year, time passing to the whir of the sewing machine and the radio in the background, a slow pavane of fast songs, the KLMO disc jockeys nattering, crowing, exhorting, explaining, laughing, nagging *Yakkety Yak,* when you got the *Summertime Blues, Stagger*

Lee playing craps with Willie, losing, natch, like *Please Mr. Postman* bringing letters to Jack that smelled like women after he'd been on construction jobs in the desert. *Splish Splash* while Joyce is taking a bath, the phone rings and the woman says, *Is Jack home?* and Joyce says, *Jack? Like, Hit the Road, Jack?* Go ahead, *Great Balls of Fire,* take up with *Runaround Sue.* Oh that man, *He's So Fine,* and Joyce would wipe her nose and tell herself *Big Girls Don't Cry* just because *He's a Rebel,* just because *To Know Him Is to Love Him.* Joyce loved him. He loved Joyce, but he liquefied women, other women, and then fell like a helpless fly into the cognac of his own creation; he loved his wife, but he needed other women, used them like quick transfusions: he made them want to *Shout!* And Joyce, waiting at home, radio on, sewing machine whirring, clock ticking because *You Can't Hurry Love,* oh, Joyce tried and it didn't work because *My World Is Empty Without You, Babe.* Elvis asked, *Are You Lonesome Tonight?* And what could Joyce say? *I'm dying of it, Elvis.* Sometimes she answered sprightly, *It's My Party and I'll Cry If I Want To,* but mostly she hadn't that kind of bravado, only blind, barreling rage, as she and Sandee, in Sandee's car, and Sandee's little kids screaming their bloody lungs out in the back, cruised up and down St. Elmo, checking out the parking lot of every bar, looking for that Studebaker Starlight Coupe, recreating a dead woman's orgy of anger. *Mama Said There'd Be Days Like This,* but of course that's not what Joyce's mama said. She said, *The graveyards are full of girls like you, Rejoice.* Are they full of women who waited? He doesn't come home, days go by, he calls, but he doesn't come home. Everyone else, even Sandee, says, *O Rejoice that you have got rid of such a man! Who wants a man who would put it in any old port? Storm or not,* and Joyce, snapping at her best friend, *Stop! In the Name of Love.* Please let the pain stop, Joyce wept inwardly as Charleen, breaking all the speed limits, raced to County Hospital not for Joyce to have her baby but only a would-have-been baby, lost and mourned, described as a fetus. As Charleen ran the stoplight at Far West, they rattled past the cemetery, which was not at all full of girls like Joyce. She was not a girl. She was, she felt like, an old woman. An old childless woman. A woman punished for her willfulness, her rebellion, her pride. The Reverend Throckmorton was right; she did regret it. Joyce had said *Let Him* to God and He did.

In April 1968, Joyce and Sandee sat on a hard bench in the courthouse hall waiting for the public defender to tell them when the judge returned to the courtroom, ready to render his verdict. Joyce was pale, and her hair hung limply, framing an anxious, haunted face. Not surprising since a courthouse is an uncomfortable place at the best of times and this was not the best of times. Joyce had conceived yet again, this time without any hope of fruition. The judge's verdict was not yet in, but life's verdict clearly was. Joyce would never have any children. She slumped against the wall and said indifferently, *I'm never going through this again.*

It's really a bitch, isn't it? We been through it before, but

This is the end for me, Joyce replied, glancing furtively up and down the hall, letting Sandee chatter, assure her that it was a minor charge, really, aggravated assault, and the other guy started it and Jack was really innocent and Jack was right not to plea-bargain, not when he was innocent. Even though Jack was the one who got charged, it was really all the other guy's fault and the judge would have to be fair, even if it was Judge Vernon Eliot, who had convicted Jack in '65 of unarmed robbery and then watched him get off on a technicality, and even if the judge was clearly pissed off, just to *look* at Jack Jackson again, still, he was a judge and he was supposed to be fair and

This is it, said Joyce.

What?

This is the very hall where you threw the rice at us on our wedding day. Right over that banister there. This is where I tossed my bouquet to the secretaries on the first floor. That courtroom we've been sitting in, that's the one where we got married.

Oh no. It isn't. It can't be.

It can. It is.

The public defender peered around the door and nodded to Sandee, who nudged Joyce. They took their places in the courtroom behind the public defender, who was a brisk, attractive woman of about forty wearing a navy blue suit with brass buttons. Joyce stared at the back of Jack's neck. They listened as the judge sentenced him to two years.

For assault! shrieked Sandee.

I told him he should have plea-bargained, muttered the public defender under her Listerined breath. She noisily assured Jack she'd file an appeal and on what grounds and legally why he ought not to worry.

The bailiff pulled Jack toward a door leading to the bowels of the courthouse: the jailhouse rock. Jack turned at the door and winked at Joyce.

This is as bad as it's going to get, Joyce said without inflection. *It's not ever going to get any worse than this.*

Oh honey. Sandee sat back down and put her arms around Joyce's shoulders. *You're so right. It will get better.*

I didn't say that. I said it would never get any worse. The graveyards are full of girls like me and as soon as I lose this baby, that's where I'm going. She rose slowly, walked out of the courtroom, down the hall, and through the dust from all that rice, all those years ago.

The phone company called, demanding payment, and Joyce said her husband was in jail and she was sick and could not work. And indeed, shortly after that she could not work because Sears repossessed the sewing machine. The water bill went unpaid month after month. They quit collecting trash. Dunning notices from the gas and electric companies, the phone company, they all piled up beneath the mail slot on her apartment door. They lay like snow that refused to melt. Joyce stayed in bed, sleeping it off. Sleeping it all off. Waking was the nightmare. There was no current Elvis Pill to take. He had no hit songs on KLMO. For the first time since 1956, Elvis Presley could not help her.

They've cut off your phone, Joycie, said Sandee when Joyce finally answered the door.

So what? She shuffled back through the dark house.

This has got to stop. We're going to do something about this, Joycie. Which doctor did you see at the county clinic?

*I haven't been to the clinic. I don't need a doctor to tell me I'm preg-
nant. I've been through this before, remember?*

*Well, Joycie, it's four months now, isn't it? Four and a half. You've
never made it this far before. Maybe this time—*

Oh, give it up.

You should go to the clinic.

*I'll lose the baby, they'll punch my butt with painkiller, and I'm sure
I'll see a doctor then. I'll see him and he'll have a nice long look up my—*

We're going to need a note from a doctor.

What for?

*Go get dressed and then get in my car, Joycie. And tell me where you
keep your marriage license.*

Joyce put her documents on the table as she was ushered into the
cubicle at the welfare department. A big woman joined her, sat down,
introduced herself as Mrs. Mason, and began asking Joyce questions
in a voice reminiscent of gears grinding. Mrs. Mason filled out the
county's forms quickly, efficiently, and with an emphatic dotting of
the i's. Mrs. Mason seemed to take it personally that Joyce was un-
communicative, uncooperative, that she showed no fear or anxiety,
that she was not overeager to be thought honest and appealing as are
the usual welfare applicants-unto-supplicants. In a testy, insinuative
fashion, Mrs. Mason asked, *You don't act as though you even want a
Family Assistance grant and a MediCal card.* Joyce did not reply. Mrs.
Mason added, *If you do, you'll have to show me a better attitude. You'll
have to cooperate with me.*

I want this to end, said Joyce, and that was all she would say until
suddenly her eyes widened and her mouth fell open in an involun-
tary gasp. She could not have been more surprised if Elvis Presley had
walked through the door of the intake booth. Deep inside, she felt a
tiny thump. Not a kick. Only a flutter, but unmistakably a flutter and
with it a protest and promise: the resurrection of Joyce Jackson and
the life inside her. This child was going to get itself born. Make no
mistake. Another fetal flutter and Joyce laughed out loud, threw her
head back, laughter pealed from her lips, breaking all the rules of the

welfare department, which demands gravity, humility, and pathos, demands sweating supplication and implicit assumption, acceptance of defeat. At least that's what Marge Mason always demanded—and always got. Except from Joyce Jackson, whose inexplicable laughter brought other social workers to the intake cubicle door to see if Marge was dealing with a lunatic.

Marge demanded to know if Joyce had been taking any number of mind-altering drugs popular in 1968; she rattled them off in a volley of abuse. Marge's questions were so preposterous and inappropriate, so completely without understanding, delivered with such rapid-fire urgency, that Joyce reached over and caressed Marge's cheek, a gesture of shared humanity, an effort to console this burly woman, to ameliorate Marge's spluttering rage. But the gesture only drew from Marge a reprimand as unmistakable as a slap. No matter. Joyce laughed all the more and the sound seemed to paint the grim walls of the intake cubicle the same golden, unpocked peach color of the beach, the sunset-lit foam, and the lights still twinkling in the lagoon.

Burning Love

Eleven

When Emily put down the phone, she went directly to the cupboard and took out all six boxes of peach Jell-O she had been saving for May 21. She turned on the hot water tap and flushed them all down the kitchen sink, one after another. The smell made her quite sick. The sweet, cloying smell, redolent of warm flesh and sunlight streaming through vanilla-colored curtains, warm petals fallen from full-blown roses beside the bed: the bed, that single central planet in their imagined orbit, the sheets tousled and love-scented, the lovers' pleasure further sweetened and condensed for its being afternoon, time snatched, stolen from the common volley of obligation; time tensed like flanks and buttocks, intense for its being so steeped in love and summer's honeyed breath: the ply of pink sticky fingers, the tongue softly scratching, seeking out that dollop of *Did you ever know of a man who wanted to do anything with Jell-O, except maybe lick it out of your belly button?*

These dreams were soon down the drain. Of course they had gone down the drain earlier, when Rick had called, surprising Emily since it was not Wednesday or Sunday but Saturday night and well before eight, Pacific time. Nonetheless, Emily was already in her oversized USC T-shirt, which she wore for a nightie, and in bed with a novel, having said her Old Maid's Prayer, though not in anything so crass, vulgar, and vernacular as words. Actions speak louder than words. Emily had plucked and pumiced and perfumed her body to perfection *(Oh Lord, send me a man!)*, manicuring her body like a garden where a lover might wander; she performed all this tweezing and painting and shaving and lotioning, knowing no lover would there wander or explore. Indeed, the cotton was still between her just-painted toes when Rick called to say he wouldn't be coming back to California for the summer vacation. He'd thought it all over, weighed the possibilities, precedents, prereqs, and priorities. He thought it best he attend summer school there in D.C. instead of coming home to California to do paralegal work for Emily's father.

"What?"

"We can get married sooner. we can have our whole lives—"

"But my father expects you—"

"I already called your dad. He was disappointed, but he understands law school. And listen, honey, what are we giving up, really? All summer I'd be working with Shaw, Shine, Brill, Syme, and Turlock there in Newport and you'd be working in St. Elmo."

Emily coughed and swallowed a great, tough, gangly piece of emotional gristle. "We'd have the weekends."

"Twenty-four days. Total. Really, honey—God, I miss you!—but I added it all up and this way I'm done with law school a whole semester earlier."

"But you weren't going to work for my dad till early June and we'd have two weeks just to be together."

"Oh, baby—you're working all day. What would I do? Lie around your apartment pool and talk to the ducks? Didn't you say you had ducks?"

"Not in the pool."

Rick told her again how funny and cute she was and how he loved her and how he was horny. He snorted and said he couldn't wait to marry her. Soon. Sooner. Soonest. 1985. Early 1985.

After she finished flushing the Jell-O down the drain, Emily went back to her room, sidestepping the piles of books and laundry, and pulled the phone onto the bed with her. She called her sorority sister who had got married and now lived in Carmel. She was joyed-over to hear from Emily because she and her husband had great news! She was pregnant! Of course they'd wanted to postpone all this for her career, but— "Oh, there's someone at the door," said Emily. I have to go." Then she called another Tri Delt, whose husband said she was out at a wedding or a baby shower, he couldn't remember which. "Oh! There's the doorbell. I have to go."

Emily put down the phone and cried her eyes out because there would never be anybody at the door. Everyone was married but her. She'd die with the Old Maid's Prayer on her lips.

Weeping, she staggered to her small writing desk and yanked open the third drawer, where she kept the secret calendar with the days marked off toward May 21, which she had decorated with stars and hearts. That was the day Rick's term finished. Less than a month away. Crying like some grubbing LMC peasant, she took the calender to the bathroom, determined to give it the dignity of a Viking funeral, drop the embers into the toilet and flush them (eventually) out to sea. But the pages flamed before they turned to embers; they singed her fingers and she had to drop them. The windowless bathroom filled with smoke, setting off the smoke alarm, and then the pages wouldn't even flush. She had to reach into the toilet to get them out. Emily dragged the kitchen wastebasket into the bathroom and churned the secret calendar among the eggshells and milk cartons, the Jell-O boxes, greasy bits of bacon, and orange peel. Then she washed her hands, blew her nose, and threw that Kleenex on top of the whole.

So, this was it. "That White Sustenance—Despair," the price extracted for dabbling in adult love, for giving your heart and soul along with your body. That a man could so diminish you. So unthinkingly diminish you! Emily began to weep and wail, afraid of doing something truly LMC like falling to her knees on the floor and banging her head against the carpet, smashing her country blue crockery, because right after the pain, running, as though to catch up with the pain, like all those little doomed oysters in "The Walrus and the Carpenter," came the anger. The pain at least could be acknowledged. The anger was overwhelming and had to be denied. *How could he? How dare he decide all this without so much as consulting me! He thought it! He considered! Alas my love you do me wrong—* She covered her mouth before the other, more fearful lyrics came tumbling out.

Emily went to the refrigerator, determined to get drunk. Closer inspection revealed only a quarter bottle of white wine. No alcohol. No drugs. No moors to tread. No rocky beaches. No stormy night to brave. There was, however, a can of Betty Crocker chocolate frosting in the cupboard. She sat down on the couch with her frosting and ate it, a spoonful at a time, feeling vaguely sick, not simply from the sweetness but a sort of seasickness, lines rolling about her mind like unsecured cargo in the hold of a storm-tossed ship, something from *Alice* about living backward and bellowing now for the pain you knew was yet to come. The pain loomed before her, the anger and, worse, the fear that this moment was but a rehearsal for larger and more unthinkable hurt Yet To Come. "I'm twenty-three years old," she whimpered between spoonfuls of chocolate frosting. "I've graduated from USC, I'm a Tri Delt and an independent woman"—she licked the spoon—"and I don't know shit."

She threw the spoon across the room, the frosting too, pulled on a pair of jeans and a sweatshirt. She could not stay in this dreary apartment. Tonight she needed to know it was possible to survive such pain. No book could so assure her. No story could so testify. They were too refined, books and stories and poems, the pain had been too processed. Emily needed to see it with her own eyes, see the old bloody-but-unbowed, raw-but-not-unraveled indomitability of someone who had already survived.

Cars lined up under the jacarandas and music reeled out to Santiago Street. While Elvis warbled *Follow That Dream,* the sheet on the picnic table billowed in a kind of random dance with the black satin streamers on the King's portrait and those tied to the crepe myrtle trees. Emily pulled round onto Sultana and parked behind a motorcycle and went in through the back gate. Laughter and voices wafted out to the back steps, and Emily had to knock more than once to be heard. Perhaps no one would hear and she would be forever shut out from shared humanity, but then Cilla opened the door.

Cilla's jaw dropped and her eyes grew big and she looked bilious.

Immediately Emily apologized for her very existence, to say nothing of her coming here at night like this and she really didn't mean to intrude and she was still talking when Cilla left her there, walked into the kitchen, and announced to one and all, "It's her."

"Who?" asked Joyce just as the phone rang.

Emily found herself in a kitchen full of light and noise and people, radio blaring, DJ babbling, kids underfoot, and the smell of hot dogs still heavy on the air. Joyce motioned to Emily that she should take a chair. A big woman with dark eyes, frosted hair, and the fleshly solidity of a school bus offered her one. When Joyce hung up the phone and introduced Emily as the family's new social worker, this same heavy woman dashed, all but pirouetted, to the radio on the top of the refrigerator and turned it off.

Everyone seemed to freeze, the expression caught somewhere between shell shock and paralysis. Discreetly Emily felt for the fly on her jeans, but her sweatshirt covered it up. She gave a halfhearted grin and said she was sorry to—"Don't be sorry!" Joyce cried, scooping a toddler out from under the table and taking him to the sink. Another boy remained under the table stacking up generic soup cans. "We're all celebrating because Sandee's just won the KLMO Memory Jackpot."

"Well, that's wonderful," said Emily, having no idea what was under discussion.

"Probably Emily doesn't listen to the Oldie-but-Goldie station." Joyce turned on the water and washed the toddler's mouth. "Do you, Emily?"

"I'm afraid I don't. I'm not that old." She coughed and looked at the faces surrounding her. She was closer in age to Cilla. "I'm sure I will be one day."

"Well, that's good to know—I mean, Sandee here just won twenty-seven hundred dollars! It's their biggest jackpot ever! Just for being the first caller with the right answer!"

"I been ready for this answer for twenty-four years!" Sandee crowed. She was a big palomino of a woman, strong of hip and haunch, broad shouldered and big breasted. "I told Cilla, hand me that phone because I can answer that question and I'm going to be number one!"

"What was the question?" asked Emily.

"Elvis's GI number. Elvis Aron Presley, Number—" Sandee's dark eyes glazed.

"You wrote it right by the phone," said Joyce. "Number 53310761."

The phone rang again, and Sandee got it while Joyce introduced Emily to the toddler in her arms as Little Jack, and under the table she said Emily would find Justin (who toppled soup cans at that moment on Emily's foot). And of course Emily knew Cilla, and that little brown-eyed beauty over there, that was Lisa Marie, and this was Charleen and her husband Bob and over there, by the fridge, that was Sandee's brother, balding, bearded, blue-eyed Phil Sloat, and "This is Jack."

He stood up slowly, all six foot four, two hundred ten pounds of him. He called Emily *Ma'am* and went to the fridge for a beer. He was the sort of man you automatically picture naked. He carried his age and weight well. His face reflected the furrows of the forty proverbial winters and his hair was graying at the temples. He wore a T-shirt advertising Mexican beer above jeans and thick motorcycle boots. A leather jacket and helmet were draped on his chair. The motorcycled, malicious-mischief-making macho—who yet exuded an air of both tenderness and energy. He made you want to trust him when you could just look and know he was dangerous.

Emily got through the introductions, blessing at that moment her mother's relentless inculcation of manners because without those reflexes, Emily could not have endured the confusion, meeting people she already knew. In a manner of speaking. She had met them all in County Case File 68-46784, and now, in this kitchen, she could not have been more undone if she'd been suddenly introduced to Mr. Rochester, Scarlett and Melanie, Tess of the D'Urbervilles, and whoever it was in *The Thorn Birds*. Here they were, all except for Stan and the infamous Dorrie Vardy.

At that moment a thin woman came in zipping up her jeans. She had lank blond hair cut at chin length and a narrow face and blue eyes. Petulance perched on her lower lip like a cherub on a Christmas card. Joyce introduced her as Dorrie Vardy and she nodded to Emily without interest. She took the one vacant chair and tentatively lit up a cigarette.

"That was Angie," said Sandee, hanging up the phone. "Down at Scents and Sensibility. That's that flower shop on Brigham," she explained to Emily. "Angie donates all her leftover flowers to Sacred to the Memory of Elvis. Before that, if Joyce wanted flowers she used to have to lower Cilla into dipsy-dumpsters at the florist's and—"

"Oh don't!" cried the mortified Cilla. "Don't tell her that!"

"Angie wanted to know how I could remember Elvis's GI number, and I said, Angie, how could I forget? I used to keep that number in my wallet. I kept it in my underwear drawer on a piece of scented paper and my first husband found it and he thought it was my boyfriend's phone number. He wouldn't believe it was Elvis's."

"You did have a boyfriend," Charleen reminded her.

"I have to go," said Dorrie, stubbing out her cigarette. She picked up her shoulder bag and told the boys to be good. She stepped over to Jack, bent and kissed him full and hard and long on the lips. The act was possessive rather than passionate. Joyce turned to the kitchen window, ran cold water in the sink. The phone rang and Joyce answered it.

"My mother will worry if I don't get back," Dorrie said. "Congratulations, Joyce—"

"Thank you!" Sandee jumped up. "And don't you worry about the boys! We'll take care of them!"

Dorrie shook her head and said to Jack, "I guess I'll see you at home in a week. Be careful going down to the desert on that motorcycle."

"I've lived this long."

Emily felt a swift, intuitive, inexplicable pang of pity for him. She had expected to hate him, to see him as the author of all Joyce's troubles, imagined him to be a sinister, slighter, and more oily individual. Her picture of Dorrie would need revision too; Dorrie was not at all curvaceous, buxom, with a Rita Hayworth shock of hair and a husky voice no man could resist.

"That was Stan," said Joyce after Dorrie had left. "They just heard the news down at the Cask and Cleavage and Stan says we should all come down and celebrate."

"I better get going," said Jack. "My job starts at dawn and it's a long ride down to the desert." He scooped Justin out from under the table and kissed him, picked up Little Jack, talked in his own language and kissed him too. He held Cilla and Lisa Marie as if he would never let them go, but he did, swung his leather jacket and helmet over his shoulder, said good-bye to everyone, called Emily *Ma'am* again, and turned to Joyce. "You know how much it means to me, you looking after the boys."

"Those little boys are always welcome here. They know it and you know it."

"I'd keep them at home, but I can't pass up this job, even if it is only for a week, and Dorrie's mother's been sick a lot lately. You know how it is."

"I guess I do," she replied in a neutral voice. "After all these years."

They heard Jack's motorcycle pull away and then Sandee said she thought she'd be going on home.

"What about the Cask and Cleavage?" asked Joyce.

"Oh no. Thanks anyway," Sandee demurred. "Ray'll be home soon and he'll want dinner and—"

"Sandee, Ray's ass has been warming up a barstool at the Monkey's Hideout. Why should you go home and fix his dinner?"

"Let him fix his own goddamned dinner," seconded Charleen.

"I just don't think we should go to the Cask and Cleaver, Joycie," said Sandee, sucking off the end of every word and glancing meaningfully at Emily.

Emily protested at once that she was leaving. In fact she'd only come at all because she had got a phone call and was driving around town—a little later, after the phone call—and she found herself on Santiago Street.

"A phone call from the East Coast?" asked Joyce.

Emily played with her engagement ring.

"Emily's coming with us," Joyce announced.

"Joycie!"

"Oh, it will be all right, Sandee. Don't worry. Emily needs us, I mean, needs to help us celebrate. Cilla will look after the little ones, won't you, honey?"

"You just tell that Justin to mind me."

"Justin, honey." Joyce got down and pulled him out from under the table. She stroked his hair and admonished him to mind Cilla. "Cilla, just put the boys in my bed and I'll move them when I get home."

"No, you won't, Mama. You'll sleep on the couch like you always do when they come to visit," Cilla replied in a snippy tone.

"Well, who cares tonight? Tonight Sandee's won twenty-seven hundred dollars! The Eastbound Express is playing at the Cask and Cleavage. Hey—it's time to rock and roll!"

Twelve

Dogleg Wilson took the mike and turned down a fan's request for a song by the Bee Gees. He added that here at the Cask and Cleaver, as long as the Eastbound Express was playing, you wouldn't hear no drizzly disco, no Christopher Cross crap either. A boo and a hiss came from the bar and someone yelled, *Disco Lives!* All this just as Joyce, Phil, Sandee, Charleen, her husband, and Emily walked in. Dogleg raised his belt over his gut. "If it ain't live music, it's dead, man. It don't live. It don't breathe. It just sucks." The Disco Liver looked ready to fly at Dogleg with his fists, when the bartender in a single Jesse Owens bound leaped over the bar and collared him, directed him toward the men's room to cool off. Certainly this was not the picture of the Cask and Cleaver Emily had had when the USC alumni had met in their dull, decorous banquet rooms.

Joyce and Sandee went up to the bandstand and confabbed with the Eastbound Express (who, as a band, had never been farther east than Chagrin), and Emily and the others got a table and ordered a pitcher of beer.

Joyce and Sandee joined them; Dogleg took the mike again and announced, "Our friend Sandee here has won the KLMO Memory Jackpot with Elvis's GI serial number! Stand up, Sandee, and take a bow!" She did this graciously and got exuberant applause. "Whatever else you might have heard, folks, it was Sandee here won twenty-seven hundred dollars! Bartender, the next pitcher for that table is on the band! It ain't often we got something like this to celebrate. Sandee memorized the King's GI serial number twenty-four years ago now, and that's more than a hundred dollars a year." As he spoke, Dogleg's three hundred pounds began to quiver in time to a beat Stan hadn't even hit yet, but when he did, they moved right into *Money, Honey;* they rocked out and the dance floor filled. Charleen danced with her husband; Phil Sloat danced with Joyce, who—Emily was rather shocked to see—moved with a grace and abandon Emily always assumed you automatically gave up when you turned forty.

Emily sat with Sandee and drank beer at the table made of thick dark wood and varnished to discourage graffiti. The bar at the Cask and Cleaver was cast as an eighteenth-century smuggler's hideaway. The pictures on the wall seemed, to Emily's inexpert eye, to be abstract expressionist pirates and the mirrored ceilings reflected a carousel of red, blue, yellow, and green lights. The bartenders were plainly clad, but the waitresses were supposed to be period pieces, skirts hiked thigh-high, a cascade of petticoats and corsets that pushed their breasts up so high they needed a periscope to see over them. Their waitress introduced herself as Traci. Traci did not give a damn for Elvis's GI number, but the thought of customers with twenty-seven hundred dollars to spend sent her into a swoon; she brought more napkins, ashtrays, and another pitcher of beer, this one she said was on the bartender, Bruce.

Phil and Joyce returned from the dance floor. Phil was breathless. "I'm going for reinforcements," he said. "I need money for the pay phone. Cough me up some cash, Sandee. You just won twenty-seven hundred dollars."

"Call Ray, will you?"

"Call him what?"

The Eastbound took their break and flocked to the winner's table, where Joyce and her friends were already on their third pitcher of beer. The band ordered another. Joyce introduced Emily to her brother, the drummer Stan Denton (who, Emily knew, had been born Noah Denby and looked exactly like Joyce except for a certain diffidence that his older sister did not share), and to the other members of the band. Charleen warned Emily not to ask how Dogleg Wilson got his name. "He'll show you," she whispered.

Emily blanched and was introduced to a rail-thin, coal black man who played lead guitar. "Demetrius Ball," said Joyce. "SEHS, 1962," she added, as though this clarified everything.

Demetrius shook hands with Emily. His fingers were so long, he probably could have played guitar with three of them and plucked harp strings with the other two. "My friends call me Meatball," he advised her.

"Hmmm," said Emily, believing this to be the better part of valor.

The sax player, Eldon, was right out of central casting: nerd, the guy who could better swing a slide rule than a saxophone. Sandee told her his real name was Wallace.

"Hmmm," said Emily sagely.

"And this is the Eastbound's bass player," said Joyce, putting her arm around a moustachioed, slope-shouldered man in his middle thirties who wore a John Deere cap sideways and whose face seemed equally lopsided, as though his features had all taken two steps right and stayed there. "His name is Mike Hershey, but he goes by Candy," Joyce explained.

"Hard." He winked, screwing his face further into a knot. "Hard Candy."

Emily took a long deep draft of her beer and allowed Eldon to refill her glass and wondered if anyone in this crowd kept his real name. Their break over, the Eastbound returned to work, launched into *Shake, Rattle and Roll* like they expected to wash everyone out the door on a great tsunami of music.

By this time Phil had had some luck rounding up reinforcements (including Sandee's Ray) and lots of other people came up, joined them; they pushed three or four tables together and the beer kept coming and it seemed as though everyone (except for Emily) had gone to SEHS at one time or another. Joyce took especial care to include her, introduced Emily to everyone as the new social worker. Everyone smiled and nodded and was very nice to her.

The men asked her politely to dance and Emily did, but she was a little alarmed at the way they let themselves go on the dance floor. Not that they were exactly John Travolta in *Saturday Night Fever*. More like *Saturday Night Live*. Emily continued to dance in her own decorous tread; her feet moved, but her arms and shoulders stayed decently put and her hips remained firmly tethered to her backbone. She was having an earnest conversation about fruit with a man named Chuck Sullivan when Eldon hit that wailing sax solo on *Return to Sender* and Chuck said they had to dance. Once on the floor, Emily felt tiny invisible manacles, shackles she was not even aware of, she felt them snap open. It's the beer, she told herself.

It certainly could have been the beer, because there was quite a lot of it; there were so many of them now that Traci was bringing pitchers two at a time. In fact there was so much beer that after two more dances, Emily excused herself to go to the ladies' room. She stood in line behind Charleen, Diana (Phil's girlfriend), and Florence Sullivan, each of whom was old enough to be her mother. She noticed this as she looked in the mirror. She wondered briefly what she was doing here with all these older people. *Older LMC people,* her mother's voice corrected her. "Oh shut up," said Emily just as, mercifully, three toilets flushed in unison and she did not have to explain the remark.

When she returned, the Eastbound had altered the mood, playing Elvis's *Are You Lonesome Tonight?*, to which Emily could very happily reply a resounding NO! Sandee's Ray asked her to dance and Emily said yes.

Ray was a man of middle age, height, and weight, his body constructed squarely and his hair close-cropped and colorless. With his graying, unshaven jaw and coarse skin he reminded Emily of a cinder block. She tried to picture him in bed with voluptuous, Junoesque Sandee, but the effort cost her considerable concentration and she missed something he'd said. "Pardon?"

"So you're the new social worker?"

"I guess I am."

"Don't you know who you are?" Ray whispered hoarsely, pulling her up tight so that her breasts pressed into his hard cinder block chest.

"I wonder sometimes. It's like I moved to St. Elmo and found this big bottle with a tag on it that said DRINK ME and I did and I just fell down a rabbit hole that a year ago I couldn't even have imagined! Of course, maybe I've just drunk a lot of beer tonight. I have drunk a lot of beer tonight. I don't usually drink beer." Too LMC for words, that's what her mother thought of beer drinkers, but Emily did not say so. Ray pressed her more tightly and murmured something else she didn't quite hear, didn't think she wanted to either. She ought perhaps to declare herself to Ray as an engaged woman, but inevitably Ray would have asked, *So, where's your fiancé?*

"Well, you're certainly an eyeful of good-looking girl," said Ray. "I thought you had to pass an ugly test to be a social worker."

After enduring this dance with Ray, Emily vowed to sit out the slow numbers, but the promise was moot because the Eastbound Express seemed to be steaming full throttle toward midnight, and with each song Emily was pleased to find herself becoming a better dancer, bone and tendon, nerves and veins vibrating like a string on Meatball's lead guitar.

Each time she went back to the table after dancing, the crowd seemed to have altered slightly, people ebbing, flowing, coming, going, maybe twelve or sixteen of them, eighteen? Gradually the faces blended in some vaguely middle-aged amalgam distinguished only by sex, and each time someone new joined them, someone always said, *This is Emily Shaw, Joyce's new social worker.* Emily got their names and promptly forgot them, wondered why she couldn't be introduced just as Emily. She remembered her mother, for years and years, always introducing their cleaning lady as *Zora, the cleaning lady,* should any of her mother's friends happen to come by when Zora was there. Sitting out *Mean Woman Blues,* Emily puzzled over this. Would her mother have identified Zora as the cleaning lady if Zora had been black? Would there have been any question then but that Zora must be the cleaning lady? Not only was Zora white, but she always wore pastel polyester pantsuits, high-heeled sandals, dangle earrings, and bracelets to clean in. *Too LMC for words,* Emily's mother declared. Despite being awash in beer—or maybe because of it—Emily understood Zora at last. Zora wore pantsuits, high-heeled sandals, and dangle-bangles so that Mrs. Shaw *must* identify her as the cleaning lady. No one could make that automatic assumption. Emily wondered what these people at her table would think she was if she were not introduced as the new social worker. Would they think she was the old social worker? Would they think of her at all? She had new respect for Zora.

"Do you wanna dance?" asked a man named CJ or EJ or BJ, Emily never got it quite straight. The music, the mirrors and reflecting lights, the carousel of new faces kept Emily giddy. The beer kept her going back to the bathroom, where she stripped off her sweatshirt, happy to find she still had on her oversized USC T-shirt underneath. *You can't dance in your pajamas,* snapped her mother's voice. *We didn't send you to USC, pay for you to be a Tri Delt, so that you could dance in your nightshirt with a bunch of LMC*—Emily turned on the water and washed her face vigorously, fluffed her hair, and left.

She went back to the dance floor, rolling and rocking, *Let the Good Times Roll, Big Hunk of Love, Dancing at the High School Hop, Whole Lotta Shaking Going On, Tutti Frutti,* back to back or all at once, Emily wasn't quite sure, not even sure whom she was dancing with, or if it mattered.

Finally the Eastbound took a break and, leaning on Sandee and Joyce, she had to crawl back to the table, where there were a couple of fresh pitchers of beer. Thank God for that because it took a lot of beer to recuperate, to laugh and listen to Joyce and Sandee and Charleen tell about some long-ago kissing contest. They pulled CJ or EJ or BJ into the discussion because he'd been a Chieftain, and Emily was trying to decide what a Chieftain was when over the rim of her beer glass she caught sight of a man in the mirror at the bar. He was a dark-eyed man with a moustache, not beautiful, but appealing. He winked. She was sure he winked. At her. He turned on the barstool and smiled at her.

Oh shit. Emily choked and Sandee patted her absently on the back, but their conversation went on without Emily. *Mr. Hansen.* Mr. Hansen left his beer and came walking toward her.

Emily had not seen Howard Hansen since the night he had taken her to Zacateca's for dinner, now several weeks ago. The day she'd first met Joyce. The night she'd missed Rick's call. The only night. She'd lied to Rick for the first time. She'd said that she and Penny Pitzer had gone to the movies, *Chariots of Fire*, she had added, hoping that the specific additive would improve the general flavor of the lie. Rick's feelings were hurt when he called and she wasn't home. Emily soothed and crooned and lulled, apologized, did everything, in fact, except tell the truth. And why not? Such an innocent evening. Why couldn't she just say: *Well, Rick, honey, last night I was out with another man, not exactly that, I mean he's really a sort of coworker, well no, that's not right because he's a Big Muck in our department, in charge of all welfare field workers and our training classes here at the county and he took me out to dinner because, I can't explain, exactly, what happened to me that afternoon, but I met Joyce and I came back to the office and I just sort of unraveled, Rick, thinking about* Greensleeves *and how people get themselves into messes screwing their brains out and you'd think they'd learn—I'm speaking here of the whole human race, Rick—but they don't. It just undid me, honey, and right then Mr. Handsome, I mean Mr. Hansen came along and scooped me up—I can't tell you what a wreck I was—and took me to this little Mexican place, a dump really, honey, nothing like La Hacienda in Newport where you always take me, but the food was absolutely great and Mr. Hansen and I got to talking and he went to UCLA—and okay, I wasn't calling him Mr. Hansen by then, I was calling him Howard. That's his name. Even though he's eight years older than me and went to UCLA, we'd sort of had the same experience, except that naturally UCLA could never be USC since it's just a state school. Mr. Hansen gave up music to study social welfare, just like I loved English and had to change my major so I could butter my own bread. I'm not saying I got pressured into sociology or anything exactly, but you must admit, Rick honey, I didn't exactly embrace Emile Durkeim or any of the rest of them, who are all, to a man, crashing, unmitigated bores. There. I've said it! Maybe this being a social worker is not exactly a far, far better thing that I do than I have ever done before. Maybe I'm really the sort of person who should make a nice fat contribution to United Way and let it go at that.*

Not try to DEAL with these people, because Cilla Jackson, young as she is, she told the truth. Poor people stink. Not Cilla and Joyce, but lots of poor people really do stink and I'm more the Chanel No. 5 or Givenchy type and there's days go by when I think: I can't take this; I really don't think I can take this. I couldn't take it that night. We got to Zacateca's and Mr. Handsome sat me down and ordered me a beer and glass of ice water and talked to me, low and quiet and reassuring, while I drank my ice water. He had just that same kind of voice in training class, where, I'm certain, positive, he waxed on that you shouldn't fraternize or socialize or go out drinking or sleep with—no, he wouldn't have said that, although he could have because there were some men trainees in our group—but even if he didn't say that, I remember he said words to the effect of don't get too chummy with your clients. Strongly Suggested. What can I say when he comes over here and asks me what I'm doing with all these welfare types? Maybe I don't have to say anything. Maybe I can just pretend that they're my friends. Why not? They are my friends and I'm out with them, here having a good time. I am having a good time, Rick. I haven't had this much fun since our engagement party, Rick. These people are as close to friends as I have in this godforsaken desert rathole of a town, Rick, and while you're kicking up your legal heels and getting ready to join Shaw, Swine, Swill, Slime and Turdlock, while you're going to hear Leonard Bernstein at the Kennedy Center, I'm here at the Cask and Cleavage in St. Elmo, California, listening to a band with people called Dogleg and Meatball and Hard Candy and watching the head honcho of my department cross the floor and say to me

"You want to dance, Emily?"

Emily and Howard flailed away on the dance floor to *Hound Dog*, to *Yakkety Yak*, to *There's Good Rockin' Tonight*, right alongside Joyce and CJ (or whoever), Phil and Diana, Charleen and her husband, whose name Emily could not remember probably because it was something like Robert and he hadn't changed it to Dogleg or Eldon, Eldon, who in the course of *Devil with a Blue Dress On* was doing things to that sax that are probably forbidden in Muslim countries. Emily and Howard danced till they were ready to drop and might have, except the next number was *Great Balls of Fire*.

"Who can resist *Great Balls?*" cried Emily before biting her tongue in half for punishment. They took a break after that; Howard settled his account at the bar, ordered two more pitchers to be brought to Emily's table, and told her the Eastbound was the best rock-and-roll band between Los Angeles and the Mexican border and he never missed a gig of theirs at the Cask and Cleaver. "Cleavage," Emily corrected him. She introduced him simply as Howard to everyone at the table, though she'd forgotten most of their names. "Oh well, win a win, few a few," she added before announcing that she had to pee. "I shouldn't have said that," she admitted. "Totally LMC, peeing, I don't mean the peeing, but the saying it. And you just have to wonder, don't you? *I've* always wondered why men can say they have to pee, or take a leak, and women can't. Are we supposed to pretend we don't have bladders?"

All the women at the table gave a great cheer and applause and toasted to having bladders and Emily went off to the ladies' room with a vague sense of having performed some inestimable service.

The Eastbound lit into the opening riffs of *Don't Be Cruel,* and except for Howard and Joyce, the table vacated. "There'll never be another Elvis," Howard said reverently, and Joyce lifted her glass to his. "To the King of Rock and Roll."

"To the King," said Joyce, floating happily on a golden tide of Budweiser. "He came to me in a dream last night," she confided to Howard. "He was young, the young beautiful man with the sad, sad eyes, he came to me in a dream."

"I'd give anything to have Elvis talk to me in my dreams. What did he say?"

"Well, it's strange, because I was his assistant or something like that and I had this letter for him, and I handed it to him, but he didn't read it. We're standing under an arch by this lake and I know he's going to be leaving and in the dream I say to him, *I can't bear what's going to happen to you.* He just looks out over the lake and tells me I shouldn't worry. *It's a gift,* he says. *You can't buy it or earn it, you just have to accept it. It's going to be all right. It's like light on water.* And then we both stand there and look at the lake and he was gone." Joyce took a pensive sip. "And I was just thinking of that, of him saying that, when they came on KLMO with the Memory Jackpot question about his GI number. Isn't that something?"

"Well, I wish Elvis would talk to me in my dreams. Closest I get to Elvis is driving to work every day, past that house on Santiago Street. You know the one I mean? Heartbreak Hotel?"

"It makes you feel close to Elvis?" Joyce's lovely face lit up.

"Close to the King. Close to the music. Close as I'll ever get nowadays, but music used to be my life."

"What happened?"

"Oh, I grew up. I grew out of it."

She regarded him critically. "If you'd really just outgrown it, then you'd make fun of it, like, well, like wearing your hair in a duck's-ass hairdo. You know what I mean?"

Howard laughed ruefully. "Well, it was a little more romantic than a duck's-ass hairdo, I guess. I fell in love with a woman who didn't want to marry a man who was always trying to support his music habit. It's a hard life. Ask them." He nodded toward the Eastbound Express. "So I did the romantic thing, or maybe I did the sensible thing. It seemed romantic at the time—and I got a master's in social welfare and went to work and she went to law school and the first thing she did when she passed the bar was divorce me. It ended up being funny."

"But not at the time."

Howard shrugged and made a deprecating face. "There was nothing lost. No kids. No one really suffered. Honestly I look back at it and I don't have any idea why I was so crazy about that woman, but I was."

"Gonads," said Joyce authoritatively. "There's a time in your life when you might just as well wear your gonads over your eyes because you walk around blinded by them anyway."

"What about gonads?" asked Emily, rejoining them.

Charleen's husband asked Joyce to dance, and never-minding her vow to sit out the slow ones, Emily went willingly into Howard's arms when the Eastbound struck up *I Want You, I Love You, I Need You,* feeling the old alchemical combustion of youth and alcohol, music, and lyric calculated to make your blood percolate up and down your veins. The music slid into Elvis's sweet imperative, *Love Me,* and Emily's arms slid up Howard's neck and she slowly tilted her head back and he might have kissed her, but LAST CALL rang out across the room.

"ALL HAIL TO THE KING!" Dogleg shouted. "ALL HANDS ON DECK BECAUSE WE'RE GOING DOWN, WE'RE GOING *WAY DOWN!*"

At the bar, Bruce slapped his towel in time as Stan ruffled out the opening riff of *Way Down,* met by Meatball on guitar, and then Dogleg hit that keyboard like he had suddenly become the Reverend Mr. Dogleg beating the sin out of it. Emily found herself in the churning midst of people with their hands raised overhead and their voices raised to *Way Down,* Phil Sloat doing the dancing decathlon, Joyce doing the shimmy,

Sandee's magnificent bulk writhing, Diana, Charleen, CJ, Chuck and Florence Sullivan, the whole crowd of them, sweat flying from their brows, vaporizing in the hot air, and then Eldon's sax was smoking and Dogleg throbbed his keyboard while doing vocals and the whole band was *Burning Love.* Emily couldn't even see Meatball because he was lying on his back, clinging to his guitar, his hips thumping, pumping up and down to *Burning Love.* Everyone on the dance floor, happy heretics all, hotfooting over coals, *Burning Love,* their sweat flying like steamy smoke, sizzling out of that short fuse: put the key of imagination into desire and start the ignition. Imagination and desire fired Emily, who danced like the floor had been torched, like her very flesh was turning on a musical spit, sizzling, smoking, and she laughed out loud to think of Shakespeare, of the violent delights, the violent ends, the fire and powder, flash of heat you could feel radiate off the Bard's immortal pages. Shakespeare, he knew all about *Burning Love,* that's why he smokes up the pages of the *Norton Anthology* while the rest of them just trundle and grump. Shakespeare could catch the throb, throttle, combustion of imagination with desire, lust, and suction. Oh, Little Willie, the Burning Bard, he'd met that general of hot desire, all right, he knew *Burning Love* and he knew what to do with it: melt it all down and pour it—molten, liquefied, and, above all, hot—into words, form them into perfect sonnets, that's why his words still smoked up off the page, singed your very fingers: because that's what *Burning Love* is all about. Shakespeare knew it. Elvis too. Emily threw back her head and laughed, imagining them both up there with the Eastbound Express, the Burning Bard and the King, that hip-thrusting hunk of—what else?—*Burning Love.* The King in sequined white and Little Willie in sequined black, each gripping a mike while the flames flared all around them, two masters of emotion, singing to one another and anyone else who cared to experience the flames you love to lick, turn you into smoke you like to die of and here, right here, with heat wavering, flames snapping all around, Elvis and the Burning Bard who knew that water cools not love, hell no, not *Burning Love.* And what other kind was there? What other kind was worth having? Emily spun into Howard's arms and out again. He caught her, pulled her up close against his hot body, and she combusted spontaneously, *Burning Love* at both ends, steaming spirit, just like Elvis and the Burning Bard. Breathe deep, *O Burning Love,* and fear not, fear not the heat, the smoke, the sizzle.

Thirteen

Time after time the phone beside her bed rang cruelly. Her arm flailed, like some drowsy serpent, searching, reaching for the phone, touched instead a tousled head. He caught her hand and brought it to his lips. The ringing stopped.

Emily opened her eyes to see Howard Hansen in her bed. His eyes were not open, but he smiled just the same. He laid her hand across the mat of dark hair on his chest and patted it. It was her left hand, and the rock of her engagement ring shone dully. Emily closed her eyes. Howard pulled her closer. She rested her head on his bare shoulder, smelling the scent of love spent: heat and light, *O Burning Love*.

Had she really kissed Howard passionately right there on the dance floor while the music and the magic yet flamed about them? *O Burning Love*. And had she, with that music somehow physically ingested, throbbing inside her, throbbed home with Howard Hansen? *O Burning Love*. And had they, trailing embers from their feet, trailing smoke, walked in beauty like the night, like light and heat and their clothes crackling off, strewing them in a path across the floor? The living room floor. And, upon reaching the bedroom, had she, Miss Emily Shaw, Tri Delt, USC, class of '81, all but unbuttoned Mr. Hansen's shirt with her teeth? *O Burning Love*. Did Mr. Hansen, formerly Miss Shaw's instructor in social welfare training classes, did he roll over and under her, over and under again and again, while Emily Shaw felt a percussive beat, a tiny point of searing light that only

Howard Hansen could find, fan, lick like flames? And did he? *O Burning Love.* And did Emily Shaw then crawl up the length of his body, head flung back, and did he trace a path with his hands and lips and tongue down Emily's body, down her throat, between her breasts, and lower, lower yet, to where that point of light embered hot and glowing? *O Burning Love.* And had she been tied to the stake of her own desire while choirs sang overhead and down under, *O Burning Love?* And had she, Emily (engaged to be married to the famous Rick, soon to join her father's law firm), whispered hot words she'd never said to Rick, indeed, words she had never had the occasion to say to Rick, whispered: *Please, please, I can't take any more?* Had she truly said that? *O Burning Love.* And had he, Howard, whispered sweetly, tenderly, *Yes, you can, honey, you can take more and more and more?* And was there more? *O Burning Love.* There was. More. Till the dawn's early light, there was more: hands clenched, bodies bowed, deep kisses, spirits soaring, ignited, burnt to ashes, to rise and do it all over again. Heat and light, *O Burning Love.*

Emily groaned, reached across Howard's chest, and quickly turned the photograph of Rick beside the phone facedown. Her head throbbed, as though her brains, like bubble gum, had burst against her skull. She fell back against Howard's shoulder.

"Hangover, honey?"

"I think so."

"I can cure that. Amazing Grace." He patted her reassuringly. "I have this surefire hangover cure. Recipe from my aunt Grace. She gave it to me for my twenty-first birthday. I'll probably have to go to the store. You probably don't have the ingredients." Howard swung his feet out of bed. "We can't face breakfast till we've had Amazing Grace."

"I thought we already had it."

Howard got in the shower and Emily lay there, smiling to hear him sing in the shower; he had a nice rich voice and he seemed to know all the verses to *Amazing Grace,* as well as *Waltzing Matilda.* Then she remembered. She roused quickly, and despite her hangover (mouth full of cotton, boll weevil and all), she flew around the apartment stashing all the pictures of Rick she had so carefully and artfully placed about when she moved in.

She was back in bed before Howard emerged from the shower. He sat on the bed and pulled on his clothes. They still smelled of smoke from the Cask and Cleaver. The pillowcases smelled of smoke. The bed smelled of burning love. Howard kissed her and assured her he'd be back with their salvation.

Emily was just out of the shower when she heard the phone ring again. She got it on the fifth blast. She stood there, dripping, towel hastily wrapped about her, and talked to Rick. Rick had called her back a second time last night. He was worried when she hadn't answered. He wanted to know where she'd been. "Out," said Emily crisply, "with some friends from the welfare department." She rummaged up enough logic to convince herself that her whole current predicament, including the hangover and her having been in bed with another man, was all Rick's fault. Rick waxed on about his love for her and explained his decision again. Emily held the phone at arm's length, as though it had farted. "There's someone at the door," she said, truthfully for once.

Howard came in, took his grocery sack to the fridge, put things in, and looked at the magnet picture of Rick, the only one she had forgotten to stash. "Is this your fiancé, the one who lives back east?"

"I only have the one."

"He's very attractive. Law student at Georgetown, didn't you say? That night we went to Zacateca's."

"I suppose I did." She could not bear to talk about Rick, not to explain or deny. She could not let Howard touch Rick, nor Rick touch Howard. She took the picture from Howard's hands, opened the refrigerator, and threw it in the vegetable drawer.

"Let me dry your hair," said Howard softly, leading her to the bathroom, where he got out the hair dryer, fluffed her hair, kissed her neck and shoulders while the warm air blew on her skin. Emily turned in his arms and, whatever Amazing Grace he had intended to concoct from what he'd bought at the store, they brewed something very like it right there in Emily's bed, as fleeting and potent and unlooked for as grace—which is always amazing. How can it be anything else?

It could also be chicken broth and lemon juice, heated to boiling, and a well-beaten raw egg mixed in, off heat. That was Amazing Grace, drunk as hot as you could bear it, chased with ice-cold grapefruit juice and finished up with hot tea.

They got dressed and went to Zacateca's for breakfast, or lunch, "Or whatever it is you eat at three in the afternoon," said Howard to the waitress. While they ate huevos rancheros with hot sauce, he described for Emily the trials and tribulations of growing up a musical prodigy in Monrovia, California, which he said was a hotbed of extras. "I could play, oh, four or five instruments well, and if I could have divided myself up, I could have been my own rock band and chamber orchestra."

"Well, why didn't you? I mean, after you and your wife broke up, you could have gone back to music, couldn't you?"

"Not really. By then, I knew myself too well. I'm not really cut out to be a musician, or an artist, or any of that."

"But you clearly have all that talent and ability."

"It takes more than that. Ego, need, drive—I'm not that kind of person and I'm not willing to suffer." He smiled and sipped Zacateca's strong coffee. "It's like the difference between being a writer and being a reader. When you're a reader, you come to words and stories and novels and they refresh you and you get to learn and live it, you get to rejoice in all that magnificent emotion—and when you want to put the book down, you put the book down. You close it up and you're finished. The writer can't do that. The writer has to live it all out, months, maybe years—the writer needs a cupful of pain to get a thimbleful of prose. It's the same for a musician, or a singer. That's what we demand of our artists. They need to live like that. If they're any good at all, they die like that. I'm not that driven. I just don't have that kind of ego or desire. Talent isn't enough."

"Maybe that's why I love novels. I always have," said Emily thoughtfully, "but I've never had the slightest wish to write a book. Except, I do have a wonderful opening line for a book."

"What's that?"

Emily smiled slowly. "HEY! ISHMAEL!"

Howard laughed out loud, which touched Emily, as Rick had never thought this a particularly funny joke. On the other hand, she'd never thought his joke about the fat lady asked to move her ass (she had to make two trips) was very funny either. She always rather assumed their different tastes resulted from Rick's being male and her being female. But last night seemed to fling a bucketful of doubt over those easy suppositions, as if her previous assumptions were calmly walking down the street, say in the eighteenth century, and suddenly a bucket of slops got tossed on them, and they all looked comic. At best. She worried, for instance, that Rick's love was like his lovemaking: swift, perfunctory, efficiently achieved, maximum release for minimum effort. And it did not soothe or calm her that this question would never have arisen but for her having committed—not quite adultery, perhaps, but— "Pardon me?" she said, snapped from her thoughts.

"You said last night you came to the Cask and Cleavage in your friend's car, and I just asked if I can take you to your car. How will you get to work tomorrow?"

The whole notion of *car* and *work tomorrow* momentarily bewildered Emily, coupled as it was with the recollection of the If Not Forbiddens at least Strongly Suggesteds from training class, that one ought not to cohere, drink beer, flail, roil, rock and roll with one's clients. Indeed, thinking of training class reminded Emily how she had imaginatively tallied up who had risen from which beds, never dreaming she might herself have risen from the same bed as the instructor, the Great Guru, Guiding Light, and Generally Invincible Leader of Family Assistance. Emily took a deep breath. "My car," she said pensively, feeling Time's wingèd chariot rattling nearby.

As they drove, Emily sloshed about in evasions, demurrals, half-truths, and neo-abjurations, admitted finally that her car was over near the county complex. Driving down Santiago Street, Howard chatted about how he went by Heartbreak Hotel every day, offered some of the same anecdotal chitchat gleaned from the newspapers that Penny had told her now months ago. Emily stifled a tinge of resentment. If Joyce's house were less flamboyant, there'd be much less chance of getting caught. While Emily mumbled, *Oh really,* or its equivalent, it occurred to her that perhaps Howard did not know that a welfare client lived in that house. He asked where he should turn.

"Sultana," she said, feeling rather more cheerful.

But luck was not on Emily's side. As they drove past, Joyce was changing the sheet on the picnic table, in much the same way a careful nurse might change the patient's bed, or an acolyte might tidy an altar, so that nothing—not the Gideon Bibles, the black satin-framed portrait of the King, not even the wreath of plastic daisies—might touch the ground. The refrain from *Peace in the Valley* blew from the speakers and into the street.

"That's Joyce!" cried Howard. "She and I were talking about Elvis last night! I told her I go by Heartbreak Hotel every—" A look of excruciating pain crossed his face. "Joyce. Is that where she lives? That's her house? That's Joyce Jackson, isn't it?"

Emily played with her engagement ring. Joyce finished up and went inside.

Howard massaged his temples. "You took over Sid Johnson's caseload, didn't you?"

"They were *in extremis.*"

Howard twisted his hands over the steering wheel. "Look, of course I'm not going to say anything to anyone, but I have to warn you, Emily. It's not wise. Really. It's not a smart thing to do. I know you can't leave this job behind at the stroke of five, but I think you're inviting heartache—or disaster. You wouldn't be the first social worker who made friends, became part of a client's life, and then found the day came when you had to make a choice between your friend and your client."

"We're not in training class now."

"I'm not talking about training class. I'm saying this as your friend. I'm just trying to warn you away from what can be a—a terrible situation. Do you know what Marge Mason would do to you if she got hold of information like that? Like last night?"

"What about last night?"

"About you being out dancing and drinking with your clients."

"Oh. I thought you were talking about you and me."

"That's personal. That's between us and has nothing to do with the office. The other is professional."

"I was being professional. They were *in extremis*," she repeated stubbornly. "They called me at the office yesterday, I mean on Friday, and they said they were *in extremis,* but it was too close to five and I couldn't go, so they called me last night, Saturday night, and said it couldn't wait, and I came over, and we talked, like you would for any *in extremis,* and then we went out."

Howard was silent for a long time while Elvis finished another gospel tune across the street. "I wish I hadn't seen this, but I have," he said at last. "You're in over your head, Emily. You're facing the very hardest part of this job, and that is keeping your reactions picketed into professional responses with your clients. You can like them as people, but you have to respond professionally, and it's tough, really, maybe it's impossible, but the other path is so dangerous." He smiled to hear Elvis sing *Amazing Grace.* "Joyce is a wonderful person, I can see that, and her friends are fun and funny, but they're your clients and it's a mistake to believe, or let them believe, they're your friends. It's a mistake for them too."

"They're not my friends. They were *in extremis.* How could I be friends with them? I'm not an Elvis fan. I'm a Tri Delt! My friends live in Carmel and Pasadena and Scottsdale and Palm Beach. And Georgetown! Yes! My friends go to law school in Georgetown and—" Emily rattled along about Rick till Howard, who looked suddenly tired and gray, made a sardonic reference to a one-night stand. Emily retorted, words to the effect that she was only doing this job till she got married to Rick, who would then join her father's firm and sail on her father's boat in every sense of that term. Emily kept talking, even though across the street she saw a shimmering hologram condense from the lavender-tinted light spilling through a jacaranda, a silvery, see-through, all-but-invisible version of herself making gagging noises. This holographic Emily was trying to strangle herself, hands throttling her own throat, eyes rolling, tongue lolling out like that of someone twitching on the gallows, screaming silently, *Shut up!* But Emily's lips kept right on flapping, finishing up with, "I wouldn't stay in this rathole of a town one minute longer than I had to. I'm going to be married in *1985*. Early *1985*, and I'm leaving St. Elmo forever and I'll laugh at what a horrible desert burg it is and how I had to live here and be a social worker to people who are Elvis fruitcakes! How I had—"

"A one-night stand with the man who taught your training class?" inquired Howard coldly.

The holographic Emily under the jacarandas gave up in disgust and vanished. From across the street, gospel songs wafted. *I Believe,* sang Elvis. Emily looked at Howard. He believed too. Not that Joyce was *in extremis* on Saturday night, but everything else. Emily opened her mouth, but no words came. She could not unsay it. She could not undo what she'd done. She could not make it undo. There was nothing for her to do except get out of Howard's car. Without looking back, Emily walked to her own car, drove home to the empty apartment, where she stripped the bed and finished the can of chocolate frosting.

Fourteen

Emily Shaw spent the next week deep in the pea green sense of having done Everything Wrong. She tried to attribute her moral, mental, spiritual, and physical biliousness to PMS, but her period was just past. She succumbed to alternate bouts of rage and groveling self-pity. And there was no comfort. No one, no place, and nothing could comfort her. She'd screwed up badly in her work. She'd betrayed her fiancé, the man she'd loved for four years. She had tasted *Burning Love* with the Head Honcho and Guiding Light Guru of Family Assistance and then said brutal things to him, things she ought never to have said, even if it was only a one-night stand. And maybe it was. Now. In every light she looked either crass or foolish. All Emily could do was wrap up in Joyce's grandmother's antique quilt and snivel, sniffle, and whine privately.

On Friday she was actually relieved, glad to have something else to think about, when she received a call from Juvenile Hall about an *in extremis*. A fifteen-year-old girl whose family was on Emily's caseload had run off with a twenty-three-year-old married man. The man's wife had found them in a downtown by-the-hour hotel, where she burst in brandishing an unregistered weapon. Emily found this shocking, but she was not dumbfounded and undone as she would have been three months before, indeed, as she might have been even a week before, before *Burning Love*, before she'd learned from experience (and not from a novel, a sonnet, a play or poem) that only two things could make you burn: love and hate. Love and hate were burning up this fifteen-year-old girl, the man, and his wife, who had fired five shots into the headboard of the bed where her husband and his fifteen-year-old girlfriend lay naked. When the police came, they naturally arrested the woman and took the man into custody for debauching a minor. Suella Nesbitt, the minor, they sent to Juvenile Hall to await the county's final judicious consideration of her desperate case.

Emily thanked the social worker who had called from Juvenile Hall and rang down to the library for the Nesbitt family file. She happened then to look up, across the amber waves of desks, and see Howard talking earnestly to Penny Pitzer. Jealousy, hurt, longing, as well as something hot—and probably white—shot through Emily Shaw, and she warred inexpertly with all these emotions. Penny sat down and Howard looked across the room to Emily; his eyes were filled with pain denied and so all the more potent.

A co-worker at the next desk handed Emily the phone, and a brusque male voice demanded, "You the new social worker for Joyce Jackson?"

Emily immediately turned, got out some paper. "Is Joyce all right?"

"Oh, she's fine." The man gave a low snicker. "She's better than you'd ever guess. She's fooled all of you, years and years and years. Fooled the whole goddamned county, fooled you and that big nigger they sent before you—"

"Who is this?"

"Oh, Joyce Jackson is just a handful of gimme and a mouthful of much-obliged. She's a rich woman. She's a bitch too, but she's smart. You got to give her that."

"Who is this!"

"I'm doing the taxpayers of this state a favor, honey. I guess I got to since none of you college types"—he seemed to suck the last phrase from his sinuses and blow it out his nose—"got any brains at all. That bitch is smarter than any of you. She sold a car for two thousand dollars. Cash. A Studebaker that don't run. Cash money, for that! And it ain't in any bank account you'll ever see. You'll never see the money she makes from her business, either. She runs a business on the side. She don't tell you that, does she? She makes hundreds—thousands, I bet—selling antiques and sewing up blankets from shitty scraps and sewing a bunch of bullshit in with it, telling people how they're family heirlooms, antiques made by her old grandma. Hell, her grandma's long dead and her own mother don't speak to her."

"Who is this? I won't listen to any more of this, this—"

"You have to. I'm a taxpayer."

"You're obscene." Emily gave a closed-mouth grimace to the social worker across from her, who looked up quizzically.

"I'll tell you something else, you goofy college girl, Joyce Jackson won that Memory Jackpot last weekend."

"No, that was—" Emily checked herself.

"That's what they want you to think! Jesus! You really are just as goofy as they say! But you can add, can't you, college girl? Figure it. Two thousand from the car. Twenty-seven hundred from the Memory Jackpot and who knows how much for the quilts and the shit she sells for antiqued. She has antique sales all the time. Sells trash for antiques, for lots of money. Add it up. You add it up. Add it up."

The phone clicked in her ear. Emily chatted into the buzz cheerfully. "Thank you for calling," she concluded, putting the phone down and looking for Howard, but he had vanished. She glanced over at Large Marge, whose massive forearms were flattened on her desk. Marge squinted with concentration over some papers, and Emily shuddered to see the tail of the mythical mouse twitch in her barn owl's lips. She took her purse from the drawer. "I'm going over to Juvie," she said to her co-worker, "to see about the *in extremis.*"

"Which one?"

"Oh, the fifteen-year-old girl who got shot at in bed by her boyfriend's wife."

A uniformed guard ushered Emily into a small conference room at Juvie with high ceilings, high barred windows, and acoustic-absorbent walls with little spitwads and pencil leads stuck in the holes of the soundproofing. Emily took a chair on one side of a graffiti-scarred desk. She fought the sensation that she was the one here against her will, the prisoner.

Suella Nesbitt shuffled in as only a hundred-and-fifty-pound, five-foot-two, fifteen-year-old girl can. She was dressed in a county-issue smock. She lowered her bulk into the other chair, sulked and splayed there as though fatigued beyond description. Her hair was a wiry mass, and she alternately stroked tenderly or yanked at it with her strong black hands. She was disappointed Emily didn't have a cigarette. She listened to Emily for a while, then she butted in and said they might as well cut the crap, that she loved Jet Macon and everything else was shit. She would always love Jet Macon, and nothing would change that. His wife could never come between them. Nothing could. Not even these prison walls. Not the law. Not death. "Dig?" demanded Suella.

"Hmmmm," said Emily, making notes.

Emily recognized here the general sentiments, lineaments, and content—if not form—of *Ballad of Reading Gaol*, as Suella raged on and on, (not sniveling in the least but) raging how love had made a prisoner of her and not these clammy, goddamned, sound-fucking-proof walls. "Love!" Suella screamed. "I am the prisoner of love! You heah me out there, you fuckin' guard? *Love* has made me a prisoner and *love* has made me a queen! Dig?" Emily suggested that perhaps Jet Macon might go back to his wife, that he might conceivably—not certainly, but could—have been taking advantage of Suella's youth and, well, inexperience, that perhaps all Jet wanted of Suella was the proverbial hump and thump (though Emily did not phrase it just like that). Suella scoffed. It would never come to that. Emily almost expected to hear Suella sing *Baby Baby Baby,* break into a Motown *Greensleeves.* Suella said she'd die for Jet and count herself a happy woman. She'd go to prison for him. She'd do anything for him. And if Jet went back to his wife, she'd kill him. First she'd kill the wife, then she'd kill Jet, commit murder—and anything else—in the exonerating name of love. Suella Nesbitt was full of burning love. Probably Macon's wife was too. Probably so was Macon. It burnt a hole in your life, love did.

Emily cleared her throat. "They're not going to let you out of Juvie if you keep talking about killing people for love. Don't you want to go back to school and have a normal life?"

Suella gave her a look of consummate triumph and pity. "Don't you know nuthin', Mizshaw?"

The blood drained from Emily's head, and she thought she might faint if she stayed in this gray, graffiti-smelling room, the grief here as palpable as rats' scratching. She hastened out of Juvenile Hall and walked swiftly across the wide, grassy expanse of the county complex, where the May wind ruffled the palms and shaggy-sad eucalyptus trees. The devil-grass lawn was already dry unto dusty, near brown in spite of the sprinklers. She sat down on a picnic bench, also graffiti-scarred, between two palms and started to cry, sob audibly, mascara streaking her cheeks. What had she done—or left undone—that Suella Nesbitt should have such contempt for her? Or that low, hideous anonymous caller who'd said she was goofy? What good was it to be a USC Tri Delt when a fifteen-year-old juvenile delinquent thought you were a twit? When a man who'd brought you to life—first on the dance floor and then in bed—when he thought you were a liar and a fool? When the man you'd pledged your life and love to would rather study law than spend summer weekends licking Jell-O out of your belly button? A dreary, rag-ridden procession of accusations stirred, scuffled, roused from the encampments of her mind, marched forward like an army of beggars, and now she had to go make the phone call that could well prove them all correct.

She walked past County Hospital's gleaming emergency entrance, landscaped for efficiency, which is to say not landscaped at all but a wide circular cement drive in front of bottle green glass walls and tidy tall palms standing like sentinels. She avoided all that and walked round to the oldest wing, where there was no smooth cement but uneven paving stones and a totally useless fountain. The entrance was arched in the style of the twenties. Dead leaves curled on the steps.

Emily pushed open the door and went in. This seldom-used waiting room was dim. A few naked overhead bulbs shone on a dozen mustard-colored chairs lined up back to back. A single geriatric

Candy Striper sat there, listlessly turning the pages of an old *Life* magazine. Even the phone booth had a droopy, derelict air, the old-fashioned kind with creaking doors and a halo of fluorescent light overhead. The phone books were all four years out of date, but no matter, KLMO's number was still the same. Emily asked the name of the individual who had won last Saturday's Memory Jackpot, the one with Elvis Presley's GI serial number. A man with a deep, unrealistic voice told her: Mrs. Joyce Jackson.

After work that Friday, Emily drove right past the off ramp for the Raintree Apartments. She was halfway to San Diego before she quite realized the distance she'd come. She took a westerly cutoff, a meandering route she'd never even known existed, though she'd lived in Southern California all her life. Eventually she showed up in Laguna Beach at her parents' home. They had just finished cocktails and were going in to dinner. They were surprised to see Emily, but set another place and said she should join them and the Turlocks and the Shines, their guests that evening.

Emily endured dinner, but only just, revolted throughout not simply by her parents' usual sniping, their cheerfully brutal way of reminding one another of their shortcomings, but by the Turdlocks and the Swines, who seemed to think it all quite clever, and indeed, they too had witty ways of dealing dirty with one another. Raking up the embers of old quarrels and fanning the flames of still-smoking remembered wrongs, that was as close as these people would ever get to *Burning Love*. Any of them.

Emily excused herself before dessert, got back in her car, and drove to the mall, where she went directly into the huge emporium of Tower Records. Here, without checking prices, without looking to see if songs were duplicated, she collected one of every Elvis album on the shelves; it was by no means the whole of his twenty-three-year singing career, in which he had recorded 65 albums and 105 singles, but she took what she could find: gospel, country, Christmas, early rock classics, forgettable tunes from the mid-seventies, half-a-dozen albums with movie music and the slick packaged hits of the early sixties, music from the 1968 comeback special on TV and the great Memphis and Nashville recordings that followed, the powerful performance at Madison Square Garden in 1972 and the *Aloha* special televised all over the world from Honolulu in 1973.

The blond young man checking her out at the cash register blanched at the total cost. "Elvis fan, are you?"

"I'm a convert," she replied, snapping down her credit card.

She returned to her parents' home, avoided them and their guests, went into her bedroom, where she played the records, one after another, over and over on the small stereo. At two, her mother knocked on her door, glanced at the paper, cellophane, and albums all over the floor. "Did you just buy these tonight, Emily?"

"Yes."

"All Elvis?"

"Yes."

"I never thought you cared much for Elvis."

"I never did." Emily met her mother's concerned gaze. "I have a lot to learn."

Saturday morning Emily called a fellow Tri Delt, Jennifer Prendergast (USC, class of '80), who lived in Newport, and agreed to meet her at the movies, *Chariots of Fire,* but Emily left long before that, drove to the beach, and walked alongside the crashing surf. Minimally she expected Gothic release, but it was May and the beach was not windswept, rock-strewn, or empty. Such breeze as there was teased dogs chasing Frisbees, and the beach was dotted with preening young women and flexing young men and ghetto blasters warbling out *Ebony and Ivory.*

After the movie, Emily and Jennifer went to La Hacienda. Jennifer chain-smoked and talked endlessly about how she planned to get the guy she was living with to marry her, the tactics she'd already tried and those yet remaining. Emily envied Jennifer her troubles, her arsenal of solutions. Jennifer was fortunate not to wrestle with questions of fraud and anonymity, with burning love and one-night stands, with crushing disappointment in the man she loved and guilt at having lied to a man she found profoundly attractive. At least no one had ever said that Jennifer was so goofy that she could be duped into believing that a blanket sewn of shitty scraps was an antique quilt. "False as the flavor in a frozen burrito," said Emily, pushing her plate aside.

"What?" Jennifer thought Emily was behaving very strangely. Perhaps celibacy had affected her brain. "Hey, how's Rick?"

Emily made a great show of playing with her engagement ring and waxing on about Rick, without quite adding that he wasn't coming home for the summer after all.

Jennifer bit a chunk of her taco and scraped the last of the shredded lettuce between her lips. "I was afraid maybe you'd fallen in love with someone else."

"In St. Elmo! That sink of poverty? That LMC sewer of desolation and despair?" Emily gave a ringing, hearty, Heathcliffian laugh. "Surely you jest, Jennifer! Don't you remember? I'm a Tri Delt, like you! I went to USC! I'm engaged to a Georgetown University law student! Could I really go to a smog-ridden desert dump like that and find someone to *love,* Jennifer! In that burg? The Armpit of the Nation! Me? Could I do that?" Emily folded her arms and demanded, "Does the eagle know what is in the pit?"

"I don't know," said Jennifer, who had been a business major. "Does he?"

On Monday morning Emily dressed in a particularly high-collared, up-buttoned, upright-unto-uptight Laura Ashley blouse and a brisk cotton skirt; she put on white stockings and high-heeled pumps, knowing somehow intuitively she would need the heels for stature, maybe even for weapons. She told herself this was silly, and with a great show of Monday briskness she walked into the welfare department, and almost immediately both her bravado and her high heels wavered because at 8:05 Juvenile Hall called and demanded she come to an afternoon conference regarding the fate of Suella Nesbitt. And midmorning, reception called Emily. The lady out front said there was someone waiting for her. "He won't give a name."

"He?" said Emily, mouth dry, swallowing hard. She wiped her hands on her skirt. She knew who was out there. Joyce's accuser. As she walked through the sea of desks and ringing phones, Emily tried to imagine how she might best handle this. The brave man dies a thousand deaths. How would Emily Brontë do it? Daphne Du Maurier? Shakespeare? Yes. That was the model. Shakespeare: to stride into the reception area, regardless of the ensemble of sulking, hulking, supplicating humanity clustered there, to meet the accuser face-to-face. But when she got to reception, there was no one there for her.

The ladies manning the reception desk grinned and pointed in a conspiratorial fashion to a florist's massive colorful bouquet, freesias and carnations, ferns and daisies. The ladies laughed and gushed that they hadn't told her because they thought it would be such a happy surprise!

"Thank you." Emily opened the diminutive card:

Love, Rick

She glanced at the sulking, hulking, supplicating humanity clustered, cluttering the waiting room. She met the happy eyes of the receptionists. She put the card back in the envelope and tried to smile. Indeed, she had no choice: she must smile. She must be joyed-over to receive flowers. Women always are. You have to downright gush, don't you? Emily must blush and flush and be so very pleased because for a man to send you flowers means he loves you, can't live without you; it means you're *Gentle on My Mind, I've Got You under My Skin, Bewitched, Bothered and Bewildered, It Had to Be You, Younger than Springtime, Our Love Is Here to Stay, You're the Top, Lovely to Look At, No Other Love.* It was a public avowal of *Burning Love.* Delivered here at the office, it was a public performance. Convention dictated that Emily must play her public part: walk back through the doors and collect the attention of all her co-workers, accept everyone's smiles, the young secretaries, who would think Emily's fiancé was just so sweet and thoughtful, the older women, who would know the bastard was apologizing for something. In carrying this bouquet across the welfare department, Emily was publicly forgiving him. This evening she would have to call and thank him and he would (metaphorically) nibble on her ear through the phone and be just so sweet and thoughtful. That was the way it would happen; it had all been staged. She bent her head to sniff the bouquet and came up light-headed, slightly nauseated, to see a sort of holographic Rick, Winning Team Smile and all, on bended knee, declaring *Burning Love,* dressed in a white spangled bodysuit, a parody of Elvis, of Elvis's expression of passion and anguish and Elvis's posture, at once humble and dramatic. One of the receptionists stepped round the desk to open the door for Emily, since she had her hands full. Emily gasped as the holographic Rick shimmered and the spangles on his suit caught the light; he jumped, spun forward. Carrying the floral chalice of his love in her arms, Emily must follow him into the huge, echoing, rock-and-rolling emporium of what had once been mere phones and paper-pushing bureaucrats. The entire office all seemed to jump up on top of their desks, providing Rick with a triumphant choir, *doo-waa-doo, ooh-waaooh,* a perfectly pitched, soprano-wailing, bass-bounding gospel group that harmonized perfectly. They danced and sang as Rick made his way down the center aisle and his music ascended the high-vaulted room and rained back down on all of them. Emily, bearing her floral tribute, followed Rick's cute little bottom, twitching away in his spangled white sequined suit, while, with harmony and percussion, a chorus line of welfare workers wailed *shoo-shoo-shoo-bee-doo-wah-wah.* Rick sang, thump-bump-and-grinding out sheer hot desire with his body; his face twisted with anguish, passion, and the pain of love he could not deny nor dismiss. And Emily must rock and roll too—right down the center aisle following his lead, showing off her flowers and showing too, to all her coworkers, the pleasure they gave her, the triumph, excitement, expectation, desire, anticipation, jubilation, liberation, those emotions that only *Burning Love* could bestow on you. When they had nearly reached Emily's desk, Rick got down, got dirty, got gritty, groaned, panted, hummed hard, sang, his voice at once sweet and searing. He was going to ignite, scorch, flame up and die right here in front of her and he couldn't stop himself. *Burning Love.* That's what it does to you.

"Nice flowers, Emily," said Marge.

Emily tried to say, *I think they need water,* but the words would not eke past the tight, closed-lipped smile she had perfected in her brace-ridden adolescence. She excused herself wordlessly and went to the women's bathroom, where she crammed the flowers down the little silver maw of the trash can. She tore Rick's card in shreds and dropped it in the toilet, and, since she was there, she peed.

She was just coming out of the stall to wash her hands when Large Marge walked into the bathroom. "I hear you have an *in extremis,* some fifteen-year-old girl hanging out in whorehouse hotels with a married man and getting shot at by his wife."

"Oh. Yes. Well. Suella. Suella Nesbitt. Suella Nesbitt is in the grip of something we don't altogether understand."

"What? What!"

"I meant, yes. Imagine that."

"Imagine, Emily? What's to imagine? Disgusting!" Marge gave Emily a look of infinite distrust.

At quarter to twelve, Emily's worst fears came to pass and the phone rang again. For her. The low, anonymous voice coiled around her ear. "Did you do it?"

"Who is this?" Emily demanded.

"You know I'm doing the county and the state a favor. You better get to it, you goofy college girl. You better get to thumping and go get Joyce Jackson for fraud."

"Fuck off," said Emily very politely. "And take your father with you. If you have one." She put the phone down and grinned ineffectually at the shocked co-workers all around her. "My lawyer," she smiled. "That was my lawyer."

They all agreed this was understandable, and satisfied, they returned to their forms.

Emily waited till nearly lunchtime, when the office thinned out, and then, knowing exactly what she had to do, she dialed another county extension.

"Disability Adjustment."

"Could I please speak to Mr. Johnson? Mr. Sid Johnson." She waited a few moments till there came on the phone a deep, rich baritone voice. She identified herself as the individual who had taken over his caseload. "Mr. Johnson, I must talk with you. It's about Joyce Jackson."

There was a short silence. "Everything I know is in the file."

"I've read the file. That's why I'm calling you. You're the only one who asked questions. All the rest of them, well, you're the only one who seemed to, who tried to—"

"Take it up with Marge."

"You know very well I can't."

"Take it up with Howard Hansen. He's a decent human being."

Emily gulped. "I can't do that. I need to talk to you. Joyce is in trouble."

"Joyce Jackson has been in trouble since the day she first drew breath. I can't help her."

"But you can help *me,*" Emily pleaded. "Please. Please." She thought she heard him wad up paper angrily. "Can I meet you for lunch? Zacateca's?"

"Are you from St. Elmo, Emily?"

"No, I'm from Laguna Beach."

He snorted and asked her how she knew about Zacateca's, and of course she couldn't tell him. "We can't meet there anyway." Sid Johnson sounded tired. "Too many people. But down the street from there and round the corner there's a little Vietnamese place. Saigon. I'll meet you at the Saigon."

Fifteen

The Phans clung to the Saigon restaurant as they had clung to helicopters rising, like noisy angels, into the smoke and burning sky of the city of Saigon in 1975. Here, in St. Elmo, those few Phans who spoke English ran the cash register and did the books while the rest of them cooked, bused, cleaned, waited tables, or simply squatted, smoking, in the narrow alley out back of the restaurant. The menu had been enumerated so the customer need only point to #12 or #34 for the order to be taken. When there was the occasional mix-up, the food was, by St. Elmo standards, so weird that almost no one noticed. And even if they did, their complaints were met with smiling, polite incomprehension.

Emily was greeted by a tiny woman who could say *please, thank you,* and *this way,* which she said over and over, indicating that Emily should follow her, never mind that Emily tried to indicate she was waiting for someone. The woman might have vanished into the wilds of the Saigon altogether except that an enormous black man entered the narrow foyer. He wore a sport coat, dark tie, and blue shirt. His hair was grizzled white on the sides and he had the gaze of a man who misses nothing—who might elect to remain silent, but who sees everything. Emily found him unnerving from the start and not at all the sort of sympathetic figure she had hoped for.

The Saigon was small, with cold tables lining a streetside window and a few booths at the back. Mr. Johnson indicated they would like a booth and the tiny woman obliged. A smiling waiter brought them a menu and Mr. Johnson ordered, "Cā phē phin súa dá." Then he pointed to #47. "You want a Saigon coffee?" he asked Emily. She nodded. He held up two fingers for the waiter "You're even younger than I'd thought," he said by way of greeting.

Emily fumbled, words to the effect that she could not help how old she was as she hadn't any choice in the matter, not very much choice, anyway.

The waitress brought them ice water and Mr. Johnson downed his in one gulp. The Saigon was not air-conditioned, and somewhere nearby a swamp cooler slurped noisily and from the kitchen came the hiss of steam; cookware clanged with foreign language.

Emily began earnestly with the fact that she had got an anonymous phone call accusing Joyce Jackson of—

Mr. Johnson held up one hand and shook his head. "I'm not sure I want to hear this. I shouldn't have come."

Emily, using a good many more words than ordinarily would be necessary, tried to describe how his questions, the ones in Joyce's case file, had moved her, but with his silence she retreated into bravado, waxing on in general terms and concluding rather grandly that she— for one—did not believe that ignorance was bliss.

Mr. Johnson scoffed out loud. "Ignorance is ignorance. But everyone in this world—red and yellow, black and blue—they all got one thing in common and it's this: They all wants to plow themselves a neat little furrow. Down they go into that furrow. They burrow down just deep enough so they can't see over the sides and then they say—*Hallelujah! We safe! In here, we know we safe! As long as we don't see outside this here particular furrow, we be the safest and the most correct people on earth!*" He had a deep rolling voice, emphatic as a cello. He never took his eyes off her. "Now—most folks—they manage to do all this, get all burrowed and furrowed up, everything comfy so they don't have to ask no more questions, nor answer questions from anyone who might think different from them—they do all this by the time they're twenty-four. How old are you, Emily?"

"Twenty-three."

The waiter poised his pencil for their order. Emily admitted to total ignorance of Vietnamese food and asked Mr. Johnson to order for her. She said she wasn't very hungry. He asked for gói súa tōm thit (#6), chá dúm (#23), and rau cái xāo gā bō hoāc heo (#39) and more water. The waiter brought their Saigon coffees and she watched Mr. Johnson deal with his, pour it properly over the ice, and she followed suit. The coffee was an altogether new experience, sweeter, certainly pleasanter than the company. She wondered if she had completely misread the file, misheard Penny Pitzer, misunderstood Joyce, Cilla, and her many other clients who so admired Mr. Johnson. This man was as humorless as a dictionary.

She cleared her throat and took the uncomplicated path of flattery. "I wanted to ask your advice because everyone says you are the best social worker and there's nothing you don't know about this county."

"I grew up here. I know these people. I hate this town just the way they hate it. I love it just the way they love it. I got one cousin on the Board of Education, one on the mayor's City Transit Committee, and one serving time at the county work farm out in Chagrin for dealing drugs. My people have been barbers and beauticians, bootblacks and bootleggers in St. Elmo County since there was a St. Elmo County. My great-grandma, Nana Bowers, she came to this town the slave of Madison Whickham."

Emily's face reflected ignorance without bliss.

"The Mormon scout who gets all the credit for founding this town. But it was my people who did all the work, my people and Madison's women. Madison took off and the rest of the Mormon men went on missions. Converting the heathen was easier than living in St. Elmo."

The waitress brought their #6, which she announced in its Vietnamese name, but Mr. Johnson said it was jellyfish salad. Emily nearly inquired after the effects of jellyfish on the human intestines, but Mr. Johnson dug in, so she warily tried hers too.

"My great-grandmother had fifteen children, and she named the youngest, my grandfather, she named him Grief. And when everyone says to her, *What you wanna name your boy Grief for?* she says she done run out of everything else. So, when you come from a family where they run out of everything except grief, you got some notion of what it's like to live on the bottom of the cage. And when you've flown up, out of that cage, gone to college, gone to Chicago, seen the lakefront from your living room window, when you've done all that and come back to St. Elmo, then you got some notion of learned humility. That's all you need to be a social worker—or a decent human being."

Emily imagined Learned Humility as an elective under philosophy: Humility 203: Practical Aspects for the Social Worker, taught by someone who looked like Saint Francis of Assisi. Or Suella Nesbitt for that matter. Emily flushed to imagine her Tri Delt sisters' judgment, what they would say if gossip ever reached them regarding Emily's involvement with a bunch of Elvis fanatics who lived on welfare and passed off antique quilts. Humility 203 indeed. Worse, think how the Tri Delts would snicker to know she'd been drunkenly bedded by an ex-musician-turned-social worker. Think of that episode. Emily flushed; the Tri Delts had a cheery phrase, The Old Fuck and Run.

"Fuhrck?" asked the waitress.

"Excuse me!"

"Do you want a fork or chopsticks?" Mr. Johnson translated, as the waitress set before them #23, #39, and their rice.

Emily opted for chopsticks and regretted it instantly as they seemed like flamingo legs, still attached to the flamingos. In one of the dishes, Emily recognized red chili peppers and green onions, as well as stranger things, flesh-colored cubes swimming in dark sauce. Sid's chopsticks clicked crisply. He was clearly hungry. So this seemed like a good time to dive into her account of the phone call, the accusations of fraud. Sid took some more chā dúm and rice and asked how much money was under discussion.

"Lots. Add it up," she said, repeating the baleful instructions. "Thousands of dollars. He said she'd sold a car for two thousand dollars."

Sid nodded, kept on eating. "I noticed the Starlight Coupe was gone when I drove by."

With difficulty and her chopsticks poised, Emily got on through the accusations of Joyce's trafficking in antiques and antique quilts, without saying that she herself was the possessor, the dupe, of such a quilt. (And what was that but a lesson in Humility 203?) "And then, a week ago, more than that, the Saturday night before last"—*O Burning Love*—"Joyce won twenty-seven hundred dollars on a radio station's Memory Jackpot. That much I know is true. I checked it."

He motioned the waitress for another coffee. "What was the question?"

"Elvis Presley's GI number."

"Jesus! Elvis! Of course!" He dropped his chopsticks and mopped his face with a napkin. He sighed and suddenly looked all of his fifty-one years. "You know, Emily, the very first—I mean the first!—Home Visitation I made when I started with the county, you know who it was? Why—Mrs. Joyce Jackson! I drive up to that house and I see those black ribbons blowing from the trees and the satin streamers blowing from the framed portrait, I see the hand-lettered signs— SACRED TO THE MEMORY OF ELVIS—and I knew, right then, I would never be rid of that man." Sid took a drink of ice water. "I may never be rid of him. Why would I be here if I were through with him?"

Emily, of course, had no answer for this, but she did remark that it must have been nice for Joyce that Mr. Johnson was such an Elvis fan.

Mr. Johnson shook his head. "I wasn't a fan."

"A convert?"

"In a manner of speaking, I guess. That concert I went to six years ago was certainly a turning point in my life."

"Let's see." Emily bit her lower lip in concentration. "That would have been 1976. He would have still been alive."

Sid studied Emily compassionately, flatly amazed by her mathematical prowess. "Well yes, Elvis was alive, but just barely. He had a concert in Chicago the week of my wife's birthday and that's what she wanted for her present. I couldn't believe it. I said to her—You're on the board of the Chicago Symphony! Why go see Elvis? *It's my birth-*

day. I want to go see Elvis. I say—Let's go see Aretha! Let's go see Ray Charles! Stevie Wonder! Why should we pay good money to go see some hip-swiveling—" He paused and passed over the obvious *honkie* and went on. "My wife says: *I want to go to the Elvis concert for my birthday.* I say: No Elvis for this bro. There was rock and roll before there was Elvis Presley. But my wife says: *Wrong, Sid, before Elvis there was black music and there was white music and when they come together, then you got rock and roll and not before.* And then she starts singing that old Willie Mae Thornton tune, *Hound Dog.* She goes all around the house for the next three days singing nothing but Elvis, till finally my son begs me—Take her to see Elvis, Dad, I beg of you. We all beg of you. You don't do this, Dad, and we are all gonna pay."

"Yours was not to reason why," offered Emily, tumbling up her Tennyson. "Yours was but to do or die?"

"And I almost did. We go there, us and a hundred thousand others, black and white, mostly white, mothers hauling their adult daughters, daughters hauling their kids, kids hauling their boyfriends. Houselights go down, stage lights come up on a whole philharmonic of an orchestra, bleachers full of gospel girls. The backup band, the orchestra, the choir, they rev everyone up a bit and out comes Elvis. All gold chains"—Sid gestured over his own expansive frame—"brass studs, white leather, high collar and cape, fringe flying, sequins catching the light, blinding everyone in a hundred-mile radius. He's got some flunky up there just to hand him scarves to wipe off his sweat, and then he gives them away like pieces of the True Cross. And he was fat. Fat! The kind of middle-aged fat man girls like you call—well—" Sid snorted and returned to his chopsticks.

"All butt and gut?" suggested Emily. Sid nodded and dug into his rau cái xāo gā bō hoāc heo, #39. Emily added politely, "Well, at least you can say you saw Elvis. Joyce has never even seen him. She's never ever—"

"Oh, you're wrong, Emily! Joyce sees Elvis all the time! Elvis spends more time with Joyce than he does with Jimi Hendrix! Elvis, he spends more time on Santiago Street than he does in the heavenly choir! Don't underestimate Joyce Jackson. She sees Elvis all the time.

But she don't see what I saw. Joyce will never see what I saw. Elvis was so drugged that he starts to talk and all he could do is slurp, stumble, slip up. He had a stutter even when he was straight, so you can imagine what he was like drugged to the gills. He's up there spluttering on, getting all misty and modest, telling us, like we're supposed to weep or cheer, I don't know which, that he couldn't play but three chords on the guitar. His face was puffy and bloated and he was sweating like a pig under those lights. He'd been poured into his clothes. Or maybe they'd been painted on, but you could hear the seams groan. He was drugged and exhausted, his eyes were like little slits in all that fat, and he looked like he hadn't slept in months. And still he was going to get up and sing himself to death for two hours. And the next day he was going to do the same thing in Duluth, and the day after that in Minneapolis, and so on. The last seven years of his life he did that—dressed up, stood under those lights, and sang his guts out for a million people—every two and a half days. He gave a thousand concerts in seven years. He couldn't talk. He sure as hell couldn't dance. He could hardly stand, but by God, Emily, the man could sing! All I could think of was Billie." Sid took more rice. "Billie Holiday. Same damn thing. Ego. Music. Hunger. Drugs. Why, drugs are nothing but torch to a tumbleweed for people like that. If you don't have that kind of hunger and ego-need yourself, then it's too easy to condemn them. Maybe the talent, the hunger, the drive, and the drugs all go together."

Maybe not. Emily excavated through her thick dark sauce, thinking of Howard Hansen and why he had not become a musician. Talent did not guarantee that you could live like that. Or die like that. People who want that, who are capable of it, do not become social workers with Howard's conviction and compassion. She understood, suddenly, the source of Howard's strength, his success as a human being. Never mind a lover.

Emily colored slightly. "Go on with the story. You were going to tell me how it was you knew you'd never be done with Elvis."

Sid laid down his chopsticks like Lee's sword. "All right, Emily, I will. Elvis couldn't talk, but he could sing—and when he sang, some spirit jumped up out of that wreck of a body and graced even those songs that were—well, some of them were just a bunch of Elmer's glue passing for music." Sid's face twisted with derision. "That kind of spineless sentimental crap Frank Sinatra sings."

Of Frank Sinatra, Emily knew nothing save that her father shared his political views, but she tried to look as though she would recognize spineless sentimental crap if she met it on the street.

"Huff and puff and pant. All smoke. No fire. *Unchained Melody?* Elvis couldn't even catch his breath in between beats. *Memories?* Ugh. *My Way?*" Sid downed half a glass of water as if to wash the very taste of those titles from his lips. "You want another Saigon coffee?" Emily nodded and he motioned to the waitress. "So I'm sitting in the audience, thinking that whole damn concert is going to be Muzak, and then he starts on *The Impossible Dream.* I am really bored by now. And *Impossible Dream* is just another hack show tune."

"What song is that?"

"Oh, you remember—" Inexpertly Sid hummed a few bars and threw in a handful of lyric, and Emily did remember. "And then, Emily, the next thing I know I'm crying. Elvis comes all the way up to those brave notes, and he hits the sad ones like they have to be wrung from his guts, drained right out of his wrists—and there I am, blubbering. I look around and my wife is crying. The woman next to me is crying, behind me—everyone is crying their eyes out, their faces all streaked with tears—and hope. Elvis unleashed that song, Emily, unleashed *The Impossible Dream,* so that you remembered it was Robert Kennedy's favorite song and you remembered the courage of everyone you ever admired, the living and the dead, from Martin Luther King, Jr., to my old grandmother. And as if that wasn't enough, Elvis goes on to *Dixie* and *Battle Hymn of the Republic.* I mean, Emily, we are dealing here with old war-horses of songs, songs that have been beat to death and yet live. Can these songs live? Can these old, spavined pack mules of songs live while they're carrying the freight, the weight, of the history of this country? All that cheerful damn democracy stained everywhere with slavery and injustice? Elvis made these songs live, Emily. We all felt it. We're all crying and clapping, and next thing I know we've all jumped up and reached out, holding hands with those beside us. We're singing, shouting! Crying out!" Sid drew a deep breath. "It was just like church."

It was not like any church Emily had been in, but she did not say so.

"Elvis finishes with *All My Trials, Lord*. He brings up all that sweetness, sadness, the hope and resignation, plumbs it right out of the music. Song's over and we're all crazy with clapping and *he* thanks us—real polite, he thanks us. Then he says he wants the houselights up so he can see the audience, now we've seen him. Houselights come up and Elvis looks us over. He takes time looking us over, like he wants to remember us, every one. And then we got to look each other over. Black and white, young and old, all our faces streaked with tears and we are all clutching wet hankies. And it was like family, Emily, making its peace for that moment. Maybe just for that moment—but it was peace." Sid sipped his coffee reflectively. "And then I looked back at him, no spotlight this time, just the, well, you might say the democratic houselights. And he had shrunk. I saw it. He did not stoop or falter, but he stood there before us, pale and puffed and fat and shrunk and stoned. And human." Sid toyed with his chopsticks. "A prisoner. I knew it then, just as surely as I'm sitting here now. Elvis was a prisoner. He was the prisoner of everything he'd created."

Emily thought of Suella Nesbitt, at that very moment sitting on the single cot in her narrow room at Juvie, the high barred window, sunlight slanting in on her, illuminating at sharp right angles the graffiti-stained wall, a girl awaiting the county's disposition of her immediate life: the prisoner of love. Was it possible that passion—whether of love or music—that passion, which offered the most freedom, might equally be the very thing that could constrain and finally imprison? As easily imprison as liberate? That perhaps the liberty *was* the prison? The possibility struck Emily with the sensation of a chili pepper unwittingly swallowed, which is what she'd done. She coughed and choked and swilled ice water, and in the course of all this she missed Sid's next sentence. Still spluttering, she asked if he really had said that the day after Elvis's concert he had had a heart attack and almost died.

"October 16, 1976. It was me or someone like me. It was a man who was forty-six years old, who had worked hard and got everything he'd ever dreamed of, everything that the grandson of a man named Grief could have wanted. My wife's face was blurring in and out, my son and daughters, blurring in and out, and there were paramedics rattling gurneys around me and oxygen tanks and tubes going up my nose and in my arms and a lot of plastic masks and cold steel. Cold steel." Sid shuddered and pushed his empty plate away. "And that was when I learned my humility, Emily. I'm lying there and I think: You asshole, Johnson. You're no better than Elvis. You feel sorry for him because he's a drugged-up prisoner of his own creation. And what are you, you asshole?"

"A prisoner?"

"Everything I'd created brought me to that moment, Emily. I was going to die for Cornibbles. You remember Cornibbles, Emily?"

"I'm a Cheerios girl myself."

"No one remembers Cornibbles. They never got on the grocery shelves. I fought my enemies tooth and nibble, but they prevailed and Cornibbles got aborted and Wheatnix lived on."

"I have heard of Wheatnix," she admitted.

"Just before I went out, or under, or wherever it is you go, I thought—*Goddamnit! I want my money back! I'm going to the ticket booth and I want my money back! I want a new movie! I don't like the end of this movie! I want a new one!*"

Emily imagined the old St. Elmo Dream Theater as Joyce had described it. The garish silver wave of a ticket booth and the ticket taker with a sort of harsh, Edward Hopperish light overhead. She imagined herself going in and watching *The Life of Emily Shaw* and coming to those scenes where the lovely heroine was living in a dog-dirt desert town, stupidly, tearfully accepting an antique quilt from a welfare mother who should have been accepting Emily's charity, going to the Cask and Cleaver with a bunch of LMC types and making *Burning Love* in a one-night stand with a man who should have known better, sitting here with a black guy old enough to be her father, in a Vietnamese restaurant eating God-knows-what. She saw herself angrily stomping up the aisle of the Dream Theater and out to the ticket booth and demanding her money back or a new feature, *The Life of Emily Shaw,* where she would do charitable works with other Laguna Beach matrons, underemployed like herself. "It must be the food," she said weakly, pushing her plate away. She took a sip of ice water and a deep breath.

"I knew I was about to die and I promised God anything, if only He would spare me, but all I could see or hear was my old granny sitting in her chair thirty years before, and me telling her I was going to play basketball. She says to me, *Sid, basketball is a white boys' game at St. Elmo High. You plays football, honey. They 'lows colored boys to play football.* And I say, No *ma'am. I don't care what they 'lows us to do, I'm playing basketball.* And she says: *Well, you young, Sid, and I guess you gonna do it, but you oughta know, it gonna cost you. Plenty'.* And me—I just laughed. I say to her: *What's it gonna cost me, granny? The world changin', Granny! This is 1946, Granny!"* Sid wiped his face with his napkin. "She just lit up her cheroot and she never did answer my question, not till I'm lying there in the checkout line, Emily, and they're jumping and thumping and pumping me back to life. Granny answered me then, but not before, because before that, well, I figured, hell, if I could play the white boys' game at SEHS, why, I could play scholarship ball at UCLA! Why not? I could major in econ and date the only black music major at UCLA and the most beautiful girl in the whole school—the world. Why not? I could get that girl to marry me! And if I could do that, why, hell—I could play the white man's game at Capital Foods in Chicago. I could get to be the first black vice-president of marketing at Capital Foods, have three secretaries, keep them all busy, set my wife up doing charity—and not taking it—see my children in private schools and, hell—if I could do all that—why, sure as hell I could beat out those bastards who thought that Wheatnix was a better idea than Cornibbles! And it was that Cornibbles struggle brought me to where I was. I'm lying there dying, and my old granny, I hear her voice tell me at last what it was gonna cost me. She says, *Sid, honey, they gonna take that basketball right out of your backside. They gonna take it from your hide, honey, and dribble it right down de court and dump you in de basket.*"

Emily laughed so loud that everyone in the Saigon turned to look at them. Sid wiped his eyes. He said his wife hadn't thought it was all that funny.

"That's when I quit. Everything. I came back here to St. Elmo, the town I hated and couldn't wait to leave. I thought, Well, all right, I'll start at the bottom and with the bottom. At least people on welfare, if they have heart attacks, it's not over Cornibbles. They worry who's gonna pay the rent, who's gonna feed these children. Oh, I saw it all different after that. You get that close and you say: *Thank you, Mr. Death, thank you for freeing me.* And you say it humble, *Thank you for freeing me from my prison and still letting me keep my poor, puny human body.*" Sid finished his coffee. "My income dropped fifty thousand dollars. Overnight."

"Well, why aren't you working with those people, Sid? The people who want to pay the rent and feed their children? What are you doing in Disability Adjustment? That's a job for a pencil pusher!"

"I'm waiting out the storm."

"What storm?"

Sid leaned seriously across the table. "When Marge Mason catches Joyce Jackson, there's going to be a storm. You know that or you wouldn't be here. You can't protect her from Marge Mason. Believe me. I worked with Ole Massa Marge. I've seen what she does to people. I've seen how she enjoys it. Pleasure. It gives that woman pleasure. She likes to see people twist and flinch under the whip—and it doesn't matter if it's a welfare client, or a new social worker like you. Anyone. Listen, Emily, I had a client whose husband left her with four children under the age of seven. She fell in love with a good man and they wanted to get married, but who could afford a divorce? She was on welfare, and he was a cook at Denny's. But he moved in with her just the same, became a father to those children, a family. They're honest people. They come to me and they admit he's living in the home, contributing. I said fine, I'd just do some paperwork under what they called the MARS program."

"Man Assuming the Role of Spouse," said Emily, whose training classes had not been entirely lost on her.

"I figured out a revised budget and a revised grant, sent it to Marge for her signature. It should have gone through like a pin through a peephole." Sid shook his head. "She spent days on it. Undid everything I'd set up, refigured his income—which was chickenshit—at a much higher figure, figured in the food he ate at work and the rent he saved now he was living with her. She pared those people right down to their bones. And a while later, after the man left my client, she came back in and I did another revised grant, no man in the house. I sent it to Marge and she signed it without so much as a word."

"She's a barn owl."

"Well, it was bad from the beginning, but as I went on, me and old Massa Marge, we were locked in a real Cornibbles-and-Wheatnix duel to the death. But the stakes were higher here. I went to Howard Hansen and he says I'm not telling him anything he doesn't already know, but on his own, even Howard can't budge Marge. She's been here a hundred years and she's protected by the institution. Institutions always keep their hands protectively over their assholes. Assholes like Marge. I said, *Okay, but I ain't picking that woman's cotton. No more. I'm not her private foot soldier. I want out of this war.* And I was out. Till you called."

"I know Marge hates everyone, but she seems to hate Joyce more."

"Don't you be getting in between those two. Joyce—well, it was just a matter of time before someone turned her in. I always knew it. Right here." Sid thumped himself in the chest. "I couldn't save Joyce. You can't save her. If you try, Marge will just get you too."

Emily winced to think of her own tail twitching in that indifferent barn owl's beak.

"This is your first job, isn't it?"

"I only just graduated from college last June."

"They should never have given my caseload to someone as young as you. Someone older and more experienced should have got it."

Emily imagined her geriatric self limping in to the welfare department with bursitis and wattles on her neck, carrying a thermos full of Geritol and wearing Birkenstocks and support hose. Too too terrible. She raised her eyes to Sid's. "Do you think Joyce is dishonest?"

"What does it matter what I think? You got to listen to me, girl! Marge, she looks like a missionary, but she's one of those missionaries puts the cannibal in the pot! And she ain't even hungry! You stay clear of this."

"I meant the unreported income," Emily persisted. "Do you think that's dishonest?"

"Is it illegal? Is it immoral? Is it justified because she hands out clean clothes to people who live in dumpsters? To men and women who do drugs in the bathrooms of the city park? Because she leaves warm coats at schools where children don't have but a T-shirt between them and the wind? Is it justified because of the job she's doing with those girls— with Justin and Little Jack, for that matter? I tell you, Cilla and Lisa Marie are fine girls. That's a fine home. You won't find a home that good where you got daddies who are bankers and doctors and lawyers. Does that mean Joyce should be able to sell that Starlight Coupe for two thousand dollars, put the money in her cookie jar, and not tell you? I don't know, Emily! I got out of there so I wouldn't have to know."

Sid rose, picked up the check, and would not hear of Emily's paying for it. She scooted out of the booth, put on her dark glasses, and took one last swill of ice water to try to banish the intestinal discomfort, which might have resulted from the weird food, or the suspicion that she had a barn owl roosting on her head, or the conviction that the coming attractions of *The Life of Emily Shaw* were anything but attractive. There was, too, the notion of learned humility, which was just as foreign to a Tri Delt as the rau cái xào gà bō hoăc heo she'd just eaten.

Sid offered her a toothpick and held the door. They stepped into the street, where harsh white sunlight twinkled up off the asphalt and heat hunkered down everywhere. Emily was suddenly desperate, realizing she had not even asked the question she'd come with. "What'll I do, Sid?"

"Nothing. There's nothing you can do. There's nothing I can do either."

Emily opened her car door and the heat inside seemed to tumble out, thudding like a dead body at her feet.

Sid patted her shoulder. "I'll tell you this, Emily. Joyce Jackson is a remarkable woman. There isn't anyone like her. She's like one of those gospel pianos. They look just like any other old upright, till you put your hand to it, try to make music. And then, you know, that piano is in such fine tune, there's nothing you can't play on it. You can do *Chopsticks* on one of those old gospel uprights and it sounds like Chopin. Joyce is that kind of woman." He sucked his toothpick.

"You don't think she's a fruitcake, then?"

"Hell no!"

"Even if she has got Elvis all confused with Jesus?"

"Oh, girl! Joyce knows who Jesus is! Joyce knows who Elvis is! Joyce Jackson is absolutely clear what she's about. It's everyone else who's confused." Sid flipped his toothpick into the street and grinned at Emily. "Don't you mistake it. You let the rest of them call that house on Santiago Heartbreak Hotel if they want. That's not Heartbreak Hotel. That's Graceland."

Shake, Rattle and Roll

Sixteen

Mama's pinning this pattern to my underwear and she tells me to stand still, but I can't. Hey! When Elvis tells you to *Shake, Rattle and Roll,* that's what you do! Martian, Venusian, or American, you hear young Elvis rocking and you know you're listening to a man who's been set free, freed to do what God meant him to. You know what he's feeling, body and soul. It comes natural. He speaks, sings, to your body and soul too, not to mention your feet, your knees...

There's a knock at the back door. "Good thing too," I say, my arms straight out at my sides. "When I telephoned that pizza place, I told them they had to bring it round to the back. I told them our front porch is Sacred to the Memory of Elvis and we're not having it smell like pepperoni and mushroom."

Lisa puts down the Barbies and goes to get the pizza, but when she comes back in the living room, she's got this weird look, like maybe it was anchovy.

Right behind Lisa there's the new social worker, Emily Shaw, who we haven't seen since the night of the Memory Jackpot, when she shows up here, near to ruining everything. And who knows why? We never did figure it out. Mama said if Emily wanted to explain, she would of called or something. Sandee said Emily's probably still in the sack with the guy she was making out with right on the dance floor at the Cask and Cleavage.

Well, she's out of the sack now. She's wearing Liz Claiborne jeans and a Newport Beach sweatshirt and she's carrying an eelskin purse and a big brown grocery bag.

"Hello, Emily!" says Mama. "You're just in time. We got a pepperoni and mushroom pizza coming. You like pepperoni and mushroom?"

"I did not come for pizza. This is not a social call," Emily announces.

"Well, sit down anyway. I'm just pinning this pattern on Cilla—if she'd stand still—she grows so fast, by the time I get it fitted she'll be—" Mama looks at Emily up close. "You look terrible. What's the matter?"

Emily pushes the grocery bag at Mama. From the look on her face, whatever's in there, I know it's not pepperoni and mushroom.

"I know everything," Emily declares, just like the Pledge of Allegiance. "I know about the Studebaker and the Memory Jackpot and the antique quilts and the antique sales."

It's only the pins stuck all over my bod that keeps me from falling down right where I stand. *Money, Honey,* Elvis sings out, like he knows we're deep in it this time. I look over to Lisa, and her jaw's gone slack and she's pressing Brown Bunny up against her chest like someone's going to take it away, take it all away, nice house, nice clothes, break up the family, send Mama to jail for welfare fraud and me and Lisa to Juvie, then to separate foster homes like that girl I heard about in seventh grade who lived in a foster home where the man had bad breath and didn't shave and kept kissing her till she told her teacher she couldn't stand it. I get kind of sick. Really.

Money, Honey. Unreported Income. Mama goes to the stereo, turns Elvis off but it's worse when you stop a song in the middle, because it plays over and over in your head.

"I know everything," Emily says again. "But I came here tonight to warn you and to let you know that I'm not telling anyone. I've decided that. Whatever happens, it didn't come from me. I'm not a rat and I'm not as goofy as you think."

"No one thinks you're goofy."

"Someone does," Emily snarls. She looks at us the way the Colonel looks at his blanket just before he tears into it. "Anyway, that's all I came to say. I'm not telling. My supervisor can do what she wants to me. I'm not telling. That's my decision. But if someone does tell, you better be ready, Joyce. It'll be your too too sullied flesh on the grill. Marge Mason hates you. She's hated you from the beginning. At first I thought it was just she wasn't an Elvis fan, but it's not Elvis. It's you. Marge Mason has hated you since 1968."

"Mrs. Mason was the woman who—when I talked to her, when I first went to the county for welfare—That first time when Sandee—" Mama looks bewildered. "I haven't seen Mrs. Mason in years and years and—"

"She's seen you."

Emily goes on, Mama too, jawing, but me, I'm standing there, pins in my underwear, fighting down all the anchovies filling up my mouth. I know I'll have to swallow all those slimy little fish before I can say, "I didn't know we were on welfare when I was born. If we were on welfare in *1968* when I was born, Dad must not have been living with us. Where was Dad? Where was Dad before I was born?"

Mama gets pale, but she stands, walks slow, goes over to the stereo, turns over a stack of records, starts it up, and out comes *Love Me,* Elvis's awful pleading heartbreaker of a song. She picks up the needle and moves it to *Good Luck Charm,* but *Love Me* goes on slouching around the room like a ghost. "That was a long time ago. And—"

"*Where was Dad?* We wouldn't of been on welfare if he'd been living with us."

"Oh, Cilla—what does it matter?"

Lisa says, real quiet-like, "I thought Dad always lived with us till, well, till Dorrie, till he left to go—"

"Oh, you girls just floor me! What does it matter to you? Have you ever been cold or hungry or unloved? Haven't you always had a nice house and pretty clothes and people who loved you? What does it matter where Jack is—or where he was? What does it matter who paid for it?" She turns to Emily Shaw. "What does it matter who paid for it?"

"It will matter to Marge Mason," says Emily.

Mama starts folding laundry, snapping it like it's done her a personal wrong. "It's all lies," she says. "It's all just a bunch of bullshit lies."

"Your saying that doesn't make it unso, Joyce. I called KLMO."

Mama starts throwing clothes, folded or not, into the boxes. "Who was it told you all this? How do you know? Who said this?"

"A man. He called last Friday. I don't know. He wouldn't leave his name. Maybe he was just having a meanness fit. Maybe it will pass. Maybe he won't call my supervisor if I let it pass."

Mama runs her hands through her hair like she's going to snatch herself bald. "Well, Emily, I really don't know what to say."

"You could say you were sorry."

"What for?"

"For everything! For lying! For passing off that stupid antique quilt on me!" Emily says *antique quilt* like it was someone else's snot got caught in her mouth. Now I know what was in the grocery bag.

"Okay," says Mama quietly, pulling the quilt from the bag, giving it a hard look. "It wasn't a real antique. It was a real gift. My grandmother didn't make it. I made it. I wanted you to have it."

"You wanted to butter me up! Oh, you must have thought I was really goofy and lonely and naive. Here I was, the social worker, here I'm supposed to be helping you, and you're helping me!"

Mama laughs. "Oh, Emily, who gives a shit who's helping who? What do you think the county pays you for? Are they paying you to be touched, to be caring, to understand suffering like he understood it?" Mama points to Elvis, really just points anywhere. We got these Elvis pictures everywhere. "They don't pay you for that! They pay you to push papers and drive the county car and scold everyone who isn't living nice, tidy little eight-to-five lives with a mortgage and two cars, two bathrooms, two TVs, two weeks' vacation. Whatever help I give you, or you give me, it's got nothing to do with St. Elmo County, Emily. They pay you to come here and see how I keep house." She draws her finger across the table in one swoop. "They pay you to make sure I really, truly am a woman without a man in my life, or my home, or my bed. They pay you to use my bathroom and check the medicine cabinet for razors and shaving cream, they—"

"I never did that! I never looked for razors or—"

"Then why does every damn social worker have to pee?"

Emily can't answer that, so Lisa butts in and says, "Mr. Johnson never did that. Mr. Johnson never once used our bathroom."

Emily tosses her head. "That's because Sid Johnson knew all along. He guessed from the beginning. He knew you were cheating. Somehow, he knew. He quit Family Assistance because he knew Marge Mason was going to get you and he didn't want to be any part of it. And neither do I!"

"No one asked you to come here tonight, Emily. No one's asking you to lie."

"You lied! You lied to me! All of you. That night—here, there—at the Cask and Cleaver—and I was having such a wonderful time, and everyone was lying to me! No wonder you always said I was the social worker—so everyone would go on lying to me!" Emily's lower lip thrusts out and trembles.

Mama studies the quilt in her arms. "Emily, this quilt is like any other gift. You can give it away, but you can't give it back." She puts it squarely in Emily's arms. She says tenderly, "Let me do this for you."

"Oh, you've done plenty for me, Joyce! Oh, how can I thank thee? Let me count the ways! Thanks to you I've totally screwed up my first job, and when Marge Mason is through with me I'm going to look like one of those hideous old Italian paintings from the Middle Ages where the naked saint walks around with her eyes on a platter: *Canapes, anyone?* Thanks to you I've tasted That White Sustenance, Despair! I've drunk the whole bottle! I've eaten the cork! Howard won't speak to me because of all the awful things I've said—"

"Howard—was he the musician?"

"Musician!" Emily eyeballs us like we are a family of muggers and then informs us, that man—Howard—was not a musician, he didn't have that kind of hunger and ego and drive and need, but he had what it takes to be in charge of all social workers and supervisors in

Family Assistance. (Mama looks weird at this, sort of glassy and gassy at the same time.) Howard conducted Emily's training classes and told all new social workers it was Strongly Suggested not to get involved with clients, not to drink or go out dancing with them, but to keep them eight-to-five clients and not friends. "And who would want to be friends with a welfare client?" Emily demands. "Who would? Do you know why there aren't any TV shows about welfare workers? Do you?"

Well, we didn't, of course, and our faces must of showed it.

"Why are there all those cop shows on TV and not one about social workers? I'll tell you why! Because the poor people on cop shows, they're doing something about their situation! They're colorful and desperate! They're out there robbing banks or ripping off gas stations, forging checks, risking their lives to peddle drugs! That's who the cops get to deal with! Who does the social worker get to see? Day in, day out? Just a bunch of women who've screwed up their lives and don't know what to make of it, or where it all went wrong or how, except that they've been screwed, really screwed. They can't do diddly about it, so they sit around and watch soap operas and smoke cigarettes and wear their bedroom slippers and wring their hands all day long. Everyone except you, Joyce." Emily gives us all a prissy grin. "You're out there making money hand over foot for all intensive purposes. You're selling cars for cash and trash for antiques. You're making money off the radio! You're giving away clothes in the name of Elvis Presley! You're keeping that Sacred to the Memory of Elvis porch so there's not one soul in this town who doesn't know this house! Oh—how—how—public like a frog!"

"A what?"

"A frog! A frog! Like so frogging what! So, thank you, Joyce, thank you. Thanks to you, I've had plenty of shared humanity, O Bartleby! I've had enough of learned humility, more than any Tri Delt ever had to endure. Ever! Enough to last my whole life, and I hate it!"

We listen and she goes on and on, but who knows what she's talking about? We just sort of sit there (except for me, I have to stand with the pins in my underwear), and we listen to Emily while the one record finishes and the needle hisses and the next one drops and *Burning Love* comes flaming out, and then she lights into Elvis, tears into the King and the general of hot desire—whoever he is—them and Shakespeare too. She's got everyone just skewered against the wall, and then she yells, "Listen to Elvis! It's obscene! Stupid! Worse than stupid! You think Elvis is so wonderful? Elvis Presley was a hip-swinging hillbilly with a head full of greasy kid stuff and tasteless, tacky sequined capes. The truth is, he was a bloated-up orgiastic toad of a drug addict, and he ought to be talked about in the history of marketing and not music at all. I lied to you too," she says proudly. "I never was a fan of Elvis. I never cared when he died. I was in Rome. Get it? Rome, Italy! What could be farther from this desert dump than Italy?" She looks like she wants an answer from us, but right then the record changes and Elvis comes on singing *Santa Lucia,* that really sweet, old-fashioned tune. The words are in Italian, but you don't need them to understand the song. Emily is about to say something, then stops. She listens, real hard, like someone is calling her name from far far away. She licks her lips and says, "That's the one, the saint who carried her eyes around on a platter. Santa Lucia."

Mama tells her that song's from *Viva Las Vegas.*

"No it's not, it's from Italy." She looks like someone is throwing bucket after bucket of cold water on her, sobs into her hands, keeps asking Mama to play the song again and again, and Mama does. Then she turns the stereo off and sits down by Emily, pats her back. Emily brings her wet face out of her hands and whispers, "It was an unmemory, Joyce. It couldn't be a memory because it never happened, but it was that day I got lost with my parents, and then I got lost from my parents, and then I got lost in this foreign country and I did not want to be found."

Emily goes on crying, trying to tell about this guy named Carlo driving her around in Italy and his mother and Elvis dying on the same day and how she'd forgotten all about it—which isn't surprising (I wanted to say) since she'd just got through saying it didn't happen—but she's weeping and wiping her nose and Mama's there with the Kleenex, and naturally Lisa can't stand for anyone else to cry and get all the attention. And then there's a knock on the back door. Never mind I got patterns pinned all over my underwear, I'm the one who has to go collect the pizza.

We all four eat the pizza and sweat ourselves into a big love bath of friendliness, and after we finish the pizza Mama cracks them open another couple of Budweisers and we all go out on the front porch step where it's cool. On her way through the living room, Emily picks up Lisa's Barbie and says she always loved Barbie and Ken. Where's Ken? Well, ten minutes later you got to nail Lisa's shoes to the floor because she's going to ascend with happiness: Emily's going to bring her old Ken doll back from Laguna and give it to Lisa. I feel like reminding everybody that she'll have to mail that Ken doll to the foster home, where Lisa will be fighting off a bad-breathed man who'll try and kiss her. I sit on the steps with the rest of them. I play with the Colonel's stick, but I don't say too much. Pizza feels like pepperoni bricks in my stomach. They're all cheerful and chummy, but I'm wondering what Emily Shaw knows that I don't. What's in those welfare files? I bet Emily knows why my dad wasn't around when I was born and where he was. Who he was shacked up with then? Maybe he's not even my real dad. Hey, maybe I don't know anything at all. I got grandparents right here in St. Elmo, don't I? People I wouldn't know if I passed them on the street. Maybe I don't know any of them. I look over to my mother, Joyce Jackson. Then I remember she's Rejoice Denby too. I think: Who's that? No one knows the future, but maybe I don't even know the past.

I been ignorant and wrong my whole life. I used to think the past was down and the future was up, when I was little, I mean. That's why you couldn't see the future, because you'd look up and the sky is far far away, and you couldn't see that high to see the future. But the past—why, the past was easy. All you had to do was look down. There it was at your feet. That's what I used to think. But now I understand: I been sold a whole truckload of antique quilts, all comfy and warm and stitched together with lies, bits of this and that, scraps of truth. I can't take no more. I stand up to go inside. I toss the Colonel's stick across the yard. Nothing happens. "Hey—" I holler, "where's the Colonel?"

Well, he's gone. Real gone, Elvis might say. The Colonel and his blanket too. By the next afternoon we're crazy with worry. "He's chop suey," says Sandee. "The Vietnamese have got him and the Colonel is sitting on some plate with a little piece of parsley by him and his blanket in the sauce." She says she's going down the street and ask these Vietnamese point-blank what they did with our dog. Mama says I better go with her.

Sandee knocks at their door, but the only Phans at home don't speak English. One by one they come to the door and Sandee tries everything she can think of. Personally, I think she's making a fool of herself. Who'd want that dog, much less eat him? Finally Sandee can't make them understand a thing and so she stands there and goes, "Woof woof? Woof woof?"

"If all you were going to say is *woof woof*," I tell her when we're walking home, "you should of just sent Ray in there."

"That's enough out of you, Cilla Jackson. Ray's not as bad as some and better than most. When you get older, you'll understand these things."

"I hope I never understand stuff like that. I hope I never understand how adults screw everything up and screw each other and still live with it. I hope I'm never that grown up."

"What's with you, Cilla? Shit!" She grabs my arm. "Shit!"

I see it. The county car. In front of our house. "Maybe it's just Emily," I say. But it's not. A short woman, gray hair, body like a torpedo, gets out of that car. She bombs away through our gate and up to the front door. I know who it is. No one needs to tell me.

By the time me and Sandee get to the front gate, Mama's already answered the door and Marge Mason is talking, chuckling it sounds like, just a sort of deep, happy rumble in her chest, while she goes on about how we've cheated and lied and stolen and we'll have to pay it all back and how the law and the county of St. Elmo and the state of California was going to punish us and make us pay and pay and pay.

Spit gathers in my mouth, like it does just before you're going to barf. I see it all before me: jail, Juvenile Hall, the shame, foster homes, and Heather Wilkes reading all about my family in the newspaper. *All My Trials, Lord.*

Marge Mason reaches over, fingers the American flag on our window. She says we got a lot of nerve, but it's finished. We're finished. "This Heartbreak Hotel you've been running at the taxpayers' expense—all this is coming down. It's coming down around your ears."

Mama steps outside, puts her body between Marge Mason and Elvis Presley. The wind comes up just then and laces out those black satin streamers and they sort of wave at Marge, like *bye-bye,* but Marge never moves. "You better get off this porch," says Mama. "This porch is Sacred to the Memory of a great man."

"Ha ha ha!" Marge croaks out. "A rock star?"

"Elvis Presley was a great human being. Elvis gave more happiness to people in an hour than you'll give in your whole life, and I feel sorry for you if you don't know that. I've always felt sorry for you."

Gray as she is, Marge turns red and she yells, "You! You feel sorry for me! You had better save your pity for yourself!"

"Get off my porch—you've said your piece."

"Oh no I haven't! Far from it! I'm going to bring you down. I'm going to see you punished for all this—" Marge waves her arms over our porch. "I'm going to see you pay for everything!"

"You see that sign on the gate? BEWARE OF DOG? Get off my porch or I loose my dog on you."

Well, there is no more dog, is there? I have to bend over, throw up. We lost our dog, and now we're going to lose our house and our family and nothing can save us from this human torpedo who wants to blast my mother into jail and me and Lisa Marie into Juvie till some man with bad breath comes to take us home with him.

When I'm done barfing, Sandee puts her arms around my shoulder and pulls me to the porch and the door. "Hush, Cilla, honey. We won't really let the dog attack this time. Your mama was only kidding, weren't you, Joycie? You wouldn't let the dog bite this woman, would you? Shh, Cilla, there won't be any blood to clean up this time. Don't cry."

We get inside and Sandee kicks the door shut and lights up a Newie. I go into the bathroom, rinse my mouth and wash my face. I come back in the living room and curl up in the La-Z-Boy, cover up with an antique quilt like it might be cold in May.

We hear the chain link gate clang shut, and the county car pulls away. Mama comes in, leans against the door, and closes her eyes. "Least I was ready for her. Emily called right after Mrs. Mason threw *her* butt in the blender. Whoever it was called Emily, they got tired of waiting and called Mrs. Mason."

"I'll kill the sonofabitch," says Sandee, stubbing out her cigarette like the ashtray is the guy's eyeball. "It has to be someone we know. That's what I can't figure. Who?"

"Give me a Newie, Sandee."

"You can't smoke, Joycie. You never could."

But Sandee hands her a Newie anyway and Mama lights up. "I better call Emily. At least we're not in this alone."

"Oh, really?" I can't stand it. "Who's in it with us? *Emily?* Emily Shaw is on our side! Oh, thank you, Lord. Thank you, Jesus, for sending us such a mighty ally!"

Mama closes her eyes, ignores me. "Yea, though I walk through the Valley of Turds—" She squints against the cigarette. She can't smoke. She never could. "I shall fear no evil: for there is a presence even when no one is present, a gift when no giver's in sight."

Seventeen

It's no joke, the Valley of Turds. We find a letter-turd in our mailbox next day, cellophane window envelope, the kind that gives you nightmares. There's going to be a hearing. On Monday at 11:00 A.M. Mama reads the letter and her face goes that putty color of refrigerator biscuits, the kind that ooze out of the can. She hands the letter to Sandee. Sandee swears and curses, but her heart isn't in it.

I ask to see it. They let me. I wish they hadn't.

The purpose of this hearing is to determine the validity and/ or extent of allegations of substantial overpayments made to you since August 1977. This is a preliminary hearing only. If there are determined to be such overpayments, another hearing will be scheduled to assess corrections, and all benefits received by you will be considered to have ceased as from the date of this preliminary hearing.

If you wish to bring an attorney to this preliminary hearing or any subsequent hearing, you have the right to do so. The County will not assume any responsibility for any fees or costs you incur in the course of any aspect of this inquiry.

Present at the hearing will be your Family Assistance social worker, Miss Emily Shaw, as well as her supervisor. It is customary in the case of a new employee that the supervisor shall accompany, be present, and oversee proceedings. Hearing your case at this preliminary stage will be the Family Assistance Board of Executive Services (FABES), the governing body of the Department of Social Welfare.

So that FABES can reach a fair and timely decision, you are requested to bring all the below-listed documentation:

1. Income tax returns, 1977–1981.

2. Bank records. This shall be understood to be an inclusive term, encompassing savings and checkbooks, August 1977 to May 1982, whether or not these accounts remain current. It will also be understood to include any time deposits, IRAs, money market accounts, and records of any safety-deposit boxes maintained. Also, any loans contracted or reconveyed between August 1977 and May 1982.

3. Vehicle registration(s).

4. Credit card statements (August 1977–May 1982).

5. Rent receipts (August 1977–May 1982).

6. Utility bills (August 1977–May 1982).

Consideration of these documents is essential to any fair determination, and failure to provide them to the FABES inquiry will be prejudicial to your case.

Please come to reception at the Department of Social Welfare fifteen minutes before the above-noted time on the above-noted date. Reception will direct you to the hearing room (224) on the second floor. You may call if you have any questions.

Very truly yours,

Marjorie D. Mason, Supervisor II

cc: Family Assistance Board of Executive Services
Mrs. Olivia Edelstein
Miss Bonita Vail
Mr. Orson Findlay
Mr. Howard Hansen

"There's nothing on paper, Joycie," says Sandee after a while. "They'll never be able to find anything on paper."

"When they finish with us," says Mama, "we will be drowning in paper."

My dreams are full of drowning and gagging and being torpedoed. In my dreams I see the Colonel hanging by his own blanket in the garage right beside the Starlight Coupe. I wake up. I go get in bed with Lisa and Brown Bunny.

At school I screw up my honors history class report on the battle of Shiloh, even though I had it all studied up. It was supposed to be an oral report, but I can't talk. I can't eat. I can't even think. I sit in class and I try to make my brain sing *Peace in the Valley,* but all I hear is *In the Ghetto.* My softball game falls to pieces. I'm captain of the team, but I just don't give a doo dah day for Thursday's game against Urquita Junior High.

I walk five straight players. The coach, Miss Mendes, she blows her whistle, calls time out, walks to the mound, asks if I've got PMS or something.

"Sun's in my eyes."

"Sun's in their pitcher's eyes too, Cilla, and she hasn't walked anyone."

I ask her to let me warm up a little between innings and the catcher throws me a couple of high ones. I was doing okay till I thought I saw my dad up high in the bleachers. I shade my eyes with my hand, trying to see if it really is him, or just my wish and hope for him, even though I don't. Wish or hope, I mean. I don't care. I don't care if I see him at all. Maybe he's not even really my dad. My real dad would of been there when I was born. He wouldn't of let us go on welfare. Besides, was there ever a grown-up who didn't grin at you and lie? All kinds of lies. How great they were in high school. How they could of gone to college and didn't want to. How much money they make. How much they can drink. How fast they can run. How much this car cost. Dad's coming back. Stories like that. You can't ever get the truth out of a grown-up who's set on one bullshit story or another. One year passes, *Dad's coming back,* two, five years and she's still saying, *Oh, Dad's com-*

ing back. Sure, Mama. But first we'll get Elvis back and Buddy Holly and Richie Valens and the Big Bopper too. Then we'll look for Warren James Jackson, Jr. Whoever he is.

Well, whoever he is, he's up there in the bleachers. He gives me a slow wave. I wave back. Heather Wilkes thinks I'm waving at her.

Coach replaces me, but we lose the game anyway. I come out of the dugout and here's Heather Wilkes waiting for me. And there, on the other side of the chain link fence, there's my dad, leaning on his Harley, smoking a cigarette. I pretend I don't know him.

Heather's just been dying to tell me her secret all day. Her mother said she could bring a few friends down to their condo at Corona Del Mar this weekend. "Oh, we'll have such a blast, Cilla! Think your mom will let you come?"

I tell her thanks, but I'm going to visit my dad this weekend, at my dad's weekend place. Lake Tahoe. I keep at it, adding cherry and whipped cream and everything to this story, till even I can't think of anything else to say. Heather looks pretty disgusted with me.

After she leaves, my dad says, "You're a little off your stride today, aren't you, princess?"

I want to say something really nasty, but I don't. I ask him what he's doing here.

"I'm working the desert again tomorrow and Dorrie's mother is sick, so we had to bring the boys by for a couple of days."

"Why doesn't Dorrie's mother just up and die and get it over with?" He asks me if I want a ride home, but I'm not going home. I'm taking the city bus over to the library to return a book and I tell him so.

"I'll take you to the library."

"Mama doesn't let me ride the motorcycle without a helmet."

"I got a helmet."

"What'll you wear?"

"My good looks." He starts to rough up my hair, but I duck out of reach.

I go to the gym, get showered and changed, and get my stuff. I'm walking back out and I see him there, sitting on his bike, smoking a cigarette, kind of slouched and easy, even though he still looks like he might bite. That must be what gets them. The women, I mean. All his women.

He puts the helmet on me and we zoom off to the library. My dad comes in with me and he sits in reference while I go to the desk. It's Miss McClusky there, my favorite librarian, and she says, Oh Cilla, there's a new book just in and she thought of me right away, so naturally I have to go with her to find it and we have a nice long jaw over *Golden Girls: Women Olympic Champions.* Then she asks after my oral report on the Civil War. "The battle of Shiloh, wasn't it?"

"Everyone lost." I wish Miss McClusky would just let me go. I look over at my dad. He is too big for the library chairs and desks. They don't fit him. He's the only one in the reference room wearing motorcycle boots, a leather jacket, and a shirt advertising Mexican beer, with chest hair showing at his neck. Every woman in reference, every woman in the library—young and old, pushing carts or pushing pencils—they're all watching him. He stands up, walks me to the door with his slow, easy walk that tells you he could run anytime he wanted to. He holds the door for me and I wish I wasn't proud of him. I wish I didn't love him. Or want him back. Let Mama do all that. Let her cry her eyes out, buy the sun, the moon, and the Starlight Coupe to get him back. Let her love him. Not me. I'll never do that for any guy.

Out by the motorcycle he makes me put on the leather jacket besides the helmet. "It's over eighty degrees," I tell him.

"It'll be cold going up the hill on the bike."

"What hill?"

"Oh, I thought we'd just take a little ride, Cilla. You and me." He gives me that deep smile that creases up his face in all the expected places. He zips the jacket up on me. "I'm real proud of you, Cilla. You are real smart, just like your mama."

"Aren't you smart?"

"Hell no. I'm sure no match for you and Joyce."

"I guess that means you're a match for Dorrie."

I can tell by his face I've hurt his feelings. I'm not supposed to talk about Dorrie now: Here it is, our time together, and maybe he'll even buy me an ice cream! I should be thrilled right down to my Reeboks. Instead, I'm snit-snotting about Dorrie. I've messed it all up. Too bad. What about my time? My five years? What if he's not even my real dad?

We zoom over to Far West, left on Brigham Boulevard, and go up into the foothills. High, past all the numbered streets, until we come to those new tracts where just a few years ago there was nothing but lemon groves. These new streets all have names like room deodorants, Cranberry Hill and stuff, but once we get past them the road narrows down and the curve starts up. The bike takes these deep curves so easy and assured and I lean into them with my dad. It's like riding a racehorse.

He cuts off the main road and takes Old Spanish Canyon. It smells fresh and peppery and sycamorish up here, like spring is supposed to smell, not like that smog bog St. Elmo. The road follows a dry creekbed. We're going so fast the wind bites right through my socks and gnaws at my knees and I'm glad I have the leather jacket because there's deep shade on this narrow road. I duck down behind my dad's back and hold on tighter. He pats my hand. Holds it. Squeezes. I don't cry.

He drives all the way up to Hammath Hot Springs, right up to the chain link fence that says NO TRESPASSING: THIS MEANS YOU. It didn't mean Heather Wilkes's big sister on prom night. Heather told me her sister and all her friends came up here and went skinny-dipping. There's nothing here but a few tumbledown bungalows and the hot springs. That's all that's left of what they were going to build but never did. We get off the bike and walk around. My dad lays it on with a trowel, telling me stories, oh, how him and his friends used to have really wild parties up here. I can't stand it. I say: "You didn't invent skinny-dipping."

"I better not ever hear of you skinny-dipping up here, Miss Cilla Jackson. You come up here with a boy and I'll horsewhip him."

"Boys are a pain in the butt. All boys."

He goes on about how Mama used to live up here when she was

little. How her old man burnt down the house they lived in. He says my grandfather is a sonofabitch all right, and I know, right then, that Rejoice Denby's father vowed to horsewhip my dad, Warren James Jackson, Jr. If he is my dad.

Going back down, we don't do Old Spanish Canyon but stick with the main mountain road, which is curvier and not so steep. When we're a few miles from town we come to Lookout Point, where you can see all of St. Elmo. On good days, anyway. Today's not a good day. My dad pulls in, turns off the bike. Either end of Lookout Point, there's a car. Teenagers. Parking and necking in broad daylight. They got the radio on. *Chariots of Fire*. Who'd want to make out to *Chariots of Fire*?

We get off the bike and I take off the helmet and unzip the jacket. "You want it back?" I can see the hair on his arms is standing up, he's so cold. He doesn't want the jacket, but he'll take a cigarette out of the pocket.

I look over as much of St. Elmo as I can see. It looks like God has dumped his vacuum bag over the sky in this town. Everything's all kind of pink-lintish. "I hate this town," I say. "Soon as I can, I'm leaving. Going to college. Some place far away."

"St. Elmo's hateable," he says, resting one of his boots on a boulder and smoking. "When my draft notice came, I was glad to go, glad to get out of this town. And then—well, you can see what happened to me." He laughs.

"What happened?" I say, real snotty-like.

"I came back, didn't I? I came back to St. Elmo and now I wonder—" His cigarette goes out in the wind. He relights it. Puffs.

"What do you wonder?"

He smokes. He says he wonders if he ever got away.

"Oh, you got away. You're a big success! You're living over in San Juan County, not in grubby St. Elmo at all! You're living uptown in Clearstream."

"I pay rent there. I live here. I've always lived here."

"Well, if that's true—which it isn't—then how come our whole family's hip deep in this Valley of Turds?"

243

"That valley?" He points to St. Elmo, stewing in its own lint.

"Don't play dumb with me, Dad."

"I don't have to play dumb, princess. Oh, come on—" He reaches out and pulls me close. "Tell me what's bugging you, princess."

"You mean you really don't know? Mama didn't tell you?"

"What? About the Colonel? Don't worry about the Colonel. He'll be back. He's just out tomcatting."

"Takes one to know one."

He lets me go. He's mad, but he won't smack me. Once, he went to spank Lisa for something and Mama told him never to raise a hand to us girls. I was specially surprised because Dorrie was there, and Mama never says anything like that around her. Oh no, around Dorrie it's all peaches and Listerine. Lisa, she was just as pleased as she could be till Mama reached over and spanked her. Twice. Sent her to her room. So, since I know I won't get smacked, I press my luck. What do I have to lose? "I guess that's how it is for boy dogs," I say. "They just smell it on someone and take off. Just whenever they get the urge or the itch. Don't think about anyone else."

"That's enough, Cilla. Tell me what Joyce hasn't told me. Tell me about the Valley of Turds."

So I do. I tell him good. I tell him so good, it's like my every word is a little spitball and hits him square in the face. I tell him about Emily's getting that phone call and her coming over and then Marge Mason standing on our Sacred to the Memory of and putting her grubby hands on our flags and telling us it's all coming down, everything's coming down around our heads. I tell him about the letter from the welfare department and the rent receipts and utility bills and bringing the lawyer and then, next thing I know, I'm telling about jail and Juvenile Hall and the foster home with the unshaved man and bad breath and the stink and poverty and shame of it, "And it's all your fault!" The teenagers have quit necking and turned their radios down. They're watching us like *The Young and the Restless* and I just don't give a popcorn fart. I wouldn't care if Lookout Point was a stage and the whole city of St. Elmo was watching me. "If you were any kind of father at all, you wouldn't of left and we wouldn't be in this Valley of Turds! We'd have a home and a mother and a father like other kids. Mama won't even divorce you and be done with it! Oh no—she has to go on loving you and pretending that—well, what does it matter that Dad's living with Farty Vardy? Dorrie gets you! What do we get? We get a bunch of damn social workers checking us out every six months, peeing in our toilet and making sure we really are as poor as we say we are, making sure we really don't have any money, making sure we really don't have a man, making sure that *dad* is just another dirty word in our house! Maybe you're not even my real dad! My real dad wouldn't of left. My real dad must be dead—or something—and you're just some man Mama screws now and then when you can get it away from Dorrie. Oh, don't think I don't know! I know when you been to our house when I'm at school. I can *smell* you in that house. If Mama's happy being screwed now and then, well let her—she's nuts! If you were our real dad, we'd all be wearing *Blue Suede Shoes!* We'd have *Money, Honey!* We'd have *Peace in the Valley* and not this Valley of Turds. You think Mama's smart? I think she's dumb. She's crazy, too! She thinks Elvis is going to save us from Marge Mason, save her from going to jail and me and Lisa from the foster home. I want to say, *Oh yeah, Mama? What's the King going to do, Mama? Come and croon old Marge up? Rock her out? Let her feel the mighty power of his burning love?"*

I got my fists doubled up and I'm beating on him. I'm punching him in the stomach and he stands there and never even tells me to stop, just takes it while I hit him and I tell him how I hate him. "I love Elvis and I hate you! Elvis wouldn't leave his daughter! Death had to take him from Lisa Marie, but you—oh no, you leave us the same night Elvis passes through—dies, I mean, Elvis died! He died and died and died! Everything died—" I cry and hit him till I can't anymore, and that's when he pulls me up against him. He doesn't even tell me to hush. Just holds me and lets me cry. He smells like motorcycles and sawdust and smoke. I hate him because I love him so much.

After a while I quit. He goes to wipe my eyes with his T-shirt. I tell him thanks, anyway, but I don't need it. I got Kleenex in my schoolbag.

He lights up another cigarette and looks out over this smog bog we live in. Finally he says, "I remember when the St. Elmo Valley was a pleasure to live in, when, spring mornings, you'd wake up and smell the orange blossoms, when there was citrus groves climbing all over these foothills. I remember when all that waste land out by the flood channel was all dairy farms and cattle grazing. You could smell those cows for miles. You still can sometimes, when there's fog or any dampness. It's like a ghost smell."

I blow my nose. What do I care about a bunch of damn cows?

"Every few years it would rain till we'd just about get washed out to sea. Before they put in the flood channel they used to call that Dogsback Ditch because it was so yellow and ugly. And when it flooded, sure enough, there'd always be a dozen or so cows too goddamned stupid to go for higher ground, and a week later you'd smell them out there. Bloated and stinking and caught in some ditch or culvert, stinking so bad you couldn't get near them to bury them. I feel like one of those cows." He takes a deep drag off his Marlboro. "Too goddamned stupid to go for higher ground and now I'm just stuck in the culvert, bloated and stinking and good for nothing."

Grown-ups always do this. They do it on TV. They do it in the movies. They do it in real life. It's Suffer The Little Children, Pity The Poor Parent Time. Here's my lines: *Don't cry, Daddy. Please. You're not a failure, Daddy. Please don't cry.* I'm supposed to make it easy for him, but I'm not buying into this antique quilt. I say, "You're right. You were stupid to leave me and Mama and Lisa for that dumbshit Dorrie and those two Vardy boys."

"They're good boys, Cilla. They are. You can say what you want about Dorrie, but they are good little boys."

I can think of lots I'd like to say about Dorrie, but what's the point? Instead I say, "Are you my real dad?"

"What?"

"You heard me." I sound just like my mother. I know it. He looks like the shock is going to send him into a coma and rattles on about how long him and Mama have been married, but I say, "I didn't ask if you were married or not. I asked if you were my real dad."

"Who's feeding you this line of bullshit?"

"I figured it out. It makes sense. My real dad would of been around when I was born. Maybe you're Lisa's real dad. You were around when she was born. I remember that. But my dad must of been someone Mama slept with and then she got knocked up and he just split. That's what really happens between men and women, isn't it? People just like to screw, and all that stuff in songs, all that stuff about love, *Love Me Tender, I Can't Help Falling in Love with You, I Want You, I Need You, I Love* You—that's just junk, isn't it?"

"You're wrong, Cilla. You're wrong about love. Joyce would tell you you're wrong. Joyce knows love. She knows what love is really all about."

"What's she know? What do you know? You've screwed up your lives so bad, what do either of you know?"

He takes my shoulders. "I loved Joyce Denby from the minute I saw her on the porch of that shack where she lived. I loved her and I went into the army and I thought about her every day and I came back to this town vowing that I'd marry her. And I did. There never was another woman for me, no matter what's happened. I knew that, and so did she. I hope when you grow up you'll find with a man what your Mama and I—"

"I'll never be that dumb."

"That's burning love, Cilla." He holds my shoulders tight. "That's love that don't burn out."

"Liar. Look at who you're living with. If you love Mama so much, then how come you're living with Farty Vardy?"

"I don't know."

"What?"

It seems like he almost laughs. "Dorrie's weak and silly," he says. "She's no deeper and just as hollow as a doorknob. She can't even spell *love,* much less give it. Joyce has love and she has it to give. If you don't have it to give, you don't have it at all." He lets go of my shoulders and puts his boot back up on the rock, looks over the city. "I'm forty-five years old and I only just figured that out. If you don't have it to give, you don't have it at all."

"You mean you don't love Dorrie?" I can't believe this. It's like the smog is lifting over my whole life.

"Oh, I don't think I ever did love Dorrie. I loved the way she made me feel. She made me feel like she couldn't live without me, but the truth of it is, Dorrie can't live without a man and it probably doesn't much matter who that man is." He takes a long, deep breath. "Joyce could live without me, but she didn't want to. I was her choice. She can't live without you and Lisa, and she needs Elvis and Sandee, but she didn't need me like that. She just wanted me. She wanted me."

"Well, you can come back home now! Mama'd take you back. You know she would! She's always loved you. She always said you were coming back."

"Well, I'm not. I can't."

"Why not? You said you don't love Dorrie. You said you love Mama."

"I love Justin and Little Jack too." He reaches in the leather jacket pocket, gets out another cigarette, and leans into the match. "If I leave Dorrie, what happens to Justin and Little Jack? I'd have to leave them with her. You think I'd do that to them?"

"You did it to us."

He starts up like I have hit him again. He says, "It was the worst mistake of my life, but I can't undo it. And I can't do to my sons what I did to my daughters. If I leave those boys, I still can't make it right with you girls, and the boys will hate me too. At least you girls have Joyce for a mother, Joyce and all she has to give. Dorrie has nothing. Nothing for no one."

He swings his leg over the bike. Picks up the helmet and tells me stand still. Puts it on tight. Tells me to zip up the jacket and I do. He stomps out the cigarette and pulls me, helmet and all, up against his shoulder. I know he's crying. I'm not supposed to know, but I do. He's like light on water and I can see right through him.

He brings my face up close to his. "I am your dad, Cilla. Just like I am Lisa's dad. You both have the same mother and the same father. I wasn't around when you were born, Cilla, because I was in jail. That's where I was. Prison."

His eyes are dark. He watches me to see if I'll blubber or gasp or snivel or cry. I know that, whatever I do—right now—it's important for the whole rest of my life. So I say, "What were you in for?"

"Aggravated assault. Well, that was the general charge, but it was really because of an attempted robbery three years before. I got the same judge from the other charge, where it wasn't a robbery at all, it was— Well, I'm not saying I was innocent this time. It was a fight. I got into it. I kept it going. The judge sent me to prison for assault. My wife was pregnant. She went on welfare. What else could she do? You were born in County Hospital. I was working in the prison laundry when the guard calls my name, tells me I have a daughter. Cilla, I never been so happy in all my life! I rode that laundry cart, shouting, singing! Because, even though I was in prison, I knew my life had been saved. Your Mama and I, we wanted a baby more than anything, and now we had a baby and I knew we'd be all right. I'd serve my time and I'd go home to my wife and daughter. All the rest of my sentence, I just kept saying to myself, *My wife and daughter, my wife and daughter...* I knew we'd be all right." He turned his key in the motorcycle ignition.

"But you weren't—" I say. "You weren't all right."

"But we could have been."

I get on the Harley and we start down the hill into St. Elmo, this desert dump of a town we all love to hate. I hold on tight to my dad, keeping my head down, out of the wind, and I hear Elvis singing *Got a Lot of Livin' to Do,* I hear him in my bones and blood and head and heart, that song just comes to me from nowhere, and I know when I hear it that it's Elvis not just singing, but talking to me, telling me what Mama's known all along. Elvis himself is letting me know. We can still be all right.

The Book of Love

Eighteen

Denny Sullivan knocked again and again to make himself heard over the music, Elvis's husky voice vowing, *Baby, I Wanna Play House with You.* Denny called Joyce's name through the screen door and she came into the living room, passing the record player and turning down the volume. She wiped her hands on her jeans and her face brightened to see him. "You've found the Colonel, haven't you, Denny?"

Denny cleared his throat. "Joyce—"

"I knew he'd turn up. That brute. Where'd you find him?"

"Joyce, I have some news. Can I come in?" Denny stooped to enter. "There's been an accident, Joyce. A kid pulled out. He was parked. He didn't see them. See it. The motorcycle." Denny drew a long breath, hurting with every word, with every syllable of pain he knew he was inflicting. Joyce's green eyes grew wide, unbelieving, her lips opened wordlessly. "Jack's motorcycle. Jack and Cilla, Joyce." Her head fell against his chest, his uniform buttons biting into her flesh. He held her shoulders tightly. "There was a kid parked on Brigham Boulevard. He didn't look. He just pulled into the lane. Jack swerved. He saved that kid's life. The kid was shook up, that's all, but the Harley went out of control, Joyce, and—well, Jack and Cilla both flew off. They're alive. But they're not okay, Joyce." He held her close while she shuddered. "Cilla was wearing Jack's helmet. The helmet saved Cilla's life."

"What was Jack wearing?"

"Jack wasn't wearing a helmet. We have to hurry. I came here to take you to County. Is that the kids I hear out back? You wait. I'll be right back." He led her to the couch, feeling somehow that Elvis was being uncooperative by crooning *Loving You.* He went through the kitchen door and lowered himself to the back step and asked the kids if they'd like to go for a ride in the cop car. With the siren.

"And the lights?" asked four-year-old Justin.

"You bet, pal. Now, you just go round the front, no, not through the house. Use the gate. My partner's out front and he'll fix you right up in that car."

Lisa's eyes narrowed; she stepped back from Denny's offered hand. "Where's Mama? Where are we going?"

"I'll tell you in the car."

"Tell me now."

"You go on around front, Lisa. I'm going to bring your mama."

Denny went back through the house, picked up Joyce's purse and her sandals. He knelt and put her shoes on her feet and his arm around her shoulders and drew her up. The record finished, rasped, and snapped off. The silence was terrible.

Before they left, Denny turned on the porch switch, and the Christmas lights framing Elvis's portrait and the flag-clad Sacred to the Memory windows twinkled as he led Joyce to the gate. Before he put her in the squad car he gave one last look to the spangled-suited Elvis framed in sparkling lights, mike held in a white-knuckled grip: tense, intense, knee thrust out in posture at once dramatic and humble.

The glass walls of Emergency were spangled with efficiency. Joyce stepped from the squad car into the smog-studded vanilla light of the May afternoon. She moved slowly, as though swimming, perhaps drowning, plunged in, powerless as seaweed. The glass doors opened of their own accord, whooshed like a clarinetist's breath as she swam toward the reception desk and the nurse who spoke, or seemed to; words certainly floated between them, got lost, the meaning emerging slowly from murk like blue water, murk, fog thick as dolphins' backs, through clouds of some arbitrary color. Denny led her toward long parallel rows of plastic chairs, repeating assurances that the doctor would be out soon. At one end of the row there was a trash can, at the other a knee-high ashtray. Gravely, slowly, Joyce asked Denny to call Sandee at Inland Trucking.

Joyce sat staring at the trio of potted palms on either side of the sliding glass doors, and each time they opened, the palms seemed to expire, wilt, rouse themselves in a slow, predictable dance. Joyce put one arm around Lisa and one around Justin. Little Jack, round-eyed and incredulous, climbed into her lap, wrapped his short arms around her neck. She pulled the children as close as flesh permitted, as though they could meld and pool their strength, let it flow, ripple under all the doors and walls and barricades. She breathed in the children's sweetness, their clean hair, their dirty hands, their salt-stained cheeks. She closed her eyes till dots swam before them, red and wet and brilliant as the pomegranate seeds that day she and Sandee had got on the backs of Harleys driven by Jack and CJ. The Harleys had ripped, roared, snorted to life as the four of them rumbled out of St. Elmo, escape made all the sweeter as it was a weekday, a warm weekday in October, and they ought all to have been at work—and weren't. When you're nineteen, like Joyce and Sandee, a hot autumn day like this demanded to be filled with exhaust and adventure.

They took back roads down to the beach, stop-and-going through small towns, canyon roads winding through rough bronze hills. They saw an abandoned farmhouse where a lop-eared windmill stood forlornly in the overgrown yard, but by the door there yet bloomed a pomegranate tree, its fruit virulent, red, and appealing. They jounced up to the house, picked pomegranates, and Jack split two with his pocket knife, handing half to each. They drove back through their own October dust, down twisting canyon roads where live oaks bent low to the ground; they drove through shadows encapsulating light the way dark water wraps itself around golden carp. They sucked on the pomegranates and spit the seeds at one another; the juice ran down their wrists and necks and chins and they never once dreamed the thin red rivulets of juice could have been their own thicker blood, that their heads (the girls in scarves, guys in caps) could have been as easily split as those pomegranates, feeling—quite to the contrary— immortal. Joyce had one arm around Jack; in her other hand she held the pomegranate, sucking on its tough red lip, laughing, believing that these were the pleasures God owed her. Now, of course, she knew quite differently. God owes you nothing. Whatever He might donate was a gift, portable as destiny or desire. Like destiny or desire, it could not be earned or denied. It could not be taken from you. It could only be lost.

"Joyce?" Denny adjusted his holster and knelt. "Joyce, the doctor's talking to you. You want him to repeat it? Joyce? Yes?"

"Priscilla's condition has stabilized," said the doctor. "She has multiple fractures of the tibia and fibula of the right leg. Those are the bones between the knee and the ankle. She has suffered a good deal of abrasion on the lower body, but that will mend. The leather jacket protected her from the worst of it and the helmet saved her life. There's shock, of course, but I think you can count—"

Joyce brought her gaze from the trio of potted palms, yellowing and wilting by the door, to the doctor's face. He was dry and sober looking with gray temples and blue eyes. "Trauma?"

"Your husband is not so fortunate, and he has suffered more than trauma. The doctor took a deep, seemingly painful breath. "He has head injuries and there are broken ribs, a punctured lung, a broken clavicle, and internal bleeding. We're trying to stabilize him now so we can take him into surgery and—"

"TRAUMA!"

"The trauma team is working with him now and we will—"

Joyce, in her old reflexive gesture, touched the doctor's cheek as if tenderly testing his fleshly validity. "Oh, TRAUMA, it's me, Starlight Coupe."

"Starlight—yes— Of course! Oh no—that's your daughter and husband?"

"Yes. Jack. It is, it was Jack's car, the Starlight Coupe. I saw it there, you know, and I knew it was his and I knew it was meant to bring him back to me, but I—well, I thought I was wrong, but I wasn't. It is going to bring Jack back to me, because you're going to save his life, TRAUMA. You said you bought the Starlight Coupe because it saved your life, and now you're going to save Jack's life."

"I'm going to do my very best, Mrs. Jackson. We all are. We're doing everything we can. You can rely on that."

The sliding glass doors parted and the potted palms nearly fell over in the gust created by a shrieking, big-bosomed, broad-shouldered woman bursting through. Sandee flung herself on Joyce, on the children, on Denny and the doctor, who said that Joyce could see Cilla briefly before they took her into surgery to set the bones in her leg.

When the nurse and doctor left her, Joyce felt suddenly dwarfed, abandoned, and inadequate to the beeping monitors and IVs clustered near Cilla and connected to her by long plastic tubes, hoarfrost webs of plastic. She could not take her daughter's hands; they were swathed in bandages. And she dared not touch Cilla's IV'd arms. The lower half of her small body was encased in a rigid apparatus and her skin was gray and muddy. Joyce watched the pulse pound in her throat. She bent her lips down to her daughter's, brushed them, murmured words of love and comfort, comfort and love, over and over again. Cilla's eyes flickered open, acknowledged Joyce, and closed again.

Joyce spoke and whispered and soothed, controlling her quaking voice with great effort. She brushed the hair from Cilla's forehead. The sight of her daughter, prone, rigid, helpless, eyes closed, was terrible beyond endurance. Joyce raised her gaze to the dreary-colored cabinets, where there hung side by side two long posters, one with a neatly labeled skeleton, his hand and foot out in a rather jaunty manner, as though introducing himself, Mr. Bones, to Mr. Flesh in the next poster, that one depicting the warp and woof, the web of muscles: structure and substance, the democracy of flesh and bone, the democracy of the dust.

Cilla parted her lips and eked out the word *Dad.*

"Oh, don't you worry about Dad," Joyce whispered. "He's going to be fine. God doesn't want Jack up there. God's got His hands full with Elvis."

A broken blue smile formed on Cilla's lips. "Dad's…coming home." She formed each word as though it were a tiny stone she must savor and spit. "You…were…right…Always."

"Of course I was. You didn't doubt that, did you? I always knew Dad was coming home. I'm right about your getting well, too. You're going to be well and up and laughing, playing softball, honey. You're going to be—"

"Dad—" Tears fell down the sides of Cilla's face and Joyce wiped them tenderly.

"I told you, Cilla, Dad's going to be fine. You're both alive and you're going to be fine. They're going to set these bones and—" She glanced up at the dapper Mr. Bones and Mr. Flesh. Fragility of flesh and bone, the loss, even the possibility of loss, so unthinkable. Cilla seemed to nod, and Joyce, because she couldn't speak or pray, began to sing. Like a shaft of light through water, Joyce plunged into a pool of song and doctrine, swimming through the lyrics, each breathy aspiration filled with hope and banishing silence, just as she had that August night five years before, when she had sat at the edge of Cilla's bed, singing song after Elvis song, singing long after she'd heard Jack's Harley start up, roar down Sultana, turn right on Santiago, and disappear under the purple jacarandas, singing till Cilla slept and, finally, Joyce slept too, curled beside her daughter.

Joyce awoke, cramped and sweating. She listened to Cilla's quiet breathing and roused enough to look over to the blue Smurf clock. It was nearly three A.M. But what day? Tuesday. Yes. August 16. She sat up slowly. She hurt everywhere. She looked for her sandals. They were not under the bed. Oh yes. Right. They were in the kitchen somewhere. They were the first thing she'd thrown at him.

The Colonel looked abjectly up from his blanket, sniffed. The dog's mute demands drained her. Earlier, his barking—added to the screams and oaths—must have waked people in a half-mile radius. Lisa slept through it. Cilla didn't. Joyce patted the Colonel and tiptoed from the room.

She turned on the kitchen light, stepping gingerly through the carnage—trash cans, ashtrays, chairs, canisters overturned, the floor a mess of butts, broken glass, cups and crockery and sparkling sugar. She found her sandals and washed her face at the sink, staring at her reflection in the blackened window. Somewhere out there in the backyard, the kitchen knife must be gleaming in the grass. In the fight to keep her husband she had used everything, including the knife. She had whined and wept; she had sworn and whimpered; she had slugged him; she had called him filthy names and clung to his waist; she had repudiated his taste in women and then begged him to stay with her. And then, of course, she'd tried to kill him. That's the way it is with love. In the end, you do everything you vowed you'd never do. You part with everything—self-respect, pride, dignity—you give them away without so much as a thought. And for what? By the time you're reduced to that, it's too late anyway. He wanted nothing. His freedom maybe. But his freedom he could take. It was not a gift Joyce could bestow.

She took a sweatshirt off the La-Z-Boy and stepped out onto the front porch, wishing she smoked cigarettes. She sat there just the same, listened to the crickets and the wind. Fresh for August. Insistently, the wind rustled through the jacarandas overhead and ruffled the two skinny crepe myrtles in the yard. Their cool sherbert-colored blooms seemed to glow, pink candelabras lighting up the dark. The wind seemed suddenly to change direction, to come round behind her; its dry fingers played over her back, blew her hair out before her, demanding that she rise. She moved slowly off the porch and into the yard. As though she were no more than a sail tethered to some puny human mast, the wind pushed, nudged her past the crepe myrtles and out the gate. She crossed Sultana and continued up Santiago. The wind urged her along to keep some unknown appointment.

At the county complex, she passed first the huge welfare building, on its "public" side, windowless, monolithic, and ugly beyond belief. She'd have to deal with welfare soon enough. Your man goes out the back door and the social worker comes in the front. The wind pushed her past welfare and toward Juvenile Hall, where the lights still shone. The lights never went off at Juvenile Hall, but electricity could not dent its darkness. She had known that, instinctively, more than twenty years ago, sitting in a sorrow-stenched cubicle with her father. At every significant turn, Joyce's life had been touched upon by some county institution: the courthouse, the jail, Juvenile Hall, welfare, the hospital, institutions that served, finally, as human trash bins, whatever their original purpose might have been. She shuddered as, passing Mental Health, a human cry pierced the moonless night. The wind carried the cry across the county complex, tangled it in the sad eucalyptus trees. Joyce thanked God she'd never had to deal with Mental Health, realizing even as she whispered that Mental Health certainly would have dealt with her if she had stabbed her husband with a kitchen knife.

The kitchen knife had come to Joyce's hand after the ashtrays, glasses, the canister, cups, after all that had been smashed and broken, the table and chairs overturned. Joyce did not believe that he was really moving out. Dorrie Vardy was but one of many women—all too many women—who had left their hands on Jack's body and their perfume on his clothes. They came and went, these women, one after another. Joyce despised them, but she did not think them dangerous. The one permanent fixture in his life was Joyce. She did not believe he would move out—until he said he'd extracted a promise from his father, their landlord, not to raise the rent on the Santiago Street house. Then she believed it.

Oh, How Great Thou Art, Jack! Are you the Red Cross of Runaway Husbands? Like father, like son. Your dirty father walked out on your mother and four children, turned off the gas and electricity and left you all there in the dark and the cold.

It wasn't cold. Anyway, I'm not turning off the gas and electricity.

Why not? You stupid bastard! How can you leave us? How can you leave me for that dipshit, that—slut!

Joyce, don't—

Can't you see? She's an empty cupcake! She's stupid and shallow and weak and—

Joyce, I didn't want to say this, but I—you—well—you might as well know—you'd know anyway, sometime, Joyce. Dorrie had a baby last month.

What?

Dorrie had a baby. It was a boy. On July twentieth, she—

She did what?

Dorrie had a baby.

The simple declarative words struck her like a crazy, careening, runaway truck, smashing into her, rolling over and leaving her dying with just enough breath to ask, *Whose?*

Mine. Ours.

You mean—all the time—these past nine months, you—

It's been real hard, Joyce, hard on me, hard on Dorrie, she—

It was then that the kitchen knife gleamed soundlessly, there by the sink, and she clutched its handle in her grateful fist.

Joyce had, by now, crossed the open, grassy expanse of the county complex while dry wind rumpled the eucalyptus, rattled the unruly palms lining the hospital driveway leading to Emergency. She avoided the pool of fluorescent light twinkling on the asphalt and went round the building, in the fringes of shadow, to the old entrance, long unused. No beacons here, no circular drive. Uneven bricks and messy crepe myrtles, their thin gray trunks turning yellow in the lamplight and their pink blossoms trembling in the wind. They encircled an inefficient fountain, long since silent. Joyce peered into the stagnant water, black as old walnut hulls. The yellow reflections from lamps winked at her, teasing, unreliable as the lights in that long-vanished lagoon.

She heard a lock turn and a burly security guard stepped from the darkened archway, ordering her off county property and adding that she should not be out alone at night. Joyce shrugged and moved on. What had she to fear from strangers? Her pace picked up, she broke into a run. It's the ones you love. They're the dangerous ones. They're the ones who can kill you.

Fighting for possession of the knife, Joyce and Jack had choreographed themselves out of the kitchen, tumbled off the porch steps, rolled *one—two—three, one—two—three,* the Colonel barking like the sonofabitch he was, but locked up in the living room. Dancing the violent, lyricless *Infidelity Waltz—two—three, one—two—three—*

they rolled over and over, wrestling in the devil-grass, the fight like a ghastly version of the intensity of their lovemaking. Joyce slugged, kicked, and Jack tried to hold and pin her, until Cilla's piping voice cut through the struggle and Joyce looked up to see her on the back porch, her little arms upraised, white nightie flapping at her ankles. As though Cilla had caught them naked, Jack instantly rolled off Joyce. *Go inside, Cilla, honey,* Joyce called. She dropped the knife as if it had caught fire. *I'll be there in a minute.* She heard the door close and, on all fours, panting, she made her way to the clothesline pole, pulled herself slowly upright. In the glare of the orange porch light she saw Jack's chest heaving. He sat, rubbing his hands on his thighs. Joyce released the clothesline pole and stood on her own.

I have a child of yours. Did you see her? I have two children! Two of your children, two of our children, Jack! Did you forget them? You have two daughters, Jack. What about them? What about me? What about us?

Dorrie needs me.

I need you!

No, you don't.

The truth of it flew up before her eyes like a regatta of moths. She had to brush them away. Joyce said very slowly, *I'm being punished for my strength. I am strong and she is not and I am being punished for my strength. That's it, isn't it?*

And Jack said yes, he guessed that was it.

She turned then, left him, walked up the steps and into the house to sing to Cilla. There was nothing else to say.

A horn blared as Joyce crossed Far West Boulevard against the light. She was still running and hadn't seen the light. Or the car, for that matter. She staggered, slowed to a walk, gasping, her sides aching. She stopped to catch her breath and leaned against a low wall bordering the city's cemetery, separating it from Far West Boulevard. The cemetery was five full miles from Santiago Street. Inconceivable that she could have run so far. She glanced over the wall, put there to protect motorists from the certainty that the dead existed, that ultimately there are more of them than there are of us.

Joyce jumped up and over the wall, continued running through

The graveyards are full of girls like you, Rejoice. "I'm not a girl anymore, Ma!" she cried, sweat and tears falling from her face, and still she ran; she ran without any goal or path, just running through and around the headstones, running so that all she could hear was her own hard breathing, the insistent throb of her heart, the pulse in her throat. Then she heard the birds. A noisy operetta of birds in the live oaks, squat palms, and magnolias. She looked down; she had a shadow. Parasol colors twirled across the sky, summer dawn, gaudy, intense. Last night's wind, like some disgusted housekeeper, had swept moonlessly through St. Elmo, swept it clean, emptied the air of smog and dirt and lint and grit. She was astonished to see the blue hard contours of the distant mountains. You never saw the mountains in August. She sprinted back toward Far West, got to the wall, leaped over, and saw a bus coming. She made it to the stop and took off her sweatshirt. Oh yes, you could see the mountains, but if you lived in St. Elmo you knew that the price extracted for this excruciating clarity was devil's breath heat.

The bus pulled up; the doors opened with a pneumatic hiss, like that of a near-silenced fart. The bus was empty, but nonetheless full of noise as the driver—chunky, balding, redolent of Old Spice and bubble gum—had a transistor radio tacked over his head. KLMO, the Oldie-but-Goldie station, blasted out *Ready Ready Ready to Rock and Roll.* The driver grinned, twitched, reached overhead and turned up the volume.

"I don't have any money with me right now," said Joyce, stepping on the bus. "But please, I can pay you back. I have kids at home. They can't wake up and find both parents gone. They'll think—"

"WHADCHUSAY?" The driver pointed to the radio as if to some bebopping transistor angel.

"I DON'T HAVE ANY CASH ON ME. I HAVE TO BE HOME WHEN MY KIDS WAKE UP. CAN I PLEASE—"

"No can do, lady." He blew another bubble. "Money talks. Shit walks."

"I'm not walking." Resolutely, Joyce took her seat by the door. The driver regarded her critically while he chomped methodically on his gum. He muttered, put it in gear. The bus and music moved on to the Beach Boys. Just what I need, thought Joyce, a bunch of warbling white boys asking the obvious question, *Why Do Fools Fall in Love?*

The bus turned down Brigham Boulevard. A working man got on, put his lunch bucket on the floor between his feet, and closed his eyes. Others boarded at every stop. This early they all seemed to be cranky and uniformed: nurses on their way to County, skinny girls in Burger King brown, surly young men in Texaco red. Sleepy and cross as his passengers were, the more people on the bus, the merrier grew the driver. He bounced and do-wah-ditty-dittied along with KLMO.

"Hey, St. Elmo!" cried the DJ, "one hundred and one fun degrees at the dawn's early light! When KLMO tells you to cool it, we're not just jiving you! All you poor working saps, up this early—that includes yours truly here, ha ha ha, I got three in a row for you. Rock and roll's trinity, ha ha, rise and shiners, get ready for a little musical caffeine!"

La Bamba burst over the bus and the driver shouted, *"¡Hola!,"* danced in his seat, sang along with Richie Valens, even though the lyrics to *La Bamba* were in a language he could not speak. He pulled the bus over and a stout middle-aged woman got on. Her uniform was Standard Matron: blue skirt, white blouse, support hose, thick-soled shoes. Her face was round and her jowls hung heavy as theater curtains suspended from her cheekbones. She was as far from *Chantilly Lace,* wiggles, giggles, and ponytails as could be, but the driver (singing with the Big Bopper) ogled the matron as if her massive breasts dripped nectar. She ignored him. She sat down beside Joyce and percolated the odor of Dial soap and rectitude.

That'll Be the Day, sang out the late, great Buddy Holly. Oh yes, that'll be—this is—the day. The day to go home and face kids' questions. Learn to live with loss. Learn to live with everything upside down. Jack would learn to live with Dorrie Vardy and commit adultery with his wife. Joyce's bed would now give him the respite, afternoon delights, moments snatched from Dorrie and domestic obligation. He would come to Joyce's bed, come in Joyce's bed, and go home. She bit her lip against the welling tears, crying, as far as the bus driver and the other passengers knew, because Buddy and Richie and the Big Bopper were dead. Alarmed by her sobbing, the man with the lunch bucket between his feet woke up. The Burger King girls and Texaco boys drew their attention from their windows and fastened it on the slender, fair-haired woman in blue jeans and a T-shirt crying her eyes out.

"Ha ha ha!" guffawed Mr. KLMO. "I bet there are those of you who couldn't answer this question twenty years ago! I bet you still can't answer it! Tell me, rise and shiners, who wrote *The Book of Love?*"

The question—the absolute lack of an answer—sent Joyce off into a fresh paroxysm of weeping. The Standard Matron, in an act utterly inconsistent with her Dial soap and rectitude, reached over and gave Joyce a hug, both astringent and comforting. "It's just the same old story, honey. We each get to write a chapter in the same old book." The bus driver downshifted, said the next stop was Brigham and Santiago.

The girls were not awake. Since she could not even call Sandee (who was in Puerto Vallarta with her new boyfriend, Ray), Joyce got in the shower, stayed there till she heard the girls stirring. She forbade them to go in the kitchen. Cilla's face wore a look of hurt and suspicion, and Lisa Marie, for all her little-girl beauty, had that shrewd, sizing-up expression in her eyes. Joyce took them to McDonald's for breakfast.

When they got home, it was 104 degrees already. Joyce faced the carnage in the kitchen, testifying as it did to last night's anguish and today's loss. To help her in this battle, she enlisted those well-known Roman generals, Ajax, Clorox, Lysol, Pine-Sol, Comet, and Mr. Clean. Parson's ammonia was the chaplain of this venture, this literal mopping-up campaign. Joyce told herself the kitchen must be cleaned before she could tell the girls anything. They watched from the doorway, holding on to the Colonel. They offered to help. Joyce thanked them, but declined. They had not made the mess; they had no part in it.

She'd already had enough of KLMO's Oldies but Goldies for one day, thank you, and switched the radio dial to KBOY, the Top Ten station, and it seemed more penance yet that as she cleaned she should have to endure Barry Manilow and Andy Gibb.

The KBOY disc jockey had a voice heavy on contempt and probably high on speed. "Splish splash! The King's been taking a bath the last few years. Whoo-hooo—anyone out there remember Elvis Presley?"

"Stick it," snapped Joyce, scrubbing all the harder.

"Hey!" countered the DJ as though he had heard her. "When was the last time you tapped your toes to *Memories*—or hey, try this, *Unchained Melody?*" He deepened his voice, sang a few goofy bars. Seriously, folks, all you rock and rollercoasters out there, you'd better unchain yourself from the old desk and get to the pool because it's a hundred and five and climbing! And if that's not hot enough for you, I'm going to heat things up even more! Listen, when the King does it right—and I do mean *when*—there's no one like him. He's done it right this time. It hasn't hit the Top Ten, but it's still climbing! Let's help the old King out and play *WAY DOWN!*"

"Elvis doesn't need your help, you little pipsqueak," Joyce muttered.

The insistent beat, opening bars of *Way Down* thrummed out, but the DJ just kept talking. "Can you dig it! The King's best since *Burning Love*, five years ago now. Welcome back, Elvis!"

"Elvis never left, you pencil...head." Joyce gave the girls a weak smile.

The task was nearly finished, and as Elvis's voice filled the kitchen (and she turned the radio up), it seemed suddenly imperative to Joyce that she have it all done—filthy bucket emptied, rags trashed, bottles put away—before Elvis finished singing *Way Down*. She felt it way down, with a kind of irrational urgency, felt herself working simultaneously for, with, and against the music. She rinsed out the bucket on that last, low groin-grabber of a note. She turned to face the girls. The kitchen was clean. But she couldn't say it. Not yet. After lunch, Joyce promised herself. She'd give them lunch and, for dessert, some puffed and confectionated story passing for the truth.

The girls watched her in silence as she began slathering bread with peanut butter and slicing bananas for their sandwiches. She could feel their questions even more poignantly in the silence. In fact, silence seemed to gather up force and invade the kitchen. "That's funny, isn't it?" Joyce reached up to the top of the fridge and gave the radio a thump. "Silence on the radio. That wisecracking DJ better pay attention, or he'll lose his job over this one."

And although Joyce did not know it, she was quite correct: the DJ did lose his job over this long, protracted silence and the four-letter word he shouted when, urgently, he broke that silence with unconfirmed reports from Memphis that Elvis Presley was dead at the age of forty-two.

Joyce took the radio down from the fridge. "Impossible."

...he suffered a heart attack and...

"Impossible." She flipped the dial to KLMO.

...Sources say the singer was found in the bathroom of his Memphis home...

"Impossible." She turned to KNX, KMPC, KRLA, all the crackling Los Angeles stations she could pull in, flickering signals from distant stations, as she sat there, all afternoon, with the radio in her arms, trying to coax from it news that did not say

Baptist Memorial Hospital has us on hold, folks, and as soon as we...

...Sources in Memphis do not deny that...

...The King of Rock and Roll was only forty-two, but...

...His weight had ballooned and there are rumors of heavy drug use...

...They have taken Elvis...

...They are trying...

...A heart attack...

A spokesman for Baptist Memorial Hospital in Memphis has confirmed Elvis Presley has died.

Joyce and the girls sat on the shaded porch. Lisa's head lay in Joyce's lap and Cilla leaned against her mother. They were subdued, pale, eyes redrimmed, unwilling to believe, as they watched the Santiago Street traffic, that life should go on. Shifts at County Hospital changed, five o'clock county workers halted, did their usual homage at the stop sign at Santiago and Sultana. Life was going on. The world seemed to be going on. Certainly it was going by. Joyce rocked back and forth, stroking Lisa's hair, watching the wind flirt with the pink-papery crepe myrtle blossoms, rise more insistently, throttle them; it blew over Joyce and her daughters, with the same urgency that had brought her to her feet last night. "Dad's coming back," said Joyce as though repeating the wind's message.

"When?" demanded Lisa. She sat up, sniffed, and asked again, "When?"

"Dad's coming back." Joyce tasted the phrase carefully. "I don't know exactly when. I just know he is. Love like that, it doesn't die or change. Nothing can change love like that. Jack will be back."

"Elvis isn't coming back," said Cilla. "Elvis is dead. Elvis is dead and he isn't coming back."

Joyce listened, acutely, to the final expiring breath of that wind that had swept the sky clean, clarified the very air it passed through. "Elvis didn't die. He just passed through."

"You mean he passed away, passed on?"

"No. I don't mean that at all."

"Passed through St. Elmo? Like he was on the train or something?"

"Yes. Like that. Like...well, at night you lie in bed and you hear the train whistle and you know it's passing through, even though it doesn't stop, even though you can't see it. You know it went through. You don't doubt it." Joyce rose, dusted off her clothes, turned and stared critically at the porch with its dog-scratched door and torn screens; she glanced at the scrawny crepe myrtles flanking her and the dusty, leaf-choked walk. The little girls regarded her with a mixture of anxiety and enthusiasm. "Yes girls, I think that's how it happened. I think Elvis passed through time. Think of it like time was a sieve or a colander, and we all get bounced in it till finally we just pass through. Elvis passed through this sieve, his flesh, everything that can suffer, all that gets thrown away—but the important things, they don't—"

"What important things?"

"Love. Music. Elvis always had it to give and he didn't die, girls. He passed through time and he's going to live forever, and he'd want his truth to go marching on. Lisa, you know in that hall drawer, the third from the top? There's all that Halloween stuff? You find those rolls of black crepe paper and bring them out. And Cilla, you bring me a clean white sheet and that big poster of Elvis from your room and the King Creole poster too."

"You want the orange crepe paper too?" asked Lisa.

"No. You girls hurry. We have work to do. I'll need help bringing that picnic table around here to the front."

Reluctantly, the girls got to their feet. The afternoon sun made its separate peace and retreated. The wind died. The dust settled. And clarity came on Joyce as it had when she'd risen from the baptismal waters of the irrigation ditch, clarity bright as the collusion of light and water, the lights of so very long ago, caught in the lagoon: the condensation of water into light, the consolidation of light into water. Joyce rose carefully, brushed her hair back from her face, ready to accept, without straining, whatever splendor might illuminate or encircle her.

Nineteen

Folders, files, and forms in triplicate were strewn across Emily's desk; they were filled with numbers, sums and percentages, calculations, net and gross, the latter word best describing her reaction to all this. Moreover, Marge Mason sat at her side virtually all afternoon, breathing metallically down Emily's neck and saying things like, "There, now you can move that figure from column H and subtract that portion of the household budget. See?"

Emily did not see. Indeed, she did not want to see. "Math was never my forte," she explained at last. "I passed statistics and college math and something else they said I had to have to be a whole human being, and a USC graduate." She drew the latter phrase out to impress Marge, but it seemed to have the opposite effect. "I can't remember how I passed them, but I must have. I'm here, aren't I?"

"Are you?" inquired Marge with as much irony as a woman like that could muster. "Shall we return to these figures, Emily? I'm trying to show you how to handle this complicated part of your job."

"Well, I abject. I mean, I object. I don't believe we should even listen to anonymous phone calls, or if we listen, we certainly shouldn't act on them. It's not honorable, a call like that. It's obscene. I read this story once where—"

"This is not a story, Emily. This is your job. In this job we must take everything into consideration."

"Maybe this caller just hates Elvis. Maybe it's that simple."

Marge laughed mirthlessly. "It's not simple. I called KLMO. This man was telling the truth."

"But that Memory Jackpot money was a gift! It wasn't earned income!"

"Our system doesn't allow for gifts. Income is income, whether earned or not. I know this is frustrating and difficult, Emily, but you must pay attention. Dealing with fraud is, unfortunately, part of our work. Ask your co-workers." Marge gestured in her broody fashion to the duckling social workers whose desks adjoined Emily's. It was five o'clock, and so the other social workers nodded in sad agreement while trying not to appear overly eager to take their purses out, tuck away their caseloads. The phone rang and one of them answered, handed the receiver to Emily.

Emily excused herself from Marge's mathematical ministrations. "Emily Shaw. Yes. Yes. I'm that child's caseworker." Her voice shook and she broke the lead on her pencil. "What was she doing on a motorcycle! She's only thirteen! Her Dad! And what about him? This is not a routine call to me! Never mind. I'm on my way."

Emily slammed the phone down, snatched her purse from the drawer. "Have to go. *In extremis.* You know how it is." And before Marge could reply, or restrain her, Emily flew through the office, out to the reception area, where she elbowed past the sulking, supplicating humanity being driven out the doors now that it was closing time. Emily thrust herself past all of them, stumbled down the steps, and ran headlong into Sid Johnson, who caught her before she fell.

"Oh, Sid! Sid!" She gripped his coat and cried, "There's been a motorcycle accident, Sid! Cilla and Jack! They're at County! I have to go. Oh, Sid, that guy called Marge and she's really doing it to Joyce, and Sid, she's going to make me do it! Oh, Sid—it's so—I can't, Sid! I can't do that to a friend!"

"You go on to the hospital, Emily. I'll be there when I can. Soon. Don't think about Marge. Not now."

Emily ran across the grassy expanse and burst into the Emergency waiting room. The Eastbound's nerdy sax player, Eldon, was already there, sitting by Sandee's brother, Phil. Charleen was reading a story to Justin. Lisa was hunched and huddled in Sandee's arms. Little Jack lay asleep in Joyce's arms. Joyce's face lit to see Emily, and when Emily started crying, she patted her hand. "Cilla's going to be fine," Joyce whispered.

"And Jack?"

"Jack's going to be fine too."

Across from Emily, Charleen raised her eyebrows dubiously and Emily blanched. She turned back to Joyce and said she'd stay as long as Joyce wanted her to.

"You know, Emily, it seems like we've known you, like we've been friends, for a long, long time." Joyce closed her eyes and dozed over Little Jack's curly head.

With the rest of them, Emily waited, straining to hear some voice, some just-inaudible call. But other than the voices of other families in the huge waiting room, all that could be heard was Muzak, punctuated frequently by a cool public voice speaking hospital codes, calling for certain individuals to come to certain places for numbered reasons. As the late-afternoon shadows swallowed up the Emergency waiting room, the fluorescent lights burned brighter and seemingly higher. Gradually, they all arrived. The word—such word as there was—percolated amongst them: Dogleg still in his Union 76 uniform, Demetrius Ball still wearing his nametag from Stetler's Ford agency, Mike Hershey, his John Deere cap and facial features pulled even more tightly to one side, and Stan Denby. Charleen's husband (whose name Emily could never remember) and CJ or EJ or BJ came too. Shortly after seven Florence Sullivan arrived, Denny's sister-in-law.

Florence was a first-grade teacher and informed them all in an authoritative fashion that she had come to take the children, give them dinner, and have them spend the night with her.

"I'm not moving," said Lisa.

"Oh, honey, please go with Florence and the boys," Joyce urged her. "Please. It'll be better and I'll call—"

"You can't make me." Lisa drew herself up into a tight little ball like a hedgehog. "I'm staying close to my sister and my dad."

"All right," Joyce said wearily. "Lisa stays."

The Vardy boys, though, went to the tune of Florence's promise of Pudding Pops and Tater Tots. "I've already got a substitute lined up for tomorrow," Florence said, patting Joyce's hand. "So these little boys can stay with me as long as they need to. Don't worry about them, Joyce."

Florence and the boys left. The rest of them waited. Those who smoked, smoked. They made trips back and forth to the candy machine, the Coke machine, the cafeteria for Styrofoam cups of the most awful coffee. Their eyes glazed and faded in the harsh fluorescent light. They leafed through old magazines and stared at the print of newspapers. They spoke in whispers and slumped, sagged in plastic chairs. Where the chairs were ripped, they picked the stuffing out and pushed it back in. They sat bolt upright each time the swinging doors from Emergency opened and a white-clad figure emerged. They wilted when none of these people brought news of Jack or Cilla. They listened to the hospital announcements and the Muzak spilling from ubiquitous speakers in the ceiling.

"Isn't it bad enough," groaned Stan, "without Mantovani?"

"That's what they play in rock-and-roll hell," said Meatball.

"While they make you drink this sweatsock java." Dogleg drained his cup. "Any more where this came from?"

Emily volunteered to go for another round of sweatsock java, took orders for seven coffees, and returned from the cafeteria with the coffees, and a milk and doughnut for Lisa. Bearing the tray in her arms, Emily returned to her people gathered in the waiting room. Lisa Marie thanked her for the milk and doughnut, then Stan took a coffee, Eldon. Emily noticed that Ray had joined them. His cinder block bulk filled up the chair next to Sandee, and Emily could hear the scratch of his gravelly voice. His gravelly familiar voice.

She took the tray over to Sandee and stared at Ray, who was wearing his working clothes but smelled of beer and onions. He looked alarmed and then amused to see Emily.

"Thanks, Emily." Sandee took her coffee. "You remember Ray, don't you?"

"I remember Ray. I'm certain I remember Ray," she added, flushing, dismayed, appalled, but convinced she'd heard the same gruff, insinuative undercurrent of her anonymous caller. "Yes. I remember. In fact," she went on nervously, "we've talked since that night at the Cask and Cleaver, haven't we? We talked on the phone. I'm sure we have."

Ray shrugged, went back to his conversation with Sandee.

Emily glanced over at Joyce, who seemed uninterested in this exchange. Why should she be? Why should any of them be? Ray was Sandee's man. Ray lived with Sandee. Why would he—? What if I'm wrong, she thought, and I accuse him and— Emily took a deep breath, and courage from Oscar Wilde, because if you want to live more than one life, well, you must be prepared for more than one death. "You shouldn't be here, Ray. You are not a friend to Joyce and all these people, they're loyal. I know you're not. Maybe they don't know it," she declared, as much to Joyce as to Ray, "but I do. I recognize your voice. I don't know why—why did you turn Joyce in to the county?—but I know it was you."

"You goofy broad, get the hell outa here."

"You did it! Admit it!"

"Emily!" cried Sandee. "What's—"

"Ray was the one! He was the anonymous caller! He called me and turned Joyce in and then he called my supervisor! I know it was you! I know your voice!"

"You goofy college girl," Ray sneered. "County paying you overtime to sit here with the riffraff?"

Emily flung the tray—four cups of steaming hot coffee—into Ray's lap.

Ray jumped up, screamed, swore, and, still screaming and swearing, he tried to pull his pants away from his body, couldn't, had to undo his belt and drop his pants around his ankles. "Bitch! Whore!"

Sandee leapt to her feet, put her body between Emily and Ray, who was about to launch himself. "Ray! Ray, stop! You can't hit her!"

"Bitch poured fucking hot—"

"You called me!" Emily shrieked. "You made that obscene phone call! And when I didn't do anything about it, you called my supervisor, Marge, and—"

"You goofy bitch! I never—"

"That's what you called me on the phone! You said I was goofy! You said, *You really are as goofy as they say....*"

Joyce and Sandee exchanged horrified, knowing glances, and Sandee's eyes bulged. She went *oof oof oof* with every breath, as though she had been kicked in the stomach. She reeled, and when she could speak, she turned to Ray, said almost wistfully, "Ray, I came home that day Joyce colored my hair, Ray, and I said, You should see the note that goofy new social worker wrote Joyce—"

"So fucking what! Look what she—"

"You did, Ray," Sandee whispered. "You did it. Why?"

"Why?" Joyce echoed.

Ray shook his fist at Emily.

Sandee tackled him. She kicked his feet out from underneath him. Not difficult since his pants were still around his ankles. She thrust her shoulder right up into his diaphragm and down he went. She jumped on top of him, and in the flail of fists and flying oaths you could hear Sandee grunt and Ray yelp as she banged his head against the floor, holding him by the ears. Dogleg, Phil, Meatball, and Mike all tried to pull the two of them apart. Ray staggered to his feet, spluttering blood and foam from his nose and lips. Sandee, with one massive, concentrated thrust, freed herself from the grip of Phil and Meatball and she ran, butting her head into Ray's stomach; he hit the floor and by then hospital security arrived, and though security guards half-nelsoned Sandee's arm, they could not silence her. "You sonofabitch! You get out of my house! You get out of my life! You lying fucker! Liar! How could you? How could you sleep with me and—" Sandee began to blubber tears; blood bubbled from a cut on her lip. "I loved you! I was good to you! Five years! I've been your woman five years! I've loved you and looked after you and you—how could you do this to me?"

"I didn't do anything to you." Ray shook himself free of the security guard, pulled his pants up and buckled them.

"What happens to Joycie happens to me!"

"I'm sick of Joycie," he snarled. "I'm sick of Elvis too. You love Elvis and Joycie so much"—he pulled his key ring from his pocket— "you can fucking go live with them! I'm sick of you. All of you!" He threw the house key at Sandee's feet. "Have my stuff outside tomorrow, all my stuff, or I break the door down, bitch."

"Woof woof," Lisa called after him. "Woof woof."

"Aw fuck off." The sliding doors opened and Ray stood there, in their jaws, as though tempting fate. He turned, shook his fist at Emily Shaw. "You're a bitch, you know that? Your boss is going to make sure you lose your job. You're going to get it, yeah, you and that big nigger that came before you. You—"

"What big nigger?" Sid Johnson stood behind Ray. "I don't see no big nigger in these parts. I know some, though. Mean ones."

Ray vanished into the night. Sid flashed his county card, dissuaded the security guards from throwing Sandee out too. Sandee and Joyce retreated to the women's bathroom while Emily sat with the others, her hands rolled into fists, the tension and fear released, but not salved, by the violence. When Stan put his arm around her, Emily cried softly. One by one they came up to her, assuring her she was not goofy. They admired her courage. Even Sid Johnson admired her courage. Courage was not a word Emily had ever much trafficked in, except on paper—novels, poems, stories, and the like. It was not a word that Tri Delts very often used. She briefly wondered if perhaps she'd been brave all along and just not known it, like having blue jeans on under a ball gown and feeling only the occasional pinch of the zipper.

Joyce and Sandee emerged from the bathroom, just as TRAUMA came out to say that Cilla was in Recovery. That the fractures in her bones had been set and her mother could see her. Tomorrow she could have other visitors. TRAUMA smiled at Lisa.

"And Jack?" said Joyce. "Jack?"

"Joyce." TRAUMA put his arm around her shoulders. "We can't wait for his condition to stabilize. There's too much swelling from the head injuries. We have to go ahead and operate now. It's risky. But it's our only chance."

"What kind of chance? What kind of chance does he have?"

"Let me take you in to see Cilla, Joyce. And then you can all go up to the second-floor Intensive Care waiting room. When Jack gets out of surgery, he'll be in Intensive Care. You wait there. It's more comfortable. Less public." TRAUMA glanced at the spilled ashtrays and coffee puddles on the floor. He led Joyce away. "It'll be better for everyone."

Twenty

Emily tucked her feet up in the plastic chair, trying hard to read a story in an ancient *McCall's* and not to look just across from her, where a grizzled old drunk snored, obliviously urinating on himself and the floor. Two drug addicts leaned against each other, the skin on their forearms veined and pale as Roquefort cheese. A handsome young Chicano ogled Emily with his right eye while he covered the left half of his face with a towel he'd been given when he came in sporting a long graceful gash that ran from his temple to his chin His mother caught him flirting with Emily and slapped his knee, glared at Emily, who quickly looked back down at the *McCall's*. This was truly not the sort of thing she had witnessed as a Candy Striper at St. Luke's Hospital By-The-Sea. Two police supported between them a black youth whose left leg dangled uselessly. Sid must have known him, because he got up, spoke briefly to the police and to the young man, whose face twisted in a mask of pain. Certainly, Emily thought, pain was pain, but in Laguna Beach the elegant frame around it took your attention from the picture of pain. And here, the picture burst through the splintery frame, burst out and fell at your feet and you could not walk around it. This is not to say you could alter or ameliorate someone else's pain, but you could not, in St. Elmo, ignore it.

You could, however, walk around the puddle of pee in front of the drunk, and Emily watched while a slender woman did just that, gasped, sidestepped the puddle to protect her high-heeled white leather boots. She wore a white sheath dress, and Emily was surprised to hear Sandee say unmistakably and with no malice aforethought— "Oh shit! Dorrie! How did you—"

"I went by Joyce's house, and the neighbors—"

"Look, Dorrie, I tried to call you at your mother's house, but there was no answer and I didn't know where else to—" Sandee looked stricken. "Your mother isn't—"

"No, Mom's fine. I don't mean fine-fine. Of course she's still sick." Dorrie's tight dress had a deep V cleavage framed by thick lace from her shoulders to her waist. The high-heeled boots seemed to crawl up her thin legs. "Where's Joyce?"

"Listen, Dorrie, you better sit down. I guess I have to—" Sandee looked around to see if there was anyone else to do this. There wasn't. "Do you know there's been a motorcycle accident?"

"Yes, Joyce's neighbor told—"

"It was Jack and Cilla on the bike, Dorrie. Jack let Cilla wear the helmet. Cilla's busted up, her leg's broke and there's some bad—well, Cilla's going to be okay. Joycie is with her now. When Joycie comes back, we're all going up to ICU and wait—" Sandee gulped—"for word on Jack. Jack's in surgery. Jack is—" Sandee glanced over to Charleen, who supplied the word *iffy*. "Jack's iffy, Dorrie."

"Oh, that's terrible."

Actually, it was embarrassing. Dorrie's *Oh, that's terrible* might have been used to describe a cake that had fallen, or an omelet that had failed to fluff. Dorrie lowered herself to a chair, trembling as she began biting her nails. Two bright spots—blush unrelated to blusher—burned in her cheeks.

"Well, yes," Sandee stammered. "It is pretty terrible."

"'How iffy is he, exactly? I mean—where?"

"Where what?"

"Where is Jack iffy, I mean—"

"Shit!" cried Stan, whose tolerance for Dorrie in the best of times was limited. "Jack's got head injuries, internal bleeding, punctured lungs, broken ribs and collarbone, and other than the fact that his brain is swelling and he's just gone in for brain surgery, Dorrie, we just really don't know a fuck of a lot!"

"I guess I better wait for Joyce." Dorrie reached into her bag and took out a cigarette, lit it, and went back to nibbling her fingernails. She bit and puffed and puffed and bit, and finally she said, "The Colonel nearly bit my head off when I went in the gate."

"He's back?" cried Lisa. "Really!"

"I guess so!" Dorrie sniffed. "He gave me a run in my pantyhose when he chased me off." She pointed to the narrow ladder, adding that she had a new pair in the car. "Then the next-door neighbors came out and told me what they'd heard about Jack on the radio, and then, while they were trying to tell me all this bad news, a bunch of these really strange-looking Oriental types came running down the street and they kept pointing to the dog and shouting at me, *Woof! Woof! Woof! Woof!* What was I supposed to say?"

"Oh glory hallelujah!" whooped Sandee and Lisa together as they ran toward Joyce, who stepped from the elevator into the waiting room. "The Colonel's back! Dorrie says the Colonel's back home!"

"Dorrie?" Joyce looked up as though expecting Mao Tse-tung.

Dorrie took a deep drag off her cigarette, slammed it into the sand of the knee-high ashtray, burst into tears, and ran, sobbing, to Joyce's shoulder. Emily and the others gave a collective sigh of relief because *Oh, that's terrible* did not, after all, account for the extent of Dorrie's feelings. Dorrie had been waiting for Joyce, Emily thought; we're all waiting for Joyce. Emily looked around her, surprised that Joyce should be so central to so many disparate lives. She glanced at Sid, who loosened his tie, shook his head. Emily tried to list mentally the number of lives in which she was crucial; there were no names amongst her Tri Delt sisters. Emily knew she was but a pawn to her parents, a pawn grown up to be an ornament. And Rick?

Joyce escorted Dorrie back to a plastic chair. Dorrie nattered and wept and chattered while Joyce spoke low and soothingly, said they were all going to go up to the Intensive Care waiting room on the second floor. "We'll wait for word on Jack up there. Can we get you some coffee or something?"

"Oh, Joyce!" Dorrie wailed, pulling a Kleenex from her purse. "You haven't heard a *word* I've said! You don't understand! I can't go up to Intensive Care! I'm really sorry but I—"

"I know it's terrible, Dorrie, and it's scary, but Jack is not going to die. I know that. Jack will not die. Not like this."

"I mean, I'm going to have to leave and it doesn't mean, well, the accident is awful, really awful, but I didn't know about it and it wasn't my fault and I already—plans, you see?"

"Holy frijole!" snorted Dogleg. "And I thought I'd seen everything!" But the rest of them were not so swift, so knowing or astute. The rest of them had a vaguely greenish *What what?* painted across their faces. Joyce mumbled and murmured words to the effect of no, they didn't quite see.

Well, it was a long, convoluted story and it came out oddly and if it had been a house, it would have been built second story first, doors upside down, shingles on the kitchen floor, but you might still have recognized it as a house for all that because, as it turned out, Dorrie had come to Joyce's originally because there was This Person waiting out in the hospital parking lot. This Person was waiting out in the parking lot now, but at Joyce's, This Person was just in the car. Joyce's house was all closed up and the Colonel attacked her and the neighbors came out and told her the terrible news they'd heard on the radio. But then the foreigners came to the gate and shouted *woof woof* at Dorrie, who had come, in the first place, to tell Joyce about This Person who was in the hospital parking lot now because of the terrible accident and Dorrie was so glad Cilla would be better and it was just terrible there weren't two helmets and when she'd left the boys off, she just figured Jack would go right down to the desert and not that he would go by Cilla's school and it's too bad now that he did. Dorrie had been so sure he was going to go straight to the desert that she came back by Joyce's with This Person so that Joyce could, well, give Jack a sort of message. Dorrie wanted to pick up the boys and leave off a message. It would be easier for Joyce to deliver the message, because she loved Jack and Dorrie always knew that. "And I don't care, really, Joyce. I did. I used to, but it's easier for you to tell Jack that Dwayne—This

Person—Dwayne has a job waiting for him in the Texas oil fields and he makes good money now, but in Texas! Well, we're going to Texas. We're getting married first," she added brightly. "In Vegas." Dorrie already had the ring. Dwayne had bought it at the Price Club and it had two rubies and two diamonds. He drove a Porsche, and in Texas, Dorrie could maybe go to beauty school, like she always wanted, and Dwayne already had a buddy there who'd rented them a furnished apartment. "Don't you see?" Dorrie cried. "I have to go! Dwayne's my chance for happiness and I'm taking it!"

She shouted this with as much vigor as a confused woman can, because it turned out that all this time—well, maybe not all this time, but some of it—for some time now Dorrie's mother had not been sick at all. But when Jack was working those gigs in the desert it was easier to leave the little boys with Joyce because Dorrie never needed to worry about them then, or even think about them, and she needed, they needed, that is, Dorrie and Dwayne wanted—"It isn't like Jack didn't know about Dwayne. He did. I thought Jack was going to kill him! I heard that story, Joyce, you know, all those years ago, Jack thought you were sleeping with some guy and he chased him into the ditch, wrecked his Studebaker, and beat the living shit out of the guy. Was that the same accident? Anyway, I was really worried that Jack would just kill Dwayne, but he didn't. He just seemed really *bored* by the whole thing. I mean, really, my feelings were kind of hurt. And now, well, I don't think he really, like, you know, he isn't too, like, broke up—" Dorrie lit up her fourth cigarette and blew out the match. She went on that she was really sorry about the accident, of course she was! But she didn't love Jack, like, you know love-love, that kind. She felt like his sister. "I feel kind of like your sister too, Joyce, and if I was your sister," she continued triumphantly, chasing her own logic like a dog following a kite tail aloft, "you'd say to me—take this chance, Dorrie! Take this chance for happiness!"

"He's your what?" Joyce rubbed her hands slowly across her temples. "Dwayne's your—?"

"He's going to be my husband. *He's* not married! He was once, but he's legally divorced and he can marry me and Jack never would."

"What about Justin and Little Jack?" asked Sandee. "What about them?"

"Well, they'll be ushers at my wedding. Dwayne'll be their step-dad."

"No, no—" Joyce faltered. "You said something else. You said Dwayne was your—"

"My chance for happiness! That's what I said! And I mean it!" Dorrie took quick, intense puffs.

"Jack wasn't?"

"I guess not."

Joyce appraised Dorrie slowly. Dorrie was about to take Jack off like a dirty shirt, to trade him for a Porsche, a Price Club wedding ring, and a furnished apartment. Jack was not Dorrie's chance for happiness. He had been bored with her infidelity. Looking at Dorrie now, Joyce found it almost inconceivable that she should have nearly knifed her husband over this woman. Could this woman have caused her one moment's anguish or sorrow? Dorrie puffed and puckered around her cigarette; she had a look of confectionary confusion; her body shook the way a Twinkie would if you took its temperature. Joyce pushed her hair back from her face with both hands. She understood why Dorrie had come to Santiago Street: it was not to pick up the boys, or leave off a message. Dorrie wanted Joyce's blessing. She wanted Joyce to say, *"Vaya con Dios, My Darling,* go and be *The Yellow Rose of Texas* and have a great time at *Rosie's Cantina, Teddy Bear!* Of course you *Got a Lot of Living to Do, Treat Me Nice, Tutti Frutti, Shake, Rattle and Roll* right out of St. Elmo and *Viva Las Vegas!"*

Joyce spoke slowly. "Well, you know what Elvis would say if he was here?"

"No. What?"

Joyce smiled sympathetically. *"It's Your Baby—You Rock It."*

"What?"

"You heard me."

"Well—fine! If that's the way you want to be about it!" Dorrie's lower lip thrust out. "I thought you would have cared about Jack, anyway."

"Good-bye, Dorrie."

"Just tell me where to pick up my boys and I'm leaving here and I'm not coming back!"

"You can't have the boys. They're not going with you. You go to Vegas and Texas and wherever else you want. You do what you want, but those boys are staying in St. Elmo."

"They're my children!"

"They're Jack's children too."

"Jack's not—Jack might not even—" Dorrie paused, acknowledged for the first time the collective hostility around her. "I do care for Jack, I just don't love him."

"Can wisdom be put in a silver rod, or love in a golden bowl?" asked Emily, unbidden.

"Like—uh—pardon me?" Dorrie sniffed. "'Who are you?"

"I'm nobody. Who are you?"

"Dorrie," Joyce stood up. "You take Dwayne, who's waiting for you out there in the parking lot, and you take your chance for happiness and you go to Vegas and get married. Adiós, Dorrie—*Tutti Frutti,* you go off and be *The Yellow Rose of Texas, Teddy Bear,* but you're not taking those little boys. They're not going to live like that. You and your friend—"

Who at that moment entered the Emergency waiting room. Dwayne was a solidly built redheaded man with a beard wreathing a weak chin, which gave him the look of a serious toilet brush. He wore a shirt with a string tie, a suit, and shoes with inconspicuous heels built into them. He called Dorrie "Sugarlump."

Joyce paused long enough to acknowledge the shambling Dwayne. "You ask old Dwayne here if he wants Justin and Little Jack. Wants to support them with all that big money he's going to make in Texas. If they'll fit into the back of a Porsche. If he wants ushers at your wedding. If he wants to share a Vegas hotel room with a two-year-old and a four-year-old. Ask him, Dorrie."

"Dwayne loves me! He loves my boys!"

"Well, I'm sure it will be a real loss, then, that they're not going with you, but they're not. They're not going to live like that. That kind of poverty and not being wanted or loved or needed."

Dorrie gave a rippling laugh. "Poverty! Is Jack Mr. Moneybags? He, like, drives a motorcycle! You drive a '62 Valiant! You have a plain gold band of a wedding ring. Where's your diamond and ruby wedding ring, Joyce?"

"I'd walk the gravel path with Jack any day. He never had to be Mr. Moneybags for me. I'd rather have Jack whole and alive and beside me"—Joyce's voice trembled, she coughed and went on—"than a hundred rings or cars or houses. And right now, I'm going to do what Jack can't do for himself. I'm going to protect his sons. They're not going with you and old Dwayne there. You go. I'm happy to see you go. But you're not taking those little boys."

"Come on, Sugarlump—" Dwayne took Dorrie's arm. "We'll get settled in Texas and we'll send for them. Hell, we'll go to court and get them if we have to. We'll have the money. Come on, let's just go get married."

"Do that, Dorrie," Joyce suggested reasonably. "You better do it now."

"You know what Elvis says," Sandee chimed in. "*It's Now or Never.*"

Charleen sang a few bars of *Suspicious Minds,* Emily tossed in a little off-key *Don't Be Cruel,* Dogleg offered the opening few lines of *Love Me,* and Stan came up with bits of *Money, Honey.* The others blurted out in shots and volleys, laughs, titles, tunes, and lyrics.

"You're all nuts!" cried Dorrie. "You know that? Jack always said you were nuts, Joyce. He did! He said you were crazy for Elvis and you had a screw loose!"

"Is that so?" snapped Sandee. "Well, Jack told us you were a loose screw!"

"Come on, Sugarlump. You don't have to take this shit."

"You don't," Joyce reminded her. "You can leave." And she did.

Emily's heels clicked swiftly down the deserted hall as she headed toward the old section of the hospital. She had promised to join the others in the ICU waiting room, but she needed to make this call and to make it alone, here in the old wing, the deserted waiting room and phone booth where she had called KLMO that day Ray had first ratted on Joyce. This small sober room had no potted palms, no sliding glass doors, no Muzak. Prewar linoleum floor, green walls, a dozen curry-colored plastic chairs lined up under a bare incandescent lamp, and here in the corner there stood the classic phone booth.

Though she was alone here, Emily nonetheless pulled the door shut behind her and a fluorescent halo flickered overhead. The air in the booth was rank with old grief and cigarette smoke. She put her coin in and kicked the butts littering the floor. She dialed and told the operator she wanted this call billed to her home phone. The operator asked her number.

"You'll have to give me a minute. I can't think of it right off."

"Take your time," said the operator genially.

It occurred to Emily that Shakespeare might not have written his sonnets if he'd had access to a phone. "I live alone," she explained, "and so there's no reason to call myself, is there? I forget sometimes "

"Take your time," repeated the operator.

I have, Emily thought: this was not a rash decision, though it was perhaps an impulsive act. It could have been undertaken in other, more fastidious ways, a cool note, say, written on cream-colored paper when there was world enough and time to think about the wording. But Emily felt an imperative that had nothing to do with Time's wingèd chariot: Emily wished, passionately, for centrality, connection, and above all to be free of the false. She slid her diamond engagement ring off her finger and dropped it in her pocket. She wanted her freedom, and (however late it was on the East Coast and however much Rick hated to be wakened) she wanted it now, here, in this deserted, liver-lighted room. She remembered her own number and gave the operator Rick's Washington, D.C., number. That she knew by heart.

The phone rang twice. In the middle of the third ring it got picked up, though not answered right away. A sleepy woman's voice came on. "Hello? Hello? Is anyone there?"

"I'd like to talk to Rick," said Emily.

The woman rolled over. Oh, Emily saw it all: the bed, there beside the desk where Rick's lawbooks lay open. The woman's bra would be atop the books and her pantyhose draped over all the precedents. His pants were neatly folded and hung over the chair. Rick always neatly folded his pants, however intense the thrust of passion. Emily heard the woman murmur and then settle back down as the phone cord stretched over her bare, pale arm. Rick sat up slowly. Emily swallowed a sour lump of déjà vu, another unmemory, *The Operator,* the story she'd read so long ago, whose elusive last line had so haunted her, though she could not remember it until this very minute, now that the story was about to become history. Emily's history. When Rick answered, Emily said, "This is an obscene phone call."

"Emily? Emily!" Did he look about for his Winning Team Smile? To put it on as one might a pair of glasses? "What's wrong? What time is it?"

"It's late. Too late."

"Listen, Emily—it's not what you think!"

"How do you know what I think? Or feel or anything!"

"Emily, where are you? You sound odd. Let me call you back. This is a bad connection."

"You and me? Yes, I think we are a bad connection."

"No, listen, honey, I can explain. It's—"

"*Now or Never?*" Emily supplied sarcastically. "That's what Elvis says, *Are You Lonesome Tonight?* That's what Elvis wants to know."

"Elvis? What's wrong with you, Emily?"

"Nothing's wrong with me! I'm not goofy and I'm not dithery and I'm not—"

"I never said you were, honey. I don't think you're dithery. I think you're cute. Now listen to me, because I can explain, I—"

"You don't have to. I don't care. We're finished. I don't care who you sleep with, Rick, I say ho-fucking-hum!"

"What?"

"You heard me." Emily consciously tried for Joyce's tone that could be both candid and demanding. "You deserve Shaw, Swine, Swill, Slime, and Turdlock, Rick! You belong with them. You'll end up just like them. You'll whine to your secretary and screw her. You'll screw your partner's wife and turn your marriage into nasty power plays and you'll make money off of money and never touch anything so real, so complicated, so difficult as a woman. I can see you for what you are, Rick, the answer to the Old Maid's Prayer. Well, I'm not an old maid and I won't live like that!"

"Emily. That girl, the one who answered my phone, is my study partner."

"I don't care who she is! It doesn't matter. I told you, we're not engaged! I don't care who you sleep with! I don't care!" But Emily wept just the same, wiped her eyes, while the tears kept coming back "I took off that ring and I'll *never* put it back on. That ring was nothing but a pair of handcuffs and you'll never drag me off to some high-class prison where everything is tidified and smoothed out and bordered in country blue and false as the flavor in a frozen burrito! I'll never live like that! I want to be an eagle! I want to be an eagle like Elvis!"

"What is it with Elvis, Emily?"

Emily wept. "Elvis is the eagle who does know what's in the pit—and he didn't have to ask the mole. He went there. Himself. He lived it! Oh Rick, you wouldn't know *Burning Love* if you walked across it in your bare feet!"

"You're too upset to continue this conversation. I'll call you back in the morning and we can—"

"Really? Where will you call me? Where do you think I am? Lying in an empty bed at the Raintree Apartments surrounded by ducks? You want my number, Rick? The one here, in this deserted phone booth at County Hospital?"

"Hospital! Are you hurt?"

"Of course I'm hurt, you dimwit! But I expected it. I had the coming attractions a long time ago, in that story. I've had the coming attractions for twenty-three years," she sighed, "so it doesn't really matter to me who you sleep with and it would not matter if you were sleeping alone. I'm finished. I'm in love with someone else."

"Oh yeah?" Rick snorted. "Who? Elvis?"

The light dimmed or fluttered, as though some reedy wind or shadow passed. Emily opened the door and peered out of the booth, looking for the security guard, who was doubtlessly hovering about and enjoying this conversation. Though she saw no one, she felt certain she was not alone, as you know the winter sun is there when you cannot see it through the clouds: light suppressed, suffused, but light all the same. Rick rattled on and on and Emily began to wish she had made this call from some more public part of the hospital. She lowered the phone from her ear. There was someone here. Sitting in one of the ugly mustard-colored chairs in the empty waiting room. His thick, slick, dark hair fell forward, obscuring his face. His elbows rested on his knees, his ten fingers touching at the tips. He had been waiting a long time. A long, lonely time. Emily's fingers crawled up the phone to disconnect Rick, though she never took her eyes from the figure in the empty room. His collar stood up high against his neck and his short sleeves were rolled up tight against his arms. He raised his gaze from the floor. His was a young man's face, a boy really, vulnerable, beautiful, bright, shy, and inherently sweet. But his eyes—and it was the eyes that held her transfixed—were an old man's eyes, old eyes that had known great suffering. His eyes were full of pain and anguish, both endured and inflicted. The tension in his hands and his expression were at once humble and dramatic; everything about him simultaneously evoked, implored, and offered pity. His eyes met Emily's eyes, as though completing a song begun a long time before, a silent refrain transcending historical tragedy, testifying to a story more interesting and ambiguous than that.

"If you'd like to make a call…," chirped the recording from the phone, "please hang up and dial again. If you'd like to…"

Emily hung up. She pressed her forehead into the hard round dial of the phone, her face against the phone's impassive face. "Don't let Jack die," she whispered, as though the connection here were of some extraordinary variety. "Don't let Jack die," over and over and over, even while she dialed information and got Howard Hansen's number, put her dime in the slot, heard the phone gulp it, dialed. But only when Howard answered did she look up. She found exactly what she expected to find: the bare-bulbed light falling on empty yellow chairs, pale green walls, the brown floor mottled, spongy as a toadstool, un-redeemed, but transformed all the same.

Twenty-one

Cuddled, huddled, heads drooping on any adjacent shoulder, they slept, snoozed, and stretched when they could. The Eastbound Express, Joyce, Sandee, Lisa, Charleen, Phil, and Sid all camped in the second-floor ICU waiting room, which was indeed a good deal less public, smaller, with curtains on the windows and lamps instead of harsh overhead lights. There were posters on the wall and glass ashtrays instead of knee-high sandboxes. The chairs were not bolted to the floor, and two vases held plastic flowers of forlorn autumnal hues.

Emily, however, was in the hallway, pacing in front of the elevator doors. Down the hall from her, in the Orthopedics office, a secretary played an unrelenting riff on the electric typewriter.

The elevator doors opened and Howard Hansen stepped out, and Emily moved into his embrace. "Is there any word on Joyce's husband since we got off the phone?" he murmured against her hair.

"No, we're still waiting. I'm so glad you came, Howard, you didn't have to, but I'm—"

"I wanted to. I want to hear your voice. And not on the phone. I want to be with you, Emily, even if it's in ICU."

"Even knowing I've broken all the rules?"

"Especially knowing that," he replied with a tender smile.

"I've gotten involved with everyone I'm not supposed to be involved with and everything's upside down, the professional is personal and the personal is so immediate and terrible. I feel so helpless and I can't really do anything, but I have to be here. It couldn't be any other way. Not for me."

He took her face in his hands; there was an intensity about him that warmed Emily. "I thought I'd lost you for good that Sunday. I shouldn't have warned you, or brought up anything at all to do with the office, but I had to. I couldn't— I let the welfare department touch, muddy up what I feel for you—" He laughed ruefully. "I can't even describe what I feel for you. It's new for me."

"It's new for me too. I broke my engagement." She held up her naked left hand. "I'm free."

"Then I want to break all the rules too." He pulled her close to him and held her while, down the hall, in Orthopedics, the Gatling gun percussion on the typewriter continued. "I was afraid it was just a night you'd forget, you'd vanish into your other life and forget—"

"I could never forget that night, and I'm not vanishing, and I don't have another life. Everything I said in the car, it was all lies and I don't know why I said it, just using lies to cover up other lies, but I'm not just doing this job till I get married, and I'm *not* leaving St. Elmo, and I'll never make fun of Joyce Jackson, and I won't let Marge use me against her. You know about the hearing on Monday?"

"Yes," he said dryly. "I got my copy of her letter."

"It made me sick to read it, sort of cramped up and cotton-mouthed and bilious."

"Like a hangover. I know just what you mean."

"She's not going to use me as a weapon, Howard. I don't know what will happen at this hearing, but that won't. I won't be used as a weapon against my friends."

"Marge uses everyone as a weapon. She's a destroyer. That's why Sid left Family Assistance, because of the USS *Marge*."

"I know that. Sid's in the ICU waiting room too."

"I might have guessed as much." Howard touched her hair, and Emily lifted her face to him as though he were a spring rain.

At the end of the hall, the typing came to a halt. The light in Orthopedics went out and the secretary locked the door. She waited for the elevator, smiling, watching the couple from the corner of her eye.

Emily and Howard went into the waiting room and sat down together. Sid stirred, opened one eye, chuckled, and went back to sleep. Joyce, who was not sleeping anyway, only dozing with Lisa lying in her lap, nodded at them knowingly. Emily put her head on Howard's shoulder until the surgeon came in.

He was older, with a seamed face and the austere air of a man who has mastered the human body, but not perhaps human nature. He seemed surprised to be confronted with such a large and disparate group. He said, "Mrs. Jackson?" throwing the name into the center of the room and waiting to see who would answer to it.

The news was grave. He could say that, at least in crucial ways, the four-hour operation was successful, but he added that Jack had slipped into a coma. "He remains in a coma, Mrs. Jackson."

Joyce seemed to roll forward and Sandee caught her before she fell from the chair.

"This sounds like very grim news, but I would ask you to consider several things. His spine was not broken. That would have killed him outright or paralyzed him for life. The worst of the impact from this crash seems to have been absorbed by the thoracic region and, all things being equal, I think we can eventually mend the worst of that damage. It will take time, but it's mendable. The head injuries—" The doctor ran an immaculate hand over his fleshy face and heavy, hooded eyes. "If he can be brought out of the coma, I would say your husband has a better-than-even chance to be a whole man again. Eventually. I say he can. I don't promise that he will. We have done as much as medicine allows. Some of it is up to him. Some of it is up to God. Some of it is up to you."

"What can we do?" they asked. "Tell us what we can—"

The doctor took a deep breath. "We don't know how this works, when it works, why it should work, for that matter. But patients have been known to respond—return, you might say—when people they know well, family, close friends, go in and talk, literally call the patient back, shout, long enough. We know that sometimes human voices, well-known voices of people the patient loves, can reach that patient where medicine cannot. I can offer you that much hope. I cannot give you a time, or certainty, just that much hope."

Joyce rose unsteadily to her feet. "Will you take me to him?"

"Just go right behind those doors, the ICU nurse's station. They'll take you. No more than two at a time. Good luck, Mrs. Jackson."

Joyce refused all offers—even Sandee's, even Lisa's—of anyone to accompany her. She insisted on going in alone, at least this first time. She suggested they all go home and get some sleep. It might be a long time yet. They might have to work in shifts.

They watched Joyce disappear behind the ICU doors and returned to the waiting room, but no one could sleep after that and yet no one made an effort to leave. They sat silently, anxiously, until dawn's milky tones fell through the high grilled window, colored the floor, the walls. Sid turned off the lamp. The night's vigil was finished. "I'm going over to the office," he said. "I'll be back later."

Phil took Sandee's house key and said he'd put Ray's stuff on the lawn, wait there till Ray came to get it. Meatball, Mike, and Eldon went with him. Dogleg went back to the Union 76, taking the ICU phone number with him, promising to do his turn if he were needed. Stan took Lisa's hand and said he'd take her out to breakfast and then to see Cilla and then home for some sleep. Howard insisted that Sandee and Charleen should go down to the cafeteria and get some breakfast, take a break, that he and Emily would hold down the fort. "Nothing's going to happen for a while anyway. I'll go down with you and bring Emily up some coffee."

They all left, and Emily rose, stretched, went to the grilled window, where she could see birds noisily waking in the fat, furry palms. In the distance, the bright shriek of a train whistle split the morning air. Again she had the sensation of not being alone, and this time she was considerably more shocked than she'd been in the phone booth. This time, the squat, bulletlike body of Marge Mason filled the doorway. Emily rubbed her eyes: surely this was one of those moments when you woke to find yourself strangled in the sheets, the dream retreating in the face of your stubborn unwillingness to believe it.

"What are you doing here?"

Marge had an electrified air, as though a few sharp jolts of voltage had, in general, improved her complexion, her eyes and hair. She wore a blouse of metallic gray and gray pants that also crackled with current, suppressed excitement. "I was troubled, Emily. I thought and thought. All night I thought—what could make that girl get up and run out of the building like her boyfriend was on fire? And then it came to me. I called County Hospital. I knew where I would find you." Marge gave a threadbare laugh. "What a little twit you are, Emily. You let that woman trick you. Oh, she's clever, I give her that, but—"

"Do you know what's happened to Joyce's husband and daughter?" Emily demanded.

Marge scoffed. "It doesn't change what's going to happen at the hearing. I'm going to take that woman and her stories and her shrine to Elvis Presley and I'm going to blast it all wide open."

Howard's notion of the *USS Marge* came to Emily: a huge female vessel, gunmetal gray, with bosoms like foredecks and eyes like closed-up metal turrets, guns blasting every which way. Emily rubbed her eyes. "Why does everyone have to be your enemy? Why are you so hateful and suspicious?"

"Watch what you say, Emily. You can be—you are—implicated in all this. You knew about the fraud before I got called in. You knew and you did nothing. It will look very suspicious to the FABES board."

"Suspicion always haunts the guilty mind," replied Emily, invoking Shakespeare's line but hearing the refrain from *Suspicious Minds*. "A suspicious mind is a terrible thing, just like Elvis said, Elvis and Shakespeare."

"Has she turned you into an Elvis fruitcake too? It's unbecoming on an educated person."

"I recognize a great artist when—"

"Oh, she really has got to you, hasn't she? Elvis Presley was a drugged-up, ignorant cotton picker—"

"Elvis might have been born to poverty, but he rose to be the

King," replied Emily, quoting Joyce, adding on her own, "he immortalized his best material and dignified even the worst of it."

"You and this woman are both nuts! Nuts! You and this woman are crazy!"

Emily regarded Marge with an almost scientific curiosity; she listened while Marge rattled her sabers and marshaled her threats and evidence, railing always against "that woman," never speaking Joyce's name. Slowly, to Emily's mind, the unspoken became the obvious. "I understand now."

Marge crossed the room with a sergeant's swagger, jabbed Emily with her index finger. "You don't *understand* anything. You don't *know* anything. You don't *have* anything except your little degree from your big university."

Emily took a steep breath. To some extent this was true. Studying sociology at USC had educated her in the dreary compromises institutions extract and daily demand of us, but her instincts remained untutored: Emily saw things in moral and dramatic terms and she trusted life to reward her in moral and dramatic ways. "You can't say Joyce's name, Marge. You've never been able to say it. You can't say it now." Bars of light fell across the floor through grilled windows, illuminating Emily's understanding, and despite Marge's spluttering, she went on. "Joyce is the only welfare client you haven't been able to beat or degrade, the only one who won't satisfy your appetite for victims. Joyce was never a victim, no matter what's happened to her, and you just really can't abide that. When I read, in the file, what you'd written when you first interviewed Joyce all those years ago, I thought, I wondered—what happened in 1968, what happened to make you—"

"She was stoned that day."

"No she wasn't. I understand it now. It was when she reached up and touched your face, wasn't it? It was that particular gesture. You don't mind if people hate your guts, but you can't bear to be pitied. She pities you, Marge."

"I pity you! When I'm done with you, you'll wish—oh, I'll make short work of your job, Emily! And I will do it swiftly, neatly, and efficiently, which is more than can be said of you!"

"Any asshole can be efficient."

"What!" cried Marge.

"You heard me. Institutions always cover their assholes," Emily added, borrowing from Sid Johnson. "You use the institution of the welfare department to cover up the destruction that you love and pretend you're just doing your job. You've lost your integrity, and when people lose their integrity, they lose their humanity. Oh, they—you—can still eat and sleep and sweat and have a grave, but without integrity or humanity, you must become a brick in an institution. An institutional brick that shits"—she considered briefly—"as opposed to shitting bricks."

Marge's sinuses quivered. "I suppose that's Shakespeare too?"

"No, I made that up. A least I think I did."

"Consider yourself removed from this case."

"Say whatever you like, Marge, but I'm going to be at that hearing on Monday and you can't stop me."

"You'll be fired, you stupid—"

"Not before I tell the board how you've treated welfare clients."

"How I've treated them! How am I supposed to treat them?" Marge lingered nasally over the phrase.

"You're not supposed to demand that they be low and groveling and abject, but you do. You insist on it. All those women who've slept with men and get left with kids, who lie alone at night and cry, all those 'Alas my love, you do me wrong' types who—"

"Alas my what!"

"You want to see these women punished—and most of them are. You want to be able to despise them—and most of them give you that satisfaction, but not Joyce. You can punish the rest of them because they're powerless and poor. They're manless and they need the food stamps, the money, and the MediCal card. But not Joyce."

"She's no different," Marge snorted. "She needed the food stamps, the money, and the MediCal card."

"But she was never powerless." Emily stepped closer. "She always had daring and strength. She always had imagination."

"You really are a fool, Emily. Those aren't words you can use about a woman on welfare!" Marge's foredeck breasts shook in an imitation of merriment.

"Then say her name. Say *Joyce Jackson*."

Marge eyed her coldly. "I sincerely hope you have another job lined up somewhere."

"Maybe the board will want you to get another job when I tell them how you went to Joyce's house that day. They'll probably wonder why you stood on her porch and threatened her."

Marge's heavy-hooded eyes narrowed up and her mouth twitched briefly. "That was part of my job."

"That's not true. You had no business going there that day. None. You went to gloat. You were so certain of victory that you just couldn't resist it. Joyce called me after you left. Did it make you feel good to watch a little girl get sick when you threatened her mother? Did it?"

"It was part of my job," Marge repeated, as if offering up her name, rank, and serial number.

"You're pathetic. But I can only stir up pity on my Saint Francis of Assisi days, and this isn't one of them. I'm not like Joyce, who—"

"Who will be repaying a huge debt and in jail for fraud if I have anything to say about it!"

"Why are you—"

"Because she's guilty!"

"Of what? Guilty of imagination and daring? Of doing things in the name of Elvis Presley? Of loving a man who's gone?"

"I assume you're speaking of her husband."

"Because Joyce has never whined, or cried, or whimpered?"

Marge's lips bent into a smile. "They all whine. And cry. And whimper."

"Yes, but you want to see it. You want it done in front of you so you can despise them. You love to despise people like Ruby Washington who can't get their kids dressed by four in the afternoon, people like the Ackermans and Santoyas. It gives you pleasure to watch them flounder and sink."

"Seeing that woman in court will give me pleasure!"

"You can't stand to see any of these women crawl back and stand up, to see them put their lives together again. God forbid they should find a new man! God forbid they should get a little ahead, or feel that life has something to offer them besides welfare! Oh no, you have to whittle them all back down to the old desperation. You can sleep, knowing they're lying awake, knowing they're thinking, *Oh shit, what's going to happen to us now?* You're happy as long as they are impoverished—in every way—or working jobs where they sling hash or mop floors, minimum wage and brutal hours. Leaving their children off in some low-rent baby barn of a day-care center. You like to keep them hungry and humble and needy. But Joyce Jackson won't let you. She refuses to act like a welfare mother."

"She cheated the county," Marge said stubbornly.

"She cheated you out of a victim, Marge. Joyce gives clothes to charity instead of taking it. You can't bear it that her daughters are always clean and beautiful and cared for, that they come from a home where they are loved—"

"And who loves them?" Marge demanded. "Their jailbird father? Elvis? I suppose Elvis Presley loves them!"

"It's more than can be said for your children."

Marge blanched visibly. "How dare you."

"You envy Joyce."

The tense, terrible silence in the ICU waiting room contrasted with the sounds of the hospital rousing for another day's routine, carts clattering and voices rippling in the distance. Emily clenched her teeth and reiterated that she would be at the board meeting Monday. No matter what.

"The board will never listen to you, Emily."

"Why not?" asked Howard, who came in carrying two coffees in paper cups. The expression on Marge's face could have registered 9.8 on the Richter scale. "Why wouldn't the board listen to Emily? She's the caseworker." He handed Emily her coffee. "I'm on that board, Marge, and I think they will listen to Emily. I think they'll call in Sid Johnson as well."

"What are you doing here?" Marge asked icily.

Howard turned to Emily. "Has there been any word on Jack?"

Emily shook her head.

"I wouldn't have guessed you to be on a first-name basis with these people," Marge glowered. "I thought you had more sense than that."

"Maybe I'm an Elvis fan." Howard sipped his hot coffee gingerly, blew lightly on the steam. "I'm here, we're here—Emily and I—on a human errand. Why are you here?"

"I'm here because of my job."

"Oh no you're not!" cried Emily. "Your job just lets you dress up all that vindictiveness in rules and regulations, in refigured budgets and net grosses! The truth is, Marge, you're trying to destroy a woman who doesn't own anything except a '62 Valiant. That letter you sent her was an absolute"—Emily cast for the right word—"a mockery! Joyce doesn't have any credit cards or loan money! There aren't any money market accounts or safe-deposit boxes! Joyce rents a house that's filled with pictures of Elvis and a lot of junk."

"Junk she sells for antique."

"You can't prove that."

With a patronizing air Marge looked from Emily to Howard. "I can prove she won money from the radio station."

"Minor," said Howard over the rim of his coffee cup. "A temporary alteration in her circumstances."

Marge gave a rusty laugh. "I can see you're out of touch with the rules, Howard. Twenty-seven hundred dollars for a welfare client is not minor."

"She won that money in May," Emily said quickly. "It's still May. All she has to do is declare it formally. She can report it to me today, and if she does that, I can refigure her grant. Her grant will be cut, but there'll be no need for a hearing."

"The car?" Marge inquired archly. "She sold that old Studebaker for two thousand dollars."

Emily's mouth went dry despite the hot coffee. "I don't think that car belonged to Joyce. I think she was just storing it for someone else. I don't think you can prove very much, Marge," Emily went on defiantly, determined, now or never, to act on the convictions she'd accumulated. Nonetheless, so that Marge should not see her hands

302

tremble, she put her coffee cup on the table. "If you let that hearing go on, the only thing you'll prove is my point, that you've hated and hounded and bedeviled a woman who had the temerity to pity you."

Marge looked momentarily bewildered. "Why don't you say it in English?"

"You're the supervisor," said Howard, stepping in briskly. "You can call off the hearing. Today is Friday. Call it off."

"Why should I?"

"So you won't have to stand up in front of the board," Howard replied simply, "and be proved a contemptible coward."

"And jealous," Emily added.

Marge scoffed, "Of a middle-aged welfare mother?"

"Then say her name. Say it."

Marge's lips puckered as though she had taken a big swill of Parson's ammonia; she muttered and mumbled and fumed, but her foredeck breasts diminished and her shoulders hunched over and her gray back retreated, leaving Emily and Howard sitting in a square of sunshine straining through the grilled windows, shadows striping on the floor.

Twenty-two

The lights are never off in ICU. The temperature never changes. And it is never deserted. This is Medicine's Last Stand, the gallant, swashbuckling medical gesture in the face of the fight we will all lose anyway. Several nurses sat before a console of flickering lights and bleeping monitors. They looked like the crew of the Starship Enterprise. Joyce Jackson followed a nurse, who walked softly on mushroom-springy shoes, down a passage where narrow cubicles were separated from one another by white, floor-length opaque curtains. Joyce glanced covertly at the other patients, who lay prone and vulnerable in their hospital beds, their mortality everywhere exposed.

The last cubicle, #6, was narrow, with a high window barred like that of a cell. Here Warren James Jackson, Jr., lay, his body held absolutely motionless and swathed wholly in white. Tubes ran in and out of his body, shackling him to bags and needles, registering graphs and squat machines that encircled him like mechanical hags beeping dispirited codes. His skin was gray underneath the purple bruises disfiguring his face. His hands were oddly unscathed.

"Call if you need anything." said the nurse as she closed the white curtains around Joyce and Jack. Her springy-soled shoes disappeared down the passageway.

Who should I call—thought Joyce—for what I need? Who shall I call? She kissed her own fingertips and ran them lightly over Jack's lips, where yet another plastic apparatus hung from his mouth; one was taped and stuffed up his nose too. "Jack?" she whispered, as though she were afraid to wake him, reminding herself forcibly that waking him was the whole point of her being here. "Jack! Jack! It's me, Jack! I love you! Listen to me! I love you. Come back here. Come back to me," she repeated over and over till she was dry-lipped and exhausted, the immensity of the task diminishing all her effort into nothingness. Words dried up before they reached her lips and she was reduced to repeating his name over and over, the single syllable resolving itself gradually into riff and rhythm, a beat that brought forth brittle, tinny melodies. If words failed her, perhaps music would not. Joyce cleared her throat and tried, futilely, the sweet, easy old songs, *Love Me Tender, Dixie, Peace in the Valley, Amazing Grace,* finishing none of them. The familiar tunes got lost and the familiar lyrics seemed to have spilled, broken and splattered, all over the floor. She wept as though she could see them, lying there jagged and useless at her feet. She was silent, powerless.

Before her lay the linear, laid-out, finite body of the man she had loved for twenty-five years. She pressed his unresponsive hand in hers, to pull him to the graveled, imperfect shores of consciousness, as though she, a small woman, could tow him—all six foot four, two hundred ten pounds—to safety. She saw herself splashing, reaching for him, as he had reached for, rescued, her straw hat from the ocean all those years ago, saved it, handed it to her, laughing. And in that moment when she had the hat in her hand, the man in her arms, and the lights reflecting brightly in the dark lagoon, she had tasted undeniable promise: not simply present happiness, but future promise, like a persistently regenerate wafer, because if the promise had, thus far, not been completely fulfilled, neither had it been altogether dissolved.

She wiped her nose and eyes. "Don't leave me," she whispered fiercely. "Don't leave me again. Don't ever leave me again."

When Jack left in 1977, Elvis had saved Joyce's life. His music, keeping his shrine, carrying on his work, helping others in his name, all that had slowly saved Joyce's life. Elvis had pulled her—dripping pain, graceless and unlovely, but alive—to this rocky, imperfect shore, resuscitated her, not in any single dramatic moment but in daily increments, a process wherein she slowly learned, as we all must, to strike that daily balance between grief and hope, to balance remembrance with anticipation, experience with possibility, coming slowly. to understand that last, most difficult balance: the cyclical and repeatable versus the linear and finite.

Tears dripped off Joyce's chin as she endlessly, fruitlessly repeated Jack's name, her voice thick with sobs. She begged Jack to hear her, let her voice through, listen. His hand in hers remained unresponsive and his body unmoving and his consciousness lost to her. But the lyrics she thought she'd lost, the melodies she thought gone altogether, came back, frail and uncertain at first, but gathering such strength that Joyce knew her own fragile alto was not alone. The music was a gift. Not only not lost. Found. Saved. Volume escalating, they sang a duet, the other well-known voice giving Joyce's a kind of clarity and confidence. Elvis's rich voice drew nearer and louder, submerged Joyce's, moved and moving beyond her abilities, penetrating where Joyce's voice could not. She closed her eyes, bit her bottom lip, quit singing. Elvis's music grew louder; he gave of himself unstintingly, the whole enormous range of his voice, from raw emotion to simple melodies, refreshing as a glass of clean water, ubiquitous as light, his voice ringing with passion, anguish, and intensity. A voice at once sweet and searing. Joyce held Jack's hand in both of hers, pressed it over her forehead, eyes closed tight against the apricot sunlight stealing in slats through grilled windows. She did not need to see. She could hear. She listened while Elvis's voice, the gift he had from God, like light and water combusted into vapor, fell deafeningly down, music filling that narrow cubicle, spilling, billowing underneath the white curtains, where nurses in mushroom-soled shoes treaded softly past the ostensible silence in #6.

About the author

Laura Kalpakian, a native Californian, was educated on both the East Coast and the West Coast. *Graced Land* is her sixth book, following three previous novels and two collections of short stories. She very often writes about people—past and present—in fictional St. Elmo, California, a place best described as east of L.A. and west of everywhere else. Her stories have appeared in magazines and journals in England and America and have collected many honors, including the *Stand* International Fiction Prize, a Pushcart Prize, the PEN/West Award for Best Short Fiction, and the Pacific Northwest Booksellers' Award. Laura Kalpakian has also received an NEA fellowship and the first Anahid Literary Award for an American writer of Armenian descent. She lives in Washington state with her two sons.